Love

Heals

Karma

Love

Heals

Karma

Jay William Smith, Jr.

BALBOA.
PRESS
A DIVISION OF HAY HOUSE

ISBN: 978-1-4525-5247-7 (sc)
ISBN: 978-1-4525-5246-0 (e)

Balboa Press books may be ordered through booksellers or by contacting:

Balboa Press
A Division of Hay House
1663 Liberty Drive
Bloomington, IN 47403
www.balboapress.com
1-(877) 407-4847

Because of the dynamic nature of the Internet, any web addresses or links contained in this book may have changed since publication and may no longer be valid. The views expressed in this work are solely those of the author and do not necessarily reflect the views of the publisher, and the publisher hereby disclaims any responsibility for them.

The author of this book does not dispense medical advice or prescribe the use of any technique as a form of treatment for physical, emotional, or medical problems without the advice of a physician, either directly or indirectly. The intent of the author is only to offer information of a general nature to help you in your quest for emotional and spiritual well-being. In the event you use any of the information in this book for yourself, which is your constitutional right, the author and the publisher assume no responsibility for your actions.

Any people depicted in stock imagery provided by Thinkstock are models, and such images are being used for illustrative purposes only. Certain stock imagery © Thinkstock.

Printed in the United States of America

Balboa Press rev. date: 6/4/2012

PROLOGUE

Welcome to the second phase of Alex Nichol's journey to heal his mental, physical, and spiritual life. The first book *Karma Affects Everyone* carried you on his journey. You witness how these external events affected his personal relationship within himself and others. He could function successfully in the business world but his personal relationship with himself was in continual crisis. Alex is a success in the eyes of the world. He has a beautiful, brilliant wife, a thriving business, and all the expensive toys a man could want. Nevertheless, Alex is not content. In fact, he is on the verge of a nervous breakdown. Alex is aware that he grew up in a dysfunctional family and even entered into an equally dysfunctional first marriage. Just *why* Alex finds himself in such circumstances is what continually puzzles him. These events cause him to seek help from a psychiatrist whose best advice is to "get on with your life" and take your medication. Instead, Alex attempts to bury his pain in sexual encounters, medication, and alcohol, but nothing he tried offers a permanent solution to the continual expanding nightmares and increasing anxiety attacks that plague him. Thanks to caring friends, Alex seeks a different kind of help, struggling to be "saved" before it is too late.

During three months of Alex Nichols' life, the karmic debts he has accumulated for four thousand years comes to a head. Through the aid of a compassionate hypnotherapist, and with regressive hypnosis, Alex unravels the mysteries of his past lives: he views his life spent in ancient Egypt, a Grecian incarnation, and another in eleventh-century in Germany. A final regression sends Alex on a visit to between lives. He learns how break "forever commitment", forgiving, and asking forgiveness that can free one from lifetimes of trial and error.

Life is a game, meant to be played to the fullest in each individual soul's quest for spiritual perfection. Alex finds many allies, both in human form and between lives. As he learns to seek help from others, he matures mentally to confront his current conflicts and, most importantly, he finally lets go of the past.

However, there were the matters of the heart and love that was not resolved because he is still not ready to face his last final challenge. Jenny is the spark plug to continue his quest to love without emotional conflict. We often consider that love evolves with the tender relationship between two people, although there is that foundation of previous life experiences that colors or distorts how love is demonstrated. On his journey of healing with Jenny, during their honeymoon, these continual flash back to other life times keeps their relationship somewhat on the edge. These events continually keep her in the shadows as to what is going on with him. Yet! He has to find the cause and resolve the distortions to convey unrestricted love. So welcome to the journey and be prepared to explore the Alex's life experiences and know resolutions are possible.

CHAPTER 1

It is May; it is May, the merry month of May where the entire world rejoices to the awakening of Mother Earth. The land along the Columbia River is no exception with its beauty and plant life. All the plants and trees are busy parading their new growth and development. Even all my nightmares of all the karmic events that happened with my family and Marian are gradually evaporating into nothingness. My mind, soul, and body rejoice that the hidden burdens are gone. The activity completed and my life is now good. Not just good, it is great; I have it all; a new woman in my life, a successful marina project that is developing, and the internal wounds from past lives and present life's journey are healing and fading fast. A few frightening memories of the past are still with me but they have no power to bring those events into my active mind or color my daily thought processes.

The rustling of the wind wafts through the forest of Douglas fir causing the river to make those gentle waves and it carries the smell of the river. I am sitting on the edge of the dock. Like a normal boy, I am busy dragging and splashing my naked feet in the water as if I was truly a young teenager. From the broad view on the end of the dock, I am looking out over the scene of tranquility. The river waves murmur soft sounds as they lap against the piers and banks of the river. My fantasy life dances and whirls with my new love for Jenny. She is what life is about and I am so full of pride she is in my life.

I can't remember a time in my life when there was such peace and enjoyment as I am now experiencing. Not in my wildest dreams have I ever thought I would be free of the nightmares from hell. Looking back, I know that I am now realizing all the rewards that I would obtain when I dealt with my karmic mess in a positive creative healing way. All that I went through was worth the rewards I am receiving now.

While I was married to Marian, Captain Jack, who operated our yacht "Ra", had made it possible for me to meet my hypnotherapist Roger. With Roger's help, I was able resolve past lives' karmic debts and I was able to divorce myself from a very dysfunctional marriage, business, and life. I am also grateful to have found a Roger who helped me to open the door to my spirit world. There I found my spirit spiritual advisor Kevin, my guardian as to speak. Kevin is the man; a real friend. Kevin continues to act as my spiritual advisor while I am on this earth journey. I couldn't have survived and worked through my agenda for this life without him. My continual soul growth and development is now primary to me. He said I would have all the help I needed to be free and free I am. He kept his word while I never believed it could really happen. I have no more karmic debt with my family or Marian forever. The 'forever' was a prison word from hell for the longest time, and now that word 'forever' represents freedom. The sound of freedom is music to my soul. There are times I could just dance or sing with joy that I am free and unlimited. I know if I did that in public, people would think that I am nuts. Still there are times I just want to scream out regardless of where I am. I often have a hard time keeping from yelling the word 'freedom' as go about my daily routine.

While I am sitting on the dock west of St. Helens, I am looking at the majestic Mount St. Helens all covered with snow. She lost her top when she could not restrain internal pressures. Still from time to time, we see plumes of steam to remind us she is still cooking down there. She is not dead yet. Under the right stress, she could blow again.

At least I did not lose my top from all my internal pressures. This marina development project began when I was still married to Marian. I needed to build a bridge to different employment when I divorced Marian and our financial investment business. My connection with Johnny, then Ol' Johnson, and the whole marina, restaurant, condos, etc. just kept on growing as if it had a mind of its own. It is developing to be heaven on earth for me. The rewards of being in the present and releasing my mind and soul of self-annihilation has allowed the pleasures of life to blossom in every aspect of my life.

The luckiest day of my life was when Captain Jack hired Johnny to work as crew person on the yacht "Ra." Johnny was one the greatest gifts that came out of marriage to Marian. Not only did he help save my life from Marian and open the door to this marina project, but most of all, he introduced me to his most beautiful and talented sister Jenny. I must have done something right in my life to have an employee that would want to share his sister with me. I think sharing is not the complete term; he wants me to marry her because in his mind we are a great match. We appear to have the chemistry to develop a good caring marriage. In my mind, I think so too.

By having Jenny in my life, she is adding the music of love and laughter daily. Yet, there is a dark thought I keep stumbling over when I think or dream about her. It does not make sense now because we fit like hand and glove. It must be just ghost feelings from the past Karmic pain I went through. If it is a ghost, what meaning does it have for me now? It still haunts me from time to time. It keeps dancing on the edge of my thoughts daily. I have not nor will I explore the ghost since I have it all. I can also admit I am a coward because I don't want to rock the boat. I have been to hell and back with my parent's and Marian's behavior that almost ruined my life. To be honest, it was me that almost ruined my live because I could not find my way out of those nightmares by traditional methods. Somehow, I became the victim of my own earth journey plan I put in motion of my own free will and accord before I was born. I wanted my freedom and that life plan was the only way out.

When my soul was still in "heaven" or the other plane of existence before I was born, I now realize that I design my life's plan kinds functions for my soul's development or evolution. Still when I get into this physical form, with all the emotional hang-ups, I shift into survival mode. No matter how many times I have been born into this physical world, I always forget how emotional these bodies can be. The emotional survival made me blind to the team of people who are here with me, to assist me to complete my plan. I am not going to let those shadow thoughts I am having now cause me any kind of grief. I will just keep burying them until they stops bugging me. I am enjoying a life that I never dreamed possible, No, I should say, I have never dreamt such a magnificent complete dream was possible, that is developing, and it could come into reality.

Our business we have developed to make a reasonable good living is moving right along successfully. We are selling most all our condos before they are constructed, so we have all the cash flow we need. We set up a screening application to insure that the person or persons buying the condo can afford it. We have them submit a financial report, credit rating, background check, references and then we take the time to insure that they can really afford living here. We also spend quite a bit of time with the buyers to insure this fits their life style. We are not just selling condos; we are selling a life style that empowers people and place where they really feel at home. We are the selling agent so the new homeowner pays the normal closing cost without agent's fees.

The project is moving ahead of schedule. Life is good, no, it is fantastic; no, it is beyond words or maybe it is just magical. To think about it, there are no real words to express or explain what it feels like to have my real life back.

In spite of everything, I reflect upon the living nightmare I was living, even with all the unemotional planning when I was in the spirit world, I knew it was going to be hell. Nevertheless! I have to remember my old soul has the wisdom of many past earth experiences and the strength to survive what new experiences I may have in this life. How easy it is to do planning in a vacuum, without the emotional activity of a human body and society. That experience is like our day dreams about life, in vacuum, where everything works without a hitch or problem of any kind.

There were times I had to laugh, I felt like Mt. St. Helens. Why am I now dwelling on the past when the focus should be on the life I want to live and be active with? We spend too much time in the past with what could have been or etc. I cannot change those experiences. I have the power to change how I view and remember them. Those events can be positive tools to empower my life when I have removed the emotional drama.

"Keep focused" is the watchword of the day. Life is about creation and this project is doing that for me. We found out a couple days ago we have options for more land west of us to build upon if we need it.

Another great gift from my ex-wife were the two ladies of the night she sent to me to satisfy my sexual needs was she refused to be involved in. I still remember the passion that seemed unending when we first married. I was a young buck that had all his teenage fantasy dreams fulfilled. Once I was totally hooked, the well dried up and I returned to frustrating physical needs not answered. I wasn't sure if it just happened to me or is the norm. Once those normal sex drives are activated, it is hell to shut them off or down.

The ladies, Judy turn out to be a designer and Frances was an architect. I remembered I had Johnny involved to insure that escorts was all that would happen for the evening and nothing more. I was their first client. They resorted to this high-class activity to raise money quickly to start their business. Besides, I made sure Marian was not going have anything on me to cause more problems in my future. During the course of the evening, they found out about our project and wanted to submit a proposal. This all sounds almost like a fairy tale, but they submitted the best workable proposal. The funds my wife paid for their evening, helped get them get started and really paid off for our housing, marina, restaurant, etc. project.

Frances and Judy showed me a very special plans for my own condo. Our condos are a row house. My row house will have extra space in the attic with windows as a bonus room looking out to the river. Steve Holland, our general contractor, had all the condos have the same appearance on the outside. Steve had the bonus room like mine on the other end of the front row. Ours was the only ones with this kind of bonus room. We need to keep the front row built with at two-story limit to gives those condos behind a view of the river wherever possible. We are working on making each unit soundproof so homeowners are not exposed to noises from their neighbors or the outside world. To think I will have a home without all that Egyptian 'Ra' reproduction stuff of my ex-wife. Jenny has been sneaking in a few ideas to show she is interested in the construction of my condo as indication she plans a future with me. Johnny, her brother, the matchmaker, is fun to watch, because of the way he is around us, trying to make everything so special for us. I guess that old saying is true: you do marry the family too.

An alarming thought went off in my head to bring me back to reality. I took a quick look at my watch and the day has slipped by. I needed to go to Portland for an important appointment with my "ex" Marian very soon. She has the meeting at my old partnership office to sign papers that was a surprise offer by her. Marian was always full of surprises but I still have to watch her motives. Perhaps this would be the final meeting with her 'forever'. There is that beautiful word again. That word use to mean a bondage to Marian forever, which she extracted from me 4500 years ago when I was her protector in Egypt when she was a male high priest.

CHAPTER 2

The afternoon drive up Route 30 to Portland was uneventful. Emotional feelings were stirring up some of my old dead feelings, as I got closer to my old place of work. When I came into outer office of my old office, Barbara, my former very dear secretary, greeted me with a big hug and kiss on the cheek. She would never have done that when I was her boss.

She showed me into my old office. My replacement was not there. All the papers were laid out on the conference table for me to read and expectantly to be signed. As usual, Marian was in control, there would be no one there to acknowledge that I existed. I cannot believe that Marian was paying me off in full. She could hold to her buyout clause in the divorce. A certified check was also displayed at the end of the row of short and brief paper work. I told Barbara that it looked okay to me. She assured me that she had a company lawyer she trusted review it to insure there were no hidden loopholes. While we were waiting for the witness to arrive, she again asked me if I would have a job for her in the future. The sooner the better were her words. I informed her I had not forgotten her request. In fact, it looked like it could be sooner than later. She made a sigh of relief and explained her husband had accepted promotion out on Route 30 towards St. Helens. They are planning to move in that direction. Maybe a condo at my project would be an answer for them. Besides she added, she could walk to work with a laugh.

Before I could reply that it sounded like a good idea, the two witnesses, one of whom was the lawyer, who reviewed the work for Barbara, had arrived. They were there to witness my signature and close the deal. Everyone signed around and it was a done deal. I told Barbara I would expect her call or I would call her soon about her job offer. I took the check and put in my pocket, while singing to myself that our entire project will have the monetary funds it needed to grow. I thanked everyone. I felt like I was floating out the door and the building, as one would say, more like walking on air. 'Good bye forever', were those beautiful words, as the door close on that indescribable emotion. It is finally over.

My next course of action was to drop into my bank to deposit the check. The amount caused the teller to raise an eyebrow. She even let out soft sound when she asked "All of it?"

"Yes," I replied my quickly? With the deposit slip in my hand, we, our development project, were closer to completing all of our financial funding needs.

About to exit the bank, my brother Matthew walked in. It caught both of us by surprise. In fact, I would say it was quite awkward since we have no love lost between us. Quickly; I asked him if all was well with the property he bought from me in Newport. His grunt was in an affirmative. He asked how I like being involved with a property development project. I swiftly replied, "It was the best thing that has happen to me in a long time."

Trying to show he was not interested in my world, as he walked away, "That is good" were his words frozen in ice. I know there is no way we can ever even be friends, so I have to let him go. He grew up with full support of our parents. Matthew even joined in with their rejection abuse of me after I was thirteen. My parent; made me responsible for him from time he was five years old until mother wanted to be a mother to one of us when he turned twelve. Of course, she chose him. While I was supervising him, I made sure he never got blame for anything that was unacceptable to our parents. That even made situations even worse for me. Oh well! I have some real friends now that treat me like family.

As I was walking down the street, I remembered that just around the corner was that coffee shop where I encountered the spiritual Tarot Card reader. She told me about my future and general information that needed to be completed by my birthday, September 26, or I would have six more years of hell with Marian. These past months flew by and where did they go? I walked briskly to the shop hoping she was still there. My eyes lit up when I saw the sign, a reader was available, and it was Tamara. I wanted to announce to her that I did it all and won, thanks to her help. I looked in my wallet and found a $100 bill to pay for another reading and to give her a big tip for her prior help. I stuffed the money into my pants pocket for quick access.

There is a whisper of some conflict inside my head. Should I do it or not, that is the question? The last time she came up with all challenges I need to face, but what the hell, why not, was now my cocky attitude. My life is on a fast track to successful loving bliss. I quickly walked in and ordered a coffee. When it was served, I walk directly over to the reader. "Are you available?"

"Yes." She replied quickly

"You probably do not remember me?" I softly asked as I sat down.

Without a second thought, she replied, "You were in here late last summer and there were a lot of activities you needed to do before your birthday. You must have completed them because here you are, looking very happy and sound."

I did not know my spirit teachers, who are God's helpers, reminded her about him to make it easier for her.

"That is amazing, after all this time and you remembered me!" I replied astonished.

"Well! What can I do for you now?" she asked. She didn't want to explain that her spirit teachers gave her the information. Sometimes she likes to take some credit on her own.

I told her to do her thing, whatever it was: to verify that everything is done and that I am totally free and unlimited from here on out.

Tamara handed me the Tarot Cards, informing me to think of my question while I was shuffling them and to cut the deck three times. I performed the task with a proud cocky attitude that she would not find any issues of the past and everything is a done deal [period].

The reader took the bottom cut of the deck and while laying out the cards for the reading. All at once, she piled the cards back together and looked at Alex with reluctant concern.

Tamara's mind was racing. "Oh my God! This guy is in for another past lives event within a year! Her spirit teachers, who were also listening to Kevin, Alex's advisor in spirit, told the reader they were giving him a year of rest. Then he would have to chose, to remove his own negative Karma that would affect or limit his emotional relationship with Jenny. How was she going to tell him this? Kevin told her the following: "I keep getting this very odd statement. Do you hear the same thought dancing across your mind, especially when you are around the new woman in your life? Tamara repeated it to me, 'I never want to be compromised again.'"

That statement stunned me. Again, I am as unprepared as the last time at what she was going to say. Where did she get that information? Was it true? This conversation with her now appears to be a bad idea, kept racing through my thoughts. What is going on here was screaming in my mind. Kevin had promised it was a done deal when I resolved the problems of my parents and Marian. Now he is going back on his word. Question after question were racing in my confused mind. My face saddened and panic feelings were beginning to raises their ugly head.

Tamara reached over, placed her hands on mine, and tried to assure and calm me. What she suggested was not or would not be as bad or painful as what I had been through since last time I was here. How could she know? She did not have to experience what I lived through. Then she tried to cover her story by telling me it is truly a choice of whether I want to do it or not. I had to decide. My mind screamed out I decided this is crap.

They tell me I decide but damn, do I really have a choice? What is the truth, phantom, or what in hell? I must be out of my mind to be here again. On and on these racing thoughts sped out of control. I was racing toward meltdown.

Tamara finally tapped my hand softly to bring me back to her. "You came in here to ask questions and get answers where you would have prior knowledge to beat the game. I can only tell you what your spirit teachers tell me and what you want to know. You have one more task out in front of you and it will truly be the end."

The end, yeah, one more task; the same old game, just one more, just one more, one more, one more, crap. My mind was racing. When does anyone ever tell me the truth? That old adage, we are just trying to spare you unnecessary pain. That's crap. Say it all and give us, I mean me, a real choice. This measuring pain out a little at a time, must give someone pleasure, but that's not me!

Again, she grabbed my hand to bring me out of my creative madness. "What I am making you aware of is that you can do something about it or not. It really is your choice. To be aware, is to be forearmed. Slow down and think for a minute. Your spirit teachers are just giving you a look at your future. Remember nothing is written in stone, the story can be changed. Your choices and your efforts you apply can make the difference. I really am here to help you to be free of past lives' damages with knowledge and understanding. You can do nothing or on the other hand, you can address your future successfully. I am really trying to help you. Does any of this make any sense?"

Without hesitation, I clumsily got to my feet and reached into my pocket for the $100 bill I was going to give her as reward for last time I was here. I dropped it on the table. My mind was racing out of control. Now she has unloaded more stuff on me. I was expecting her to tell me, I was a winner and there were no more activities like that in the rest of my life. Jenny and I would sail through life like a perfect dream. What crap! I have to get the hell out of here – now. Before the reader could say or do anything more or create more havoc with my life, I need to do a great vanishing act before I really lose my control.

I was filled with conflict and rage while staggering down the street to get to my car. I must have seemed like a drunken man to those who were passing by. My mind was divided between getting the hell out of here and while fighting thoughts about there was more trouble ahead. At least this time I did not give her time to tell me much about what the hell it was. I really did not want to know. I needed a break from all this crap. Is there no end?

There was my car. I came through the fog of confusion, I got in and drove back to my apartment. Arriving at the apartment, what in hell just happen to me. I don't remember anything since I left that reader. I need to get in my place, going directly to my bedroom and crash on the bed. The light went out to my escape land. I was floating in my quick deep drug like sleep. My whole world was fading into darkness, thank God. Without knowing, I found myself traveling to that space where Roger Strong, my hypnotherapist, had taken me to talk to my spirit teacher.

Kevin, Alex's spiritual advisor, called to Adrian, Alex's spirit name, "you will have to listen to me. You are in a deep sleep which we helped to induce because of your training with Roger Strong. While you are in this state, I am going to lay out a plan for you to deal with the next phases in the healing of your soul. You have completed the first task way beyond our expectations. Your body did take a beating dealing with it but because of the love with and around you, you have healed also faster than expected" were Kevin's gentle words.

"These past months I have given you hint of the opportunity to heal your heart with 'I don't want to compromise.' The work with your family and Marian were what was happening against you. As result of past lives, you have internalized a heart fear, pain; you are not sure how you call it. You will never really share your love emotion with anyone unless you can relearn how to again love unconditionally and get past abandonment issues.

Now you need, I think, to heal that deep pain of lost love and family abandonment issues that only you can do that. You were granted that healing opportunity when you were in Spain 300+ years ago. As fate would have it, an unexpected wild card [an unexpected player] shattered you to core of your being on both issues. You have not been able to love or to be that vulnerable to love since then. All those painful events have been experienced over time, but that event in Spain tied them all together. You have survived it by building a barrier against the pain of love so permanently to insure it will never happen again. It almost destroyed you. Spirit healers had you in a healing comma for 100 years. You have built the barrier; therefore, you have to release it. The worse part was Marian, then a man, was major player to teach you a lesson of obedience and doing so, almost destroyed you. You chose love and family over your obedience to her [him].

We had no idea when you developed your life plan 300+ years ago and as it unfolded in Spain, that Marian's soul would be your area. Your spiritual team have always talked or should say, or hinted about your barriers, obstructions, in passing but never to the point. You were always saying you will **never** be able to relate to others with any kind of love emotions let alone to yourself. Love, acceptance of yourself as an evolving soul, and the depth of that love determines the depth of the love you will share with someone else. Jenny is in your life to take you to the place of complete unconditional love healing, if you let her. With the healing of unconditional love, you will finally experience the thoughts of your Creator made flesh" were Kevin's instructions.

"Remember, you witnessed souls when you were on soul plane working, helping wounded loveless souls, they were unable to love unconditionally, and they were unable to continue their journey of completion? Without internalizing unconditional love in human form, you could not be able to accept the unconditional love from your creator. There is so much more your soul hungers for and these last few events can be removed forever. Then you truly will be free. I have never met a soul that was so hung up on the need for freedom" were pleading words of compassion from Kevin.

Kevin continued with "I checked your soul's experiences and it appears when you lived during the fifth century B.C., your soul quest was to be open to love. That soul quest was also to bring dignity to human kind and a capacity to love unconditionally. You changed from a warrior protector of property to a warrior for the protection of human rights and people. That is what happens when you moved into the sixth plane of the spirit world. One of the major activities of souls on the sixth plane is humanity. Therefore, for the past 2,000 years, you have moved through and around in this plane to learn and then demonstrating that learning on the earth plane as a human. I am glad you are in the altered state because I am not in the mood to debate any of this information with you."

"Furthermore," stated Kevin, "What I am going to do, with the permission and consent of the committee, is to give you one year from your last birthday to just enjoy the thrill of being alive and feeling life without any past lives' stress. You have earned that. I really have to say that truly you have only 5 months left of that year's time. Sept 26th is your birthday. Should you marry Jenny? Should you take your honeymoon in Europe? That action will be the signal to us that you are going to face the events that prevent you from loving unconditionally. You have tried it twice since Spain to heal the pain to accept someone and I mean some love, and you wouldn't let it happen. Again you will have lot of help ready for you and we know you can do it."

"Adrian, [Alex] you will slowly come out of this deep sleep you are in and you will remember nothing that happened after you came around the corner to find the coffee shop and the reader. Your mind will not send you messages to awaken to any of the pain of your past lives during this time. You will continue to sleep for a least another hour so your body will be repaired of any damage you might have caused from being distress about being more work to be done."

"Adrian, we all love you because you are really lovable. We have assigned some new spirit teachers that will help you to be fully in the moment. They will also assist you upon your request with any earthly venture you seek to perform. Sleep well, my very dear friend, and we will talk again in 5 months or so." as Kevin voice fades off.

CHAPTER 3

Sleep slowly evaporated and I am waking from what seemed like a drug or alcohol hangover. I am staggering into the bathroom, turned on the water in the tub to soak and undressed from my damp sweaty clothes. Why did I lie down to sleep with all my clothes on? I have not done that activity for a long time. Without realizing it, I am pouring sea salt into the hot water to prepare to soak like the old days. I threw my damp clothes into the hamper. I walked over, gently sliding into the nice hot water to reflect on the events of this day. Why am I in this shape again?

"Being a working man sucks," I screamed out. Having servants pick up after you and all the things they do for you really spoiled me.

Let me think about what happened today, I began to trace my day's activity in my mind. I was on the pier, went to town, got my entire buyout money from Marian, and drove home. I don't remember anything, wait a minute, I went to the bank and deposited the check. Oh yes, come to think about it; I met my brother in the bank, and that still very sad. Then I must have been flying high on success, I don't remember getting into the car, driving home or falling asleep on the bed with all my clothes on. To think of it, why were my clothes so sweaty? I know I don't have any windows open and the sun heated up the room. That's why I would sweat with all my clothes on. Crazy me, I keep thinking those panic attack days are back. Am I having hard time thinking or accepting all the hell of the past is over? Wake up, wake up I keep repeating to myself for self-assurance as I spent time soaking. I need to keep reminding myself I have great new life out in front of me. All I have to think about now is developing, completing, and enjoying our new project, not to mention the new growing love of my life. I never ever thought there could ever be a woman like her in my life. Damn, I am one hell of a lucky guy. After an hour or so, I had enough of this. I took an additional shower, dried off, and got ready for rest of the day. It is time for supper and I don't cook. Besides, I need to support our own company restaurant. I need to drive over but soon I will have my own place there. My office for the company will be completed soon. Just think going to dinner or any meal will be just a short walk from my new home. I really hope they will have my condo completed very soon. Then I will have Jenny help me buy furniture and stuff as a test to see if our taste matches in furnishing. Another way I can spend more time with her.

Arriving at the restaurant, there is Johnny working and enjoying it all. Of course, Judy has become a permanent fixture here too. I think they will make it a match when this project is completed. I know one thing for sure, she will not give up her business should she marry; it keeps her radiant.

There is Ol' Johnson at his usual table. The place has mostly the same customers and growing. We still want to draw in the middle class people for the condos, the marina business along with the restaurant. It will be great to have that pier restaurant in operation soon. We need to tear this place down and begin another phase of our project.

Johnny yells out every time he sees me. I believe we finally captured the friendship and trust we had together in the 5th century B.C. in Greece. I motion for him to join me at Ol' Johnson's table. We did our usual men's greeting activity and sat down. I do believe that Ol' Johnson is growing to like this buddy, buddy-feeling activity. Now they were looking at me with such forcefulness to spill the beans about what happened today. They knew I was called into my old job to pick up some money. Like business partners, they were all ears to know all about it. I looked at them as if I had no idea what they were talking about. That wasn't a good move, they both were about to let me have it. I wasn't sure I knew what "it" would be and I was not ready to find out.

Now I have a chance to build some drama. "Well partners, it's hard to believe but it is true, Marian paid me off in full because she wanted to break all ties to me. I think it happened because Lizzie put the pressure on her to make sure I stayed out of her life. No one was there except my old secretary Barbara to show me that I don't exist anymore at the company. I signed all the papers; they gave me big fat certified check, which I put in our business account. I want you to know, there is nothing in this world going to stop us now." It all came blasting out in almost one breath demonstrating that I'm back and ready to get it done.

Again, there is another excuse to celebrate. Johnny runs and gets a pitcher of beer this time and glasses and he sits all of it on the table. Ol' Johnson did the pouring because us "youngens" spill the good stuff when we pour. We all raised our glass as we stood up around the table and made our usual toast to our present and future success.

The server came over and took our order, which is always the special for the night. That made the choice easy. The food came with hast. We spent the next hour eating and just bragging about how our lives will be when this entire project is complete. I thought I would drop it into the conversation the idea that we really name this project "Johnson Landing". I got no response. Then I tried jokingly "Stastue Knocovich Marina and Landing". That got Ol' Johnson's attention. I thought he was going to throw his dirty dishes at me. I think, I hope he was joking too, but I not sure, because that is not really a joke since it's his real name. However, seriously men, I told them, we should get with the others to give this project a proper name. We have sold quite a few condos so far, we can't operate without a formal name.

CHAPTER 4

[Some time later, we got hold of everyone and the name that was finally agreed upon within the week it would be "H.O.M.E. on the River". H.O.M.E. being acronym for "helping ourselves master everyday." A community of supportive people would be doing just that. Isn't one's home the place to help us to develop our skills to be successful for our journey out into society?]

Jenny showed up along with Judy to round out the group. The evening just melted away and too soon, it was time to go home and sleep. Saying all the goodbyes and a little kissing with Jenny, which is nice, we went our separate ways because she was going to work. As I was driving home, I really want this relationship to grow, yet I have to allow Jenny to let it happen in a comfortable way for her. She has expressed that I have to be sure, that she not a "rebound". It is very important that there is a real love and friendship between us. The waiting game always seems to be hanging around in my heart.

Driving home has been a blur lately. When I got home, went directly to my bedroom. When I emptied my pockets, I checked my billfold to see if I enough money for a while. I counted the bills and I seem to be missing $100 bill. Did I count my money this morning wrong or what? I will have to deal with that issue another time because I need to get some sleep. I stripped this time, took a fast shower, and dried off but when I hit the bed for sleep, my head would not shut off. I kept thinking about Jenny. I have been divorced since last October and yet we really have not made our relationship into a twosome yet. She keeps saying she needs time since she doesn't want to be a "rebound person". In addition, she really wants to know me to develop a healthy friendship before we get physical and or married. When rough times come in all relationships, we need the glue of healthy friendship to keep us together. She wants a marriage that grows and the security of a lifetime of love. Those requirements keeps running around my mental track. I guess that is how women are. I am inexperience and I sure haven't had enough experiences to know if those activities were normal. We men seemed to have different agenda or drive. When I think about her, my agenda disintegrates. She is all that I want. I often wonder if she was in the plan for this life before I got here. Whatever the reason, she is in my life. I am so happy because she the best thing that ever happened to me. In the next breath, darkness flooded in and I am lost in sleep. This time, it was pleasant restful sleep.

The days fly by when you are so busy. Our office building is about finished, so I can offer my old secretary a job soon. The construction team that is working on completion of new restaurant is ahead of schedule. We were to have a floating building. After lot of consideration; we elected to build a pier building that heads out towards the center of the river. The county was also pleased. The pier allows the public access to fish from the pier, which has a riverside walkway. The building construction is above the flood plain. We also threw in a breakwall the entire length of the riverfront. This will prevent erosion since we have over 20-foot high embankment. There was also some funds from the government to help with that project. The new restaurant's has rustic waterfront appearance, with windows around three riverview sides to give the customers full view of the river.

The second floor laid out as the first floor with lots of windows, except, it has bandstand, dance floor, and geared more for entertainment. We had thought about a walkway around second floor but cost and insurance made it prohibited. There is food service on this floor as requested. We have elevator to bring up the food and those who are handicapped and unable to use the stairs. The design allowed for rented parties for additional income. It appears we have only one more inspection. It looks like we will be open for business Memorial Day weekend.

After Memorial Day weekend, we will be busy tearing down the old restaurant to complete the launching ramp and parking for the marina side of this project. That project should only take a couple of weeks and it should be ready for all the Fourth of July activity. We have all contractors ready to go to meet our dead line.

The condos section will have a walkway and park by the break wall. We will plant Japanese Cherry trees because their blossoms in the spring will make it look soft and very homey. We will have park benches to enjoy it all. The residential project will be set off from the Marina with its docks, restaurant and parking lot. A small wall will separate the two projects with a gatehouse person to insure public parking does not flow over into the residential area. The wet lands on East side will have a six-foot chain link fence to keep the people out and the critters that live there out of our area. Ron Collins, our legal advisor and investor, did a great job with the county to make all this possible. If our community keeps growing as it has been; we will need those acres west of us for another condo community. It will mirror the East side development.

Our general contractor, Steve Holland, is going to meet with me this afternoon to keep me up to date where we are and submit a general progress report. He has also bought a three-bedroom condo here for his family. His unit is on the other end of my townhouse row. He is one hell of guy, keeping us on or under budget with excellent quality material. With Judy and Frances setting up different interiors with standard and upgrades, that activity has really inspired all the sales. Our standards are above the normal standards in the area for the price. We are keeping on target to attract the average annual income people and families who want to develop support community with normal standards of living. We have permitted our suppliers to use our condos to help promote their new home products to the area. As payment, we get a better break on the cost of upgraded material.

Even the school district is happy with us because we will bring in revenue for their new school. They are just building a new grade and middle school within a mile of here. I am so happy to be doing something like this and seeing it coming alive. It is more satisfying than helping the wealthy acquire additional wealth.

CHAPTER 5

Time just keeps marching by, and here it is full summer. My place is complete. Jenny and I have had great pleasure finding furniture and furnishings that meet our likes, needs, in my price range, which is nice for me. It is all those great items for my home for less than full price. We shop well together. I never bargain hunted before. It is more fun than Easter egg hunting. It's fun to live on a hell of lot less salary when you are doing your passion. We also found we had lot in common when it comes to household furnishing and decoration. It is strange to move in without her doing so too, but she still taking her time. What can I say, but its o.k.. I have to tell you, rented furniture is not like having your own. Temporary is fine and that is all it is. The major room for me is the bonus room in the attic, which gives me an unobstructed view of the river and all its traffic. The soundproofing makes my home a quiet place to do the work I need to do.

The office building has been completed, all landscaped and furnished. I had Francis and Judy furnish it and set it up for me. Barbara will be starting work here a week before Memorial weekend. Her first act of business was to get our purchase plan streamlined and on track. She has found some real wonderful buys to develop this project as we envision it at the beginning.

She and her husband bought a condo in third row back and they will be moving in that same weekend. My old secretary is great organizer. She will fit in with great ease. Marian was "madder than a hatter", still she should have known that my secretary would follow me if I could find work for her.

Marian never liked her anyway because she could not obtain any personal information from her.

Memorial weekend is on us. We have a big promotional activity for restaurant, half-finished marina, and sale of the rest of the condos to keep us busy. I have to tell you we should have been committed to state hospital trying to do all at once! It's one big learning exercise. The Thursday before the weekend, we had run through dinner with the investors, a number of friends, and those condo families that had already moved in, for the staff to practice their skills. There were a few minor problems but overall it went off as if we were always in operation there. That Friday night, the restaurant was by reservation only because people were coming out of the woodwork. We had four young persons running the parking lot. We were serving meals up to 10 p.m. We had the usual crowd from the old place with big new group, which was great plus. The new restaurant was about double in size and I think we should have made it larger. The upstairs section will be open tomorrow.

I can't express how great it is to live without personal nightmares. Every day is busy but no mental - free for all. I always wondered what a normal life would be like and now I know. Yet, there is a strange growing feeling I can't put on finger on it in my heart. The more I want to be with Jenny, the more it keeps growing. Maybe that is what love feels like, I sure don't know. It's no big deal but it still there.

The whole summer Jenny and I are growing closer and closer. More hugging and kisses between us, but that's all. She is sure, but she still wants to be very sure. In fact, we were dancing around with the idea of maybe if she is sure, during my birthday weekend we have a small wedding and reception in restaurant. Jenny told me the other day, she make the decision 1 September whether it is a go or not. The suspense or drama of it all could drive anyone crazy. It is doing that to me.

Johnny is also driving me wild about every time he sees me, "Has my sister made up her mind yet?"

My answer is no and I keep reminding him it's not Sept. 1st yet.

We have all condos either sold or committed, the whole place landscaped including a waterfalls with a pond at the entrance to the place. The walkway and park turned out to be great support to the project. We picked up the option on the other area west of us and we are beginning to develop it. We have a section on the river, which is like a spit of land with wetlands behind it. We can't seem to come up with idea what to do with that large chunk of land. The community around us is very supportive of what we are doing, which is great endorsement. The marina with its boat docks, launching ramp, and public fishing off the pier has everyone around here enjoying the access to the river. The Fourth of July weekend we almost had to go to reservations for everything because it is really working. We even had a small fireworks display out front of the marina on the river. That pleased everyone, me included.

I can't say it enough Barbara is the best thing that ever happened for the office and me. She is on top of everything. Barbara is such a great conductor of all the work that flowed through the office. She had me working on schedule all the time to keep up. She also reminded me that by September we would have a rhythm down so it will not seem so hectic. We finally got our rhythm and it happened just as she said. We had to hire a couple more staff because we were still responsible for showing and selling the condos too. The work seems to keep doubling, the more we do, and the more there is to do.

Although the staff and the construction teams worked well together, we had a few rough times. I believe it was taking off so fast that we did not have time to breathe. It's now coming up on Labor Day Weekend, the last hurrah and maybe we can settle down, maybe.

It seems, the way Jenny is reacting to me, it appears it will be a go for the wedding. One firm note, she will not move in until after we are married. What is another month? Still that unknown knot in my heart seems to be growing. Maybe it is cold feet or something likes that that is causing this. I love that woman. Still when I say love, it sticks in my throat. Maybe I need to see Roger Strong and we can explore why that is happening. I had called and he is not available because he out of the country and be back until the first week in October. What is a person to do? I guess I will keep doing what I am doing.

Jenny had a break in her work schedule; she had a Wednesday free and by coincidence so did I. A special day with no one around and we can just be in love. I got a friend Steve to rent his 25 ft. cabin boat, which has a small kitchen and a head. There are bunks but we will not go there because I know the answer already. It turned out to be one of those really mellow days. The whole world seemed to melt into soft quiet gentleness.

Jenny dressed in full cowgirlclothing, snap button blouse, blue jeans, and boots. I kid her that we were going boating, not horseback riding. She gave me one of those indescribable looks that women give men and for some strange reason we get what they mean.

Then she asked me, "Where did I think I was going dressed like that?"

I had on white slacks, white tennis shoes, blue stripped t-shirt – short sleeves, and white cap. I believe I looked very dashing.

"I hate to burst your bubble, look around you. This is not the yacht "Ra" with the entire servant crew waiting on you. It is not that gleaming white ship and all the bells and whistles you used to have. This is a boat with no class, just a plain fishing boat, and a bit rustic at that. So I ask you, which of us are dress for this cruise?" were the laughing words flowing out of her mouth.

"Damn, you are right; we both are little out of touch of where we are. I guess I am a lot out of touch when you think we are going fishing. I got a clear understanding that you will not be baiting my hook or taking off my catch. Conjecture is as I see it, there is really nothing we can do to change it now but laugh about it" laughing back.

We loaded up the boat with the lunch and wine Johnny's restaurant provided for us. We were only going to travel down the river past the old Trojan atomic power plant and anchor to do some fishing. In addition, we will have time to learn about each other with some depth. During the journey, we have to watch for half sunken logs in the river because they can shear off the propeller very quickly. The view from our anchoring, the view is a valley kind of scenery; mother earth gives you that protective feeling. Every tree, rock, and landforms embrace you with a gentleness that you have to feel to understand. You can still hear the cars and trucks racing up and down Route 5 across the river in Washington State. The sounds from manmade toys didn't seem to intrude into our world. Even a train sang its song with the blowing of its whistles accenting the beat as it went by across the river.

What a setting for me to tell Jenny my deepest heartfelt love for her. That love growing every day and every way without me doing a thing. I need also to express my fear that I don't understand, maybe, she will able to tell me what it is. Love is a special something. They sing, write poems, stories etc. about love still you have to be there to feel the freedom, blending, and knowing without truly knowing. Is here a test to see if we are?

We spent lot of time laughing how crude things are now compared to the life style on "Ra". We had to do everything, no one to wait on us. We were like teenage lovers, laughing, giggling, and being goofy. How to get started talking about these deeper feeling hoping it will not offend or? I never had this opportunity before even through it's somewhat nerve racking and the same time so refreshing to have someone enjoy it too. We did not catch any fish but that was all right by us. It was such a strange loving time where we just enjoyed each other's presence. I got a little amorous which she allowed some but still she drew the line.

Jenny broke away from me. There was this solemn mood coming over her and with her face demonstrating expression of searching for the right words. She finally said, that she loved me the first time she saw me. Somewhere deep within that knew I would someday be her husband. I am still having a hard time with those thoughts. There is no foundation for them. "Alex, you were a married man when we met. That violated all my rules about dating men, especially, if they were married. It was unthinkable to consider any possible interest in them as possible mate. When you got the divorce, this relationship has been all over the map for me. I love you more than any man I have ever met. That scares the hell out of me. My girlfriends keep pushing to go to the next step in the relationship. I am sorry; I cannot violate my heart. It has been as hard for me as it must be for you. I do not know where all this comes from, still I want both of us to be sure. I will be yours without question when I am sure. Can you still give me time to find my peace with all of this? Your touches, kisses, and even your presence, my whole being hungers for you, and that scares me even more. Does this make sense to you?"

"Jenny, you have expressed my perplexed feeling since I met you. I know you, yet I do not know you. Does that make sense? I really want this to be really, really right for both of us. There are times when I am afraid to love you and I can't understand it. I even hunger to see you, still I am afraid that something will happen and all of this will disappear. Honey! These past months have been a wonderful exportation on how wonderfully you will complete my world. I really do not want to be with anyone else or alive without you. That simple thought, alive without you, I have no explanation to it source. That may seem so mellow dramatic. There are times I want to cry because I am so happy you are in my life and other times I want to cry because I am afraid something will take you away from me." I concluded

"I have something else I need to tell you. I am student and I am working for degree, which will be Physician Assistant [PA]. That is why I was not always available to date because of either classes, schoolwork and soon will be an internship. Some call it practicum, which I will begin this September. Should we take this relationship further, I will have to schedule it around this last final part of my degree. I finally have all the courses behind me and this is the last requirement, then I will be done. Therefore, if you get sick, you will have a PA in the house. Anyway, would you want me to quit my job if I decide to marry you? Can I have a professional life too? Will you, who have been spoiled with servants, be humble enough to do general housework? I want a husband who co-creates life and willing to share the load. Therefore, the cat is finally out of the box, I even had Johnny swear that he would never tell you of my goal occupation until I am sure my world can exist in our world. What do you think?" declared Jenny.

"I have often wondered why you were not available for dating beyond the time your normal job duties, but it was really none of my business. We were great together when there was time. It seemed to work into my busy schedule too. As can you have a professional life, I never thought of you ever giving up that. You are alive being you I would never change that. I have had a professional marriage, but the only thing I want, is we make time for each other every week somehow. I never want to lose courting and or loving in our marriage should we go that far. I want both of us to bring new challenges and ideas for co-creative growth into our daily life. You are not dating old shoe kind of guy, where you settle into routine and every day gets lost in yesterdays nothingness. However, I have to admit missy, that I had thought you might have had two of us guys on the line and you were stringing us long until you make up your mind. That was why you were not always available" I broke out laughing.

Jenny playfully gave me a playful push away, and that look "how dare I even consider those last remarks". Then a gentleness was expressed when she drew me close and just held me. That unknown secure feeling grew that we both can have a creative life within a marriage.

There was this strange silence from what happened. Internal feelings expanded causing the silence to expand to deeper unknown comfort level of knowing. We just looked at each other and grew real close and melting together on the bench seat. It must have been a couple hours; we did not move or say a word. That was so weird. We were lost in time and space. A description one would know if you have similar experience. If this love is really like what I describe, I want it all at any cost.

Finally, we broke out of that trance and half-heartily prepared our picnic lunch. We just kept looking at each other with our own thoughts. Not saying a word still is a knowing it is o.k.

Finally, Jenny broke the silence. "Alex, I have wanted to talk to you about what did just happen. There has never been a private or right time to tell you this. You are giving me so much comfort knowing I am not alone with these kinds of emotions for you. I am not dragging out our relationship for some hidden pleasure. I really want to be real with my feeling for you. Your patience with me has been the greatest gift you could ever give me. You are my diamond engagement ring. We are the symbols of a committed unconditional love for each other. I feel you in my soul and I know you belong there. You will never cause me negative pain there because who you are."

My eyes are cloudy with joy, I spoke very softly, "Jenny, you have said all the feelings, emotions, and words I cannot describe, I feel about you. I feel like I always knew you. That is corny but it is true for me. I am one-woman man and I have been waiting to find the person that fills that real relationship void. Marian was karma problem for which I could not control. When my eyes danced over you the first time we met, I knew you were it. I will wait as long as it takes. We will have something so special, it really worth waiting for. We both feel it and that is major importance to us. I also know there will be times there be some rough water ahead, knowing the sound foundation of friendship we have built over these months, will keep us together. I am sometimes afraid to tell or say how much I love you from a place I never thought I could.

They realized had to awaken out of their dream world. The demands on their time for now were up. They had to come back to reality. Weigh anchor and return to the real world to see and feeling how their personal world continually evolves every day now.

"I want you to know this day has been one of the most complete days of my entire life," I whispered.

"Jenny, before the engine roars drown out any normal conversation, I want you to know I really do love you from my soul. Our real love is superior for me than any just physical heated love. When we merge after marriage, it will satisfy every part of our being. There will be no hidden hunger hiding in the shadows of our lives." This was my last declaration before firing up the engine and racing back to the marina and the real world.

Tying up the boat, there was the eager beagle Johnny charging towards us. "Well! Have to two decided on a date yet? There is lot of work planning a wedding and parties, and celebrations and parties, Oh! I said that twice didn't I? A brother needs to know, so spill the beans?"

"Sorry to disappoint you, we did not even get around to discussing that subject. The saga drags on and you still have to just wait," replied Jenny in brother/sister conversation. In addition, the day moves on.

Labor Day weekend was just as busy as July 4th, weekend or I should have said more. We expected to be successful, but we have been working full out everyday just like week days were weekends. People have been asking if we would build a motel on the river for those who would want to spend their vacations here. That one thing we have not thought or planned as an option. Yet, that would be a great building for a spit of land that we have that has river on front side and wetlands on the backside. That kind of building would fit in there nicely. We will have Ron talking with the county about getting a permit to build and see what happens.

First weekend in September on Saturday afternoon, we have our first meeting with the condo owners about rules and regulations they agreed upon to buy in here. They gave us some ideas of modifications and few others rules that support the quality of life they all wanted to enjoy. Afterwards, we sponsored a block **get acquainted** party for all the residence. It appeared everyone had been busy doing that when they moved in by the way the party flowed. We were sold out all the units in phases one. All the new owners were in residence. The one clause they all liked was the owner could not sublease or rent their unit. The project would buy it back at fair market price if they wanted to move. This was residential community, not rental money making activity. I was also surprised the number of families with children that were involved.

That evening, Jenny and I were dancing a slow dance in our restaurant dance floor. Boy! I was in the mood. I whispered, "Will you marry me?" Without hesitation, she replied back "yes". I wanted to jump up and down with joy; still I contained myself, and just held her closer if that seemed possible.

As we walked off the floor, there was Johnny beaming from ear to ear. "Well! Are we going to have the reception here?" was his first words. We were astonished by his question and how did he know so quickly. Before we could say a word, his replied to our thoughts. "I knew it happen by the way you two melted together during the dance. The universe had me look up just then and there was that glow. So was I right?" were his joyful forceful words.

We could not deny it and we both said it would be Friday the 10th. We both looked at each other with shock that we picked the same day in our own thoughts without asking the other. My reason was I was tired of waiting I wanted to be married. Jenny's reason was she knew they were going to celebrate his birthday on 26th, so they had to be back by then. Of course, this was a supposed to be a surprise. It is strange it had not leaked out yet. Everyone also wanted the celebration to mark the closure and completion of the 1st phases of the project. Again this is hopefully kept a secret, but who knows if it possible with this crew.

Jenny and I went back to our table in the corner with Johnny tagging along as wanting to know more about what is going on. We both agreed that we would be married at county courthouse with few witness. Again, a surprise we were on same track without discussing it. Ol' Johnson came over because he was wondering that Johnny seemed awful excited. He was glad to hear the great news. Then we all began dancing around with thoughts of: should reception be open to our community, just few friends, or every one that frequents the place. After round robin debate, the question was who to invite. The list got so long, we finally agreed to an open house reception was the only answer. We would furnish music for dancing, refreshments, and snacks. We would use the second floor because that is why that space was created.

Before long, it turned into potluck dinner with all condo families and friends. Jenny and I did not have to plan a thing but decided to go with the flow. It boiled down to all we had to do was to get married. We decided that we would have our witnesses: Bev & Ralph, Johnny & Judy, Ol' Johnson, Barbara & husband, Frances, Ron & wife, Steve Holland & wife and Captain Jack who was flying in for the occasion. When the 10th arrived, we looked like an army invading the courthouse. The county judge offered his services to tie the knot. What a day of days!

Jenny still did not find her way to my bed before the wedding. In some respects, I was content that she did not. Those chest tremors were growing. The more I wanted to be emotional and maybe physically in love with her, the worse the tremors were. Maybe those feelings are what happened to person who is truly in love. I was forced to cool that feeling but damn, I did not like it. I used my prayers to ask Kevin what the hell is going on but silence was the reply. I kept making the best of it within my ability to handle because should I push the plate, I damn well knew a panic attack would happen. Been there, done that, don't want to do than any more. After we are married I will get with Roger Strong and find out what in hell is going on now with this new activity.

Chapter 6

Here we are at the County Court House at 4:30 p.m. with our entourage. Jenny and I decided to dress in plain blue outfits with white shirts. She wanted a wrist corsage with two white orchids. We agreed on friendship design wedding band of white gold. The rest of the crew was very colorful. Captain Jack and Ol' Johnson dressed in uniforms of old sea captains.

The county clerk put us in the conference room. We got that room because we had developed friends at the county. They wanted to witness the wedding too. The conference room was the only space where we could accommodate such ever growing witness group. There were people jammed in there I know visited the restaurant. The vows were short and sweet all to the point. Could you believe it was only 6 minutes and we were all done? The witnesses signed our licenses. You know what happens next with all the hugs around. I thought the hugs would never end. When we got out to our car, well, that was sight to behold. They had it decorated with everything that would stick to the car. They did give us one door to get in the car. Then a surprise, we became a small parade with the local cop leading us back to our "HOME on the River". We had planned some time alone, and that was not going to happen because we got there at 6 p.m. just in time for the reception, potluck, and party. Johnny and Judy rushed us to Steve's condo so we would get out of our blue suits and into our peasant Greek clothing to be comfortable. That was the excuse for us to be wearing Greek clothing at our reception. Then we rushed over to the restaurant to begin the reception. Nothing stopped all night long. Such contentment flowed through everyone. At midnight, it was opening presents, which was not to happen. We listed no gifts on every sign and invitations. We still got items that finished our home. Judy and Frances accepted donations from everyone. The names were on the big card with a picture of each gift. The gifts were all ready in our home where they should be, that is why they would not let us go there.

It looks like we will not have alone time until we get to our hotel room in Athens Greece because we are on the red eye out of here.

As I would reflect on this reception from the start, it was just a dance in the rhythm of joy. What a grand night to celebrate a union that symbolizes love. However, there is that damn uncomfortable feeling dancing in my heart again, but I am burying it until we are on our honeymoon. Everyone decorated the space over the restaurant. There were ocean of food and people. Everyone was on high on love or being around good people, because no one got drunk. To our surprise my bar bill was about half of what I expected. Johnny was honest by charging me what the guest drank. It was strange that most of the guest bought their own drinks. The music by our local band was just great. Many slow dances and then occasionaly, they would cut loose variety of songs, the Texas Two Step and swing dances. The grand magical time we were having past with great fantastic speed.

Then at midnight, Johnny brought some Greek Musicians from Portland that showed up and on with the show. They had ribbons and flowers for my wife's hair and the same for my hat. The musicians brought along some singers to sing love songs to us in Greek language. We were pulled into some of the dances. I did not know the step but all I had to do is follow the leader. It was the most fun I have had, I do not remember when. I even forgot the time and passion to be alone with my bride.

It was 2 a.m. before we knew it. We raced to get home, freshen up, and change our clothes. The women were busy with Jenny in one bathroom/bedroom and the men keep me on schedule in the other bathroom/bedroom. They never left us alone a minute and then the gang of cars paraded us to the airport. I have to tell you, I am glad that guests are not allowed to the loading area, a great rule. They way they were hugging and kissing us, it were as if we were never coming back. I kept saying, we will see you in two weeks, but that did not stop them. In my heart, the magic of this day, I did not want it to end either. Now we are on our own and on to - - - - - the unknown, a world we will create and what will that be?

We were traveling first to New York City to get our direct flight to Athens. Our plane was scheduled to leave at 6:30, so we had a short time to settle down for our honeymoon. On the journey, we were still on cloud nine. Jenny asked me, "Weren't we supposed to go the Amsterdam first". There was that look again and I had to be honest about the change in plans.

I had built her up with a day tour of the city, food and tour of the diamond factory. Now, after our talk on the river, I was never going to try to con you into having a diamond ring. I explained my plan to sell you on idea of seeing how diamonds were cut and faceted as part of using up the time between flights. We will take a tour of the diamond factory to see how it is done and I know they have display and sales room. I would have the chance to woo you into having a ring. We have come too far in our relationship of commitment; I could never have done that now. So we will miss the sights of the city. It is not important now. If we are ever going to make this relationship develop and grow, I can't start it out on a false pretenses. We just grew closer together. There were three seats in our row but great that we were the only one there. We took some sleeping aids to insure we would be awake and rested when we got to our first stop. Even when we were a sleep next to each other, when I touched her, my heart would seemed to be afraid. The closer we were to New York, the more pronounced it was. Our nap did not help much although it was 2:30 p.m.; the time zones eat up the time. We travelled across the airport to sign in because of flight will be leaving around 4:30 p.m. on Olympic Airways for our direct flight to Athens. During the 2-hour layover, we did have light lunch, no coffee. We are in hopes to sleep most of the trip. We will be there around 9 a.m. the next day.

We were not as lucky to have our row of seats to ourselves. We were packed in with every seat taken. We had the window seats, so no one had to crawl over us to get in and out. The guy on the end was full bodied; glad we could pull up the armrest between us and it was an excuse to cuddly. We just could not get back to sleep. We were neither a sleep or awake. When the coffee came around midnight, we gave in to being awake. Jenny was concerned that we really have had people around every minute since we said our vows and how that is affect me.

"Jenny, we have full life ahead of us to be alone. Having you here with me seems to satisfy everything I need. Does that make sense?" I whispered.

"Maybe we should have spent time together before we were married because I had no idea of the flood of activity would burn up all our time before getting on the plane? I would not give up what happen, but still I have been thinking about you and me." Jenny whispered back.

"So far, I would not change a thing. We are great the way we are." was my quick response.

We did not seem to talk much after that. It was strange but nice at the same time. Occasionally, a whisper of "I love you" bounced back and forth between us. That guy on end did not sleep, spending his time reading a book and keeping an eye on us all night long.

It seemed like no one on the plane wanted to sleep. Another reason why it was impossible for us to sleep, there was large group of people of all ages traveling together to go back home for a visit or something. They were not speaking English and they talked very fast. They offered us wine because they thought we were going home too. We accepted, I guess, a glass or two. It was like being at our reception again. No sleep, I don't want to get drunk now. Oh well! This journey will not last long, but right now, I really want silence. It seemed we finally able to close our eyes and they were waking us up because we were coming in for a landing.

We arrive at Eleftherios Venizelos International Airport, Athens, Greece little after 9 a.m. The group wanted to have us come along with them to their village. With lot of polite 'thank you', we finally broke away from them, yet it might have been great time too. Like all newlyweds, I could not retrieve our luggage fast enough and get to the shuttle that was taking us to our hotel. We were now alone and who knows how this will play out.

At the hotel, I thought they would never get us checked in. We were early for regular check in time. They finally they found us a room facing the beach that was ready. It was almost 12 noon when we were in the room. I tipped the bellhop, and finally we were truly alone.

"I would like you to have chance to clean up first, because man you look fried. I want to stare out from our balcony to look at the beach and feel that gentle breeze." as Jenny yawned out the words.

"Are you sure?" and I watch her head nod yes. I did not need second invitation. I was in bathroom, out of my clothes, and hot water of the shower was dancing all over me. I soaped down, rinse off, out, dried off and with a towel wrapped around me, I paraded into the room.

Jenny only replies were "that did not take you long, I will join you shortly".

I pulled back the covers, dropped the towel, and slid into those velvet cotton sheets. Someone turned out the lights and I was gone.

Jenny came back into the room and found me fast asleep. She took her time drying her hair and using her special body cream. It was her turn to slide into bed, and the sleep dragon got her too.

CHAPTER 7

The daylight crept softly into my eyes. I felt drugged from the lack of sleep. I could feel a gentle warm body next to me. A very soft sound of breathing at a very gentle rhythm came from that body. I moved closer and aware she was still sleeping. For just a moment, I closed my eyes and the lights went out again for me.

Some time later, a gentle warm floral pungent breeze flowed across the bed, bring us to our consciousness, and we pulled slowly together. Our whole world melted together and we were one. I never experienced such a complete loving sexual intimate experience. We laid there in the afterglow, not wanting to disturb the moment. I was the luckiest man in the world at that time.

There was rattling sound of the phone that shatters loving mood. Jenny was nearest to the phone, she answered it. For a short while, all she did was laugh, and finally handed me the phone. On the other end was Johnny and the friends on speakerphone so they all could talk at once. They were shouting to make sure we heard their questions. I put my hand over the mouthpiece and asked Jenny if it is alright if I just hang up. She smiled and slide back under the sheet. I did not need any more encouragement, I yelled in the phone, "Call you guys in a couple of hours." I hung up the phone, just as those soft arms pulled me graciously towards her. When you are totally in love, you know what happen next.

There were shadows of lights from the balcony that added a warm glow to the ceiling and softness to the room. We decided it was time to get up because we realized we have not eaten all day. It's 8 p.m. by their clock radio, or about 7 a.m. our time. It is hard to adjust so soon. I jokily said to my new wife, "which did we miss dinner or breakfast?"

Jenny just slipped out of bed, dashing for the bathroom and sound of the shower boiling away filled the room.

"Was she ignoring me or what?" I said slowly to myself. It is just nice to lay here smell us while I am waiting for my turn. I can never remember ever being so satisfied completely having sex or loving time. It always seemed like a release or exercise because both parties were not very involved. I read about these kind of experiences did exist; I never thought I would have the opportunity to enjoy it. Marian was cross between let's getting it over, exercise, and or enjoys my faking it. Those kinds of experiences left me unfulfilled, and her reply was always, this is the best it will ever be. I was expecting too much out of love making or sex.

Jenny entered the bedroom in terry cloth bathrobe pointing to the bathroom, "next, make it snappy buster, you have a starving woman on your hands. I do not care if it is breakfast or what meal. You need to feed your new bride. If you don't hurry, you will be meeting me down in the dining room." was her final prodding words.

I didn't need much prodding, because I was in and out of the shower, dried, and almost all my clothes on when she turned to say something. When she looked at me, she had one of those surprised looks that was priceless.

The hotel restaurant was elegant as advertised it. The place was pretty well cleared out but for a few straggler diners. There is nothing like great restaurant smells to stimulate your appetite.

After spending what it seemed like forever looking over all the choices, we finally settled: for appetizer – goat cheese and crostini with fruit. We were going to have plain salad but Jenny decided on chilled almond soup and for me was spiced eggplant salad. Then for the main course, they had leg of lamb with juniper berries with fresh vegetables, which was the house special tonight. The waiter, Frank, set us up with wine because we couldn't make up our minds. I don't remember the name of the wines; so many different kinds, what was chosen was great with every course. We killed one special bottle with the main course. I asked the waiter why he had such a common name. His reply was for the benefit of the customers. My Greek name is Juno to avoid all the lighthearted remarks about my name, I use none descriptive name Frank. Very few customers ask about that name. After over two hours of enjoying the favors, listening to live music that seemed to dance through the hotel everywhere, we were truly alive. Finally for dessert, my most favorite: Lemon Tart I thought I have had the best in the world and I was wrong.

We had greatest intimate time during dinner, sharing food, and talking about our never-ending reception. It was so hard to believe we enjoyed so many things together. During the reception, she would take the lead when I looked like I was overwhelmed and then she bounced the lead back to me. There were so many loving sharing times with all those new friends and neighbors, it was hard to believe we have known them for such a short time. We will have mountains of memories to build on from our special day.

After dinner, we took slow, very slow getting to know you walk to help us to work off some of that stuff feeling from eating too much. The pool seems like an activity we must do the next day. Without much conversation, we agreed to just hang out tomorrow and do whatever during our 5 days here. It is going to be two weeks about us, we are not trying to see everything, on the go on a tight schedule resulting in going home exhausted.

We even took the stairs up to our room for exercise. When we entered our room, we were greeting with very large bouquet of mixed flowers and the bed was made. Aren't we lucky as we looked at each other? Without saying anything more, we undressed, freshened up, and slid into bed. Within minutes, we were in our love land of peaceful quiet sleep.

It was 8 a.m. when I staggered out of bed and retreated to bathroom to freshen up. The world came back into focus as I walked back into our bedroom. I had a surprised double take to see Jenny, in her bathrobe, out on the balcony with tray of fresh coffee and sweet rolls to enjoy. I must been dead to the world not to hear food being delivered and the sweet smell of coffee. In fact, I didn't realize she was up.

Her voice was like music to my ears inviting me to join her and the food. The day of being with someone, you trust and love causes the clock to push the hands of time. After spend quiet time with breakfast, Jenny left and came back in a knock out two-piece bathing suit. It was arousing for me.

She gave me that look, get your suit on we are going swimming now. Do you hear me as she ran out of our room? The day was delicately warm; the pool was splendid and relaxing. Jenny was just getting golden brown and for me, it was more like pink to red, so under the cover I had to go. I will not spend the vacation with a sunburn.

They furnished food and beverages at the poolside. The pool area was not crowded. It was as if we had the area to ourselves. The food sampling required you to eat more. I didn't realize all the great food they had available. We were in heaven without realizing it. For dinner that evening, our waiter, Frank, was instructed by us last night to just surprise us. There wasn't one item we didn't like. I thought our chief on the "Ra" was great, but these guys in this kitchen are magnificent. During our almost 3-hour dinner, we were charting out what to do the next day. We also had plenty of help from our waiter. We decided the walking tour was in order, down to the beach; look at their marina, and shops and taverns where the tourists don't visit. We wanted to blend in, so we bought clothes to wear that was local and Jenny's command of the language helped before we started out on our journey.

Because we decided to tour the harbor at supper last night, we asked Frank, our waiter, if he was aware of someone who had a boat that went around some of the islands that was not touristy activity. We just wanted to do something different and away from the tourist crowd. Frank told us "he had a friend that has a sponge fishing boat that makes trips around the different islands looking for sponges, fish, or whatever to make modest living. He sometimes takes passengers for a fee. It was something like $100 U.S. dollars each more or less, which is not much for the whole day. I will also have the cook pack a lunch for you for the trip. They usually don't feed the tourist."

I asked him to look into the opportunity for the next day. Frank also reminded us to buy something to wear that has long sleeves and pants that are disposable were his words of caution. My friend's boat is not a passenger ship, just small working boat. This is working vessel, and I am sure they will want you to help too. Gloves and hats would be necessary just in case.

Jenny was so thrilled, "what a treat to go out on sponge boat. We are going to be part of history that still alive. I read somewhere there are only 10 to 15 of these boats existing. The whole sponge business has been damaged by infection plus man made sponges are cheaper. Even if they don't dive for sponges, you could not give me a greater gift. My dad used to tell us about sponge gathering and this will be like having him around though he died almost 10 years ago."

"Let's notified Frank it is possible. I will check in with you tonight at dinner." I stated. Then I softly spoke to Jenny, "we will have your dream come true".

As we walked down the streets, the people who pass us would just smile; I guess it showed we were in love. Window-shopping was not my best suit but did not bother me now. We did find a place that Jenny was able to find what we need for our next day voyage. I looked like a real deck hand with my wide brim hat to keep me from being more sun burned than I am right now. Jenny laughing saying, "you look like my brother when you had him over the side cleaning river scum off your *pure white* yacht. I will have to take your picture to show the gang and my brother that you have been reduced to deck hand."

The walk along the marinas was a revelation with all those luxury yachts, which were much larger and more costly than my ex-wife's yacht "Ra". I also know the cost of operating such crafts. You either have to inherit lots of money or build great revenue income or maybe both. I am glad that I am not in that rat race any longer were my thoughts. My mind wandered back to my past marriage to think of the cost of being married to Marian to have it all, that it is not worth it to me now or ever.

We had late lunch at a tavern on the waterfront where we could eat outside and enjoy the view. I have to keep asking myself, does love make everything seem grand? Even the most common activity is so impressive. Maybe it because it the sharing, I don't know. This a very new territory to me. We must have spent 3 hours sitting there, sipping wine, and eating stuffed grape leaves. I do believe they stuff them with everything possible. I will never look at grape leaves the same after today. When you leave a hefty tip, no one seems to mind how long you sit.

As we strolled back to the hotel, we were talking about everything we could find running loose in our brain to compare and or share with the other. The more the exchanges we had, the closer we grew. That is a great feeling but also frightening because that ghost of something keeps dancing in the back of my mind. Right now, I'm not going to let any ghost ruin this for me. Life is wonderful and the past be hanged for now.

After we got back to our hotel, we decided to push our intimate relationship. We took our first shower together. I must admit to myself I felt like a teenager bubbling between doing something naughty and extremely pleasurable. I have to quit comparing this life with the lifestyle I had with my x-wife, because this never happen like this. With a quick wipe down, yet still damp, I pulled back the covers; we just let our passion run free on the bed. In the after mellow glow, we slipped off to sleep while in our close embrace.

Nature call, interrupted my mood, but what is one to do. Jenny was in deep relaxing sleep and I had fantasy of slipping back into our mood upon return. Again, I was shocked to see Jenny sitting out on the balcony waiting for me to return and informing me to get dressed for dinner. I am not used to this kind of treatment, but I can learn fast. When I was dressed, she was ready in minutes; this kind of action is new experience for me. This is great too.

Frank was waiting for us at our usual table and he had all the arrangements for us to have a day on a sponge boat.

For dinner, he recommended Cacik, a salad, a made of refreshing yogurt, that has cucumbers, garlic cloves, mint, dill, etc. served with pita bread. We really enjoyed that. The main course was Stuffed Squid, which is one the Greek delicacy. For dessert, pistachio halva ice cream, what can I say; you had to be there to taste it all. The gentle wine was sipped through the meal. We cut out one course, because we were unable to consume so much food.

The walk up to the pool to let our meal digest because we were stuffed and it was our own fault. The food was excellent. The walk was the right idea before we hit the hay. We have to be at the dock at 7 a.m.

The hotel phone call made sure we were up in time. The hotel also had packed two large basket of food for lunch for the crew and us. Coffee and rolls were consumed in the cab ride that Frank ordered for us. We were on the dock at 7 a.m. sharp

There was this 32 ft. sponge boat with two small masts for sails, a cabin amidships, where I believe the captain lived, painted white with blue trim. The captain and crew appeared to be in their late 50s or older were waiting for us. The captain motions us aboard. When the crew saw we had two baskets of food, they were eager to assist us.

The captain's name was Andreas. He introduced his three-crew members, Ayres, Julius, and Tassos, who acknowledge themselves as their names were called. I had the pleasure of introduce Jenny, my wife, and I was Alex.

Andreas informed us that they were planning some fishing, or fish netting, or whatever to make the day profitable. He was thankful that we honored him by wanting to spend the day with them plus our payment helps a lot. I slipped him his fee while he was talking to us.

Ayres said something to Tassos in Greek with smile and Tassos smiled back.

Jenny replied, in Greek, "Thank you for the complement".

Their jaws dropped in surprise. Jenny went on to say, "her father and mother came from this area. When their both parents died, they went to America. My brother and I were born late in their marriage and we were required to think and talk in Greek and English. That is why I do not have accent when I speak English. It is great pleasure to be with you today, for you remind me of the pictures my father brought with him to America." Jenny exchanged some more pleasantries in native language to warn the crew to mind their words. This activity helped make a greater connection with them.

Andreas spoke up say, "we know a little English. We were concerned as to how to spend a day with English speaking people. We spend most of our time among ourselves. I had told Frank the other day, we are having hard time making ends meet lately and now he send us, you. It is an extra special pleasure because you speak our language too. Alex do you speak our language?"

Alex quick reply, "no, but do not let that bother you, Jenny will keep me informed when necessary. We are so pleased that you are giving us this opportunity today." They acknowledged I said something, but I am not sure they understood most of it.

They shoveled off, hoisted the triangle sails and we sailed quietly as we left the harbor. Jenny and I went to the bow to enjoy the scenery unfolding before us. We felt like we were on bow of the "Titanic", the movie. Love is grand.

We spent time watch them fishing. It is always thrilling to watch all the action and activity. We ran on to school of fish, so the captain turned about and made a run with the net out. They caught many fish. The crew and the captain yelled out we were their lucky charm.

They also ask if we could help pull in the nets. It was something neither of us has ever done, but sure was fun. I am glad we brought along gloves. We were soaked with smell of seawater and fish. Some of the fish got out of the net. We had to catch them and put them down the chute to the locker. I never realize how slippery fish are to catch. I don't believe I have ever laughed so much from the fun we were enjoying together. We were like kids. Jenny would relay instructions from time to time from the captain so we all could work as a team. We must have brought laugher to the crew watching the two kids enjoying themselves doing what most people would consider work.

The midday was upon us and the captain pulled into small harbor of this almost totally barren island. The lunch was just great and Jenny acted as host through it all.

The captain told us tale about this island. It seems long ago, a very rich merchant of Athens had a young son. The boy was kidnapped and held for ransom. His father refused to pay. By accident, a trading vessel pulled into this harbor and they saw a cloth up against the cliff in sort of cave. They climbed up to the cave where they discovered the skeleton of the boy. The clothes and necklace revealed it was the missing boy. The men bundled up the boy's body. It was taken back and given to his parents. The father was so bereaved that his mother had to see to the burial. The owner of boat was rewarded for his deed greater than the ransom demand. That makes the story even sadder. It was said for the longest time, that when any one passed this island, they could witness the ghost of the boy looking out waiting to be rescued.

I felt something strange happened to me during the story. With all my iron will, I was not going to go there. I was on my honeymoon and nothing was going to ruin it for me.

It was about 2 p.m. when they lifted anchor and started to head home. They had good catch and a very happy voyage. The crew interacted with Jenny like long lost kinfolk. To hear them interact in their mother tongue was almost like music, especially when Jenny would break with one of her uncontrollable laughs. What a pleasure to witness your lovely wife being free and open with friendship. It was not just an act, not for money either, but just because she enjoys being with them and them with her. Jenny seems to bring the best out in everyone she meets. I am one hell of a lucky guy. That thought keeps scaring me from time to time.

When they pulled into to the dock, Jenny and I said our final goodbyes quickly because the crew had to get their catch unloaded. I gave the captain an extra $100 for the day because it was great gift and pleasure for my new wife.

Jenny lead me to the closest tavern. We sat outside because we really smelled like fish. The waiter just kept smiling at us. Jenny asked him in Greek why was he smiling. His reply was the smell of fish on us means someone boat had a very successful day. He was happy to know it happened. Jenny took the time to tell him of the good fortune to find this school of fish that are not usually around this time of the season, and the captain made a great catch. We had lots of fun bringing it all in.

We remained at our table sipping soft white wine for a time to reflect and enjoy the pleasures that flooded us all day long. She now understands the longing her parents had for this area. Yet, it is sad they were unable to return but she enjoyed it because it awakened the love that lived in her family. I just sat there enjoying the glow of the day, silently, with my wife. I understand her better today than yesterday.

We decided an easy slow walk back to the hotel would give us time to settle in with the pleasures of the day and maybe air out the smell of fish. The full day was special. The whole day flooded with overload on the senses. Most the time, words were not necessary to carry rapture of the happening. Everything, every observation flowed with hearty pleasure excelling beyond their dreams of expectation.

CHAPTER 8

In the room, a quick shower to rid of that fishy smell and a naptime. It was again a time where Jenny sneaked out of bed and was spending some quiet time on the balcony. I wanted to give her space, but still I wanted to be with her. She saw me, and yelled out, "better get ready for dinner for I am starved. What kind of husband are you to let your woman starve?" with the biggest smile on her face. Obeying her command, I was ready in short order. I took her by her arm, escorted down to main dining room via the elevator. I was stiff from all the exercise today. As we entered the dining room, Frank greeted us.

Frank was so pleased that the day trip turned out so wonderful for everyone. His friend made enough off the sale of his fish to pay the crew for the month. Also it paid for the dock fees, supplies for the vessel and some left over for a little wine. He was very appreciative of the company and your generous gift. "I really want to thank you for helping my friend. He was beside himself of what to do. Who would know you both made such a difference. They were all so pleased to have you with them for the day as friends. Thank you both." Then he showed us to our table.

The red wine flowed gently into the glass. The first course of sweet-crusted lamb started the appetizers. The meal waltzed around lamb, which was most delightful. I have to say we had an exceptional dessert: berry brulee tarts. What part of the meal was better than the rest, it was impossible to compare, but I have to tell you those tarts were heavenly. When we finally finished, again a walk was in order before we turned in for the night. Outside, a gentle warm breeze carried the delicate bouquet of the evening flowers that were in bloom. Evening had cooled off to comfortable 72 degrees. The clear sky was flooded with diamonds. The moon had not made its appearance, and all was right with the world.

We retired for the night. Later in the night, moonlight entered the room and as it touched me. I began a silent scream. The nightmares are coming back. I am lost some place. Fear of being abandoned slowly crept in. Strange but knowing pictures flashed very rapidly that did not make sense. Boat, water, island, boat, water just kept flashing away. I try to escape out of these seamless strange collages of pictures that caused my heart pain. My mind tries to swim with great effort out of that black hole into consciousness. Finally, I am back as I look around the room. I find myself beginning to sweat and shake. It is coming back. I had better get out of bed. I quickly grabbed my bathrobe, cell phone, and escaped out on the balcony and closed the door. I swiftly dial Johnny's phone and on second ring his voice explodes into my ear with joy. Before we get lost in conversation, I told him I am having a nightmare and it is scaring the hell out of me.

"Alex, remember what Roger Strong told you that you could have flash backs from time to time. You know that what they are. Don't you remember him telling you that?" was the stern reply from Johnny.

"Yes, but this is something I have never experienced before. There were pictures that were frightening. There are feelings in my heart that I thought my heart would break. It is different. I want to just cry from inside out. I really have not experienced this hopelessness and despair" was his anxious response.

"Come on, let's not lose it. Why don't you get into a tub of hot water and give yourself permission to just let it go. You are on your honeymoon. You have to pack it until you get home. I will hold you in thoughts of strength until I see you. If you need some pills you used to take, I packed them in your soap case in your shaving kit. Second thought, why not take one, no take two now and go and soak. Okay?" Johnny's sterns softly reply.

"I will do that right now. Jenny is still sleeping. I can do this. Johnny, I am just scared because I thought I was over all this pain. I will call you later, thank you." The words melted faintly out my mouth as I hung up the phone.

Quietly, I opened the door, walked as inaudibly as possible into the bathroom. Went directly to the tub and started to fill the tub with hot water to deal with this unexpected event. The pills were there where Johnny hid them. What a relief as I washed them down and slipped into the tub filled with hot water. That nightmare was evaporating slowly.

Gently a voice awakened him and as he opened his eyes, there was Jenny looking radiant. "I heard the water, and I knew you needed time by yourself. However, you have been in there for half an hour already. Therefore, I decided to see if you were alright. Johnny told me sometimes you have nightmares and hot water is a solution to help resolve the problem. I want you to know I am here for you if you need me to deal with them. It is alright to have them, because it is a way for the body to heal. If you need me, I will be right here. Now just go back to your healing activity" were her comforting words.

About half an hour later, exhausted, I finally crawled out of the tub. Jenny came in to help me towel down, walked me back to bed and I was asleep as soon as my exhausted body hit the bed.

Is this the beginning or the end of his nightmares were Jenny's thoughts. Johnny had informed his sister of nightmares caused by his parents and Marian so if something as if that happened, it just house cleaning. Not to worry, he will be alright very shortly.

CHAPTER 9

On Wednesday, it was a planned tour of the city as a tourist. We met the bus and off we went to see the important sights of Athens. For four hours, we traveled the streets taking you past the Tomb of the Unknown Soldiers to Parthenon. Since the tour was about over we decided without saying a word to each other to take more time studying and looking at all the wonderful art at the Acropolis Museum. It was strange that we both liked similar art work.

We got back to the hotel still in time for late lunch. What a joy to have our faithful waiter greeting us as we entered the dining room and showing us to our table. He suggested a cold lamb sandwich, salad and some white wine to give us pleasure. It was just what we need to take the edge off of our hunger but not filling. We asked him where we could buy some copies of ancient Greek statutes where we are not part of tourist trade. He had a friend that had a shop off the beaten path and he wrote down the directions to get there. It was about nine blocks from the hotel, which is just the right distance to walk off the lunch. We arrived are the shop and it had almost everything. The owner also displayed his wares as a street vendor to supplement the income for the store. We found about five items that would really fit into our new home and couple or so items we can give as gifts. They were cheaper than on the main streets shops and better quality. The shop owner even packed them up and shipped back home for us. He was happy to hear that Frank from the hotel sent us. Frank has not given us a bad experience yet. We were enjoyed the pleasure of getting the gifts and items for *our* home. It was also pleasant to find someone who looks at nude statutes and enjoys the form, and the mind does go into the gutter.

We seem to take many naps lately or just look out over the world from our balcony. The days have been so comfortable and pleasant, or was it the company that made it so.

It was after seven when we return to the dining room. It seemed like that all we were doing, but the food was great. Frank asked us if we found what we wanted and was pleased that his friend was so helpful.

I could not decide between fish or duck for the main course. Finally duck breasts with walnut and pomegranate sauce won out. Jenny decides she would have the same thing since Frank said they were going to have some special seafood presentation tomorrow. The five-course meal with the duck just made it more magnificent. We were charging everything against the room number. The hotel told us that they put 20% tip on the bill for the service, which has been worth more than that to me.

We did our usual evening walk and with quiet time on the balcony, before turning in. This activity has become almost like a ritual with us. We cuddled and I was aroused but Jenny knew by now, that did not mean a need every time.

The next morning, a full breakfast showed up at 8 a.m., to my surprise. Jenny told me that she had Frank put in the order last night. She wanted a morning of leisure and enjoy a 'whatever happens day'. We had no definite plans. Jenny also realized that there was something bothering me as we walked around. Something I was not aware of, so why put me through whatever it is by bringing up these nightmares. The quality time they were experiencing so far was fuller of life than being busy with normal tourist activity.

We decided to take afternoon walk. As we pass through the lobby, the desk clerk calls out to us to that there was a message for us. It was from Captain Andreas and he wanted our company for dinner at 7 p.m. He included a phone number for a quick reply. What a pleasant surprise. That is the way life should be, filled with pleasant surprises. We called him and informed him that we would be there.

The afternoon evaporated as we wandered the streets and looked for something special for Jenny in a blouse to remember this trip. After a few stores, she finally found one that she really wanted. It was very indigenous in appearance and the right amount of blue trim on the white cotton cloth. We took her treasure back to the hotel, cleaned up and on to evening with the captain.

We walked to the boat to find the captain waiting for us. He said he had a surprise for us and we needed to follow him. We walked along the waterfront and up a side street of the old part of the city. We came to a house that looked like most of the houses, white, but this one had a green door. Andreas lifted the iron ring on the door and threw in back against the door to announce we were there. When the door opens, we viewed the men from the boat and their families in interior courtyard. To our surprise, Frank was there too with his family. All of this dumbfounded us. Frank spoke first; we are having a Greek celebration for you both as wedding present. You both have been so kind to all of us, we want to share back. [If you never been to such a party, there are no words to describe it with justice.] As we looked around, even the shop owner and his family were there. The gift was they wanted for this night, for us, was to be our adopted family and celebrate as a family. Jenny was so happy that she wore her new blouse to fit in. Everyone there demonstrated love, which went beyond language or words. It was a night that was memorable by all who attended because everyone's cup flowed with such unconditional family love. Jenny whispered into my ear, "I now understand what my father always talked about that he missed not being here. The music, dancing, singing, wine, food, and friendship brought everyone together."

I sang along with them, not knowing what the words meant. Most of the time was holding the tune. It was time to go. Some of our new family walked us back to our hotel, parting with hugs and check kisses as one does with family. They were still singing as they walked on their way back home.

When we got to our room, we went out on their balcony and sat there hugging each other. Sometimes crying with such joy and hoping it will never end. We even drifted off to sleep on the settee. I found myself wishing my parents were like what we shared today but that would be wishful thinking. Still my heart ached for those experiences. I fell into deep dark sleep. A nature call helped us find our bed for the night.

Our last day activity resulted in just laying around the pool and just enjoying the pleasures of being in a place that makes you feel real and loved. That evening, Frank was true to his word. The full seafood meal was really worth waiting for. I asked Frank how we could repay his friends for the gift of love they gave so freely last night. We are still bubbling inside from such human a gift and yet so content. My wife really understands her father's and mother's stories of the friendship and love they had here. Now she is truly a part of it. They are no longer words, but a true real emotional feeling that give you comfort and warmth. We want to share back in a true way of appreciation and love that was shared with us. Frank said he would think it over. Later during the meal, Frank talked to us about a gift if we want to do something. The hostess of the party always wanted something from America to put on display in her home. Many of her relations went to America, but for some reason they would send money to help the family but no gifts. Frank gave us a few suggestions, so it was up to us what we want to do. Our new family believes your presences brought good luck to them. They had a very successful fishing trip the day you were on the boat and the next day, they had similar luck. Besides, when you were on the boat, you worked just like family. They were so happy for what you brought them. Even the storeowner, in his store and working the streets, has had best sales than what they have had for the past two months. Therefore, they truly wanted to share back.

When we get home, I know Jenny has a good eye and she knew a few things the hostess would be pleased with. We will have fun time putting the gift together for her. We probably find something to share with them all. Never having this activity in my life, this will be Christmas with love when we do.

CHAPTER 10

Here it is Saturday and we need to be checked out and get on to the next leg of our journey. I had the hotel give a 30% tip for Frank on our bill because all the help he gave us. He made our stay special, beyond words of utter pleasure.

On to Rome aboard the Olympic Airway at 9:00 a.m. and arriving Da Vinci Airport at 10:10 a.m. Now those time changes are showing up the other way. I gather up our luggage, and we took the shuttle bus into Old Rome. We had the driver leave us off at the train station, because our hotel was short way away. A friend stayed here told me try it, I will like it. He like it because was in center of old Rome which gave you the advantage to walk to major sites.

When we checked in, a walking map of the area was furnished to find many points of interest. We were settled in and had to laugh if this is truly a three star hotel. I asked Jenny if she did not like it, we could find another place. We were on the third floor and it only had a shower. All the rooms with tubs were already reserved. This shower is going to be a trouble for me. This place is not sound proof like the hotel we had in Athens, but it will do. Jenny stated, "We will have to be a little quieter when we are making or being lost in love."

"This hotel will be fine because we are only going to be here for 2 or 3 days. I need exercise and this place will serve us well" was Jenny's quick reply.

It was lunchtime. We walked down stairs and out the front door. To our left was a mom and pop's restaurant. I understand a little Italian and so did Jenny. The easiest thing was to order the special for the day. We placed our order. The owner went next door to get the food and brought back for momma to cook. I was facing the kitchen and she was fun to watch. When the husband was busy with the customers, she would sneak a small glass of wine out of the keg. All our meals there were very good, not fancy, but good in the best way. We had litre of house wine and liter of mineral water so we had all the fluids we need. The house wine was only 3 or 4% alcohol, so you could enjoy the flavor without getting drunk.

We gently walked down a couple blocks to Emanuel Tomb. A block or so away was the Colosseum where we visited. We enjoyed walking up to different levels and trying to visualize the glory and horror that were demonstrated there. We found a coffee shop as we head for the Fontana di Trivi. As we sit at a table of sidewalk café, we enjoy pasting time just people watching. The coffee was great along with few sweets. Afterwards, hand in hand, we trudge onward to the fountain with our coins to make a wish. The tourist and venders consumed the fountain area. Everyone seemed to be in festive mood, not an unhappy or sad face in the area. We threw our coins over our shoulders while making a wish. Who knows if it truly works? After that, we were on to the Spanish Steps, where we found that place was full as well with people. We took more pictures as we have done from the beginning of the trip, to build memories and show everyone where we had been. The top of the steps gave you a great view. We just hung out there for hour or so. Being together was more important to us then trying to see everything. We worked up appetite so as we walked slowly down the street facing the steps, we found this intriguing restaurant that had a cooked suckling pig on displayed in the window.

The dinner hour was just beginning, so the place lacked customers. The waiter showed us to a table in the corner to give us space to by ourselves. I wonder how he could tell we were newlyweds. The menus were in English too. While we took turns to fresh up, we tried to guess what are partner would want for main course. We split an appetizer of prosciutto with melon which was very pleasurable. Main course, we both could not pass up the roast pork with red wine and pan cooked vegetables. It was just wonderful!

We decided to pass on the salad and go for dessert. That option became a trouble basket for me. The waited brought out this three-tier cart. You name it, and it was on the cart. Jenny decided on Sicilian cassata. The waiter understood my dilemma; he stated he would take care of it for me. When he came back, with a platter of slice of every dessert that could be sliced. What a treat and I ate it all. Without saying, we had glass of wine with each course. I left our waiter with 30% tip, which opened his eyes. A reward for everyone who makes your life better, isn't that is what life is about? That dinner romanced away over 2 ½ hours and the moderate stroll back to the hotel was welcome pleasure and reduce the full stomach.

The next morning, I needed to shower, but I never shower in the morning. There has always been this deep-seated fear within me about taking a shower in the morning. My family was always taunting me about it. Baths were safe. Therefore, I always use the bathtub in the morning, never a shower. I can't really tell you why. Jenny began to gently tease me about my phobia. That did it for me. I went into the bathroom, turned on the water and prepared to shower. I kept saying to myself, whatever reason for the phobia, I want it removed now. I stepped in, the water was flooding over me, and as I began washing something happened. Suddenly, the water turned blood red as I looked down toward the drain. Then I was horrified when I saw what looked like old Roman soldier's sword sticking out of the front of my chest. I was gripped with unknown fear, anger, and emotions I can't describe. What in hell is this? I have to get out of here I am not safe. I quickly opened the door, staggered out and sat on the toilet expecting to fall dead. I looked at my chest and there was no sword sticking out of me. I looked around me and there was no blood anywhere. Now, what the hell is this?

In a flash, I saw myself in countryside outside of Rome. I was a general in the Roman army and we were camped just outside this small town. It is morning and the general [I] was standing under a waterfalls in nearby stream taking a predictable shower. I watch the general's junior officer come up behind me and with my own sword, stabbed me in the back. I witness as I looked in state of shock; the water was turning red with my blood. My own sword blade was sticking out of my chest and such disbelief was flooding over me. I was dying. I looked over my shoulder to see the man I trusted staring back at me. I turned to move toward him but life drain out quickly and I was dead. The movie continued a short time later. I witness this cowardly junior officer later being paid off for doing the deed. It appears I was standing in the way of a local official, who was abusing the town's people for his own gains. Then I am witnessing the junior officer being slain by that same official and he was taking back his money. Serves that bastard right for what he did to me flooded my thoughts. I now know why that activity bothers me. I have to remember I am no longer a Roman Officer, so I have to let that emotional trauma go. That trauma was my productive life was cut short by that death, but I have to let the emotional trauma go because I can't change what happened. I have to remember that my soul life lives on in other bodies and lifetimes, maybe I have completed all the tasks I was supposed to do in that lifetime. I hope so, or maybe I should be more definite by saying I know so. I have to realize all the talents I have to be successful; I learned them in previous lives. Nothing is lost when the soul learns how to do it in material body.

Jenny came in to see why I had not come out since shower noise had stopped. "My God, now what in hell is going on with you? You are white as a ghost and you are just sitting their dripping everywhere."

"Oh! Jenny another one of those flashes back in a past life. At least I know why I can't take a shower in the morning. Before you ask, let me tell you. It appears that I was Roman Officer who was trying to protect the people in the community from an unscrupulous official of the government. This official paid my junior officer to murder me with my own sword while showering under a waterfall. I think I have worked it through my head, I was dead again, but I am here now and I am okay. I now believe that unknown fear, anger, or both are gone. We will know tomorrow won't we?" was my nervous laugh.

"You are looking better every minute, and as long as you say you are okay, you have to get ready for your bride is hungry. I wonder why I have to keep telling you – your bride is hungry. Aren't you hungry too? Remember we have planned a day at the Vatican and the Sistine Chapel." were Jenny's words as she turned and left the room. I quickly got my act together and I was dressed ready for the day and to answer the urgent request of my "wife" [what a beautiful sound – my wife]. We journeyed to the Hotel's

Roof Garden to enjoy a complimentary Italian breakfast before going out to enjoy the City. You name it; it was banquet of breakfast foods. The fruit always seems to taste like it was just picked off the tree or vine. The meal was refreshing besides we were not in hurry to do anything. It is great to have partner doesn't have to be on the go every minute.

At 10 a.m., we caught the bus out on main drag for the Vatican. The bus was not crowded, so we were able to sit together and be lovers. The ride seemed very short. We walked into St. Peter's square and it appears round to me. In the middle, we found Egyptian Oboist, which seems strange since this was the entrance to the Christian Church. The oboist had Egyptian writing on all sides. I can see why when the news was reporting a big event here St. Peter Square, this area can handle a half million people or more. The church building is massive.

As we entered the building, on the right was the famous Pieta. It is hard to visualize that Michelangelo was only twenty-three [1498] when he started carving such a magnificent statute and it was completed when he was twenty-five [1500]. Now it is protected behind clean plastic shield. To think of all the years it was there almost touchable and then one person's action moved us away from something so beautiful.

The next couple of hours, we walked around the church, looking at all sculptures, painting, etc. It is very impressive, but I kept felting an odd sensation. I could not put my finger on it because it seemed to be related to something long ago and far away. Had I been here before? It feels familiar. We even walked up the stairs to top of the dome. What a treat.

We found the crowd of tourists that was on their way to Sistine Chapel. We followed them, which turned out to be a short walk, and we were there. The movies and pictures just don't give it justice. We found a bench to sit for a while and enjoy it all. It all seemed so impossible yet there it is. What a vision for all of us to enjoy as long as the building stands. In our guidebook, it says it was completed by 1512. There are over 300 figures on the ceiling. What a talented man Michelangelo was and also considering the tools and equipment he had to work with. What amazing creative passion he demonstrated in his work. Our stomachs started to rumble, the next activity to find something to eat.

We found a great sidewalk café, served excellent sandwiches and coffee. We must have spent over an hour people watching, holding hands and enjoy our time together. From out of nowhere, an unruly group of young people were pushing and shoving their way up the street. Everyone seemed to give way to them; I took Jenny and moved her into the shop to be out of harm's way. There was a lot of shouting, yelling and pushing as they made their way past us. Then sirens were screaming as the local police drove up to the group and the police were out in full force quickly. The group broke loose and they were running everywhere.

"Well! Jenny I am trying to make this a memorable trip" trying to hide my own fear.

"For me, I can do without this kind of activity. You never know what boils out of these kinds of commotions. I had seen enough at the hospital where peaceful demonstration went bad. When people are in that uncontrolled activity, the primitive behavior comes to the surface abruptly and things happen beyond belief. Let's get out of here and head back to the hotel; I want no part of this." Jenny's voice seemed to force the words out.

I did better than that, I hailed a taxi, and very shortly, we were at the hotel. I asked the driver if he knew what was going on. His reply went something like this in his broken English. "There always a group who are unemployed and they are out to cause trouble. You see them coming, duck for cover. You never know" were his parting words.

We went into the hotel bar and ordered a tall drink. We then when up to the Roof Garden to spend the rest of the day. As the shadows of night stretched out, it was time to cleaned up and adventure out for dinner.

We found a restaurant near the hotel, had the special, which was with pasta, veal, figs, and whatever else that blended in. While dining, we decided that we would go back to the airport and take a plane to Florence, for a day or two tomorrow morning. This seems strange, here we are in the Eternal City with all its history and doesn't inspire us to stay. I guess we are getting homesick but not ready to admit it yet. The party we were involved in Greece, just made us want to be home with our new friends and family. Maybe we can develop that kind of friendship family love where we live. My heart seems hungry for the human feeling or belonging. I am not sure which one, both would be nice.

Chapter 11

The next morning, with great trepidation, I walked into the clear glass shower stall and began the usual body washing. Jenny stood there watching to see if I really had a handle on this haunting fear. I was nervous I have to report there was no blood or sword sticking out in front of me. I have to tell you I did not spend much time in there either. It was also strange for me to have my new wife watch all of this, also exciting. She told me we had get dressed for the shuttle, so put get a move on.

The hotel arranged for shuttle back to the airport and we were able to hop a flight to Florence and quick trip to Strozzi Palace Hotel. The room greatly out did the Apollo. Besides it had oversize bathtub. You can tell we were on our honeymoon, for we sent the rest of the day just being with each other in our room. That little ghost fears kept dancing in my head and I was busy shutting them down.

By eight, we walk slowly in the warm gentleness of the evening to an over decorated Italian restaurant a short distance down the street. It appeared it was there since the Italian Renaissance period. As we opened the door, we were greeted with musical aroma of magnificent food. The atmosphere and every decoration made you feel how glad you were there. This was our dream wish of the kind of places we wanted to be in our memories bank. The headwaiter directed us to our table and introduces our waiter for the evening. I decided I would have the specials for the evening, which was Ricotta mousse with bell pepper sauce appetizer [which we shared] Jenny had asparagus and shrimp quiche while I tackled sweet and sour calamari pie. I had roast veal roulade and Jenny went for the Florentine beefsteak with stewed vegetables. You would thought we had not eaten in weeks and we slowly savored each bite as we devoured our meal. I was not sure what exact kind of wine came with each course but they were very enjoyable, which included Chianti for which the area is famous for besides other wines. Two hours later we allowed the chiavari cake complete the whole meal. Good food and company makes everyone happy, especially me. After paying the bill, we returned to our room for comfortable night sleep because we are off again tomorrow.

After a light breakfast at the hotel, we were off with our map to visit the city. We were in the city is often considered the birthplace of the Italian Renaissance. Uffize museum is world class, which concentrated on sculpture, and works of art because of large bequest from Medici family, which we really enjoyed. We have no explanation why we skipped the huge Pitti Palace. I guess we are not into tombs because Santa Croce basilica had Michelangelo's tomb. We skipped that too. What was important to us was to see "David" and the bridges with all the shops. I have seen copies of David, they were good, to see the real thing, that was even better. As I was standing there looking at him, another one of those odd feeling crept over me.

CHAPTER 12

Time seemed to stand still and I was in another time and place. I was standing in with my friend Giovanni in Michelangelo's workshop behind the cathedral. We had heard that he had a City Council commission to create a statute, a very tall statute. My friend and I were strapping young noble men who were asked to come to Michelangelo's workshop. We were very curious as to why, so here we are. When he saw us, he gave us a big hug as he always did. He informed us he was going to carve a statue of man and wanted to know if I would pose for him. Michelangelo looked at me and said, "Mario, would you strip off your cloths so I can see if you have the body I am looking for as a model."

"Are you serious?" was my reply.

"Of course," he said, "because this will be a statute of nude man of power and command. He will be bigger than life. I will first need to draw sketches of your naked anatomy and then I will turn you into stone. As you have heard, I am going to display my statute in the square. Do you want the job?"

Cocky I was, of course, and before anyone knew it, I was standing there naked. Michelangelo started making sketches of me in different standing poses. Giovanni kept taunting me all the while this was going on. I think he was jealous because I was chosen and he was not. A little playful rivalry between us always existed and especially who has it all together to get the woman.

After a short time, Michelangelo turned and asked Giovanni if he would pose also. Giovanni jumped at the opportunity. Before we knew it, he was naked as day he was born. I have to admit he has good physique, but mine is terrific. Michelangelo set about sketching him in different upright poses.

The workers in the yard looked us over as they passed by. We were proud of our physiques. They must see lot of naked people working for Michelangelo. We know we must be the most handsome men their eyes have ever seen. He again asks me to stand up near my friend and for some time, Michelangelo kept walking around us, looking us over and sketching.

"As matter of fact, Giovanni, I would like you to be my support subject. I want you to understand, the statute will not look just like you and it will have a different name as you know. Therefore, you will not be able to strut around town when my work is on display declaring that is you. I will also tell everyone that he is my own creation" were Michael's words. He offered us coins for our time, but our pride of being a model for such an undertaking, was pay enough.

I was still angry that I was not chosen. Yet, happy my best friend would have the honor and still glad it will not look totally like him. As we were getting into our clothes, the picture faded away and I was left with disappointment feeling. The best words I can describe it was why not me. Is this why I have that feeling every time I see reproductions of David? When I seem to come back into focus, Jenny was staring at me.

"Where did you go, I was talking about the statue and what an honor it must have been to be chosen to pose for Michelangelo. There you were looking in space and ignoring me" stated Jenny.

I was still not totally hearing Jenny. My thoughts were still rambling on about David. When you look at David, little over fourteen foot tall cut down from nineteen-foot block of marble. It represents an athletic, manly character, very concentrated and ready to fight. The extreme tension is evident in his worried look and in his right hand holding a stone. David truly is that symbol of heroic courage. I have to admit he doesn't look like Giovanni or me but mixture of both of us. It was finished in 1504 and to think of all wars, whatever destruction plagued this city, he is still there for us to see and enjoy the passion of the artist.

"I had a flashback again about something I will tell you later" was the only thought that came to mind. I was still trying to get back there to ask the question. I couldn't, but the thoughts kept haunting me as we walked along. Was this really truly another one of those flashes back? Would I dare to believe what my mind's eye displayed to me? These flash-back are happening everywhere we go. Can't I control them? I need to really get with Roger Strong when I get back because I can't keep having this stuff happening.

We went on our way to the bridge and the shops. In one of the shops, we found a 24" bronze reproduction statute of David. As I was holding it, I told Jenny that they have bronze casting of the original David in a park in Buffalo, N.Y. Looking at my face Jenny insisted, "I will buy this reproduction because seemed to be important to you as a wedding present from your bride." Then Jenny blurted out, "we really don't have room for original bronze casting in our living room." We both had a laugh over that. We did buy the bronze statue of David anatomical reproduction and had it shipped.

We found a few pieces of jewelry with her birthstones in them. We could not resist. I also bought a bronze canon about 1850 vintage. It was only 7 inches long for Johnny. However, every time the thought of David entered my mind, there were those troubling unanswered thoughts. Oh well! I just need to let it go and enjoy the day. The whole day was gone by the time we got back to our hotel to freshen up to eat again. I must have gain 10 or 15 pounds already. Jenny isn't saying a thing about gaining weight, and I think I knew better not to ask.

Again, I had the same feeling of being here before, and I am not interested in looking at the splendor of the city. Maybe that flash back about the creation of David is the answer. Who knows? I can't wait to see Roger and see if I can sort some of this stuff out.

We had a light supper at the same restaurant as last night. While we were dining, we decided we needed to head back to Rome airport to catch our flight to Madrid, Spain. Our days are going fast. Maybe we need not stay for the two weeks. These strange happenings are wearing us down and I guess we just want to be home with our own family. That experience in Greece, really made us realize what we do have and we in truth miss that. Loving friends in faraway place is not as great as those who are on your doorsteps. As much as I want that love attention, my heartaches of something that seems to be cross between abandonment and loss. I try as hard as I can to define that feeling, it is just beyond words to me now. I have heard of people that hunger for loving family but still they are terrified when it offered. I guess I am in the same boat they are in. Still I am going to resolve this as I did the other crap that almost destroyed me.

CHAPTER 13

The next day was a blur, get to airport, fly to Rome airport to be there before 10:30, get to the Madrid gate because we were off at 12:15 and arriving Madrid Barajas International Airport at 14:36. The more I think about this honeymoon trip, the next time we go anywhere, it be to only one place. Trying to take in too much of Europe in to short of time, has been to stressful. Maybe that is what is causing those flashbacks in time. Who in the hell knows?

We took the shuttle to Tryp Infanta Mercedes Hotel in the heart of Madrid. We settled into our room, which was great. The hotel has an inside patio were we could chill out and feel the heart beat of the city. We strolled around the hotel, looking for a restaurant, which we seem to spend a lot of time looking for some place to eat. We found the one recommended by the hotel and it was very pleasant place. Jenny was getting moody, and I have never seen her like this.

"Jenny what is the matter?" I inquired

"I do not know but I feel funny, strange. I don't know what is going on. The closest I can compare it to is a feeling when you are lost and afraid. There is no justification for this. It might be jet lag since we are moving into different time zones. Maybe I just want to go home. I want to live in our home and enjoy each other. It can be sign of homesickness. I have never had it before. After dinner, let's go back to our room and whatever. Maybe I am beginning to catching your flash back illness or whatever you call it" was Jenny's frustrating response.

We ate very light meal, a salad with little wine. If we spent an hour there, it would be about it. We left the restaurant and headed back to our room at the hotel.

Jenny decided she was going to turn in and see if by morning, she would be ready and able to take on a tourist tour of the city. They will be picking us up at 9 a.m. The bed felt wonderful, all was right with our world.

It was midnight, I found myself in the bathroom, and suffering from what I thought was Montezuma revenge. Nothing stayed in and everything escaped through every opening possible. I stayed in the bathroom all night. I kept drinking water to have something passing through or coming up. At six in the morning, I found an employee of the hotel and I was able to get four bottles of warm coke cola. Drinking them slowly and they helped in slowing down the process but did not stop it. Jenny slept through it all. I suspect that she was having something going on also and sleep is way to deal with it.

At 7 a.m., Jenny came in the bathroom and one look at me she was shaken. "What is going on? You are as white as sheet. Alex, answer me." She demanded.

"Jenny I do not know, but I have been suffering what I thought was dysentery or Montezuma revenge. However, as the early morning wore on, it is like something else because you ate the same things I did. You are all right. I need you to get me something from the drug store to settle my stomach. With water in there, it just hurts. I have no idea what is going on." I replied the best I could.

Jenny pressed on my stomach, felt my head, listened with her ear against my stomach, and slowly shaking her head, for she did not have any idea either. Jenny got dressed, went to the nearest drug store, and brought back over the counter medicine for dysentery. I took it only to have it come up as fast as I put it down. I added water to it and that did not do it. We need something stronger so I got dressed to go with Jenny. It is interesting, my clothes that seemed to be getting tight on this trip, now they were very loose again.

As we went through the hotel, we cancelled our tour request. I went with her to see if the druggist would have any suggestions. He gave me some drugs that he thought would help. I was able to have a couple of hours before

I needed to be in the bathroom. Jenny was going to get me to a doctor or hospital, but I told her I want to go home. With the drugs I have and be able to have a couple hours relief between bouts, I can make it. "Please I really want to go home" I begged her.

I did not need to say much more, Jenny went to the front desk to check out. The hotel got us booked out at 1P.M. to Newark, Chicago and then home, arriving at 11 p.m. The total travel time 19 hours with almost a 3 hours layover. Anyway we were on way home; that is all it mattered. The travel time seemed long but I know I can tuff it out because that best we could get.

As soon as the plane left the ground, I felt wonderful. My color returned to my face and my stomach did not hurt. Jenny just looked at me astonished asking "are you really alright? You look better, but gaunt."

"I feel like I have been through hell, but all I can say now is I am hungry. Do you think if I told them of my problem, they could give me something to eat? My stomach is making noises that it is hungry" were the pleading words that came out of my mouth.

Jenny reported, "She also no longer felt funky too."

The flight stewards were more than helpful putting together something that would fill me up but was not hard on the stomach. That seemed to be the best meal ever, and I can't remember what it was.

Jenny had made a call in to Johnny on the way to the airport and he told her he would meet us where we would pick up our luggage. We called him again when we were in Newark, to tell him we were doing fine and eager to see him. We had window seats and we just cuddled and slept most of the way home. Sleep is what it is called but not restful kind of sleep.

We arrived in Portland on time and we made it to the turntable to pick up our luggage within 10 minutes. There was Johnny with couple of friends to help him. Johnny was surprised to see me so gaunt, but did not say a word. I could tell by the expression on his face, his face tells his thoughts. He can't hide anything.

We gathered up our luggage and we were on our way home. We had very limited conversation. The driving time home, seem to take forever, maybe because we were exhausted. We were in the back seat, just cuddling. Johnny's friends filled the rest of the van seats after they stored our luggage.

It was after 2 p.m. before we pulled up to our home. All we had to do was walk into our home and the boys brought in the luggage. As we open the back door, you could smell fresh cut flowers and baskets of fruit.

"We heard you were sick, so we will be on our way and catch up with you both later today" were Johnny's kind words. We were standing alone finally in our home.

"Well! Here we are in our home. I really don't know about you, but I am sure happy to be home" was my quiet reply.

Jenny just took my hand and we went up stairs to our bedroom. Invitation of the bed, found us fast to sleep. We were finally home.

CHAPTER 14

The phone rang, bringing both them back to reality from our deep sleep. I reached over and picks up the phone to hear a very loud voice scream out, "Hey you guys! It is almost noon and we want to visit" was the full booming voice of Johnnys.

Before I could answer, the doorbell rang and again the phone voice said, "Are you going to answer the door?"

"Jenny, it appears we are going to have guests whether we want them or not. I'll put on my robe and greet them and give you a chance to dress" were my remarks to my new wife. I hung up the phone, put on my robe and ran down the stairs.

Opening the door, I found Johnny with a big tray of food and Judy grinning from ear to ear. "You guys just can't sleep all day. We prepared a great brunch, for all of us. So make way for us to set the table for food" in Johnny's matter of fact and strong words.

I walk slowly up the stairs to get dressed only to find Jenny standing there amazed that all her clothes were already in the closet in same order she had them at her apartment. "Come on ol' girl, we have company whether we want them or not" rolled out of my mouth.

We quickly got dressed and presented ourselves to my in-laws in the dining room. My clothes really reflected my weight loss. Maybe they won't notice. When we got downstairs, everything was ready. The table was decorated and the food all served and waiting to be consumed. Johnny and I pulled the chairs for our women and then sat down to enjoy the meal.

The conversation never stopped all during and after the meal. We acted as if we were gone for months instead of couple of weeks, and it was less. We shared the highlights of the honeymoon but did not go into depth about problems we encountered except that I had Montezuma revenge to cover up my weight loss.

Judy saw the clock that told her they had used up over 3 hours of our time. She took Johnny by the hand and pulled him out the door. They calling they would see us for dinner at the restaurant. They never mentioned once about how gaunt I looked. I am sure they were too polite to say anything even after we explain what happened.

As Jenny and I looked around our home, we found all the items Jenny was going to bring to our home. Everything was arranged in the proper place as we would have selected. What a family we have! It looked like we always lived here. What a way to start out life. I kept finding myself having the excuse to sneak a kiss or two but there was no resistance. The rest of the afternoon was unpacking, doing laundry and general miscellaneous items. The best surprise was our packages from Greece came today so we could put our treasures around in our new home. Jenny reminded me that we would have to go shopping for house gift for our new loving Greek family before time gets away from us. We agreed to have something for all of them.

I should have known when we showed up at the restaurant, the welcome home party would happen. I am not sure that if we were the excuse for the party or whatever. The rest of the evening was spent table-hopping, hugs, drinks; one would have thought we were doing our reception all over again. It is nice to have family even though they are not related. The band even played some Greek music so we could do some folk dances. This kind of life is a real treat and a blessing to have so much when love rules the day. I felt embarrassed about my appearance but no one said anything. I had lost over twenty pound in Spain. I was now fifteen pounds below my normal weight when I left on the trip. After many thank you, we finally made it out the door by 11 p.m.

What a pleasant way to live here at our development. Where you can walk home which is about a few hundred yards away. We were ready for sleep. Jet lag or something caused our world turn dark very fast for both of us.

There is a creeping feeling flooding over me as I fall deeper and deeper into a hole. The smell of something sinister begins to flow into me with every breath. Where am I going? Thoughts saturated my mind and my eyes rapidly searching to see where or what is happening. I am here, but where is here? The walls were of stone, there were no windows, wooden door, where am I? Then my mind's eye sees a human lying on some straw in the corner. Again, why am I here consumes me with every increasing rapid breath. The door opens with a bang and two oddly filthy dressed men, rush in, grab the reclining figure, and pull him to his feet. There are no words but for lot of grunting sounds. They exit dragging this person out of the room, up the stairs and into room that had a chair in middle of the room. He was slammed down in the chair that faced a table that appears to have three chairs behind it. I can begin to feel and see the terror flooding from this man. The feeling emanating from me was fear but not of death but of "can I not yield." The door behind the table creaks open and three figures raped in same color of clothes march into the room with great determination. This victim screams out "No".

I find myself sitting up in bed, covered with sweat and lost to what is going on. My wife was sitting up next to me with a startled look on her face that was revealed by nightlight in the room. "Alex! What is wrong? You screamed so loud that I was frightened awake. The word "No" came blasting out and kept repeating itself in declining volume until it is a whisper. Are you all right? Is it nightmare?" Jenny was lost to say anything more but to grab hold of her husband and hold on tight to a very cold wet shaking mass of a man.

"They are back. I need to get into a hot bath and salt water. That is what I have to do. Will this never stop?" was my crying voice. I staggered out of bed and headed for the bathroom and sat on edge of the tub in lost daze. Jenny came in and quickly turned on the water and grabbed the box of sea salt that was on shelf above the tub. I couldn't make myself do that simple task. Jenny watched the salt dissolve in the whirl of water. Steam filled the room along with the soft sobbing sounds from me. When the temperature was right, tub was full. She helped this helpless mass into the water, and he laid back in silence. Seeing him being lost in his world, she returned to the bedroom and the phone. She called Johnny who answered the phone on first ring.

"Hello," seeing the caller I.D. he said, "Alex what is it you want?" However, he was taken back with the sound of his sister.

"Johnny, Alex had another very bad nightmare. I have him soaking in hot sea salt water. What else do I need to do? This scares me because he had few on our honeymoon, but not like this. I am loss of what to do for him". cried Jenny out of fear.

"Jenny, I will be right over in a few minutes. In the mean time, be sure he does not slip under the water and drown. Take two of those pills out of his soap dish that I packed for your trip. They will calm him down. If he seems safe to be alone, gets some water boiling for tea. I am on my way" was Johnny's parting word.

I appeared to be just drifting with the gentle flow of the water jetting in the tub. Jenny got the pills from my traveling case I had not unpacked yet. She got some water and pulled me out of my stupor enough for me to take and swallow the pills. I appeared safe to go and get some water cooking for tea. In the kitchen, Jenny began to pace back and forth waiting which seemed eternity for her brother to show up. The fierce sound of boiling water in tea kettle brought Jenny out of her helpless fear thoughts and same time, there is Johnny at the door. Jenny raced to the front door, flung it open, and embraced her brother who was charging in.

"I told you sister that we were not sure if he is over his nightmare. I thought when he got rid of Marian we were done. However, don't worry; I have already made appointments with hypnotherapist Roger next week. We talked some and he was aware that there maybe a few more hidden issues of his past lives that might come to the surface now he had gotten the worst ones resolved. So my dear sister, it appears that trip to Europe brought some more unknown fears to the surface. When this happens, we just have to not panic, get the salt water going in the tub, and just be there for him. I know when this batch is dissolved; you will have hell of a great husband. For almost a year after the divorce, he did not have these events. I wonder what in hell is triggering them. When you resolve marriage and family nightmares, what is left? I want you to know we can do this sis, so let's get our water soaked mass out of the tub and down here for herbal tea." were the firm light hearted words expressed by Johnny.

Jenny just hugged her brother and whispered in his ear, "I love you. I will never be afraid as long as I have you to help me. I will never give up on Alex. I will not lose him again." Why did I say "again" plagued her thoughts? Life seems so confusing since I met Alex. None of it makes sense to me, but all I know I love him from a special place in my heart. Maybe I lost him before, it will not happen again. All this past lives stuff is getting to me, I hope in good way.

"You see how gaunt he looks, he lost it all. It was no Montezuma revenge he had in Madrid. Something must be terribly wrong in that city for us. I felt lost or very sad; I could not put my finger on the emotion. When we left the ground on the plane, we both felt normal. He was hungry and his body did not feel racked with pain. Now, he screams out NO and is soaking wet. The only difference is he is not throwing up. Do we will have to do more than what we are doing? Do we need to get him to a doctor? The training I have had so far I have not a clue to this physical activity. Of course, we are lucky he is not throwing up or any of those other problems in Spain. Maybe it just nightmare" resigned Jenny.

They both walked up stairs to see how their patient was doing. There was Alex looking serenely thin in the bubbling water from the jets. Johnny reached down and placed his hand on Alex's shoulder to gently awaken him with assurance of his touch.

My eyes slowly droopily opened, and there was Johnny's happy face staring into mine. Between joy and sobbing sound, I blurted out "Johnny those damn nightmares from hell are back. I am scared; I thought I was all through with that. Johnny what am I going to do? I can't be like this with Jenny." Just then, a horrified look came over his face as his eyes brought her into view.

"Don't worry, Jenny understands that this only temporary and besides this adds spice to your marriage." Johnny's light hearted off the cuff remark. "I have made arrangements next week with your hypnotherapist to tackle this problem. He assured me that you could have a few buried past lives' experience that could come to the surface now. They are will not be as traumatic as those that whirled around with your family and Marian. So my friend, are you ready to get out of the hot water and come have tea with us? Let us not make mountains out of a mole hills, old history does not make current events the same."

Without replying, I got up with the help of Johnny and stepped out of the tub. Johnny quickly wrapped me in a large bath towel that Jenny handed him and with smaller towel, she began to dry me. Jenny got behind Alex with terry cloth bathrobe and helps him put it on as large towel hit the floor. I was shaking even though the room appeared extra warm from the heat of soaking tub. No one seemed to be talking. When I appeared stable, we all went down to the kitchen for tea.

I had gotten this special blend of herbal tea from Roger to help him balance out after one of those cannon battle bouts nightmares. It always seems to work before. As we seated around the table, tea has been served but dead silence still dominated the room.

Finally, Jenny could not handle it any longer, blurted out, "that was fun, I hope we don't have as much fun in the future". That broke the mood and everyone began to laugh. I was caught between the laugh and a cry as I tried to dismiss what had just happened.

Johnny asked, "What was it about? Do you remember anything that happened in this nightmare? Is it related to the other ones? Do you know what set it off?"

I was searching my mind as the questions seem to attack me for answers. Then there was a quiet thought that expressed itself when Jenny touched me in my sleep. As it started, let me think. Was that part of the dream or did she really physically touch me? This has nothing to do with those past nightmares except there seems to be some sort of semi-hidden loose end thought about Marian, but that does not make sense either. How would she be in this event? I was shaking my head from side to side and finally stated. "This does not seem to be related to anything. By the clothes and the area, it was some time back in time. There was just me and I was dragged into a room where three strange dressed men came into the room. The next thing I know I am sitting up in bed screaming, 'No'."

"I really want you to know, that scream sure woke me up with a hell of a start. I have never seen you like that, but Johnny told me that you used to have these kinds of events before working out your past history. There are parts of me that accepts past lives stuff and some parts of me really don't want to go there. That phases 'don't want to go there' bothers me more. I just want you to know, this is not going to scare me off. I experienced you telling me about having a shower full of blood that only you could see and you recovered from that. What just happened can't be that terrible. You did not do well in Europe and I, for one, am glad that we are home again. Johnny told me that he had some experience with the statute of David, but he will have to tell you about it. He did not give me too much of the details. However, I bought him a bronze twenty-four inch copy to remind him to tell you about it. He went some place when he saw the real thing. You know my dear husband, you know how to rock a girl's boat to keep her interest" those words came rolling out Jenny.

"Didn't I tell you once, I told you a hundred times, that you needed to marry this guy. Why you would always ask, and my reply was because your life will never be boring. [Pointing to Alex's heart] There is lots of love locked up in there, which I know you will enjoy. Therefore, we are now starting the wild ride of life. One would say, you, dear sister, have a chance to ride on wild side of life, isn't that great" were questioning the lighthearted flowing words from Johnny.

"It is alright for you to say, but I am the one on the ride." Jenny quickly replied.

"Hey! You guys! I am sitting here. You go on as if I am not here. Jenny, I am sorry that you have to be exposed to all of this, but honestly honey, I will work real hard to get whatever this is out of my internal world so we can be in that loving serene world. How does that sound?" I replied.

"Okay! That is it. I am leaving. It appears everything is under control for now. I need some sleep because all our supplies for the restaurant are coming in at seven. Alex, I leave you in good hands. My dear sister, I love you, and enjoy the ride. But honestly, I love you both very much and I will always be there for you both whenever you need me" were the words that followed Johnny as he got up and was out the door before Jenny or I could reply.

The door shut and I looked at Jenny, "I can get through this. Next week, I will in earnest, work hard with Roger so I can be that loving and caring husband I want to be for you".

Jenny was getting up. "Before this conversation gets to deep and maybe out of control. I need to get some sleep since I told Johnny I had some spare time and would help him with stocking first thing in the morning." She grabbed my hand and led me up to bed. Within minutes, there were soft sounds of two lovers breathing quietly together in unison.

CHAPTER 15

The alarm went off at 10, I quickly killed the sound by pushing down the button. Looking around the room, I was alone. I remember, Jenny was going to help her brother this morning and isn't kind of her to let me sleep in. Boy! That event last night sure knocked the wind out of me. I seems so out of sorts as I try to recall it. Hell! I think I will just let it go, beside that is why I go and see Roger. He helps me get to the problem, understand why it is happening and the permission to heal whatever it is to get on with my life. Going to my psychiatrist and whole activity of pills with the goal of living with dysfunctional thoughts, dreams, and life was not the future for me. I am the kind of a guy that needs to know *"why"*, to move on. When you know *"why"* it is so easy or easier to let it go, thank the person for the experience and enjoy the rest of the journey you designed for your own soul growth and development.

Hopping out of bed, look out world, here I come, ready or not. With those thoughts, I began to greet the new day. My thoughts were lot stronger than my physical body could demonstrate. When I put on my underwear, which my pants now hold up, would drop to the floor for they are excessively big for me. My pant's belt I had use first hole. Damn! I better get eating. I can't keep looking like this.

The days evaporated. My birthday passed without lot of fuss, and I am filling out again. Just a couple more days, and I will begin the journey with Roger. I will not even speculate how it will happen. I haven't had any bad dreams or sweats lately. Therefore, I have no idea what to expect this time. This activity feels different. The more I romance these thoughts, it appears to be more from within than what was done to me. Romance these thoughts, that odd way to think about the journey that is about to happen. The problem when you don't know or understand the "why", you truly can't let them go. When we, Roger and Kevin my spirit teacher, journeyed through my ex-wife's relationship with me and we broke that pledge that was over 4500 years old. How could I have been so stupid to make a pledge "forever"? Well! I did and we finally resolved that. Damn, I have to say that is a long time to be on the hook. Then the committee had me help my ex-wife of nine hundred years ago. Now I did not phrase that statement right, they finally made me an offer I could not refuse. Because I knew, it was going to be hell on wheels if I did not have all the positive help doing it. They came through with that. Therefore, that cleans up those family issues. Now what is this activity? Shut up, my busy head, didn't I say we are going to park this roaring confusion and work it out with a professional? I sure as hell not a professional and I make a bad patient for myself if I was.

I spent my time checking in with Barbara to see if there was any work for me at the office. She runs a smooth operation. She even blocked out my time with Roger, per Johnny's instructions. When I showed up, there is all the work, which is mine, in the middle of the desk for me to handle. Sometimes she has me do the presentation about the condos we have on the drawing board. I am glad we took up the option on the track of land west of us. Everything is running like clockwork; it is great to be alive. I find time to visit with Johnny and Ol' Johnson over coffee or dinner. There always lots of time socializing at the restaurant. I have gained back almost ten pounds, and feeling great.

Jenny has been working the 3 p.m. to 11 p.m. where she gets home by 12:30 or 1 a.m. I try to make time to have lunch with her before she goes to work which is nice. We still find time for each other with our own schedules. The great part of it all I have not had a nightmare since that last one. Still the unknown with her is still in my heart, but that is Roger's job to help me find the answer. Jenny and I have clicked with doing housework so that work smoothly. One thing, I am not a pack rat or a slob and neither is Jenny. Everything has it place and every place has its thing. With the electric filters on the furnace, that cuts down the dusting. When I am cleaning, on comes the filter to remove any rust I am raising. I am really doing great for a man that had servants. I had people lay out my cloths. I was spoiled, and that kind of spoiled is gone forever in this relationship. This house cleaning and laundry experience is getting better every time I do it. Of course, Jenny shows me where I need to improve in a good way.

I spend some of my time in my office on the third floor of my condo, which gives me great view of the river. There is a lot of river traffic as we come into full fall season. Our dock work is slowing down. I am not sure it was good idea to have my office up here. There goes grain ship with Panama flag racing down the river to feed some hungry people somewhere. Just an hour ago, a car ship from Korea traveled up the river to bring new transportation to our population. A yacht went up river with her side curtains, getting ready for the cooler weather and rain. I am so lucky to have so much and greatest part of it is sharing with people who understand sharing. In the hustle job I had working with and for x-Marian, there was lots money, but there was always that personal void caused by just working for money for money sake. Now I have my life in some kind of order, every day is a pleasure to be alive. There are chances every day to empower people with tools of life to make the journey of creation instead of just existing. Our plan is developing, as we envisioned it. A place where no one here is drowning in their trouble basket. I have been informed that a few of the families are developing positive support group for themselves and others even if they didn't join the group. One support group they have is for families that have a member in the National Guard who have been deployed. We, our organization, have found a way to help cover some or all as need be of their mortgage payment during their deployment. That is what families do for each other. We not going to take away their responsibility, just make it possible they can have chance at being responsible. I have to stop the mind wandering I have worked to do.

Barbara called to bring me back to reality to inform me of a pending meeting. Steve Holland the general contractor of this operation wants have meeting with the principle members to see if everyone is satisfied and are we on target as we thought we would be at this point. We need to have Judy and Francis to come up with plans for our Motel, so we can get Ron Collin started walking the permits through the system with the county. I guess a general meeting, progress report, and projections to meet our target will be required. We have done a great job so far, but we did add on the additional land and there is lot of work that needs to be considered. Barbara always sees that the meeting will happen.

This project has been working right along. What seems to make this work for us, we have enough start up work for all the crews that they are almost working exclusively for our project and us. Steve has done great job with suppliers, contractors, and county teams that this is becoming a dream operation. This construction operation is great because the contractor workers are watching out for potential problems to avoid waste and confusion whether it's their work or another contractor. I always dreamed there was a model out there to assist groups developing support systems where it is win / win for very one. Here I go again, getting off track.

I need to get back to drawing board, scheduling systems and plans, setting up communication lines and getting everyone on same page. Once I have rough draft completed, I give it to Barbara and she does her magic. Everything works like clockwork or we find a way to solve the obstacles and get things moving smoothly again. It only took me an hour to plug in everything into our design. That design is flexible to meet the needs of the time. I had better get my material down to the office before Barbara leaves for the day. As always, I just make the deadline, and Barbara gives me that look she does when I do this.

When I walked into the office, late in day as usual, Barbara states, "You know this will not be worked on until tomorrow morning. I have heard you state that you were going to do the projects that you handed me and I already got some of it in the works. All I will have to do is see if I guess correctly" as she walked out the door and closed it before I could reply.

You know, she always seems to do that with me; get in the last word and being ahead on getting the work completed were words wondering across my thoughts. I guess I will go back home and get ready for dinner with the gang at our usual watering hole. The phone rings and it is Roger on the line. "Hi Roger, I knew it was you by our caller I.D. and I am glad that you are back and to hear from you" were my very excited words.

"I got a call from Johnny, that you are back having night mares and you need some more help. I have looked at my calendar; I will be available on

Friday say 4 p.m. I know that seems late, but I have lot of work to catch up on and I am free until seven. I think we need to get reestablished and determine what I can help you with now" was Roger's manner a fact words.

"Four will be fine; my wife is off to work by 2:30 so I am free. We will be meeting at your place on the river?" I inquired.

"Yes, and I will be expecting you at four and I will have the tea on. I have to run; I am looking forward to see you. Until then, have great day" was Roger's closing words.

I can't believe it; I will be able to get all the new crap behind me. Again, I really thought I was done, but that is life. I guess it is like peeling an onion, I guess I have not got to the core of it all. Well until I do, I will be living less than a full life, and that is unacceptable. Loose end words just keep roaming around in my head, I think I will be cleaned up and meet the gang. I will have to put all speculation on the back burner until I start the process. I wish Captain Jack was here. I just have to stop doing this. Wishing, making mountains out of molehills, but losing all that weight in one day in Madrid is more than a molehill. I have to get ready and get out of here before I talk myself into being a fruitcake.

In half an hour, I arrive at the restaurant and everyone we have dinner with almost every night was already there.

Johnny was first see me and yells out "I think the last one here should buy a drink for everyone."

"Yeah you own the place! You are always coming up with something to build up your business" was my reply. I think we hassle each other almost every day since I came back for the honeymoon. He truly is great brother in law. I walk up close to him and whisper, "I have appointment tomorrow, Friday, at four with Roger. I am so glad that he is finally back and I can get these monkeys off my back."

"I know what you mean. You know I will be there for you whatever you need. These issues have to be end of the parade of karma stuff you courageously came here to resolve as 'The great warrior'" Johnny just broke up with laughter with those words.

"Wise guy, you are not the comedian you think you are" as I make a dash for the table to end this dialogue with Johnny.

As I was in easy speaking voice to our table, I asked "Ol' Johnson, can I borrow you sixteen footer tomorrow around four p.m? I have a run up the river to meet with Roger if you don't mind and if you are not using it."

"Of course, I have told you once, may be a hundred times, it just sits there all covered up. Someone might as use it; it will be good for the engine. Naturally you will fill the tank and the spare gas can while you are at it" was his usual rough voice.

I replied, "That is cheap deal any time. Is the key in its usual place?" With those words, Johnson just knotted his head.

"What is the special for today?" I asked the waitress, Kathy, who saw the table was full and it is time to give them some attention. "To begin, let's have a beer for everyone I need to celebrate."

"Read the menu on the back board, or did you lose your sight" was her reply.

"Men, I have to tell you, when you let women call you by your first name, you get all these kind of remarks" were words came tumbling out and I had to duck because I believe she would have cuffed me in the back of my head.

"Man! You have to be crazy carrying on like that with the help, your life could be shorten with those remarks" remarked my single neighbor Frank.

"Okay, I will behave myself, Kathy. I will have what everyone else ordered. Thinking that was easy way out," I gave a half apology thinking everyone had ordered the special. "The chef does great job with those clams."

Kathy smiles, "that will be half pound hamburger with everything and onion fries; shrimp basket with curly fries with a tossed salad; broiled salmon with baked potato, mixed vegetables and salad, and the special of fried clams, curly fries, salad with garlic bread. Are you sure you can eat all of that?"

It was like eating crow. "No, I guess I will just have one special. I have no room for all of that. Will you also bring round of beer too please?"

The evening was used up with usual men just talking and eating with a little beer drinking. No one gets out of hand because this is family dining.

I was home and in bed by the time Jenny got in. She was late, so I figured she was caught with overtime again. She kissed me on the cheek as she slid into bed and the lights went out.

I was up before Jenny because I had to get up to the office to answer any questions Barbara had for me regarding the work I piled on her last night. There she was working away with the help of the staff. Everyone seemed to have good routine and the work seemed to just flow. We have wallboard where we have all the condos listed and we "x" out those sold. I look like we will be completely sold out of 1ˢᵗ phase. All is well in "Camelot" and our meeting with investors and planning committee will be a breeze. I bet my x-Marian is cooking, because she never believes I could pull this off without her. That was yesterday and now on with the show.

Barbara interrupted my day dreaming to ask, "Which would you like to happen first, meeting with the investors or planning committee. I would recommend the planning committee first so you will have not only performance to date but where we are with the project and what are the next phases of the project. It nice to whet their appetite to see how all of our dreams are unfolding and this action will keep them more involved."

"I can't object to that. Besides, it is harder to get everyone one here for a meeting than it is for the planning committee. You set it up and we will get with it. By the way, I will be leaving early this afternoon. I have an appointment with an old friend and I will not be back. Do we have any appointments to show the model unit tomorrow? I can cover that if you and the staff would like to take a breather," I stated.

"That would be nice. We have been running but thing are slowing down now and we could use a day off on the weekend. Week days are nice, but shopping is better on weekends and us girls would enjoy it" was quick reply "and thank you".

CHAPTER 16

Later that day, I made my way to hiding place of key with my two five gallon cans of gasoline. I went out on the dock to uncover the boat, untie her, put in the cans, hopped in and started drifting out with the current of the river. The engine fired up on the first try and I heading up the river on crystal clear day, with gentle smell of fall in the air. The geese are honking across the sky and all seems right with the world. A short trip and I am at Roger's dock. I tied up the boat and took the key with me. I don't think there is anyone around here that would steal the boat but why give them temptation.

I walked off dock, upon the ramp and onto mossy bank. I always stopped for a few moments as I always done in the past, to enjoy seeing that safe haven residence ahead of him. I always like what I saw because the house appeared isolated from neighboring residence and was surrounded by mature trees of many varieties. It was a joy to walk slowly up the meandering graveled path to the house. All the usual flowers sent their fragrances soothing on the wind mixed with the restful earthly aromas of mother earth, makes you want to stay in the moment.

Glancing toward the house, I saw my middle aged friend waiting for me. He was waving and smiling broadly.

I picked up his pace and soon found myself shaking Roger Strong's hand. I really wanted to give him a hug but don't think we are in that kind of receptive relationship.

Roger began "I have your favorite tea ready for you and I must say this past year just flew by. I figured everything was working well with you by your letters you sent. It must have been the greatest moment of your life when you told Marian that you were through with her forever. The way you got her to release you from your pledge of 4500 years was work of a genius. I know she and her lady friend will live happy ever after.

Come my friend; let us get into the house and to work. Johnny told me you had yourself a wife, on your honeymoon and some old ghost really rocked your boat. He told me that you reported that you lost well over fifteen pounds in one day. I could use that to get rid of this little pot belly I have been carrying around."

They continued to walk through the house down the short hallway to where a small room where we had our sessions. I really enjoy the walls and ceiling being made out of glass because you felt like you were among the comfort of the plants. The same two recliners, each with a small oak table placed strategically next to it to place the ice tea glass on a coaster I have been carrying.

"I cannot tell you the freedom you helped me obtain with hypnosis. Unbelievably, while I was in Europe, there were a couple of times, I slipped into another time and space. Just like being here, I saw what was happening, who the players were, and how I was affected. Some of it did not make sense, some answered questions of unfounded fears, and some left me in a state that brought me back to you," I explained with sense of joy being here and trepidation over what is hidden yet to be uncovered.

"Remember, I told you that this may happen and you can do what we have done in past sessions. The only problem is if you get into something that you should need someone to insure your safety, you don't have that support. I know you must have followed some of the rules we discussed before or you would not be here. Was the Madrid part of your probing?" inquired Roger.

"Hell no, I made it to the bathroom and Montezuma revenge consumed me. I had to keep drinking water to have something to pass through or throw up. I have had food poisoning before but this was different. It was beyond description of chaos flooding my mind. There truly no words in my mind can explain it. It went on for hours and finally a light came into the room from the window and those thoughts just stopped. I got some warm Coke from the clerk at desk at 6 a.m. and it helped slow down this disruptive activity. I had hard time trying to figure out whether it was coming up or going out. My stomach hurt something awful, chest burned with pain, there are no ways to describe it. I would say I was on fire. That is why I here to find out 'what in hell is it'? I know you can take me there and back so I can let it go. I have some faint roaming thoughts that in some ways Jenny is involved. It does not make sense to me either" the words came flooding out of me as fast as the body could deliver them.

"Alex, we can get past this. I know if we go slowly at the cause, maybe it was accumulative of many or lots of events. I would not even care to guess at this point. I would like to take you back to your spirit friend between lives and maybe he can shed light on what is going on. I really want to play this safe because your somewhat grueling description of what happened plus the loss of weight. Can we take my route?" was final question from Roger.

I just sat there agreeing "Roger I came to you because it is beyond me. You solved the problems with my family and Marian. My life is in your hands. I will do whatever it takes to get this behind me. I have Jenny and she is best thing that has ever happen to me. So you are the doctor, I will follow your instructions."

"We'll begin slowly," Roger announced, carefully studying me, who was sitting opposite me. In the past, I talked about Kevin, my spiritual mentor or teacher. "Let's start us maybe start with Kevin. He has walked us through many events before. Does that sound okay with you?"

I nodded my approval.

As always, using a gentle, reassuring tone, it was only a matter of minutes before Roger had me in deep trance state because he had begun to relax every muscle, working his way up the body, beginning with my toes, and continuing up to my head.

When I was totally relaxed, he announced, "You are entering an altered state of consciousness. You are not asleep and you are not unconscious. If I say anything that goes against your belief system; you can bring yourself back to complete awareness by counting to five. You are now at a level in which you can remember everything that has ever happen to you. You have been between lives before, so trust yourself."

Roger remained silent for a moment, giving his words time to be in harmony with Alex's consciousness.

"You are giving yourself permission to travel to that time and space where you and Kevin have worked with your other problems," suggested the hypnotist.

I announced "Hi Kevin, Man I need to talk with you. As you know, we solved all those agreements. However, my honeymoon trip to Europe set off some things like in other lives and they are bothering, troubling me. I thought I was through with everything a year ago. I really want to get on with my life. Jenny is best thing that has happened to me, but there are strange going on even with her. I am really totally blown away, confused. I know you must be aware of what happened to me in Spain."

The conversation with Kevin, with only the one side of conversation is being recorded. I will remember what was Kevin's conversation was but it will not be on the tape. [We are privileged of being in that time and space with Alex so we are listening to both sides of what is going on.]

Kevin slowly looked at Alex [his spirit name is Adrian] "Adrian the committee realized that you had taken on great tasks with Marian and your family. We did not go into the other events or task you wanted to search out and cleared up at once. The groups of events that are facing us in truth are the ones that affect your behavior and interactions with people when you are in the body. Between lives, as you know, without a body, all the words experiences of every events and the emotional are not involved. However, when you get back in physical body, all those events, and emotions come alive with all their experiences from other lives. They are not just words like in a dictionary; they are alive with all damaging experiences you had, that injured your soul. We talked at great length that those traumas are like slivers of earth energy fully loaded that pierced your soul. The only way they can be removed is to have parallel experience where you can release it from the soul, into the body and get rid of it. Those past events can color every deed, words, and actions of your present life. Many of them have diminished your ability to love. When that happens, it diminishes your ability to feel unconditional love of your creator that you can only truly feel only when you are in physical form. We, without recording physical body, understand what it is but we hunger for the ability to feel it. That feeling gives depth dimensions beyond words. You helped with the healing of your mother with your work, which was one of the obstacles for you to feel love. I have your attention; I want to show you why it was one of the obstacles. When you courted your mother, who was your wife back in 11th century, you were in truly in love. You felt love that your heart hungered for and yet was unable to experience up to this time. In the first year of your marriage, remember you were walking on air. All you wanted was to be with her. Her father was still around running the duchy and you could develop your desire to feel love again. As in most marriages, a child forth coming, this really expanded your hopes to re-heal family love. With the sudden death of her father, you had the full responsibilities of protecting and running the duchy. Your child consumed most of her time and in way of things, this fairy tale of healing your love needs died again. Time and events slowly but surely, devastated your desires like raindrops collecting until you have stream, river, and an ocean. The basic love was there but human element events buried it again. Do you remember between lives, the plans that you wanted that marriage to do for you, how she wanted them too, and how it was shattered?"

"The memory of the plans and high hopes we both had before we were born. Everything seemed to be working as we planned and then it just eroded a way. That was the only basic reason, I accepted the assignment of having her as my mother to heal the pain of it all. Everything really got out of hand, and for why. When this life began, I really did not believe I could live through the experiences with her but I did. You know Kevin, now I am glad that I did. There was something inside of my heart that shifted or something. I became to feel different or I would never have married Jenny. God knows why to all of this. I don't know totally but I suppose you will tell me one of these light years" was Adrian sad reply

"I know you have come to Roger to open the door to some of your past to solve what just happened to you. You have not always been the most patient person when I have worked with you. I hope you will trust me to let me take the lead on this journey to resolve the pain in your heart that you wanted to heal in 11th century. Are you all right with that? If you are, I would like to cover something that is known and look at it different. It was the events that you worked through last year," asked Kevin.

"At this point, I have no agenda. That experience in Spain did me in and it has taken all cocky rebellious attitudes out of me. I need you, though I hate to verbalize it, when you consider all the years that you have put up with me. [In almost a whisper] I am so thankful you never gave up on me. I really don't understand why you haven't, but truly I thankful you haven't." almost sad reply flowed in heartbreaking breath that dropped from Adrian mouth.

"Let us be more upbeat, if you don't mind, because I don't want this to become depressing. Remember back in 5th century B.C., when your name Tarius and your very best companion friend Maricus [Johnny in this life] had your estates and families were totally joined together. That was first critical times in your evolution in development of love and really defining it as something you really wanted. Up to that time, being a warrior was your most important occupation plus saturation of your desire of physical lust on earth. In that life you tasted, felt, enjoyed, created hunger for more love that was developed with your wife, children, and Maricus and his family. As you know, the pain of your commitment to Egyptian Priest made you blind not to live out that life and deal with commitment to the Priest at another time. Your death, friend's death, life not completed, you promised to try, but failed. Because of your obsession to erase your commitment to the priest, to open the door for that opportunity, it was not in the plan. It just caused many more problems for you. That whole lifetime was to build foundation to journey from warrior protector to humanitarian that feels the Creator's unconditional love and can be a "way shower" by demonstrations to other souls in human form. You have been all these 2500 years trying to get back what you lost. Sometimes we were close but those dam wild cards, those events not planned, destroyed everything. They caused problems between us, because you always thought I can fix everything and it was my fault" exhausted words flowed from Kevin.

"I don't mean to interrupt you; maybe I am a slow learner. When you are on earth, you learn from your religious leader who says they are speaking for God; those kinds of experiences were God punishing me. When I come back here, you say God did not do that, but is wild card. I know you explain that wild card to me hundreds, no thousands of times, but dam I mad having experiences I hunger for go up in smoke right before my eyes.

You would be mad too if it happened to you. That time with Maricus really made me see the world in different way. I wanted more, I admit as I had been doing this life now, I sure as hell stupid. I should have lived that life out fully. I know beyond a doubt that I would not have spent the last 2500 years trying to get out of that Priest commitment. To think I would take on the task of protecting that priest forever for physical lust that was so void. Every time he wanted to have earthly experiences, I had to be there as his servant. All those unlimited earthy lusting desires were so beyond doubt empty and unrewarding. My heart and soul injured by these endless lives of barrenness. That time with Maricus was supposed to be turning point of my evolution. My abstinence was taken out on you. Dam I have been a fool and here I am with my hand out for help" pleading voice of Adrian

"If nothing more, I really believe you finally understand what we have been trying to help you. The reason I believe you this time because the energy of your soul supports this positive change. I have a request of you, trust me as we walk you through this process and it will be hard from time to time. I would like to build on part of the awaking that took place in Greece in 5th century B.C. However, I now I want to conclude this session because you body needs to be adjust to changes of consciousness to prepare you to have strength to continue the healing process. Will you be all right with that? I will be working with you between sessions to help with the whole process," stated Kevin.

Kevin kept looking at Adrian, this will be a big jump, but if we can change the way, we deal with events that happened which caused us these agonizing undefined outlooks we can be set free. I know you have the strength and courage because your soul has power from the experiences of warrior. You were a warrior that was successful winner against great odds, even without the help of that damn priest. There are times I wish I had the power to undo some of the commitments souls make when they are in the physical body. They have to eliminate that physical earth energy from their soul. Every soul has free will because it is the basic premise of the creation of life on Earth. This is an experiment of the evolution of soul matter. By understanding the negative down side of a situation, and the positive up side of situation, to strike a balance evolution moves forward. There has to be unified balance to move forward, evolution, or whatever term you wish to subscribe to, that has to happen. Oh well! One can dream dreams and maybe some century they will come true.

"Kevin, I think you are right. I need to go back and rethink each activity we worked on. What you had me look at in my relationship with Maricus, my family, and his family. Right now, I bet my human form is crying. I will try to get another appointment next week; it will be up to you and Roger. I know you can reach him" was Adrian parting words.

There was this dead silence in the room, there was more going on than recorded because two hours had passes away. Roger just waited for Alex to come back because he didn't have to bring him back. By the conservation, Alex is on his way.

As always, I looks at the clock through a flood of water and I'm always amazed that it seems only minutes and here a couple of hours flew the coop. Looking at Roger, I am aware that the flood of water is indeed tears of crying. Not sobbing, but a sense of relief, a sense of burden being lifted off the heart and mind and even the soul. Being in the physical has so many avenues to experience whatever you want to, but there are costs. I need to undo some of mine by starting to see Roger. Those experiences are about frustrations and emptiness. Now it about coming home to myself, home to the path I want to complete my evolution and find true freedom. The silence was a throbbing agonizing of nothingness but there was unmistakable sense of life in that silence. A void life that stimulates a quest for more; coming home to what should be, not what is.

"Roger, whenever you have time for me, I will make time from what I am doing. I did not go where I thought I was going to explore, but to some place I been but this time I witnessed it all together different. There are not words in my head to express the jangling scrambling emotional free-for-all of unscrambling of what has been if that makes any sense" were Alex quiet words.

Roger stated, "Alex, I am not sure of my time next week. My scheduling is at the office in town and my secretary has my agenda, I just got back when I called you. Therefore, I are not settle in from my trip and so not sure, where I am at. I will call you as soon as I can schedule you in. By the conversation you had with your teacher Kevin, it appears it must be more than you asked for. It was not what you wanted, but it appears what you need. I have this new recording system on disk; I used it before I thought to ask you if you have such a machine."

"No problem, I can schedule whenever you have time for me. I have also wanted to get one of those new recording equipment that does everything now. Now I have an excuse to buy myself a present. I better get going" with those words, I got out of the chair the same time as Roger. I was going to shake Roger's hand, but Roger gave me a hug.

"I think we both needed that. It's great to be working with you again" as he let go and they continued the journey to the door without any additional words.

I was on the path back to the dock and I turned to see Roger still standing there watching me. I wonder where all of this is going but since he is part of program to make sure I make it this time. What do I have to be worried about? Now, I need to get in the boat and head for home, I ordered myself. I think I will eat at home tonight because I am not sure how full my cup is right now. The gentle ride back with the sun bouncing off the water, plants, earth as it slowly descend from view. What a pleasant sight. Back at the dock, I tied her up, slipped on the cover of the boat, and hid the key then started for home. I walked along the path to the break-wall and the park in front my home and across the lawn, which smells so sweet this time of day. Entering my home, I went upstairs like a zombie, undressed, and slid into bed. The world closed in around me for the first time like a soft cotton blanket. The world was totally at peace for now and the resolves are on their way.

When Jenny got home, she went to the restaurant because they have live music tonight and she figured she would get in a few dances before hitting the hay. Looking over the place and greeting everyone she knew, she finally caught Johnny's eye and made the motion 'where is he?' He just shrugged his shoulders with that blank look of 'I have not seen him'. She decided even though the music was great, she needed to go home and see if he is waiting for her. Maybe he is waiting there for her to come to the dance. Light heartedly she headed for home. She should have checked there when she parked the car in the garage. The walk was short. After getting into the house, it was very dark but for a couple night-lights. Turning on lights in every room downstairs, he was nowhere to be found. There was that panic feeling. She ran up the stairs and charged into their bedroom turning on the light. There he was sleeping on his stomach, dead to the world. There was a softer sense about him as she came close to the bed. He seems to somehow different, but in very good way. She retired to the bathroom and got ready for bed. Turning off the lights except the night light Alex needed to sleep, she lifted the covers and gently slid into bed. Lying on her side facing her man, wondering about him and she was not trying to worry. His hand slid almost motionlessly over to touched her arm. His hand very softly encased it and nothing else happened. That moment, she felt like they were always connected. No matter what goes on in his life, I will never leave him. I would be lost again without him. The words "lost again" echoed smoothly off into space. I am not going to chase after that for an answer, I am with him now, and that is all that matters. He makes the feelings of love in my heart and that is actually all that matters. Two souls were now safe in sleep.

CHAPTER 17

Barbara was able to make arrangements for Wednesday around 1 p.m. for the builder's meeting to discuss Phases Two of the project. We are sold out on present condos except for the model. There is a pressing need to have a meeting with all interested parties to get going the next phases as soon as we can. On Friday afternoon at 1 p.m., there is meeting of primary investors to keep them up to date on what is going on with the project.

On Wednesday, Barbara had the conference room set up with coffee and hot water for tea. The oblong table was arranged so the sides would face the presenting boards and the flat screen to view the proposed project. There would be Steve, general contractor, Judy & Frances designers, Ol' Johnson; he has to be in on everything, Ron Collins, friend lawyer and implementer, the two reps. from the County Planning Commission Joe and Larry, and Alex.

Judy and Francis were there early to set up the hard copy of the design of how the project will look when completed. The plans were same for the condos that had been approved but the motel building plans will have to be approved. Ron was their watchdog with the county. Because Ron ran everything above board and in the open, it tends to be smooth sailing.

The rest of the members came in together, because they were all down to the restaurant for lunch. The presentation schedule was placed at each chair with also included place setting arrangements. She had the county workers in center so they will have full view of the presentation. This was the requirement of Ron to insure that they can see and visualize what this second phase would really look like. If there are any concerns, we need to address them now.

Judy and Frances were first on the schedule, which began as soon as the rest of the attendees were seated.

Frances began showing a sky view picture of the present completed project and the vacant land that is proposed for development on the flat screen. With the use of her computer, she did a fast presentation of the building of the 1ˢᵗ Phase. That was ended with a picture of the "Certificate of Occupancy". All present enjoyed the journey down memory lane.

The next phase was first showing closer an aerial view of the undeveloped land with overlay showing the area of the condos and how it would look finished. In fact, it mirrored of the completed phase. Included was a wall running along the highway, down the side and across the front. This wall will keep day visitors out of residential section. There will also a chain fence that will run from the road down the west side to isolate the wet land from the residency. The only different on this side is a proposed three story motel with about 28 units that be located on the spit of land on west side and it will have access to the marina and restaurant via the park that runs along the water. There will be also 6-foot fence on top of the break-wall for the safety of the people. There will be concrete steps in the middle section to allow access to the river. The landscape will match the other side. The motel will be designed, as you can see, to match the total development. We are trying to keep it as clean in appearance as possible," Frances explained.

There are plans for the motel building, landscaping and of course, the condos which you already approved on the original phase one. We are now ready to answer all your questions as to the designs and plans for phase two.

Larry was the first. We have seen the design before the meeting to give us heads up. The plans for the motel were included. Our whole department went over them to insure they will meet all the specs of the county building codes. You guys are really thorough. We found a few small problems, which have to do with an entrances and egress. In plain language, you need to have roadway to the motel and we did not see one.

"That is right," replied Frances. "I don't know how I missed that because we have plans for the parking area for the motel. Thank you for bring that to our attention. That will mean the roadway needs to be two way in front of the condos' wall. Would that be acceptable solution to the county?"

"We had already put our heads together and that seemed to be the only answer except if you want to enter just behind the wall on the road traveling west and then north to the motel. But that did not seem as viable. If you can move the condos back up the hill few feet and with proper landscaping between the road and the park area, we believe it will not detract from the esthetic appearances."

"In fact, again with a few minor modifications that really only pertain to the motel, every one of the involved agencies found no fault with your plans. You guys have thought of everything to make this place as green as it can be. The fence between the condos and the wetlands we had not thought as necessary originally but now seeing how effective it is now that it's completed. It was the only answer. It keeps the critter out of your area and people out of their space" was the reply from Larry with Joe physically expressing his support.

"Then by your words, we can expect to receive our building permit soon?" asked Ron.

"I have to laugh, Ron," stated Joe. "It appears that we granted your permit to begin with due to a clerical error that was added in the first permit and which included all additions on land that you own. Since the county commissioners had approved the first permit, it is a done deal. The only problem that I could that would hold this project up, if you changed any of your plans, goals and objectives that you had approved the first time. The motel might cause some concerns. However, if you bring that in separate, the Commissioner can have their hearing and we believe you have the support of the community. It is a done deal. I might add, that if you purchase any more land on the river to link into this project, we are submitting a rider to this permit that you will not have to go through the whole process for approval. I hope that does not upset you or make you mad at us. We just have to go by the book.

"We hear you and I am here to tell you, we have to thank you for all your help to make it happen. I am very pleased that error was on your side, I must admit. I also believe we can get the proposal together in very short time for the County Commissioners to go through the process. We are or never can be mad or upset about this. It is the checks and balances that we need. When you are on the up and up, what is there to sweat?" I stated.

"You will have my request for permit of the motel by the end of the week. We need to get it on the agenda of the Commissioners for Tuesday and get the ball rolling. Is the permit for the rest of the project a done deal?" inquired Ron.

"You can start work as soon as you want. We had the foresight to bring the permit with us because as we said, every agency and unit could not find anything that would prevent the beginning. As long as you follow the work covered in the permit, there are no problems" replied Larry.

"Now it's my turn, I guess, to ask a question", inquired Steve. "What I am hearing is that we can begin to get rolling, weather permitting, as soon as we want to because we really have the permits?"

"Steve, I thought you were right with us. Of course, that is what we are saying. The error is in your favor and I believe you still have a month or so where you can get some real work done before the rain begins", laughed Joe. "We have worked with you quite a number of years and I have to say this is a first for me to see you looking so dumb-founded!"

"I have to say, since I threw my hat in the ring with these guys. I am learning to believe in miracles. We have had and will have the best luck in every aspects of this project. I have never had subs that really worked together and helped each other out. We have had the smallest number of deficiencies of any project I have worked on or supervised. It has built a great reputation for all of us. Beginning this week, I will get the crew in to prepare the land for building. This soil has been as solid as a rock, so we can really build great foundations and the rest is easy creation. The landscaper we have, I don't know where he gets his dirt, but it is like all of this was always like this. I have to tell you, every day is delight and surprise. However, the one you handed us just blew my socks off. I thought I had experienced that magic touch to the max. Now you give me something beyond that what I thought was possible. I hope I can always keep you laughing at my disbelief keeps me working," concluded Steve.

Judy and Frances also could not believe that their dreams had come true. Their company, "M & J Enterprises", was now on solid ground. "Who would have thought that when we took that first stupid job for an escort service it would bring us back to the goal we had worked for since college? I am so glad we did not have to work as the escort service. In truth, I was ready to bolt at the first suggestion there was to be more than a social evening." Frances whispered to Judy.

Everyone was talking away, drinking coffee, and enjoying the feeling of what teamwork will do. See what all can be accomplished when the right attitude, right wind is blowing, and we can make it right with the world.

Barbara entered the room to announce that "Alex has a very important call that he will have to take. I am sorry."

I excused myself and as I passed Barbara, I reported, "We are in." Her reply was "I was listening on the intercom". I grinned, thinking to myself, I never get anything past her. That is why she has always been my right hand.

I picked up the phone, "Hello, can I help you?"

"Alex, it has been a long time since I talked to you last. This is Ned B. Nyman, one of your first investors when you started with Marian. I called your old company but I was informed that you were no longer employed at the firm. The receptionist states they have many other qualified employees that handle investments and I can refer you to one of them. [While she was talking to him, she pulled his name up in her computer and realized he was very good investor] Maybe Marian could be made available."

I told her, "I was just tracking you down for personal reason. Her reply was, "I really can't help you there." Her office procedure reply precluded giving out such information but softly she did tell me where I could find you if I was interested. So here, I am on the phone with you. It rather long explanation to jar your memory" were the ramblings of Ned.

"Sure, Ned, I remember you. You did some great investments with us and I had also heard you did quite a few long shots and they came in. I was very glad for you. The point is what can I do for you now?" I inquired.

"It is more like, what can I do for you? I was curious as to what you were doing. Remember when you were my advisor on investments, you gave me some great information that I used on those long shots. Mainly, I wanted to thank you for your help and to see what was going right in your world. Your secretary said you headed up this project on your own lead. She answered most of my questions about this project you are involved in operating. It must be great to leave the position and the company you had to find something you can put your creative juices to work" stated Ned.

"To make long story short, I divorced my wife. She bought me out, and I am now doing my passion. You need to come down; I mean come up, because St. Helens is NorthWest of Portland on the river, to see it. That is if you have time and I am still confused. What do you mean, 'you can do for me'?" baffled by this conversation I was lost for words.

"I am in town for couple of days. I can be down, or up there for I know where it is tomorrow, any time that you are free. I want to have some business conversations with you. So you tell me when," was the inquiry from Ned.

"Friday at 9 or 10 a.m., I am available. How is that for you?" I replied.

"That would be fine and to take some of the mystery out of this meeting, I have been more than successful. I was looking for place to lend money to make a difference. Just making money any more is not fulfilling to my soul. I have more than enough. Now I want to see you as to where I can do this activity because without you, I would not have what I have now. I have salvaged few companies and turned them around which was profitable for me too. My investments are still yielding more than I had ever expected, so I am set. Maybe you might consider letting me help you, if that is alright with you. I sorry I have to cut out; I will see you Friday. My car is here and they are double-parked. I want to keep this call private if you don't mind. I will see you on Friday at 9" were Ned final words.

I thought that conversation was stimulating and still it raised more questions. Is this the source of the final backing of this project? Could this help hold the mortgages and help our mortgagees that are activated to serve our country? Questions were falling over each other.

Walking back into the room where the meeting was winding down. Joe and Larry had to excuse themselves because they had to get back to the office to finish their part of the permit process. There stood Judy, Johnny, Frances, Steve, Ol' Johnson, and Barbara who wanted to know what that phone call was all about because it left me in a dazed appearance.

"Crew, I am not sure, if I heard it right, but an old client of mine had just called and was coming out tomorrow to talk business. He even mentioned that maybe he would invest in this project if it were possible. I am not sure what kind of money he is talking about or if this is something he would want to do but he could be another answer to the question of how to make this project complete. He has made mega bucks on some highflying deals in the past. I really can't tell you much more. I only ask that you keep your fingers crossed for me. I am only kidding, we all looks nuts walking around with our fingers crossed and that does not do it. "I'll keep the vision and it will be doing so; as long as we always do our part", was my very direct statement.

That was our formative statement we always lived by and a reminder to help to raise our spirits higher than they were before the phone call. Everyone was packing up their paperwork and leaving.

Barbara motioned to me "You have more than the luck of the Irish. That is why I always want to work on creatively positive team. We work through every activity with "why not" and it had worked for us. There are so few people out there doing this simple practice system. We really don't have any competitors with the same goals. I can't tell you how your attitude has made a difference in my husband since we moved here. Not to exclude all the people who are involved in living, working and just being here. The attitude of this environment just moves you down that positive creative path whether you want to go or not. You giving this job to me have been the greatest present of my entire life. I better shut up because your eyes spin big time when I get mushy. Oh, your wife said she left you a note on the kitchen table and hoped you have time to do the errand before the store closes."

I escaped with joy because my secretary, now office manager, gets awful sickening sweet and just upends me. It is very short walking distance home.

As I entered my home through the back door, on the table was big vase of roses of mixed colors and note. I quickly picked up the note and thought, "what the hell". It read, "I love you and more" Jenny. Reading her note, I just sat down and cried. She is the world to me; I have to find out what is driving me in all directions instead of deep into her arms. My heart, no my soul, just aches for her but it scares the hell out of me. Why? Why? I can't find it in my mind, it must be buried in my past. I mean really past, because there is nothing in the world that would cause me this confusion. When I not only forgave my parents for what they did to me, thank them in my prayers because I am more because of those experiences. When I was in spirit world before I was born, I wrote my life's plan for them to be my parents. I knew it was crazy to do a life with them and there was fear that I might not make it. Nevertheless, I did make it; especially with all the spirit help. That experience helped me find the strength to be more. That more is a deeper understanding of a soul driven purpose of my evolution. Still with all I have gleaned from them, I don't have a connection of that experience to this confusion that is now torturing my life. I love my woman who should be sweet and fulfilling but it causes me insecurities beyond knowing.

I need to get out of here for now. This mood is depressing me and I want to keep the upbeat my love has for me. I think I will do a soaking and then "dinner in the diner, nothing could be finer" plays that old song in my mind. I had better get with the program or it will be too late to have dinner with anyone.

CHAPTER 18

Thursday morning Jenny and I have set this morning aside to have quality time together. It seems like we are caught up with business, work, and being on site at the mercy of the project, we have no alone time. I will be glad that soon Jenny will be off that 3 to 11 shift, so we can find quality time. We have plans for the morning, to have breakfast somewhere else, time alone to remember we are newlyweds, and time to develop personal intimacy between us for when we grow old together. Barbara and the rest of the employees understand this is reserved time for us and everything can wait until 1 p.m. So far, it seems to be working with everyone. The only problem is it is developing more approach avoidance conflict within me. I need to get the time with Roger moving because every day seems to be less instead of more lately. Maybe it is because Kevin. By helping me, has me more aware of my own deficiencies and why they exist. This morning we are going to breakfast and do some shopping.

Friday is upon me quickly. I wake up at 7:30 to get ready for meeting with Ned. I am more than anxious to know what that is about. I have a 1 p.m. meeting with the investors to report on our progress to prove that we are moving and getting this whole operation completed within an ideal time frame. Again, Friday night I will be alone with Jenny at work. Roger called to confirm and he will see me on Saturday at 10 a.m. That will shake up my world again in good way.

The time is flying as I ran out the door at quarter to 9 and Jenny wasn't up yet. When I have meetings, I know it is her time to sleep in. I left her a note last night about the events of the day, and I may see her before my appointment and maybe not, time will tell.

I was waiting in the office when a new Caddy drove in right on time, and I knew it had to be Ned. I went outside to greet him and to determine his pleasure. Would it be a visual walk around my new world, meeting first or what? It will be up to him.

Ned had his hand out in greeting as I came near him. I must admit his world had not aged him one bit. He still had the same looks and he dressed the same, as if he was beginning to seek his fortune. I was completely caught by his surpriseas he grabbed and hugged me instead. That action from him was new for me, but I hugged him back. He let go and stood back "You have not changed a bit. Being divorced and new life seems to really agree with you. I would like to stretch my legs, so why don't we walk around a bit if you don't mind?"

"First I have to say, you haven't change any so life has been kind to you too. I would be honored to show you around so you can have a feel for the place and what I am trying to do" came forth my excited reply.

The next hour we walked around the condo area and toured the model unit that was fully furnished. Without question, we made the restaurant the next stop for coffee. I was opportunity for him to meet Johnny and Ol' Johnson who were visible. Ned began asking Johnny about the restaurant operation and Ol' Johnson running the marina. The three of them appeared to hit it off very comfortably. The final tour was the marina and looking over the area for more condos and we walked to where the motel would be built. Ned seemed to be impressed with my goals and objectives for this place. He, as well as I, need to answers nature's call for drinking too much coffee, so back to the office.

We again met in the conference room, where Barbara had more coffee waiting for us. All the presentation material was still on the wall, and everything was set up for the flat screen should I need it. She is a jewel.

Ned began, "I am very impressed with what you are involved in. The goals and objectives for a community that supports it as well helps the resident if they so chose. The business end is very impressive which keeps the cash flow moving. The new development and motel are capital ideas. You and your team have really moved in the right direction. As I look at your projections on the wall, they confirm to me that I have made a good decision and I want to present something to you."

"Coffee or water?" I asked to tend to his needs. "I am all ears to what you want to propose. Since we talked on Wednesday, I have wondered about our conversation. The ball is now in your court; I will listen and answer any questions you may have. If I don't have the answers, I know my office manager does. By the way, did you realize that I brought my secretary with me to this project which I suspect that it must have given my ex-wife something to brood about."

"Water for now is fine and I see it has been poured so I will help myself. I thought your office manager looked familiar to me. You know she used to sit in with us when we were in working sessions before, and if it okay by you, why you don't invite her in now. She used to come up with some great ideas too. I always had great respect for her and I know why you brought her along on this. You are successful for all the good reasons. You always need a great...[you notice I used the word 'great'] support team to make goals materialize in your world. You can invite her to join us, I would be honored" were words of a businessman, who wanted to get down to business and Ned was always like that.

"I would like that", I reached over to the intercom and invited Barbara to come in and she gave her affirmative quick reply and was sitting in room as if she was always there. Ned welcomed her and told her he was glad she was there. "Again, Ned, I turn the conversation over to you to tell me or us what you are thinking about and how we fit into your offer or not." as I gesture to him to begin.

"I have in what I call my slush fund about 10 million or so. I never keep an exact record. I want to use these funds not to build capital but support ventures that help build something better for tomorrow. A place where the workers get the support they need to be all they seek to be in their work, personal and family world. Investors are for building business to give people work, and for profit on their investments. Now there is a trend to do something like what you are doing but it somehow doesn't work. There has been some deal where the company built a neighborhood around their business to make travel time to work almost none existent. These projects look good on paper and seem to work when first start. These businesses forgot that people who work together really might not have anything in common or the same values to develop into friendships outside of work. The planners didn't take in consideration the family's values, goals, or lifestyles, as 'part of the necessary basics to help develop a homogeneous world. Many factors have caused the majority of these projects to fail. They did not to really function as designed and in reality; they fail to come close to the purpose the project as designed. In truth, the human factor and their needs were not the focal point. We are not alike or on the same path in life. Maybe what you are doing here, the diversity that will help stimulate the balance we all seek can be the answer. At the present rate, we are dividing people rather than helping them to develop effective communication skills. We need to build an extend support system that once lived in extended family situation. They spend whole lifetime in same place and with the same people. Now everyone is too mobile, the designers need something that will replace that extended family feeling. I have to say, not after what I saw today of your plans and in speaking with Barbara, you seem to be headed in the right direction. Focus on needs of people, instead of convenience of the businesses. Most of the population spends their whole lives next to each other and they don't know anything about each other. It is not that they need to be up close and personal with each other, but supportive, and with a willingness to expand their own horizons. Diversity that balances is what I think I am trying to say. I have witnessed the beginning of that here. I knew you would have something like this developed here and that is why I was seeking you out. You are my kind of ideal man with the creative motive to empower people. That's what you did for me, and I knew you would understand what I mean.

"I have rattled on and, so briefly, I would like to put my slush fund to work in your project with no strings and should there be any return, I want that plowed back in the operation or used to support the project. I am questing an opportunity to invest in designing and developing a model where we find some answers for the needs of 21st century citizens and I don't want to make money off of it. So, I ask you what do you think of what I said and if everything is what you say it is, I want in." assured statements from Ned.

"You are over whelming; you are my kind of guy. That is about what I am trying to do here. I don't think I could express it better than you did, and I am not saying that to get you to invest. I too have seen examples of complexes that were to do something, but most of the people involved didn't have a vision. They want to do something without really working through with the model. Just 'thinking it through', doesn't work because there are so many critical variables to deal with. We are always up grading what we are doing almost weekly because we need to deal with the unknown variables to assist in their integration or we will not go there because we cannot address that aspect. Barbara can attest to that statement because she has taken that on as project manager. She is working on her master's in social development programs to address these kinds of problems."

"We are having a meeting with my investors at 1 p.m. I welcome you to stay and meet with them. In fact, I want you to do that. Besides, it is almost noon. I want you to be my guest for lunch. We always make it to the restaurant before the meeting. Truly, I would be more than honored to have you as an investor. We will have everything gone over by Ron; he does all our legal stuff, so what you say or agree to, that is what happens. You can have your "legal beagles" look it over also. Nothing is done by the seat of our pants around here. That way we all know what page we are on and there are no surprises. I maybe the point person on this, but all the principles have input with the majority ruling. Say, that you can make the time for lunch and join the afternoon meeting. Barbara pretty much runs the meeting to keep social conversation out of it. Business is business and social is social is her motto and it seems to work." I stated.

"I had marked out the day, so I will take you up on both of your offers because I always want to meet and have some interaction with your other principles. You can paint any picture with words, but the kind of people that are involved reflects the true story." Ned replied.

I excused myself to make a call to Johnny to tell him that Ned will be there for lunch to make room for him too. This time I gave Ned a chance to talk with Barbara. I went back in the room to tell them. "I was going to go over to my home to get my new wife, Jenny. I want you to meet her. We have not talked about my being married again. So will you, Barbara, escort Ned to lunch and I will meet you all there?"

105

I was out the door in flash. Damn, this is part of world to pay forward and it is working. I have no doubt he will be on board. Barbara will fill any empty time or answer questions he may have with their time together. She is great doing the work and supplying the proof. I need to see if my wife, that sounds nice – 'my wife', can join us.

Arriving at the house, Jenny was in the kitchen having a cup of coffee. She was wondering if or when I could join her for lunch. She was ready to go if I was free. She was delighted for me that we may or have another investor who wants to be a part of the action. Of course, we have to have a little kissing, she had to get her coat, and we were off to have lunch and see what this day has to offer us. She also informed me, that she was off tonight because her friend asked to switch for Saturday night because she wanted to go to her parent's anniversary. Of course, I think it is great she is free tonight to help celebrate another great milestone in our world.

Johnny had a private dining room all set up for meeting members for lunch before they go into their formal meeting. He also had menus that listed the choices without prices because this is one benefit of being an investor in this project. Knowing the likes of the clients, Johnny and Chef put together the following menu.

The choices for this day are: Soups: Fish soup Normandy, Almond Cream Soup, Gulyas; Salads: Ratatouile, Fresh Garden Salad, Seafood Medley,: Main Course: Beer-Batter fried Fish, Fish Fillets India, Pork Chops with Butter Noodles*, Broiled Sirloin with Mushrooms* * includes side order of steam vegetables; Desert: Pecan Ice-cream Balls, Sherbet, Chocolate Igloo, Apple Pie La Mode, Coffee Dessert.

The members and the presenter always know that the meal precedes the meeting and where it is served. Present were Bev & Ralph Whitmore, Steve Holland, Judy and Frances, Ron Collins, Ol' Johnson, Johnny, guest, Ned and Alex and Jenny. Other minor investors are involved as only an investment. One would say that those present are the inner circle of this project.

I introduced Ned when everyone was present and were milling around the open bar or looking out on the river. "Ladies and Gentlemen, I would like to introduce a past client and friend, Ned who has come to look over our project, to meet the principle investors and will decide whether he wants to be principle investor too." I then took him around to meet each one individually. He spent some time with Jenny too.

After about fifteen minutes, I asked the guest; to please be seated for lunch and the waitress was there to take their orders. The meal soon floated in with a ten-minute delay after each course. The hour always appears to hasten by. When the meal was completed, we all walked up to the office conference room where Barbara was waiting for us.

Jenny always dismisses herself from meeting because at this point she felt she had nothing to offer the group. Being married to me was not justification to be a member. She enjoyed being a part of the operational meeting where she could be an active participant to develop this project to meet the group's goals. I really understood her position and never pressured her to join even when some of the members were trying to pressure her to attend.

After everyone taken his or her seat in the boardroom, Barbara was in charge of the meeting. She summarized the Wednesday morning's meeting of our progress with construction, permits with the county, and projects. The floor was always open for further information, discussion and any interesting points. When the meeting was about to conclude, I introduced Ned again that he could ask any questions that he needed to know in order to make his decision and if they wanted him not just for his investment but active part where ever necessary. Some specific point questions that were opened to the floor and I asked that everyone would please participate.

Next, I was surprised with Bev. She not only told why she and her husband [invested because that they believed in my dream] but she took it a step further. Because of their financial position, they want all returns to be placed in a fund to cover the programs that are offered here. Further, they want this to link in with Barbara's program. We want to see if this can really be a model. Furthermore, if there is a condo that could be sold to us, we are considering retiring and want a more simpler life where we can help make a difference. Ralph stood up and stated my wife speaks for me and he wants in it too.

Before the meeting was over, Ned was over whelmed with educational level of this group and their commitment to be an active part of it all. Especially when he realized that Ol' Johnson was the foundation of land in this operation and he plowed his money back into it to insure its success. I am convinced that I will, no, I want to invest my slush funds money into this venture, if you'll have me?

Ol' Johnson was first to speak, "as long as Alex vouches for you, I have no objections."

"I also want you to know that we have a clause in our agreement that any time you want out, we have up to ten years to buy you out. Therefore, you have an escape route if this doesn't measure up or you have change of heart. Barbara can explain it more in detail. I want you to know this is long haul commitment. We expect that in refining this community. We could develop similar communities elsewhere. I want to be first to welcome you aboard" announced Alex.

One after the other supported what Ol' Johnson stated, and welcomes him. Ron went on to speak for the group. "There will never be any hard feelings should he decided to change his mind. This is not buying time-shares or other investment schemes. We have a three month cooling off period should you change your mind. The money will be given back to you because we will not invest it into the project until the grace period is over. This grace period is to insure that everyone is on board. I have to say, during the grace period, we decide that you would not make a good match. We will offer you investment position, if that is not what you want; you get your money back. This is like a marriage, once you are committed, there will always be adjustments going on, but the goal is greater than the personal desires. I also hope that cleans out some questions you have from a legal point of view."

Ned again addressed the group, "I heard you and I completely understand the grace period and I am thankful to be considered to join the project. I also truly understand the most important part of all of this; it is a marriage of people from different backgrounds and experiences. If you are not committed to the goals and objectives of this marriage, it should not happen in the first place. My work life has been fulfilling and successful for me, now I want more. There is a part of me that wants to be a part of something that is alive and developing. Something that growing and would feed my soul so to speak. That is why I made my offer. Let the grace period begin and I look forward to be at your next meeting three months from now."

That address made everyone speechless. Still at the same time, said it all. The proof is in the involved resolved commitment, not just the money. Barbara, in her parliamentarian way, informed the group that formal part of this meeting is concluded. Barbara welcome everyone to stay and talk with Ned to get to know him better and him us. The group slowly broke up and began to go their separate ways.

Ned went with Barbara into her office to sign the commitment letter with Ron to get the ball rolling. Then Bev and Ralph entered Barbara's office to look over sites of their future home.

Ned walked up to me with his copy of the agreement in hand. He expressed it was time for him to leave because of other commitments. I walked Ned to his car and we just stood there looking at each other. Ned was first to break the silence, "Who would have thought that our first meeting a number of years back would bring us to this point in the road of life? I always liked you as a person because of your ethics. I know this will help me with all my ventures in the future. For what I learn here will be easily transferable to every other operation I have. So thank you for bring me on board. I will be in touch with you all during these next three months because it is my down time at my work." Ned gave me a hug and was in the car before I could express myself to him. It is so hard in this culture to express feelings between men without raising questionable preconceived thoughts about that action.

CHAPTER 19

I was feeling a strange feeling of loss and I can't tell myself why. Therefore, before I get lost in my trying to understand, I better go and see what Jenny is doing. On the way to the house, all I could now think about was romantic evening between us. We could have some time together and then try out new restaurant in Astoria. It will be nice easy drive down and back. We haven't done that yet. I hope I can sell the idea to Jenny.

Coming through the back door, I called out to Jenny with no reply. There was a note on the table with instructions: to bathe and get ready. What the hell does that mean, but I guess I will do what the little lady wants. Going up the stairs, I can enter to master bathroom from the hall or master bedroom. I decide I take a shower, probably Jenny has my clothes laid out for me, and maybe a message will be there to tell me more what is going on. I made the shower short because my mind crazy with anticipations or what are the options participations. I left the towel behind in the hamper and came into our bedroom to get ready for whatever is going to happen.

There was Jenny lying in bed, with big smile on her face. I know what that meant.

About a couple hours later, she likes my idea of romantic dinner away from all the eyes here. The Fish House in Astoria was nice change. We were afforded a table by the window to enjoy the evening, and night lights on the river. After dinner, we drove back on the Washington side and crossed back over at Longview. I have to say that was such a great late afternoon and evening dining. We did not make it to the dance because we did not get back until almost midnight.

Saturday morning I got up and out of the house without waking Jenny because she has to be at work at three. I went to the restaurant for breakfast. We do so little cooking at home that there always very little food to make a meal. I borrowed Old Johnson's outboard and was on my way up the river to be at Roger's home by 10.

The fog surrounded the day covering everything lightly. The sun is fighting to break through to brighten the day. The river is still busy with Saturday fishing boats and few ocean-going ships entering and leaving. It was eerie coming up to Roger's dock, the fog was moving like large ribbons as result of the wind picking up and sun penetrating through the trees. There is this halfhearted desire to know more and fear of knowing beating in my chest. Again what really do I have to be afraid of since I here alive again. Maybe knowing I caused my own problems, that time in the 5th century and I guess I might have done much better in 2th century B.C. I wonder what I messed up in this next segment of my therapy. I want to get well. I want to have a full life with Jenny, I know Kevin will help me through this; still I am afraid I could make things worse. I remember I took a good beating physically before I was able to free myself from Marian. I am not sure how much I can take in this physical body before it breaks under all of this. Maybe I put too much on my plate for one lifetime. Can I make it? Here again, I am lost in thought, instead about being present in what I am doing. There is Roger looking at me from the porch with big question mark on his face.

"You look so preoccupied coming up the walk. I thought you would never get here" stated Roger.

"It seems that there has been lot of adjustments going on relating to the last visit. I have a deeper understanding how 'bull headed attitude, non-of-your business, and arrogance' caused a lot more additional problems. I should have just lived out the life as designed instead of try to do something else too. I am ready to continue the journey; I need to be free to enjoy the life with Jenny that I suspect is a reward for putting my life together. We shall see won't we?" were my last remark.

Roger and I journeyed through the house. Down the hall, to the session room, and as usual, tea and the comfortable chair waited for me. The chairs that will help me understand my past world to free me up now. I settled into my chair, took a sip of tea, and Roger's permission words floated at me. Working with him, I slid very quickly into between lives where Kevin, my friend, teacher, was waiting for me. I was come this time with greater appreciation of his patience and love or this would not be happening as successfully as it has.

Kevin begin with "Adrian [Alex] I have been giving it great thought since we exposed you to what happen in the 5th century B.C. I decided before we go to the 2nd Century where we will spend a great deal of time giving you a complete overview of what happened, it is necessary to slow the pace at this point. Before you break in, I heard your thoughts coming up the path and with your record of past behavior; the committee decided we would not present the events of the 2nd Century B.C. today. We, including you, need to be able to look at the event with an open mind because this event is truly the pivot point on your journey to understand love but mostly the importance of unconditional love."

"I have to be honest, do you think "we" can make this journey. You read my mind; you know the fears I have. I want it all like all humans. Still can I pay the price? If we could remember why we do the journey on earth in the first place, maybe we would not have so many dumb events that we have to clean up later. I know wisdom equals knowledge plus experiences. Those experiences sometimes have a mind of their own. I can blame all of it on something or person, yet I know I am the master of my life and my soul's journey. Basically these problems are of my creation." Adrian resigns himself to his created fate.

"You are doing very well. Without all these experiences, as painful some are, it is necessary for your evolution. It is like going through school. It is knowledge given as the student's ability to handle and the student continues to advance the knowledge to develop different dimensional perception. The student keeps improving on the new knowledge learn to convert it to wisdom. It takes many life times to master the vast dimensional knowledge to convert to wisdom. That driving force for all of us is wisdom. To boil this all down, you cannot be hard on yourself because believe it or not, you are right on track with your plan of exploring knowledge you learn while in spirit and applying it to have experiences. In the business world, you are more than on track. As for your personal life, you could have quit after solving the problems with Marian. You elected to clean up distortions created by Marian [the keeper & your commitment over 4500 years ago for earth pleasures] on your lives together that affected your knowledge and experiences. We, the committee, believe without a doubt, that you can make it through these final adjustments to win your freedom your soul's wants and needs. We can belabor the points but best we make a commitment right now, to quit or go on. You will not be held in any kind of disregard, because you mastered the major projects you came here to do this life. This issue with Spain and feelings with Jenny can wait another lifetime. Your marriage life with Jenny will have to be adjusted or terminated. We keep hearing your arguments like coming up the path today. You have to decide, because you have to live it. Once you decide, there is no turning back. You have realized no matter how tough it gets, you have the ability to master it. We have people in spirit and on the earth plane to assist you. You will not do this alone. You have to live it, experience it, resolve it; we cannot do that for you as much as you may want us to do so. It is time to put up or shut up, as simple as that. So dear friend, our relationship in the future as now, will not change if you decide to abandon this project?"

I sat there stunned "that took the wind out of my sails. I may be wimping and whining, that just being a human, but at my gut level, I know I can make it. So don't listen to my bellyaching. My bellyaching is a way for me to let off steam, it doesn't mean anything. It is just a human processing system. I really want this all to be over where I can be back in total balance. I want to deal with life's challenges without historical imperfections overtones. Therefore, I am in regardless of what you heard bouncing around in my head. If this body can't take the shock of what is going on, my soul always lives on. I will have to find another physical body to continue what we have begun this day."

"I accept your commitment as your bond. We will not pay attention to any of your bellyaching, but we will be monitoring your soul that no further damage is done in relationship to what you are healing. This meeting has been concluded until next time. Know we are with you." Kevin stated without any emotional expressions.

I was back with a jerk. Even Roger was caught off guard. "I guess you heard most of it. I believe I will be seeing you until this mess are over. I appreciate your time and commitment to me. I think I need to get my house in order to prepare to live up to my commitment." I stated in half-dazed verbiage

I staggered up, Roger followed me out, and I just kept on going, no looking back. I must have been like a zombie. Getting into the boat or remembering the journey back to the marina was lost in vapors of time. I came back to reality as I pulled into the dock where Ol' Johnson was ready to catch the bowline to pull me in and tie up.

"Did she run okay for you? I had her tuned up again last week. It appears that I must have gotten into some old gasoline at the marina up town. I had thought I did not have enough to get back so I bought tank full and for some reason it fouled up the injectors" explained Ol' Johnson

"She ran like a charm. I really appreciate you lending me your boat to make these trips. It seems I still have few more sessions with Roger, so I guess I will be hitting on you for your boat. It is only 15 minutes by water, to drive there it would take 45 minutes to an hour, so you know I really thank you for your favor" I replied with difficulty because I still wasn't totally back in focus yet.

The cover was placed over the boat and motor and we walked over to his houseboat where he offered coffee and wanted to talk with me for little while. Ol' Johnson must have expected me because the table was set and coffee made. I sat down and he did the honors of serving the coffee. He also had some sweet buns in the cupboard he put on the table. He knew my weakness, almond bear claws, are the best in the world. He sat down and started "I need to ask you some questions that have been bothering me. I have never been involved in high finances as we are in now. We are on such a pace it makes my head whirl. You guys still seemed to know what you are doing. The money just keeps bouncing around to cover the expenses. You have put in lot of money and investors seem to come out of the woodwork. One of my questions: are we over building and if we are not, can we survive a cool down economy?

"At the present time, we are just keeping up with the demand. Ned's commitment of funds, should he keep that commitment, will be the cushion to give us protection should the economy cool down. Our debt load is very low because we are selling as soon as the condo is up waiting for customizing. We have real good compatible mix that exists in most stable businesses. The new owners are not over their head in debts. We did a study to insure that we are possibly under the demand of the market. With very low debt load on this project, we are almost paying as you go. We have answered needs, so far, for the surrounding population. We have a good eating-place and a marina that is very functional. I am glad we finally got the fueling dock completed this week and operating. That reduced many headaches. Overall, it looks as a fail-safe operation as we can make it. Ron and Barbara keep their eyes on cash flow to insure we are not walking on the wild side. I hope that answers your question and I suspect you have more?" I inquired.

"I have been offered an opportunity from an old friend, who is retiring and wants to leave the area. We have been friends since I opened for business. He has that land across the street you have looked at and made a verbal wish that you want might want to own. He wants to sell me the twenty acres on quick sale for cash where it is done deal within a month. Are you, or I should say, are we interested in the offer? The price is below market value around here. He is giving us the deal because he likes what we are doing here and his granddaughter lives here. She has nothing but glowing remarks for our venture," stated Ol' Johnson.

"Damn, I cannot believe it. I have had Ron check into the idea that if we own that, could we have it zoned mixed, commercial, and residential. This has been going on for over a month behind closed doors. We were looking at small supermarket, gas station across from us to serve us and surrounding area. Then, maybe, a small plaza if that is supported by a "need" study. The rest could be developed as residential homes should a need arise in the future. We know that the marina and restaurant could support their needs too. We have been working on a plan that this project would generate cash flow that will support itself. We can do this because it appears the commissioners would support such a plan based on how we are working toward our goal. They want to be a part of this experiment. We would not need to build on it right away, but it will be there for a possible spring project. What you presented has my mind spinning; I can't believe it is happening sometimes. I would like to meet with him as soon as possible to listen to his offer and should it be something we can swing, it is a done deal" flowed with great confidence from me. "Can I imagine, if I didn't get my ass out of that marriage with Marian, out of our business and working on getting my life together, I wouldn't have my passion this project. This isn't work; it is play time that is the best game in town. What has been major for me, no matter how the personal life has been, I have been able to park the problems and function successfully in the business world. I guess being a Libra helps you keep a balance and keep swimming down the stream of life.

"Hey! Young feller, where did you go? You have that silly ass grin on your face, you sure as hell are not present with me now" questioning Ol' Johnson.

"Sorry, to be so rude, but doing a little pep talk to myself. I needed to pat myself on my back to enjoy the rewards for cleaning up my personal life. Back to my statement, I did say it out loud, didn't I? When can Ron and I meet with him to see if this can happen?" I apologize.

"Sit still. I will call him now and see when he is available and where." was his quick reply. Ol' Johnson left the kitchen and you could hear the conversation being carried on in the living room but it was not auditable. He comes back after a few minutes and as he entered the kitchen. He said, "Monday at noon, where you could throw in a lunch and it would be fine for him. He would come prepared to do business. If this will not work, I am to call him right back."

"Even if Ron is not available, I will have Barbara meet with me and hear him out. She would know if we had the funds available or are we able raise it on a short notice. I will reserve the private dining room so we can have privacy. I called Johnny, take out his cell phone, punching the keys, Johnny answered immediately and affirmed I could have the room for Monday. Johnny said I can have the room. Therefore, it's all set for meeting this guy. I will also expect you to be there because you already know about it." I informed Ol' Johnson so he knows he is invited.

"I thank you, and I will be there too." was his quick reply.

I spent a few more minutes to close up loose ends. I had to get home and spend an hour or so to park my head's thoughts from session with Roger. As I got up to leave, I said, "thank you, for this gift you have given me and I hope that what I answered your questions helped. Anytime you have questions on what going on, Barbara is there for you. All major investors and supporters should know by now, that she is available to answers your concerns honestly. The internal daily workings may not be included because some information is sensitive and it is important it doesn't become public even by accident. I hope you understand."

"I do. You better get, or we will be talking for another hour." a he shoos me out his floating home.

At home, and Jenny had already left for work. That is okay for me, I can go up to my study on the third floor and maybe crash on the couch. I made my way up and as I got closer to my couch, the sleepier I became. When I finally reached, my destination and I dropped on the couch, grabbing the blanket to pull over me at the same time. The deep black hole flooded over me, there was Kevin talking quietly "you need to park the any activity of the 2nd Century B.C. for a couple days because to have free time with Jenny and finish up the deal on Monday. We will help you control this until then. Jenny is being shifted to nights 11 to 7 so you can work this out without dragging her into the activity." My brain went silent and just darkness prevailed.

Jenny got home a little after 11:30 and reading her husband's note. She very quietly sneaked up the stairs to his hideaway and there he was, dead to the world. His color was good, so he is sleeping the sleep instead those nightmares. Jenny goes over kneels on the floor by his head and bends down, giving her husband a soft gentle kiss.

From out the deep of nothingness, I came floating to the surface to feel love touching my lips and I wanted to linger long. However, once the elevator to awakening begins, it is full out until you are awake. There was my beloved coming into view through my fog clearing eyes. I was able to whisper peacefully as her lips drifted away from mine "I love you too". We stayed frozen in the moment and finally I was fully back. We talked for a few minutes. We decided we would not go over to Johnny's for a dance or two. We elected to go to bed, and in short time, you heard gentle breathing in rhythm coming from the bedroom.

Chapter 20

Sunday was uneventful because Jenny took her day off to catch up on all her chart work and related work assignments. She has only this one course to complete, which has been mostly an internship to become a PA [physician Assistant]. She has been working on this degree for sometime without any real directions where she was going to use it. Now she can see maybe there could be a clinic here for the residents, customers and for emergency needs.

I was trying to learn to cook while Jenny was busy. I have to be honest, a couple of times, unbeknown to Jenny, the meal was thrown out and started over, sometimes from a can. The day seem so pleasant just the two of us being together. The very refreshing experiences kept on growing. We have a few disagreements, but we have a system we designed for time out and that certainly works for us now. That evening I retreated to my office to prepare information for my meeting tomorrow. When my mind is free of negative, busy, monkey mind activity, I am focused. I use my energy and that of my environment energies works as magnet to attract creative positive events into my life. It is apparent that "like attracts like" the more creatively positive I am, the more there is. That statement "win, win" really works.

I can't wait, and I have to, to get these last destructive limitations out of my soul, heart and mind, because every day I will decide how I will live it. There is no doubt in my mind, I have earned the right, and I am putting that right to work for me. Now I am entitled. I want to be all I came to this life to be expressed in positive physical way. The best game in this world, and sure is great to feel it. I better stop myself rally talk and get back to work.

The night melted into gentle togetherness and another day is gone.

I was at the office at 10 a.m. to confirm my work schedule. I check to see what Barbara needed me for, and to get few things ready for the meeting. There really isn't much. We have looked at the property without telling the owner and we were considering making an offer to insure the success of our program. Ron just pulled up with his car and I know he will be in here soon. I need to go over other things before we get lost in this meeting at noon.

Barbara buzzed me on the intercom to tell me Ron was here and my reply was to show him in. "How are you Ron?" was my opening question.

"About the same, everyday is wonderful since I joined this project. Having you call me to come to this meeting was a stretch for me because I thought we were going to talk to the owner after the first of the year and he is calling us for a meeting. I am glad that I got all my research work done and walked around with the county workers. We will be able to know if it is good deal or not. If we could get it for appraisal value, it would be a dream. With the appraisal, we would have the information we need to know about how much to come up with for a counter offer if it is high. This has to be the best game in town", Ron joyfully expressed as he sat down on the sofa.

"Don't get to comfortable; it is almost 11:30, so we might as well take a slow walk over. I checked with Barbara and she has given a cash figure we can draw on because he wants to be cashed out within a month. We can swing $250,000 without borrowing any money. I am open; I never set myself up for a price. Not doing that, I have found they always offer me a better price and usual less than I expected. So come on, get up and let's get there early, I'll buy you a drink if you like." I was anxious to get this moving.

As we walked over to the meeting, we just talked about this journey with all its ups and downs, in our own lives and with the project. All of it calling to us to be the best we can be and dig into our true selves to give that to our commitment. The day was like all autumn days except in Oregon, they last longer and when it is not raining. It's most enjoyable.

As we entered the restaurant, Johnny informed me that they were already in the special dining room. "They were having a beer. What would you two want? I will bring them in together," asked Johnny.

"We will have the same" was our unison reply as we continued to the dining room. Upon entering, we witness them looking down the river at something that had attracted their attention. Ol' Johnson motioned us to come and look at what they were watching. "Look, there is a newbie trying to sail and he is all over the river. I am glad there are no other boats out there for him to run into! It appears that there are two of them learning by doing. They seem to be trying to tack against the wind to get back up the river. It appears they are losing ground, as their boat appears to be going away from us. That has always seemed like lot of work. This is why I will only man a 'stink boat'."

The men watched for a few minutes. Finally, it appears they were taking in the sails and going to use their inboard to get back up stream.

"Alex and Ron, I would like you to meet, Fred, the owner of the land across the street I told you about." stated Ol' Johnson. The men shook hands as a greeting. Just then Johnny brought in their beers and motioned that did they want the beer on table or in their hand because they were standing. Ol' Johnson motioned Johnny to put the beer on the table that way it forced us to be seated. With that action, it will give them reason to begin the meeting and get down to business.

Johnny had menus for them, but before he could set them down, they all chimed in "we'll have the special", [1/3 lb of hamburger with the works and curly fries with salad]

Fred sat down first and took a sip of his beer as the rest of us took our seats. "I want to get to the point. I know you have inquired about my property. You have to know this is a small town. Nothing much gets past anyone. I have retired and I am on my way to Florida where I have vacationed many times. I have decided to live in the Keys but I do not want to get tied up with this property. I have sold everything else. There have been a couple of guys that have been fishing around trying to see if they can steal it from me. It appears they want it for speculation because of what you have been doing across the road. I may be a farmer, but I am not stupid. I have twenty acres and it is pretty flat. The land as you know can be rezoned and has a good soil base.

It was something I inherited, and all I did with the property was paying the taxes on it and let it grow into weeds. I have seen what you have done to Ol' Johnson's place and how he has thrown in with you all. You must be nice fellows for him to do that. I don't want any more than the appraised value. I know your development has increased the appraised value on lots of property around here. The value of appraisal is $5,000 an acre because it unimproved land. I have been informed that they will increase the appraisal this next time because of your operation. This means they will want more taxes from me. If we only go through a title company, where we don't have to deal with realtor's fees, I will sell it to you for $5,000 an acre and you pay all closing fees."

I looked at Ron trying not to be blown away by the offer. "You are right. Ron had to been looking at your land and checking it out to determine how we could use it if it were for sale. It is rezone able. We were considering a market and a service station since there is neither handy to us here. Since I am the leader of this operation, I want to accept your offer of the sale price and we will pay the closing fees. Ron will see to the details after lunch up at the office. This has to be fastest deal I have been in long time. You will receive a certified check as soon as all the transfers are completed with Title Company. I will deposit the money with them this afternoon to get everything rolling. Can I shake your hand to consummate the deal?"

Before I could get my hand above the table, there was Fred's hand reaching across the table. I took it and it was done deal. "Now that is how I like to make a deal with a hand shake. I am glad that is over and I can get busy getting rid of the things I am not taking with me and be on my way before winter sets in."

Ol' Johnson was first to chide in "Fred, I am so glad that you sold the land to us. We appreciate it. This has always been the matter of fact way we always do business."

Ron, with a very pleasant smile on his face "I knew you would get wind of what I was doing. I am glad it didn't offend you. It looks like my investigation about that property opened the door for you too to get rid of it. We can go up to the office and do the formal stuff to begin the usual paper work that is necessary with these transactions. I will call Barbara to prepare everything, so it will not delay us."

"That will be more than fine with me. Now I see the food coming through the door. Let's put away the business talk and have some social talk which I enjoy" was Fred's straight-forward statement.

I raised my glass to toast the deal. We spent the next hour eating, drinking, and enjoying the companionship, which was easily developed.

By three that day, all the paper work and the check was on its way to the title company whom we always did business. Another stepping-stone along the way completed. I thought he would at least ask for 7 to 10 thousand an acre. I am glad I kept my mouth shut.

Later, that day, Ol' Johnson told me via the phone, "those boys had offered him only three thousand an acre and they were trying to over sell their offer as 'one hell of a deal'. Fred was more than happy you accepted this offer. He will soon have his money and he is one happy camper to get the hell out of here. All he has been talking about is his future life in the Keys. I am happy for him. So we all came out okay, didn't we?" The phone went dead before I could answer to his statements.

I had better get home by 3:30 as requested by my wife, which are pleasant sounding words to me, "my wife". Jenny should be up since she is going on 11 to 7 shift this week and maybe next week too. I also realize that this week could be used to be able to catch up with her schoolwork. I guess I will know what the day will bring as soon as I get home. Maybe our honeymoon time isn't over yet.

Walking through the back door, the aroma of food filled the air, and there was my lovely wife in the middle of the kitchen whipping up something on the cooking island. "Jenny whatever you are doing, it smells great. It reminds me of little of the smell of food in Greece. You wouldn't be treating me with something special for a purpose or because you are wanting to impress your special husband?" flowed from my lips in playful loving way

"You caught me red handed. Johnny sent the meal over and I just making it look like I did it. What can I say? No really, I have this passion to try out Greek Lamb Sausages with Tomato Herb Sauce and spiced rice. I bought the Olive Bread, stuffed grape leaves, and baklava, so I have no claim on them. I made your favorite salad, spinach and roasted garlic. You have to choose the wine. The meal will be ready within a half an hour. We are dining in the dining room, so you will have to set up the table. Remember that 50/50 deal, and of course, you will be responsible to clean up and put everything away after dinner. This is a test." as Jenny busted out laughing.

My quick reply, "you mean to tell me, that this is not our usual restaurant, where you eat and run."

"Of course, but you have to pay up front. That will be $60.00 with the wine" was Jenny's rhetorical answer.

"You have my number! I am cheap, so I elect to set up, clean up and put away "as I hustled into the dining room to begin my duties.

They were busy dining at four. "Why are we eating so early, you should have warned me. I would have eaten a light lunch? I know your shift doesn't start until 11. Have you something in mind for your very, very, loving, caring husband? I know I can be up to the task since I have nothing planned. Besides, I will be fast to sleep by 11. So let me in on the secret. On the other hand, are you just going to keep rambling around about everything or will you finally get to the point? The suspense is killing me. My good news; we now own the land across the road at a price cheaper than I thought it would cost us. He only wanted $5,000 an acre. We should have possession of it within a week. So what is your good news?" I pleaded. It has to be romantic time because she spent most of yesterday with her school related work.

"Don't you really enjoy the lamb sausages? I have to say, I think I could have done a better job with the baklava. Your choice of wine just complemented the whole meal, not too sweet or dry. You are truly a dear. I do have a secret that I want to share with you. Because you are major player in it, it will call upon you to be more than your best. I have no doubt that you can rise to the occasion. I have been thinking about it off and on over the weekend and I can't put it off any longer, can I? Before I let the secret out, remember you have promised that our marriage would always be 50/50. I know you may suspect that I may not be carrying my full share but you are my strong, loving, hero and you have sufficient reserve to deal with my request. You have been more than acquainted in the past to meet my needs, hopes, and desire." Jenny tone of voice and teasing continued. She was watching her husband's face to determine how far she could carry out this love-teasing charade.

"You have me. I am your knight in shining armor, and I am ready to do your bidding. I can leave the clean up until after you leave for work. My full and cooperative self is at your disposal. Wait just a minute; are we on the same page? I have never heard you beat around the bush about making time for lovemaking. I think something else is cooking. I know Johnny doesn't need a place to stay. We haven't received a request for any from our new friends overseas, since we get all our mail at the office and there hasn't been any mail from them. Did they call while I was out? Who is needing a place to stay for short time, and I hope it is just a short time. Okay, I give up. What is it? I surrender unconditionally to your request." I was just played out. If it's time together, I don't want to waits another minute doing this word dancing game.

Jenny, realizing it time to put up because she has about 10 minutes before she needs to leave. "Dear husband, I love you more than anyone in the world. Knowing that, you will, without a doubt, look upon my request of you, as very normal for any wife would ask of her loving husband. Maybe it is more like your support. No maybe, it..."

"Enough, come out with it, the suspense is too much for me. What is it, time is wasting away, and can we afford it?" I pleaded.

"Well! I was informed this morning that they will expect me to do my intern assignment at 6 p.m. today and for the next two week. I will be required to be reporting for duty from five to 10 p.m. and the nights I am not working, I can volunteer 4 to 12 midnight to get my hours caught up. I really want to get this done by end of January. So can you support me in this activity for the next two weeks? I really have to get going if I going to make it to work on time. What is your answer?" in very loving pleading way that Jenny can do to my heart. Besides, she is grabbing her coat in a motion to leave.

"First, you know I support your educational path. What about me?" I pouted.

"I knew you would accept the challenged like a real dear loving man you are. I have to leave, give me a quick kiss. I am gone, and by the way thank you. It is only a hassle for two weeks. I will be caught up with the requirements of this part of my degree and I could not miss this opportunity. I really love you." with gentle loving whisper that tumbled from her puckering lips. They did a quick kiss and she was out the door.

Here I am. I better get this mess cleaned up and do my duty to God and my country. Damn, I should have known it has nothing to do with intimacy time. There goes those old male hormones of mine, racing out of control when there is slight hint that there could be time. I can't complain because we have it all. We have been enjoying greater loving and caring life that is more fulfilling than I ever had with Marian even on our best days. Besides this may work for me if I get into my pain. I really don't need her around witnessing the painful healing process of letting go of my trouble basket. I need to concentrate on getting healing duties done. Maybe I can go over to the restaurant to see if there is anything I can do to help or hang out socializing to fill this void for now. In the meantime, what do I do with those raging hormones of mine?

The days were filled with the normal duties of running and operating the project. Steve has made great headway preparing the new area for the condos. The set back of the front row to make room for the road way worked out because we have a deeper lengthened development area on that side. Should the weather hold for another month, maybe we can get in foundations in too. Who knows with the weather here? It is fickle and the weatherpersons have hard time staying on the mark.

Most nights were the usual small adjustment nightmares where the soul, subconscious and conscious mind were trying to incorporate all these concepts, events, emotions, etc. to bring about my healing. In many ways, I am glad the hellish nightmares related to family and Marian are finally over. They were really to up close and personal. Without all the support of my friends, I am sure I would not be here and if I were, I would have been a shell of a man.

CHAPTER 21

The sunlight crashed into the room this Friday morning so intensely that it caused me to sit up in bed to see who turned on the light. I looked around, realized it was only sunlight, and had a few chuckles to myself over it all. I am awake, might as well get up, and get ready for the day. I wonder what Kevin will have in mind for me today.

As I was beginning my day, shower, and dressed, my thoughts seemed to keep singing to me, 'when will this be over?' I want to live a normal life. I really desire to develop a deep love relationship with Jenny. At one level, I want it more than life, and on another level, for some strange unknown reason a fear of losing and fear will I be strong enough to save her. What in hell does this all mean? It is driving me nuts and I want it to be all over now? Still I have to trust the guidance of Kevin he has never failed me. I have failed him but he has never given up on me. I often wonder as why we still work together. I am sure I would have given up on me a long time ago. Here I am talking to myself. It is a test I must be crazy.

I am too lazy to fix my own breakfast. I guess I'll go over to the restaurant and have some social time too and I had better get a move on because Jenny will be home soon. She has been really dragging this week working and the internship. I don't know how she does it. She needs her rest; I am getting out of here to make sure she does. A couple of mornings back, I waited for her and she felt obligated to spend time with me. She shouldn't have to feel obligated today, I am out of here, so that won't happen again.

The day is clear and little on the cool side. Like all autumn days, Mother Nature is getting ready for her long sleep in order to have a bright spring next year. The short walk always stimulates desire for food, as if I needed an excuse. Ol' Johnson sitting at his usual table. I don't believe he has cooked a meal since we open this new place.

As I walked up to his table, "are you expecting company? Do you mind if I keep you company, if you are not?"

"Sit yourself down, I haven't much new stuff to visit about, but company is always welcome. As you know, eating alone is very boring; besides, I think we all spend too much time alone. It makes us old and cranky" Ol' Johnson's country sounding dialect.

"As you know I will need to borrow your boat again today. I am still seeing Roger on Fridays. I still wonder how long I need to keep going. Nevertheless, as you told me before, I will be done when I am done, quit moaning about it. Still I am like the rest of the world I want everything over - yesterday. Then I will be bored with nothing to do. To change the subject, how is Fred coming along with his moving? He will be able to pick up his check today, in fact, around 1 p.m. The title company called us that all the paper work is completed, being filed today and they will contact Fred when the check is to be released to him. I am grateful, for your help in helping us to railroad this purchase through so quickly." I stated as matter of fact.

"First, Fred called this morning to tell me that the payment is available and he is as happy as rooster in hen house full of hens. He rented a U-Haul and it all packed up, ready to go as soon as he lays his hands on the check and signs any last minute papers. He hopes to be down in California before he calls it quits for the day. He finally decided he would take the southern route, rather than risk any freak snow or ice storms that sometimes comes dancing up or down the Mississippi valley. I can't remember hearing him sound so cheerful. I am very pleased for him. The last couple of years he has found it harder and harder to come back here after being in the Keys. Maybe I will drive over to the title company before noon to say my final goodbye before he leaves" these words just flowed out of his mouth in a sad overtone of saying farewell to old friend that he will not see any more.

"I bet Fred would like you to be there as goodbye. You know it doesn't have to be an ending. You have free time where you could go and visit. If my memory has not failed me, I believe you were headed in that direction when you originally were selling out. Then we had all this activity and you decided to stay. I, for one, am glad you stayed because you have been such a fixture around here for so many years. Many people see you as an extension of their families. Again, I think that would be a great gesture on your part to be there for him." I encourage him to do it.

The rest of the breakfast conversation was spent just keeping him up to date on what is going on and keeping him in the loop. The time to go was upon me and I got up to leave. He came along with me to see me off and prepare to see Fred off. He gives an aura of hard liner, but his eyes are giving him away. This is going to be hard for him to say goodbye since they have been handy friends since he came here so many years ago.

It was like minutes after getting into the boat, I was heading up stream on my usual path. The river was smooth as glass. Not a breath of air was stirring, yet sounds were bouncing everywhere from the trains and traffic noises on the highway I-5. As I came up to the dock, shut off the motor and silently drifted up to the dock. I looked behind to see the very smooth waves of my wake moving ever so slowly across the river and with gentle splash against anything in its way. This scene makes being human a wonderful experience. I began my rhythmic walk up the path to my waiting mentor standing with the cups of tea. I sometimes wish I brought a camera to take copy of this picture because it most tender moment of welcome.

Roger greeted me, handed me my tea and gestured for me to lead the way. As always, through the living room, down the hall and into my uncertain room. I guess the hesitation is deep fear of not knowing what we are going to venture into today. I quickly sat down in my assigned chair, had long sip of my tea and laid back. I was beginning to hear Roger's voice fade away.

Then right on clue, was Kevin's voice "Welcome Adrian [Alex]. Are you prepared for the next phase of your expiration to understand how past lives affect your present state of being? I am ready to take you on your journey to comprehend your conflict with feelings of love in your present life. By your appearance, I see that you survived the emotional activity of the last exploration. Now you will really understand how your arrogance, failure to justify your action, caused the domino effect on every earth lives you have lived so far. Let us now understand how your actions prevented you from completing the life of understanding the love of a family and friends of the 5th Century will now play into this life of 2nd Century B.C.

Ethan [Maricus of 5th century] decided come back in Palestine that is far from Greece as possible. His goal was to be born into a family where a loving relationship didn't exist. Palestine would be a safe place to begin healing of the events that had taken place in the 5th century. He had been born about seven years before you were born in Greece. His family was making a living on the sea by trading between Palestine and Egypt. His father would be gone long periods. As a result there was no way to develop a relationship with him. The mother was left to raise the children with whatever funds the father left until he came back. It was a life of feast or famine. During the deprivation times, the children were sent out into the streets to beg to provide for the family. The mother was significantly punitive to her brood if they came home with not enough to provide for them. She would eat in front of them with not a scrap for them. They all would go hungry as a lesson. That was one of her many methods of punishment.

Ethan was the oldest and the man of the house when his father was away. This gave him very demanding responsibilities for young boy growing up in such an environment. Still he knew what he was getting into when he chose this life. To him, it would be safe from a life where love feelings could or would exist. He needed to learn to control the emotional aspects of the human body. "And what a life he chose" commented Kevin.

We now hear Ethan tell his story. When I became fourteen, my father required me to work on the boat with him so he would not have to pay for my services. The work was hard and I was treated just like crew. When I made mistakes, I received the same or worse harsh treatments as the crew. Sometimes I was made to be an example for the crew. Being a family member or thinking of getting on his good side, the treatment was always worse. This was very hard work – working a two mast sailing cargo boat. I was learning seamanship by doing the work. By the time I was eighteen, my father now started to teach me navigation and the business of earning a living transporting goods. There was never praise when I did the job right, but hell was to pay when my father caught an error.

When I arrived home from time to time, my mother wailed into me of the hardship the family was going through because I was not here to help her. I had to be crazy to pick such a life but it was better than the pain of love lost, and the destructive feelings of it all. This still felt safer than trying to live a life where love existed. I wanted no part of that life again; those experiences had shattered my soul.

Ethan continued telling his story. I was walking down the street of my town when I was twenty and I heard a stressful sound coming from the alley. I looked to see what was going on. Behold, there was an old woman in rags being hassled by some young boys. They were trying to steal her purse. She was trying to fence them off with her cane. It appeared the assailants were winning. Without a second thought, I charge down the alley, picking up heavy stick and screaming at top of my lungs as I charged. I was hoping that this fierce action would scare them off, but only one ran. The four remaining turned to meet this intruder, who was ruining their pleasure and desire for loot. I was like a tiger, my heavy stick smashing against them. My force against theirs, as one by one, they fell under my blows as I cleared a path to the victim. I quickly turned to face them head on again. This time my swinging pole found no challengers because they were busy dragging themselves away.

"Are you alright?" was his first concern. "These young vultures are pretty brazen to attack in the daytime. I will see you home" were my forthright words of her new champion.

"I am fine, but very tired. I thought I was lost; no one was come to my aid. How can I truly thank you?" was questioning words from her very trembling lips. She finally crumbed to the ground.

I bent down, picked her up in my arms, and asked her for directions to her home. She couldn't weight more than two small sacks of grain. She just pointed the way and we were off to her home. She lived on the second floor of this very old run down house. One would consider it more of a building than a house because it had seen too many hard summers without any care. I pushed open the door, and entered into the space that was a very small room. She asked to be placed in the chair by the table and it was done.

"Are able to take care of you? Where is there water that I can get you a cup?" was my concern because this is worse hovel I had ever been in.

She pointed to jar which held a cup on its side on a shelf and I went and fetched her water. She sipped it very slowly. Finally, she said, "truly you are a God send, for they would have done me in. I have only a few coins that I earn telling people who want to hear about their future. For most of them, there is not much change in their daily, weekly, or yearly life but they just hope there might be something better. Can I offer you my coins for saving me?" were her pleading voice for she had nothing else of worth.

"No, I have enough. I must be on my way for I have to get back to work, thank you anyway" as he tried to disengage and leave.

"If I have nothing of value I can repay for what you have done for me, would you accept whatever words of wisdom I receive to help you on your journey into the future" were her pledging words.

Oh I guess I can give her some satisfaction and listen, as I thought over her offer. I have heard of this fortune telling stuff a lot around the market but nothing I really would consider any value for me. I am stuck in these endless days, months and years she spoke of where everything is the same.

"If it gives you pleasure, I will accept your offer" in gentle voice, for what do I have to lose but time. I couldn't offend her by not accepting something, which is truly cruel.

She motions me to sit in chair that was opposite her. Then she asked for my right hand. I complied looking very puzzled because I never did this before and didn't understand what is going on. After looking at my hand for few minutes, she began "I see you as captain of a vessel very soon because of unavoidable accident of the captain. Let me see, the men, the crew appears to respect you even though you are younger than they are. Then let us see, you are in Egypt, you will hear rumors of a great need for grain in Athens, Greece. You have never been there. Although it will be very profitable venture, please don't go. If you do go, this you will open the old pain in your heart that lived there for the past 300 years. If you physically kill the person that caused the pain, it will cause greater damage than before. You are not strong enough to face this challenge. You came here this life to be void of all that it offers" her words were growing stronger with warning. "I wouldn't go for the huge profit and keep the trading life you now have. I also see a death, great sorrow, a family, and strange vengeance forced on you. That retaliation will not be satisfying for you. Again, I plead for you to not to go. You should never have or be connected to any activity that would take you to Greece, especially Athens. You have been warned young man. Please do not take this warning lightly." as she pointed her finger at him. "I have never had thoughts like this before, please, please take my warning seriously for you have saved this old woman from great pain. The pain you will experience is far greater than whatever could have happened to me". With those words, the frail old woman just sat there in daze looking at him with glazed eyes.

I was in great state of confusion from her words and emotional threats. There was very deep knowing what she said had truth in it. Fear raced through every fiber of my body. I could not control it; I had to get out of here. I bolted from her place and with great haste returned to my father's vessel. From that day on, I kept trying to erase her present ominous words from my head.

Kevin looks at Adrian and began to talk "You can see we did try to warn him through her, but he would not listen". He continues, "and why is it when you get into a physical form, many of these life's plans the person designs to live with the active support we offer, are just pushed aside?"

"I guess you have forgotten the emotional impact on the person's life. While in physical body, you have to fight off normal physical urges of the body, D.N.A., past lives' events that creep out because you are again in a body, etc. The list just keeps going on and on. You, in reality, have no idea because if you have not been in physical body for such a very long time, it is in fact hard to explain," replied Adrian [Alex].

"I guess you are right. That is why I do not seek to be born again in physical body. All my assignees have such a hard time trying to get through their chosen assignments, their experiences, etc. outweight the advantages of trying to make words flesh to feel knowledge to gain the wisdom. My existence I have chosen I find it takes me longer but I don't experience the scares my assignees had experience in their quest. Let's get back to events at hand for we are running out of time," explained Kevin

Kevin continues, "In the meantime, seven years after Ethan was born, you [Adrian] decided you would again try living a life in a very loving environment. This activity was to help your soul shift from a warrior protector to one of a compassionate warrior. This would be your second attempt at a compassionate endeavor. This is the journey for all souls.

The city was Athens. Your father, Adelfo, very much in love with his wife Xander, who was a loving kind of woman. You entered the family marriage after about a year. They named you Altair. Your father was very well liked and respected successful business man and trader. His employees that cared for the house or the business were honored to be in his employment. When you were two years old, a brother, Lidio, was born. It was indeed a great family environment to be born into. You were living the life where love abounded everywhere. You grew up in life similar to that which you had in the 5th century. Your brother was your best friend. Life could not be better. When you became thirteen, your world was shattered again unexpectly."

Kevin continued the story with Adrian to set the stage to witness the tragedy. The scene now shifts back to Ethan where the old woman's tale is about to unfold to bring the tragedy to life. "As strange fate would have it, Ethan's father died unexpectedly when he was twenty. [Ethan again presents his life journey]

I [Ethan] am now the captain and had finally earned the respect of the crew. The old woman's words, I thought were gone forever, now played with my thoughts almost daily. She was right. I grant her that about my father but he always lived on edge, or it could be just a coincidence.

On my latest trip to Egypt, I was informed that the grain harvest was not ready yet in Athens area of Greece and there was great demand for grain. Egypt now had a very large surplus. I was ready to gamble to make some real money, which would break me out this marginal living lifestyle and the possibility of becoming an owner of a larger and better ship. I invested all ship's funds in grain. I loaded my ship up with as much grain as I could buy and carry and decided I would make for Athens. The journey across the sea was swift and uneventful. I had never made this journey before, so I had to rely on the maps I was able to acquire.

To my amazement, I arrived at Athens without any problems. Upon entering the harbor, I found a dock space, and was off my ship to find a trader. The first person I met, I inquired as to the trader who would be the most honest. He and as other who were questioned said, Adelfo and pointed to his business warehouse. As fate would have it, I tied up to the pier that leads to Adelfo's warehouse. I had left my crew on board to guard the grain and made my way back to the warehouse. I did take one of the crewmembers who understood more Greek words than I did. Being a trader you learn lot of different languages but most of those words that have to do with business or little cursing."

As I approached the warehouse, I kept on inquiring where I could find the owner, Adelfo. I walked up to a man who appeared to be a worker for the warehouse to ask my question. To my surprise, the man stated, "I am Adelfo, at your service. What can I do for you?"

"I am the captain of that ship" as he pointed to my vessel "I am load with grain from Egypt to sell. I have a full cargo load of Egyptian's best grains. I am seeking a fair price for my cargo" I replied in my native tongue because Adelfo greeted me in my native tongue.

"Come in, let us talk" was his kind words "Coffee or what can I offer you?"

"Coffee would be fine" was my reply.

We sat at the table just outside the shop that was connected to the warehouse. The employee heard his boss offer of beverage and brought forth the coffee for them. My crewmember asked to be excused because he realized his ship's master was able to carry on business without him.

"I have heard that the grain harvest is still a month off and the granaries are running low on grain. I want to sell my cargo at reasonable profit and I have been told you are the most honest man" was my comment. After my statement, after tasting the coffee and we began opening the bargaining session. This is one of the activities of this business. I enjoy the haggling sometimes but sometimes it so frustrating, but that is life.

"That is true" was the trader's quick reply. "I am willing to offer you 100% profit what you paid for your cargo if it is as you say it is. I am not in the mood for bargaining if you do not mind. Our city is in need and I run an honest business, asks anyone" was gentle words flowing out of Adelfo mouth.

I was really taken back by this kind of trading. It usually takes most of the day and then sometimes it is a no sale because there is no profit for the work performed. "Come, then, look and taste my grain and you see it is what I say. I will also show you the invoice for the purchase to prove what I paid."

The men got up from their chairs and walked down the pier where my ship was tied up. I gestured for Adelfo to go up the gangway first. The men seeing their ship's master coming prepared the samples of the cargo for viewing.

Adelfo looked at the grain, stooped down, pick up a handful, and tasted the grain. It was dry and sweet to the taste. I have not tasted grain like this in a long time to himself. "You must not have had any storms or rain on your journey."

"We had fair sailing with great wind from the desert to carry us here in very short time. We had the cargo well secured and protected to insure its quality" was my quick reply.

"May I see where the rest of this is stored? Should it be as you say, my word is my bond, the offer stands. I will check from time to time to insure that the same quality is in all the bags if you do not mind" in very business tone flowed out of Adelfo. "I have not seen you before, and you look very young to be the captain of this vessel."

"My father died last year and we always traded between Palestine and Egypt. That way we were able to provide for our family that lives there and be with them from time to time. This is my first trip to Greece and it is adventure for me and the crew. I would be honored if you will check the cargo to prove my word. But I have to tell you, this is great way to do business and is the first for me" I very proudly replied.

"I will get my men and if your crew will help, we can get her unloaded in very short time. I probably have it all sold by the time I get it into the warehouse anyways." The word was sent out, and because of my reputation, they will come. "So let's go to my shop where we can complete the transaction and let the men bring in the cargo. I will pay you in silver or gold, which will you prefer? Come, let's go" motioned with his hand toward the warehouse.

The crews' eyes reacted to the magic words of gold or silver. There was no mention of brass or iron, which means our share, will be greater. This inspired the crew to put their backs into the work. The hours vanished quickly with the crew and his workers unloading the cargo in shorter time than usual and the grain stored in the warehouse. As the owner stated, the customers were at his shop purchasing for their needs. He was also able to make a fair profit without causing hardship on his customers.

"Ethan, will you have supper with me and my family tonight? I know your crew will want to have some time ashore. There are so very few ships in the harbor and I know the merchants would enjoy some company and a little business too" was his jolly laughter.

"I will be honored but I have to say, this has not happened to me before. Am I safe? Is my vessel safe is my main concern. I hope I have not offended you with my questions. I have been in some real situations that cause one to be nervous. You, in all appearance, appear honest and forthright but there lot of money and …. I do not know what kind of harbor this is "in my questioning voice.

Acting as if he heard Ethan's words, he gestured towards him to strengthen his words by saying, "You truly have nothing to worry about on the pier that you are tied up to, and I will vouch for your ships safety. I am very well liked in this community and everyone looks after protecting what I claim as mine. You see I have some power and no one violates it. You can have your money now or I can give it to you in the morning. However for now, come, my family will welcome you as a long lost relative. I very seldom take any of my business customers to supper for the same reason of trust but for some reason, I like you. So inform your crew of your pleasure for them and I will have two of my crew guard your vessel until you come back. If some of your crew want to remain, I will still have my men there to insure there will be no trouble" in his best commanding voice.

It becomes apparent that this man wields lot of power and respect in this community. Hearing his words created a strong feeling confidence and safety. I excused myself, and returned to my vessel. I gave instructions that two crew members would remain on board, when the other crew members returned, they can have liberty. The warehouse owner will also post two men to insure the safety of the vessel and you. I have been invited to his home for supper. I will finally have a chance to wear my new clothes I bought in Egypt. However, I need to bathe first, and to my surprise, the bag of water was ready for me to do that. After a quick cleaning and placing fragrant oils about my body, on with my clothes and stood proudly before his men to get their approval. They agreed I looked great besides I needed to be gone so they can have some shore fun too.

I hurried down the gangway and pier. I arrived at the shop where Adelfo was waiting for me. They had a slow easy journey up the hill and after a short distance, we entered through the gate in the wall to a very modest but beautiful home with its gardens, and statues. Everyone one was busy preparing for the supper because it was so commanded. His wife, very beautifully dressed in white with gold accessories, was first to greet him. Besides, she was curious why her husband would break his rule about trader guest and what's more, she heard about this rather handsome captain was coming to supper. Before she could say anything, the two sons dressed in white tunics crashed in to see who this person was too. Their father had never brought home a ship captain before. He must be special. He was young and handsome, but still looked a little odd to them dressed as an Egyptian. The whole family seemed to instantly accept him. That was a very difficult unconditional feeling for Ethan because this was nothing he had ever experienced before in this life. It was just weird.

Adelfo excused himself to clean up before supper. The poor captain was left to his own defenses in dealing with this new family. It was also surprising that they were able speak his language. His mixture of Greek words caused a lot of pleasant laughter. Altair now beginning his teenage years with manhood just around the corner. He was very handsome lad. His body was developing with supporting flair to be adventurist as his fantasies. Altair, for some strange reason unknown to the family, took an instant liking to him. Here is a real live person of what I want to be some day. Altair had to sit by him during the meal. He was continually trying to engage him in conversation from time to time, while he kept touching him.

"What is it like to be captain of your own vessel? You must be able to travel all over the known world. Have you sailed to the end of the world? What is it like?" blurted out from Altair without taking a breath. His actions insured he was not disengaged from the captain or let anyone else have chance to talk with him.

In addition, the never-ending questions never seem to cease until father finally tried to the Ethan's rescue. It was apparent that Ethan seemed to be over whelmed by all this attention and still he was trying to reply before the next question was fired at him.

Adrian [Alex] witnessed this, as one would be watching a play. I keep wondering why Kevin was presenting this activity. I know better than to butt in, because I really need to know why it is so important. It must be essential to find out why I am still having strange unexplained feelings when I am with Jenny. I have not a clue to how this is related, but I promise Kevin I will follow his lead. While watching this, my heart aches for the love that seems to flows so freely and honestly here.

The time was flying by and I started to make statements that I needed to get back to my vessel. Altair just kept on engaging him to the utter surprise of the whole family. Yet they thought it was amusing since he has never done that before with any stranger.

The father interrupted his son finally by saying that he needed to have a few minutes alone with Ethan and would the family say good night. The mother and Lidio just said good night with a wave, but Altair had to have a hug and took one. Everyone's was surprised by Altair's action as well as mine. I really did not respond because it was out of my comfort zone. Altair realized maybe he really over stepped his bounds, quickly disengaged, and ran to catch up with his brother.

His brother whispered, "what is all that about?"

"I don't know, but for some strange reason, I like him very much, almost to point of being uncomfortable even for Altair. Why is this? It is the strangest, weirdest feeling I have ever had about any one. I just want to hug him, be with him and I don't have a faintest idea why. The more I talk about it, the more confusing it is for me. So let's not talk about it," he whispered back as they went to their bedroom.

Altair lay on his bed looking at the ceiling trying to understand these very unusual feelings for this stranger. Trying to get to sleep, but these unexplained feelings kept him involved. He was also recalling the feelings of all the adventures he had dreamed about when he would spend hours looking out to sea in the past. Finally, just exhausted from his exploration as to why to all of this, caused darkness of sleep to quiet it all.

As Adelfo walked Ethan to the gate in the wall. "Will you consider going back to Egypt and bringing back another load of grain for us? I will pay you the same offer" as he faced the captain.

"I will think about that and give you my answer in the morning. No, I will give you my answer now, yes. I will see you in the morning for my money and we will make up the agreement then" was my proud reply.

"My servant here, who held a torch, will see you back to your ship and I will see you in the morning and we will make the agreement" was the parting word. Adelfo watched him as he walked away thinking he had strong impression on my son. Why did that happened, I wondered? This will be very good business venture for both of us. Now, to sleep was his only thought. As he turned back to the house and his loving wife was waiting there for him.

Upon arriving at my vessel, I found most of the crew had returned in very good condition, which was unusual. I told them that the trader offered him the same deal if I would obtain another load of grain. The new Contract for grain was welcoming news by the crew, which meant more money for them. The ship was ready and they will be ready to shove off in the morning as soon the agreement is signed. I made my way to my cabin, undress to my shorts, and then dropped into my bed. The night vanished. The crew was at my door at break of dawn to receive orders to prepare for sailing. I told them I had to get the money, and will be right back. I had better get dressed and be on my way. The crew was ready to leave upon my return. All they could talk about was what they could buy with their share.

I was waiting at the shop when Adelfo arrived by 8 a.m. We had coffee and wrote up the agreement and I was paid in gold, for Egyptians love gold, for my grain. As all of this activity, it just eats up time.

By 9 a.m., they shook hands as they rose up from the chair. A new friendship was created. I took my leave and with a short walk, I was back on my vessel. The guards from the warehouse left upon seeing me coming their way. I still could not believe that the crew was in such great good shape considering most the time I would find them wiped out with wine. They wanted to know if he had the money. I quickly showed them the bag of gold and the agreement, which met with their happy approval. The first mate looked at the crew and said I guess we have successful captain. The crew did not need think about making the round trip because their share made them hungry for more. They were on their way with speed with a favorable wind and tide.

The journey back to Alexandria was as quick as the trip to Greece. The crew voted to get the grain instead of hitting their homeport for fear they would lose the prize money with any delay. They sailed in the port, loaded, and set sail for Greece again within a day. The crews were dreaming about their share and were going to spend it. The fair winds were with them again and they made as good time as the first run. They again were blessed with no rain or rough seas. Everything stayed nice and dry which insures maximum payment for the grain.

Coming into the harbor, Altair was first to spot them from the top of the ridge. With great speed, he was also first on the pier as the vessel moved in to tie up. As the gangway was put in place, he ran aboard, seeing the captain and ran over to me and embraced me. The crew was as shocked as I was. Just then, I looked up to see Adelfo coming aboard and expressed the amazement of his son's affection. I wonder what is going on between those two. It does not seem natural even for me was the father's thoughts.

"Come Altair, this man has lot of work to do. The people of the town will be soon upon us because the harvest is still not in and they are in need," commanded the father.

Hearing his father words, he released his grip and stood back with great smile on his face. He watches his father and I get everything organized to get cargo unloaded as quickly as possible. The quality of grain was as before. Everyone turn to and very quickly, the vessel was riding high in the water. The warehouse was full and the town's people busy getting their needs.

All day Altair just hung around me every chance he could. He was trying to engage in conversation about anything just as excuse to be with him. His father finally sent him home because he was becoming a nuisance. With a pouty face, he retreated home, still wondering why he is so attracted to that man.

I was growing angry with him at the same time. This kid has some way has waking a deep dark secret that I don't want or will not face now in my life. I never experience this over whelming free flowing very caring emotional interaction with any one, let alone with any one in my family.

During the course of the day, when Adelfo offered him another trading deal, my reply was I was ready to go that day. The father had oil and other merchandise that needed to be in Canakkale, Turkey but not at critical speed. It was agreed on price this time for just carrying the cargo there. Adelfo informed me could make run home first and then deliver the goods. He also had shipment of goods that were ordered to be brought back with me to Greece.

As the vessel sailed out of the harbor after being loaded with its new cargo, Altair was watching it all from his vantage point on the hill. There was a sadness flooding through him as vessel dropped from view. He just wanted to spend some time with him. What was wrong with that? I still don't understand why I want to be around that stranger. There must be something wrong with me. He doesn't speak our language well. Yet, there is something deep within that I want to interact with him. I have a brother, but not that feeling. I have male friends but not that feeling. It seems to be mixture I want to share it with him. I wonder how long it will be before I will see him again.

That evening, when father came home, he informed the family that we have warehouse full of grain for the city. Ethan, the captain, agreed to take my items to Canakkale, Turkey but he is going to travel home first and then to Canakkale. In addition, he agreed to bring some items from Canakkale to here for me to sell. I guess we will see him within the month. Trading with him has secured our finances for this year.

I decided with the first mate as they looked at the chart, it would be better to sail to Canakkale first to unload the merchandise, pick up another load for home to make even more money. Then there would be additional money back to pick up the cargo for Adelfo. A fair wind has been working for us. I wanted the crew's assurance that will be the plan. With the willing and accepting crew, plan of action, things happen successfully.

When I arrived home at Tyre, I was able to sell all merchandise I brought from Canakkale. The crew was overjoyed with their new wealth as they departed for their home for a week.

I wanted to get home to see my mother and brothers and sisters, my family. I had visions of maybe it could be somewhat like after being at Adelfo's home and how they treated each other. This could happen especially since I have lot of money that should last the family in style for a year. I also have enough to consider a larger vessel or new equipment. I have not made up my mind about better ship yet. With full expectations of a hero's welcome by the family, when I went through the door, it was all shattered as my mother looked at me.

Her first words were "Where in hell have you been, you unfaithful bastard? You are turning out to be like your father. You don't give a damn that we are starving or what happenings to us. Tell me, you ungrateful pup, how much do you have us to live on? What the hell is this you are dressed in? You can buy yourself nice new clothes while we are dressed in rags. Well! You better give me money now and I warn you, it better be good" in her hostile demanding voice.

I gave her a bag with enough gold coins to pay for everything for a year. She took it in her hands and weighs it, "I bet there are metal coins that are not worth much. Why do you torture your mother, who gave you life and always loved you most because you were the first-born? I warn you [as she shook her fist at me] there better be enough in there, to pay back the money I borrowed and for us to live on. I have no idea why I have to have two of most damn able men in my life, even if one is dead. You are turning out to be just like your father" her voice intensity increased until she was screaming at me.

Screaming and shaking the bag until it fell out of her hand on to the table and a few of the gold coins flew out on the table. She stood there in shock and quickly opens the bag and poured out the rest of the coins. [In shock of disbelief] "They are all gold coins, [and then still she screamed] is that all I get?" Her voice reflected that it was not enough.

I was thinking to myself, I should have known, regardless what I give, it will never be enough. Why do I try, when I know the answer? That Greek family life just makes it harder for me to endure this kind of ungratefulness, as those thoughts continually ran across my mind. I think I will go back to the vessel and spend the time there until the crew returns. I can't stay in this hellhole.

To his surprise, soft words were being said. "My boy, I am sorry to yell at you like this, but you have no idea the hardships I have been living under for past months. Look at your brothers and sister. They are all huddled up together in the corner because they are cold and hungry. You have no idea that they have been so hungry and so sad because you had forgotten them too. Come my precious children, you will not have to beg in the street for a little while. Come and give your big brother a hug for the good fortune he has given to us this day" in a very demanding coarse unfeeling words.

They left their corner. It is the corner where I used to be when I to didn't obtained enough money from begging. Very quietly, they got up, came over, and as command gave their brother a half-hearted hug. [As always, we never show any kind of affection to each other.] I understood that even with all that money, very little would be spent on the children for clothing and other needs. While everyone was invited around the table to look but do not touch, this gave me the opportunity to very quietly creep out of the room. I couldn't run fast enough to get to my ship. Once in my cabin, I threw myself down on my bed and cried my eyes out because my hunger was awaken. The desert-family love of his mother just drove the dagger deeper into my heart again and again. As I lost my consciousness, my world went into the usual dark pit from hell. That disconcerting dream comes charging back to vex me.

My dream is almost the same with few variations from time to time. It always starts with blood all over my hands and on my tunic. I am screaming, "What I have done". Then a sword stabs into my heart and down the dark tunnel, I am falling into an abyss. Great feelings of guilt and remorse rapped round me like tight wet blanket. Is there no freedom from this hell that always danced away until I am lost in time and space?

Kevin steps in to explain the last statement "This is the pain he is trying to get out of his heart which is result of killing you, Adrian in the 5th century. He thought if he could come back in loveless life, it would stop, and it hasn't. We have tried to have him to understand that if he came back in a somewhat dysfunctional loveless family, maybe we could remove the earth energy pain from his soul."

We believe "that action would lessen the pain intensity, and then try to heal love lost and tragedy that happened. So far, he hasn't done it. With these dam able nightmares and the words of the old woman, we thought we could prevent this "*wild card*" of trouble. As you can see, he thinks she has put a curse on him to make it happen. Now watch what he does with our help which is nothing."

"Adrian, do you want to stop for now because the worst part is coming very soon?" asked Kevin.

"You know, Kevin, if I ever going to get well, I need to deal with whatever that interferes with my ability to love. If I am Altair, it seems like I have found my ticket out for me" was Adrian reply

Kevin stated, "You will see if you do or don't, we will continue. If not, you will understand other emotional issues you are dealing with in this life."

[Ethan continues his story]

The next day, I found a few men who needed some money and they would help me beach my vessel. This way they can clean off the barnacles, re-caulk the seams and any other work below water line where repairs are necessary. They worked hard getting all the work done on one side and then the reverse side. The week was up and vessel is back in the water and ready to begin to work.

I was able to get a cargo for Canakkale to begin the leg back to Athens. All the crew reported back to work in good condition, ready for next assignment, and it appears all was well in their world.

During the week of repairing my vessel, I witnessed that none of my family came to see me, and I sailed out on the sea with a heavy heart. I now vows I will never to return because there is nothing for me here. His younger brother was now of age to hire out to pay to support the family. He didn't come to me for a job to escape my mother's wrath. Those were the last thoughts of my family for rest of my life.

I dropped off my cargo and picked up what Adelfo wanted and we were headed back to Athens. When they entered the area where there were many islands, we ran in to small squall that blew us off course. When the storm subsided, we found our bearings. We also passed this barren island way off the normal trade route. It had small beach with a high land plateau. It appeared deserted. One of the crew said he would never want to be stranded there. It is like a ghost island, no, more like ghost ship.

They reached Athens and there was Altair meeting us at the pier as we tied up. He asked to come aboard, but when the gangway was slide into place, he just ran on board looking for me, without permission. Finding me in my cabin, he ran up and gave his greeting big hug. "I missed you, you were gone a long time, but I knew you were all right. I even prayed to the Gods for your safe return. Here you are. I want to be the first to invite you to supper tonight will you come? Say you will" was pleading voice of this young kid.

Before I realized it, "I would agree to come. I still have to ask your father if it is okay."

Adelfo's crew and my crew were already busy unloading the cargo. I made my way to his employer's shop to collect my fees and the check on the supper invitation.

Adelfo did not have any thing that needed shipped now but if he could wait a week, he would have now surplus grain to ship back to Canakkale. In the packet with the invoice of goods I brought, was a request for grain. It seems that they are running short. I thought it over and agreed I can do that because I could also do some additional work on the vessel. They ran into a bit of a storm, it did not do much damage, but enough that it needs to be tended to before shipping out again.

I arrived in Greek-style clothes this time at Adelfo's home, for I have found a shop in the harbor that fitted me out so I looked like I belonged here. Everyone was at the doorway when the servant announced my presence. The meal was very good, but my troublesome feelings resulting from my own family clouded the enjoyment of the meal and the fellowship. As like the last time Altair sat next to me, but this time with lot less questions. He seemed to enjoy the general conversation that went back and forth with his father. Couple of times, he would just reach out and touch my arm. However, I ignored it and kept the conversation going with the father. The night grew late, I excused myself because I need to get rest for this been a hard day and need to work on my ship to get ready to sail out at the end of the week.

Altair begged his father to walk me back to my boat with the servant. After lot of pleading, the father gave in. He now had a chance to hold my hand almost all the way to my ship. There were times he would talk a mile a minute and then there were these period of dead silence. I could not make out which was worse, talking or the silence. The silence seemed to bring about intense feeling of some sorts, way beyond my understanding. When they got to the vessel, I told Altair that we would be very busy tomorrow, so he could not come and visit. Altair seemed to understand but asked when or if we could spend an afternoon together because he wanted to show me his favor hiding place and few other things. To dismiss the boy, I agreed I could, how about tomorrow, no, the day after. I could spare him any afternoon, if that would be enough time. It appeared to be agreeable to him. The boy and the servant vanished into the night.

I spent an additional hour in my cabin trying to make some sense of this kid. Why did he spend the evening touching me, what is the attraction? It is not sexual, because I am not into boys or men. It is not that word "love", because I am not giving any signals or vibes in that direction. In truth, I know not of his emotional world. In fact, I don't want anything to do with that world call "feelings". Finally, exhausted from all this mental confusion, I lay down and was dead to the world.

CHAPTER 22

The next day, the crew was busy with the rigging and stringing new lines for the ropes damaged in the squall they experienced coming here. The sails had to be mended in a few places. The men worked as a team, as they should. One the great things about this crew, they are not strung out with emotional crap. I don't even know if they have families or what, none of my business. We keep our personal business to ourselves and I like it that way.

The following day, at noon, Altair, shows up with lunch bag and ready to take me on an adventure. I thought I would have another day, but it appears that will not happen. We hiked up on the high ridge overlooking the harbor and over the plateau that were covered with olive trees. We finally came to his special cave where he has his own place. His father owned all this land anyways, but he feels like it something special for him. I suggested since it is nice day, why don't we spend the day out under the trees and in the sunshine. I spread a blanket and we sat down. Altair was busy spreading out the food and very soft wine to go with it. The meal was basically goat's cheese, olives, bread and very watered down red wine. He was so proud of it all since he was the one to pack this picnic meal.

Before they got into eating the food, Altair asked, "Ethan, do you like me?"

"What is not to like? You are young handsome boy from a very loving family. Your dad is best business man I have done business with. I have never been this close even with my family. My brothers and sisters just take each other for granted. There is really no "love" in my family like yours.

Therefore, I have to rephrase your question to understand it. If you are asking me if I like you as person, then I would say yes but beyond that I have no answers" in very doubtful reply by Ethan. "I have never been exposed or involved in family relationships like yours. I don't know how to interact with something I do not understand. Your demonstrations of affections towards me, I really don't have a clue to how to react to them. Does that make sense to you?"

"I truly don't understand why I like you. The first time I met you, it seemed like you were always a part of our family. As you were connected with us, now I realize it is a problem for you. I can't tell you why, you seem so naturally to fit into our family or with me. I never had feelings like this before with any one, not even my brother, whom I love dearly. What you say and how your indifference does not make sense to me does it to you?" in very declaration young man voice of Altair.

"Before we get lost in these feelings, let's go for walk, and enjoy the day together" were my words as I got up and began to stretch from sitting so long. This is becoming very difficult for me. We have to do something else before I say something wrong and it may affect my business dealing with his father.

Altair picked up the remains of their lunch and placed it in the cave. Then he had to run to catch up with me because I was walking slowly but I seemed so far away. They spent the rest of the afternoon just sightseeing allowing the boy to be the guide. Altair took him to his look out place where he could watch the harbor for ships. It was a pleasant time, but somewhat uncomfortable because of all the closeness the kid offered me. He was forever holding my hand and sometimes wrapping around me while holding my hand. They arrived back at Adelfo's home and we did our goodbyes. Altair had to do his hugging stuff and I just stood there not really knowing what to do. I did finally put my arms around him too. I even rubbed his head in a playful way. That seemed to please him. They disengaged and I walked by myself back to the ship. What happen during the hug he gave, just jangled my mind with uncontrollable confusion.

On board, the men were busy storing the new cargo, getting ready to ship out soon. I went to my cabin, such as it was with very little room to pace but I kept walking back and forth. At one point, I was arguing with myself, I could have sworn I could hear that old woman's voice warning me. To shut off my head, I buried his mouth around the neck of a jug of wine to kill the pain. Shortly I was dead to the world; the black hole captured me and I was gone from everything. However, a drunken stupor did not free me from the hunger that was swimming around in my heart.

The morning came in on me like thunder with all the noise from the crew loading cargo and the throbbing of my head from the drink. Grabbing the pitcher of water, I poured it over my head; it did little to kill the pain. Going on deck the blazing sun burned my eyes. I hid out in his cabin waiting for the pain to go away during the full morning. By noon, I felt reasonably stable. I appeared on the deck to witness laughing or just smiling when they looked at me. Damn! I don't think I looked that funny. I quickly looked over the side to see my reflection on the water. There I saw that my hair was standing straight up in greasy tangled mess, and my face was white as ghost. I guess I would laugh too at this facade. I retreated to my cabin and set about grooming before the next appearance.

The first mate reported they were able to get all the cargo on board sooner than expected. Should I want to sail with the morning tide, we are ready.

I needed to escape from the madness of this place and that, which is haunting me. "We will sail at first light, the tide will be running, so get ready to leave by then. If you need a few hours to say goodbye to the city [with a laugh] see to it. I am going to see Adelfo to pay for the cargo and I will be staying on board this night" were my hangover commanding orders.

Later with all business completed with Adelfo, I said my goodbyes for I will not be this way again maybe for a year. I was now in position to purchase a larger vessel and wanted to do some trading with Sicily and the areas west. I refused another evening dinner very graciously and soon I was on my way back to my ship.

The evening was uneventful. I turned in early for I still had a throbbing headache. To sleep is the cure of a headache was all I could think about. The whole night flew by in minutes. Out of the darkness of nothing, his first mate was trying to revive me to the needs at hand. I arose slowly, trying to figure out what was going on. Then it dawned on me they were to sail with the tide, I responded to his first mate. I hollered from my cabin door to cast off and let her run with the tide. I slowly got dressed and out on the dock to see the city slowly dropping out of sight. The whole world was alive with sounds of morning, but the sun has not raised its head. The air was warm and breeze was sweet as the red sails filled with its breath. All was going well.

The two goats aboard decided to cry out for food and attention. When the crew member went to feed them, he found Altair fast asleep in their bedding. He called to the captain to come quick because he feared this was not a good sign. Sailors have many strange superstitions. When one warning sign appears, it spooks the whole crew. The captain came on the run and his eyes open wide to see the boy. "What the hell! We" before I was able to say anything more, the crew member blabbered out "We have a curse, this is a bad curse! The sky was red in the morning. The birds were flying to land. We are in for hell. Captain what are we to do?"

The crews gather around to witness the trouble-brewing problem. They just stood there looking at the boy. The tide is running fast, the strong wind is off shore, they could never make it back now. Now what! The signs are true. This would be hanging on them as kidnappers. They were now all lost in their own trouble basket.

I had to save the day. Very sternly, "I told the men to return to their duties and I would deal with this problem". I motioned my men away but they kept mumbling among themselves and shaking their heads. "Altair wake up, come on boy, wake up."

He rubbed his eyes hearing the command that brought him out of deep sleep. He was mumbling, "It is not real morning, and he never gets up until it is real morning. What is all the fuss about?" He was continually coming out of the darkness of sleep and his eyes came into focus, he cried out "Ethan, what a joy it is to see you. I wanted to be here to wish you the protection of the Gods on your trip and pray that you will come back soon. I wanted this to be big surprise before you sail" were his rhythmic gentle remarks.

"Boy! We have sailed, we are now far from land. The strong winds are off the land and the tide has carried us on our way. Damn! Does your family knows you are here?" was my desperate plea.

"No, I was very brave, I snuck out of the house before the crack of dawn, and your guard was a sleep as I walked very so very quietly past him. I did not want to wake you, so I crawled in with the goats because it was a soft place to wait for you. I must have fallen asleep. I just couldn't have you leave without a chance to say good-bye. Now it seems by your harsh words I have done something wrong" as innocent words dropped from his lips.

Ethan just looked at the boy, trying to figure out what to do. We can try to tack back to the port that could take a day if not more if the wind does not turn around. I have already told his father I would not be back for over a year. When I get to the port, the family will be in state of panic, the town's people been searching for him. Would they believe that it was not our fault, if they didn't we find ourselves dancing at end of a rope to a mad crowd's justice? I have seen this before, and it was not good sight. The crowds will jump at any chance to vent their anger or their frustration. As bonus, looting is good for them too. We have cargo of grain and they have the knowledge that money is hidden in my cabin. They would tear the vessel a part in short order to find it. His father is very important person and this is truly not good.

"Altair will you go to my cabin and wait for me there. You will find my meal on the table. Help yourself, but I need you to stay out of sight. So please do as I ask and get there quickly, now" were the commanding words flowing from Ethan. The boy did as he was told.

What will I say to the men? I have never experienced this before, even with my dad as captain. I have heard these superstitions can destroy everything, and if strong enough, cause the captain to face mutiny. I better get my first mate up to the bow and discuss what options we have with this situation. I really don't know what to do. Damn, there goes that thought of the old lady again. I don't need her words coloring my thoughts now, for I am in over my head. This boy and his actions already confuse me. The closer he wants to be the more nightmares destroy my sleep. All this and more were arguing in my head as I motioned the first mate to follow him to the bow.

As they gather close under the eye of the crew. "Well! We are in for a storm. I need you to give me some advice. You have been at sea longer than I have. Can you give me some options to deal with this before the crew gets out of hand" asked Ethan.

"My captain, this is really bad news. If we could have gotten the kid back before nightfall, no foul. That is out of the question because that is not possible with the winds and tide. The crew is so spooked. They want to throw him over board now before the curse really sets in. They saw three bad signs this morning. You heard about two, the third was wind pick up speed, filled our sails the moment he was found. We need never go back. The town's people will surely do us a hanging and the crew wants no part of that" was his very forceful statement.

"Could or would they be satisfied if we leave him at the first port?" my reply. As soon as I said it, he knew that would not pacify them. Even if the boy made it home, we would be hung. I have so many dam mix feelings about the boy, I can't think straight.

"Captain, you know that is not the answer. When he gets back home, what will be his story? We will be hunted down like dogs. His father has great power and as kind as he was to you, the opposite exist too. You have to throw the boy over board. That will be all that will appease them now" was his stern reply.

"How about we leave him on that deserted island we found? Then if he lives or dies, not blood on our hands. If he is found, then it is the work of the Gods. The Gods will therefore protect us because we did the right action. I've never killed anyone, you know I will in a fight but this will be murder. [A shutter ran rampant through his body, the world went spilling out of control, screaming, and then silence] I will talk with the men, this is the only action I can honestly live with for now" pleaded the captain.

"Come then, let us face the crew" was the reply of first mate.

The first mate motions the men to gather around and the captain proposed a solution to this pending doom. The men argued and almost came to blows if it was not for the quick action of the first mate.

Finally, the oldest member spoke; he would cast the stones to see what would be the right action. The crew all agreed. Cast the stones and what they say, we will do. Over the side or abandon on the island, this will prevent the curse upon them. The crew member, who owned the stones, went to his space and return with them very quickly. He was opening the pouch as he was in motion. When he got back to the men, he dropped to his knees and offered his stones to the Gods for the right action. Then he held the purse up to knee high of the crew and the stones poured out on the deck. A couple of the crew members could read the stones too, so there would be agreed upon reading. All three read the stone saying the same thing, maroon him on the island. That would please the Gods and the curse would be lifted. "Do you men agree with the findings of your crew members? Will marooning give you peace?" The first mate looked them all in the eye. There had to be an accord.

With almost immediate reply, "Marooning is the agreement and we will make for that island. Captain, do you find any fault with our decision?"

"No, set course and be smart about it, the sooner we unload the boy, the sooner we will be free" What else could I do? I too would be relieved of the pain this boy caused me, day and night. As another after thought, did the Gods whip up that storm that blew us off course where we found that deserted island, because they knew this was going to happen? Did they fill the sails so we could not return him? This is beyond me, I need not think about it anymore.

Ethan went to his cabin, there the boy had eaten his full and again was taking a nap. There was turmoil in my heart, I wanted to kill him on one level, and I wanted his love on another level. The war within was gaining strength every day, no, every hour. Why didn't I listen to that old woman? Did she put a curse on me to make this true or was it because the Gods made it true. Damn who knows, but fate is at hand and sadness rides over the conflict with the words. Those words were "not again". "Revenge is not sweet", and what to hell does those words mean to me.

Altair opens his eyes, with very sleepy motion gets up, staggers over, and hugs the captain. "Maybe you will teach me to be a sailor and I can be your first or second mate. Wouldn't that be fun? When I got home, I could show them how grown up I am in the couple months it takes us to return."

"Let's not talk about the future, why don't you sit here and I can show you what charts I have as your first lesson. The route we will take to get to Canakkale and what problems to expect along the journey. We can have our meals together in here and we have some time together. Do you want to do that? To be a good sailor you need to recognize landmarks and know where you are on your journey. We do not want to run aground and all will be lost" I was trying to keep it light hearted and make sure the boy was not on deck causing his crew any more stress. However, this closeness will be and is causing me more stress.

Altair agreed with my statements and finally let go of me. I walked over and sat down while unrolling a map. I expected him to sit next or stand looking over my shoulder, but instead he wants to sit on my lap. We spent a consider amount of time pointing, talking and planning the course of the journey. On some level, I wanted to hug him back for, what in hell is going on, and I need to get up to break this mood. I got so I couldn't bear it any longer, I told him I had to move because my legs were going to sleep. The rest of the day, we practice tying knots that seaman needs to know. Now he had to wear same kind of clothing as crew, his tunic would not work. With those words, he took the tunic off and wanted his crew cloths. He was walking around the room in his shorts. I called to the first mate to get me set of the smallest crew's clothing, which he did post haste. Here put these on, and you will look like a sailor.

"Look at me first. [He is standing there in his shorts] Don't you think I have the muscles and body for a good seaman? This is going to be the life for me. I will look big and strong like you. I wish my brother could see me now." As he started to put on the clothes that were a little large for him but the smallest outfit of his crew, Altair kept chattering away about his past hopes and dreams that will be real now.

"Come, turn around, and let's see how our newest crew member looks like. [As he slowly turns] You will make good sailor as soon as you grow into those clothes" the captain could hardly contain his nervous laughter.

The first mate asked the captain to come on out. He wishes to check with him if it is okay to make anchor in this inlet of this island. As I stood on the deck, I could see that they were there already. Why not, the night was about to close in on them. I want the two goats put ashore now or at first light. We need also some food supplies that will last him at least a week. Some fishing equipment and usual items to protect himself or cut up his food, what would you need it if was happening to you. Just see to it.

Altair and I had supper in my cabin. Then they did a short strolled around the vessel and looking up at the stars that were staring down us from the heaven. It was indeed a very pleasant night. The crew were down below, those who were not on watch.

"It is time to turn in, so let's go to my cabin and get some sleep because tomorrow is going to be a busy day. Are you not sleepy? Your eyes seem to be dropping", inquired Ethan

Altair headed for the cabin after he relived himself over the side. As captain entered his cabin, there was the boy lying out in my bed with just his shorts. This will not do, I do not sleep with anyone. "Altair, the crew has made this bunk bed for you on the floor, that is my bed" as politely as I could.

"Ethan, why can't I sleep next to you? This is first time I have been away from home and I am unsettled. Please, I will lie in one space and I will not bother you" was his pleading words.

"Okay then, I guesses I will sleep on the floor, you stay where you are. I roll around a lot when I sleep. Neither of us will get any sleep. I know my moving around will keep you awake. [I blew out the candle and stripped to my shorts and slide into the temporary bed on the floor.] So good night, my friend, and I will see you in the morning. Maybe we can explore the island before we sail" were my closing words as I drifted off to a troubled sleep.

Deep in my sleep, I felt a warm body next to me. Ethan's brother would often cuddle with me when he was cold. We did not have enough blankets and the younger kids needed them more. We just had one blanket for both of us, which was all my next oldest brother and I had. So how in my troubled mind, the words, or feelings were dealing with this warm body, his brother felt different, just dismiss it for now. The time was slowly moving on and I felt this body rapping itself around me. We did not do that and it is not that cold. Somehow, I couldn't pull myself out of this deep dark sleep because it fed a hunger of love from another time and space. My soul is drinking this in but the anguish of my mind threw me into deeper state chaos because what I had to do the day. Abandon the boy on island, raised my personal abandon issues that I suffered from growing up.

From that hole of deep darkness, the old nightmare seemed to charge out. The scene began to unfold and the pain of it all flood over me. This time I could feel that there was a person there who professed his love for his family, my family, and me but still he was going to abandon us for his own gratification. He would not give any logical justification for what he is about to. My head was wheeling; the world about me was spinning faster and faster. I could feel the anger building up in my mouth like steam. I began to shake, without thinking; I drew my sword and killed him. There was so much blood. The anger vanished. The room stood still in deafening silence. Then I am aware I really killed him. This was not dream. Some part of me knew it was true. It was more than I could bear. I ran the same blade through me and the world went dark. I was wrestling with sleep to come out of this nightmare. It was vivid, now there was acid taste in my mouth. A feeling of being crushed drained left me drained, sick with rage blossomed, and the emotional list keeps growing out of control. Finally, I forced myself to swim out of that hellhole and as I came to the surface, again I felt this very confusing warmth from his brother. No, my mind screamed out, I am not home, who is or what is this? With all my might, I broke through the sleep only to find Altair wrapped around me and I was holding him too. I let go with a start. What the hell? From the moon light through the window opening, I could see the boy was still dead to the world, he would not wake up, and I had to pry myself out of his grip. Getting up, covering the boy, then grabbing a blanket to cover myself, I staggered out on the deck. I was greeted by the night watch and I waved him off. I went and leaned on the railing trying to find my balance. The only thought of survival raced in my head, I needed to be rid of that boy too for I am going mad. I can't keep dreaming like this at night. What I saw was beyond words, description, just beyond me, I needed to be free of this. It is too painful. To think I was hugging the boy back, it raised an unknown feeling in me. Enough, enough, I will go mad. I need this to be over. I also grabbed the blanket the watchman had draped over him against the chill of the night and went to goat's bed and to sleep.

The morning broke with pleasantness that all was well with the world. The men made ready for me to take the boy ashore. All the supplies were already in place in cave on the plateau. I was awaken and told all was ready. They will have breakfast ready soon and he can be about his commitment to the crew.

Upon entering the cabin, Altair was waking up and surprised to see that I was out of bed. "I was so lonely; I hoped you did not mind me sleeping with you. It has been the most restful sleep I think I have ever had. How about you?"

Ignoring the question, "we have a little time before we need to set sail, why don't we explore the island together. It is a surprise. I thought you would like. So get dressed, let's eat, and be off. It looks like the special place you have back home. I know you will enjoy it."

"Okay, it sounds like fun. I will wash up and eat and we can be off." was the easy reply.

They went ashore in the skiff and spent a couple hours exploring the island. I made sure to be separated from him, rushed back to skiff, left instructions of where food, clothing etc. where, and they will come back for him in shortly. He can't come with them because there is a problem in port where they are going. They want to keep him safe. See you very soon. I signed, 'Your friend'.

The vessel was leaving the harbor; I could see the boy yelling to come back. Don't leave him there. His voice cried carried over the sea in a mournful sound. We continued to hear it as we kept sailing away. It seems forever before it was not there anymore. Such fear and anguish in the sound of his voice filled our ears I swear I could hear it when we were out of sight.

What does this all mean for me? I will know in the days ahead. Right now, I feel nothing but an empty void; I pray the Gods do save him. I do not want his blood again on my hands. What do I mean by "again on my hands?" I will never know for I will never sail this sea around Greece again nor will I ever go home.

Kevin spoke to Adrian, "I think you have seen and heard enough. You need to get back to your real world now. At least, you can see how your arrogance 300 years before causes the pain of this period. If he had stayed out of Greece, you would not have been stranded on island. You would have finished healing your heart and love. In about two my life times, you could have helped us remove the horror love issues of the 5th century that was crippling Marcus [Johnny, your friend in this lifetime], your best friend and family. For your information, that is why you was uncomfortable on that island when you were on your honeymoon. That was the same island where you were left to die on. As Altair, you lasted less than a week, you died of loneliness and pain of abandonment. You refused to eat or care for yourself. You were lost in abandonment and why was your love rejected. It has taken you and Marcus 2500 years to heal that unfortunate mess. Now get back and do your homework, we have two or three sessions before you will understand your questions and resolve them.

My eyes flash open; I am always surprised when I am back so quickly. Roger was handing me the recording so I have something to work with until the next visit.

"It seems like I maybe able to see you again next Friday, but I will have to double-check my schedule. I have some speaking engagements that might interfere. I should know next week how or when the following session will be" Roger stated as he got up and started to lead me out. "Alex, you are one of my best clients. You get in and get things moving. This Kevin seems to be great help and I wish I had him for my other clients that refuse to face past issues and waste time. Well! Here we are at the front door, I will look forward to see you next week, maybe." was his encouraging words.

I walked off the porch, and half way down the path, turned and Roger was still standing there watching me. I wonder what he must think at times. It is still hard to believe that he was one of my team members that agreed to help me on this journey. He has done that and more.

As I reached the boat, quickly untied it and slipped into the seat, pulled once and the engine fired up and was on my way. The breeze had picked up and few more crafts were motoring about. Not enough wind for sailboats, still there is one begging the wind to move him up stream. The current was winning that challenge. As I passed I waved but he seemed to be frustrated to acknowledge, then it occurred to me that he may be in trouble.

I came closer and yelled did he need help. That got his attention, and his quick reply he could use a tow. His engine had failed too. He was on his way up to landing about mile upstream. I threw him a line, he tied on the bow of his small 20 footer, and we were off. Upon arriving at the landing, he quickly untied and coasted into the docking area. He signals me an offer, but I just waved him off and was on my way. It is game of paying forward for us; you can never tell when in the future, you may need help on the river or anywhere really.

As I pulled into the dock, I can't tell if he hears his engine and knows I am coming in or what. Ol' Johnson was there to assist with the tie up and covering the craft. When we were done, he told me that Barbara needed me up at the office. I thank him and beeline it to see what she wanted. I forgot to take my cell phone, and I can't imagine what would be important on Friday.

"Alex, there is a man here to see you and wants to talk with only you. He has been waiting about an hour. He came unannounced; I don't know what he wants or why he is here. He just sits in the conference room reading the paper and magazines I have supplied him and of course, coffee." Barbara almost whispered as she showed him the way and opening the door to let her boss in.

"I'm Alex; my office manager stated that you wanted to see me. I sorry if I kept you waiting, I was doing other task. Of all days, I forgot my cell phone. So what can I do for you?" was my questing voice.

He was nicely dressed but his appearance doesn't seem to be the usual businessman. "I have been informed that you were the lucky guy to buy the property across the road from here. I could never have been able to purchase it and build too. Now, I have not built my credit up enough for the banks around here. To get to the point, I have degree in business management. I want to be able to go into business for myself. If you decide to build a gas station, grocery store on that land, I would like to be considered to sub-lease it from you or even operate it for you. I work as manager for grocery chain now and I so ready to go on my own. Oh, damn, my name is Russell Samuelson I forget my manners. [He put out his hand to introduce himself] Today is my day off, and I have heard rumor that you were able to purchase that land. I know you maybe not going to do something right away considering the operation you are working on now. I wanted an opportunity to present myself, prove my abilities, and possibly to be consider." was his rapid nervous presentation.

"Well! Russell, it seems secrets around here don't remain secrets. I like your style. I have M & L Enterprises doing the major designing of this operation. I have not approached them about anything yet as you may have guessed as to what to do with that land. I will tell you what. I would like you to fill out information application form and with your permission check you out. Should we be a good match, we can do business together. You must have some ideas as to how you would like your store constructed and how to maximize the space. You must have an idea about what this area could support to be profitable. This research takes time, but it seems like you were reading my mind or had good hunch as to the need of this operation to be successful. That reminds me, I need to make a note to myself about getting a traffic light permit to assist people in and out of this place. Russell, if you don't mind me calling you by your first name, I think you are forcing me to get busy now in considering the land use and your proposal. I can get our crew on it now. I truly appreciate your offer. I am taking it serious, and so I will turn you over to Barbara to get things moving. Should this all come together by April or May of this coming year, would that be a problem for you?" I asked.

"No, Sir, I have a job and I finished up my degree work last spring going to school part time. I just want to get on with my life and make things happen. I appreciate you seeing me without an appointment and I will be honored to have you check me out." was Russell's joyful proud reply.

"Well! I will send Barbara in and we will get things moving." as I left the room and I see Barbara had everything ready since I notice she had the intercom open to know what was going on and how she could help me. Again, she is best thing that ever happen to me in business.

She passed me in the hall with her hands filled with paper and pen, "I have to talk with you later about this" as she disappeared into the room and shut the door so I could not ask any questions about her statement.

It was well past lunchtime, I had better get something to eat my stomach is making noises and I don't want to wake Jenny. That is a good excuse to journey down to the restaurant and spends sometime with Johnny if he isn't busy.

I walked in and he was on me already. "What is it with you? I am not totally in the building and you are right on me with that question look?"

"You know we are small community, and nothing slips past us who are rough and ready businessmen. I saw Russell going into the office and I bet I know why he was there. Do you want to test me out? Or admit defeat without a battle of wits." was Johnny's smart-ass remarks.

"You know you can be a pain, and I am too much of a gentleman to tell you where. Well! You can tell me your story as I go to the table by the window by the river to have a seat for lunch where I can watch the river activity for distraction. [We walked out to the farthest corner and I sat down and so did Johnny] I guess you are going to be my lunch partner or someone to keep me company until you get your stuff off your chest." I very directly stated.

Here comes the waitress, who took my order for I always order the special on Fridays because it is always great seafood. When she left, Johnny lean over and started "some of the women of the office live around here, knows him and his family, and with Barbara's permission let the cat out of the bag to him. Now this is not a conspiracy. Most of us, who already know him, know he is a worker and a doer. He has completed his degree work, did he tell you? All on his own, without financial help or hand out from his mother, his father is dead, and Russell did it all. Everyone around here likes him. He is smart and a worker, and we, in the broad general sense, would really like you to consider him. So there, he has my vote already, because you will not find any negative information on him." Johnny was pretty cocky when he presented his case.

"I was impressed when I first met him. I have to tell you I did not know I was being set up. My personal life from time to time is in the toilet, but my business world has the maximum of my 100% attention and application. I know how to keep my trouble basket out of my business world. With that said to vindicate me, I always-welcome help that embellishes our co-creative team. I could never do this [as I point around the space, which included the whole project] without guys like you helping me carry the ball. You have to say, we are one hell of a team. Regardless how my toilet operates, I glad I have you all on the team and I am on it too."

Just then, my lunch came "pickled herring platter", with lemon sauces, small boiled potatoes, and green beans top off with light beer. Johnny said all he had to say and needed to get back to work stocking for tonight. He would talk with me later. Man, there is nothing better than boned mackerel with lemon sauce and pleasant view. Before I finished, I looked up and there was Jenny.

"I wondered where you were. I should have known you would be here. Especially because of the fare that is offered as the special today. [She bends down, kisses him, and at the same time pulls out a chair to sit down] This has been very busy week and yet it has been fun. The best part, you have given me all the space I need, for which I love you. I am taking Sunday off so we can have the quality time I miss you. It will be reward for both of us.

She added the down side is that, I have to leave now to make up some of the time and probably an hour or two extra on Saturday. I was going to leave you a note, but I wanted to see you. The bed smells so nice and it is warm when I slide in, in the morning. She whispers in my ear. "I have to go, love you very much." as she got up, gave him another kiss and was on her way.

There goes my life, my love, and all I have ever wanted in a partner, wife, I have to be one hell of a lucky guy. The door closed at the far end and she was gone from view. However, her love is dancing in my heart, now and for as long as she wants me.

The rest of the day was lost in normal busy work of living life. My mind kept exploring with what to do with our Sunday off throughout the day. I went over and inspected the ground being ready for building foundations. It appears that Steve is going to begin work on back row of condos first. He has his motives and so far, he was right on the money. The rest of the day and night was uneventful.

CHAPTER 23

Saturday marched in with nothing to do when you have a wife working and doing an internship. I stopped by the office and there wasn't any mail for me to answer. We always have one of the office employees to work Saturdays to act as sales representative or get any work caught up that needed to keep us on schedule. I finally went home and fixed something light to eat. We really don't keep much food in the house. I wasn't in the mood to go and listen to the live music. Took a long warm soaker bath with sea salt, listen to soft music and did some internal housekeeping by releasing any stress buried in my mind, body or aura [the energy around the body] to keep moving towards my goal of freedom from the past. After an hour and half of that work, I was ready for bed and tomorrow's surprise time.

Jenny realized either Alex was not home or he is in bed early as she drove into the garage. There wasn't a light on in the house except for the usual night-lights. I am getting used to night light in the bathroom, but I hope someday he will not have to have night light in the bedroom. Upon entering the kitchen, there was his note that he retired early and hoped I had a great day.

Jenny thought to herself, I am somewhat hungry, and I wonder what is in the kitchen cupboard or the refrigerator for something. Either furnished any quick solution, I think I will have peanut butter on some crackers and milk. That has always been a great back up food for me. In fact, it had been the best comfort food for those lonely nights in the past. Now that is not a problem, I have someone to be with, it just takes away the edge of hunger.

After about six cracker sandwiches, and 6 oz. of milk, she was ready to retire and to see what tomorrow will bring.

Jenny got ready for bed, slid quietly into her side, and was fast asleep. The morning shined through the window, hit her eyes to cause her to see the clock flashed nine o'clock, and slowly aware her husband was laying with his back against hers. That seemed strangely pleasant, she laid there for few minutes absorbing in the beginnings of a day with soft breathing floating in the air, but no longer can I linger, nature calls and I am starved. She slipped out as quietly as she entered last night. He never moved nor make a sound that he was awake.

When she completed getting ready for the day, she was fully dressed and reentered the bedroom. There was her lover still sleeping now on his back with arms spread out across the bed. I guess the passion is dying, as she chuckled to herself. She sneaks over and bends down to give a very soft kiss and the monsters arms wrapped around her. She was held very tight and her soft kiss has blossomed into full out passion. When she was released enough to catch her breath, she cried out, "no you don't. You have a starving wife on your hands and nothing, you hear, nothing is going to happen until I am fed. There is nothing in this house to make breakfast with, so get up buster, and get dressed. You should have stocked the house if you had other things in mind." She kept laughing like the sounds of little bells tinkling, playfully in the wind.

"I cannot have a starving wife. Give me a few minutes, I will be ready but I have to warn you, you have a hungry tiger, hungry for you." were his growling laugher words flooded back at her. I have never been so happy was the thought racing in my mind as I quickly exited to get ready for the day.

I met my wife at the foot of the stairs when I was ready and she had the door open where she was charging out with the attitude, 'catch me if you can'.

I have to say she sure can run. I will not play the game "catch me" if I was in the mood for love, because I know hands down, I would be so out of wind, I wouldn't be able to do anything. Jenny was polite enough to wait at the door of the restaurant so I could open it for her.

"Woman, you will have me worn out before I begin the day. If this is the pace of the day we will be doing, I am not sure I am up to It," my winded voice stated to her.

"Come on silly, I did not marry a wimp. We better behave ourselves because we are in public place." as she bolted across the room to empty table in the far corner [laughing all the way and teasing – catch me if you can]. I was chasing after her in hot pursuit and she still beat me to the table.

"Now children, we don't allow running or racing in here. If you can't behave yourselves, I know the manager will be asking you both to leave." Came out of the waitress' mouth as she dropped the menus in front of us in very infantile way to stay in the mood of the moment.

"Helen, you tell that boy that he has to behave. I had to run to keep out of his reach. He was trying to get fresh. I kept telling him, we are in public place, but as you can see, he doesn't listen to me. Maybe you should call the manager to put him in his place. It appears he 'had his oats and is very frisky today'" came back at Helen in Jenny's very humorous tone.

At the moment, out of the corner of her eye, she saw Johnny walking across the room. "Johnny, you need to come over here. We have a problem" in Helen's demanding playful voice. It was sure loud enough to get everyone attention in the place.

Johnny was in the mood to "Jive" with them. "Helen, I will throw them out, you say the word. We can't allow such immature behavior in such a sophisticated establishment as we operate here. If you can't do it, I know I have lot of helpers here that will gladly volunteer to throw them out. We just can't have unruly behavior while these other gentle folks are trying to enjoy their meal." Laud enough that everyone in the place could hear what he was saying.

The place was beginning to ripple with laugher as everyone knew the people involved and they wanted to enjoy playing along with the humor.

"Please don't throw us out, we will behave, won't we Jenny." I pleaded, playing to the game.

"Speak for yourself, it is your fault we are in this predicament, you think being a married man, you would finally grow up." Jenny joined in the game.

"I surrender, do what you want, I will leave quietly if that what you all want?" I think I had them with that.

Jenny spiked back "so, when are you leaving? I have never been so embarrassed in my life. In front of all these people, think of my reputation." Laughing so hard she could no longer go on with the game. To her surprise, I jumped up, bent over, and gave her a big kiss. The whole place just hooted laughs and applauded at this playful love making of their neighbor.

When the place calmed down, Helen went on as if nothing happened. "Now! What can I get you for breakfast?" Johnny pulled out a chair and stated he would have coffee with them to insure there would be no more outbreak of childish behavior.

"We both will have the Johnny's special." I replied.

Speak for yourself, "I want two eggs over light, order of ham and bacon, home fries, pan cakes and large orange. Thank you very much. Add in a coffee too" Jenny yelled out in demanding voice.

"Well! What have you two been up to so early in the morning? I am not implying anything, but it leaves a man to speculate." Johnny broke out laughing.

I came back fast, "boy! You are off. Your sister proclaimed that food comes before anything, the first thing this morning. You, as a man, can understand the hardship that places on newly wedded man. Take pity on me, even though she is your sister."

"You must think I am crazy to jump in on your side. That would be family suicide." Johnny replied.

They all broke out laughing with that remarked. The next hour they spent time talking about what is going on with each other, continually building a stronger bond of friendship. Johnny was need in the kitchen, and he excused himself and left them to decide what to do next.

To Jenny's surprise, I wanted to take an hour boat ride on the river to enjoy the beauty of the day. We will not have many more of these where even the soft wind was warm before winter grips the valley.

They got Ol' Johnson's boat ready and they were out just cruising down the river almost at the speed of the current. A few cargo ships were journeying out to add to the pleasure of the day. After over hour traveling down stream, Jenny asked about turning back. "I am enjoying this very much. While we are in this mood, I would like to do some shopping for the coming week, prepare a nice dinner and spend the evening together." Jenny presented to me. I agreed.

Upon returning to the dock, we spent our time doing just that and it was great day. The evening was journey down the tunnel of love. It was blending, melting, and fulfilling; what a real loving relationship is truly about. Having had our cups filled with completeness, I could never settle for anything less. I still have hard time believing the life I am having with Jenny. I keep telling myself, nothing will ever take it away from me. However, when I make that statement with power, there is something deep inside still causing me to fight the ugly monster of fear. I hope Kevin can resolve this for me, because I can feel my soul crying in the shadows of doubt.

CHAPTER 24

This week journeyed by like last week. Here I am sitting in my office looking out into space running thoughts and ideas. Jenny was busy with work, internship, and sleep, so I was unable to spend much time with her.

Tuesday, Russell's resume application checked out and I decided that I would have him meet with Steve, Judy, and Francis to see if this next step will work for us. I set the date of getting together to get the ball moving for Wednesday because it was free time for him, Steve and the girls. On Tuesday, I filed a petition into ODOT to have a signal light installed at the mouth of our road coming in to our business that was drawn up by Ron. We are still on the pay as you go basis even though the bank has offered us construction loans and etc. The sales of the condos are keeping the cash flow in balance. We have nice income from the marina, docks, restaurant, and monthly condo fees. We have been able to keep the overhead within reason. Steve is keeping his subs busy to insure we keep this teamwork going and continual keeping the waste cost at a bare minimum.

When I have everything completed at the office, I have the afternoon free. This is the time I take or make available to do some organization of my own personal thoughts. In the past, it was crash time. Now it is evaluation time and integration time with knowledge and understanding coming from the experiences resulting from my time with Roger. I play my recording when I am alone especially for more clarity. I swear there is more information added to the recording every time I listen to them. Maybe it was there all along, but I wasn't able to understand or listen to it before.

During the working part of my life, everything is working like clockwork. There are the usual challenges, still have great team that are there to help, but when I am alone with me. That is still a problem for me.

As I review the recordings of the sessions with Roger, it is hard to believe that I would make such dangerous self center choice in the 5th century and get mixed up in that hell-hole mess in the 2nd century. Those activities' unresolved has cumulative affect on each life that keeps rolling along lifetime after lifetime. Here I am, with everything any person would ever, ever want, and still there are events that damaged my soul that I trying to work out and heal. I often read about people that appear on the surface that they have it all. Their friends can't justify why their friend stepped off into the deep end. We all shake our head because we don't know what was buried in their friend's soul that needs to be removed. This person can't live with it any longer. Nothing, just nothing, that can drown that pain or void. Those painful events have to be recognized, comprehended, and resolved to be free. Life time after lifetime with accumulative painful experiences and void, those physical feelings become unbearable. The experiences in a body just magnify what was and if you can't resolve it, you can't stand the pain of it all. There are not enough earthly "things" to mask the pain and allows you to stay in some cases. A person can find so many ways out of the game of life besides dying. When you are lost in history of unknowns, you are either blinded to help or unable to find help.

I am glad that I found a door through time for me to get there, look at it, and actively work it out. It isn't easy, so far, the pay off far exceeds the inconveniences of the pains of the events. At least, I am using those devastating dreams to drive me to find a solution, instead of quitting. I could have drowned them in drugs or alcohol but they still are there as I once did until I found Roger. Those dysfunctional choices kept preventing my peace and they deprived me of new life experiences, and wisdom. Those dysfunctional choices are like living in a vacuum, which makes life truly unbearable. I guess it's the vacuum where you are numb to feelings and sound which is the worse part of it.

I remember as kid, when I wanted to drown myself, the voice in my head demanded I stay. I did stay, I am glad that I did. I have to say life's conflicts never end makes you want to leave. There really aren't any peaceful feelings, it like total disassociation from everything. You push the physical rush of all kinds, still there isn't any lasting a reward feeling afterwards that satisfies one's soul or heartfelt needs. Still, without resolving and dealing effectively with those events that caused the vacuum activity in your life, there is no freedom. I guess when you finally have had enough, given in to resolve, the answers are there waiting for you. Of course, there is zombie life or termination, which have no appeal to me. I am glad my heart and soul remembered my plan for this life, or I would never be where I am today. I am not all the way back, but I working on it. I've never been a religious man but knowing the plan and God had truly assigned a guardian or spirit angel to watch over me the days of my life; you have to work very hard at being a loser. The loser takes as much or more effort as it takes to be a winner. How lucky I am. I have to keep pinching myself. I know I have fought against the journey from time to time because of my ignorance but now, I could never go back or stop. Still I have to keep giving myself pep talks to keep going.

There are still some very small nightmares and I can put up with even these nightmare flashes take place during the day. Right now, the hardest part is being persistence with fortitude when I have had a history of miss use of my strength in the application of ignorant conceit. When my spirit angel warns me or tries to guide me, I was to head strong to listen even when I was for my own good. I still don't understand how Kevin put up with me all of these centuries. I wonder if we are joined at the hip, or are his development connected to the outcome of my evolution. That has to be a half bake idea. Or is it? I have to trust my hunches, because when I do, I am a little better prepared to deal with them. As I am coming to end of the week, I became aware that something is changing. The nights had been rather up and down with nothing much happening except on Thursday, the night before going to see Roger, was stormy.

The intercom called my attention: it was Barbara, who stated, it was time to close up. "Do you want the front door locked, since you will be here alone?"

"No. I am leaving too. I need to get a few drawings and ideas I have up in my home office ready for the meeting tomorrow. I would like you to sit in for information only. We don't need notes, it just an exploration meeting and preparing to get things moving. It will be more of a 'think tank' activity. We should maybe tape it, in case; we come up with some good ideas." was my response.

As I left my office, I could see Barbara was just going out the door and had left it ajar. I followed close behind and locked up, I was yelling good night to everyone else who was getting into his or her cars. Barbara and I, we just walked home.

After fixing something light to eat, I went upstairs to my third floor office just in time to see an auto cargo ship go sailing up the river; bringing new motor toys to us Americans for our prestige, comfort, transportation, the list goes on and on. This one must be completely loaded, because she is riding very low in the water. I am not so sure it is good thing to have my desk facing the river. It faces northeast, so I don't have to deal with sun light too much, but it can be distracting.

Let's see, I have a few ideas for plotting out the use of the newly acquired land. I think Steve was right with the suggestion that we set off a commercial section and sell off the rest as private residence. That way we can get our money out of the land, make profit off the sale of the homes and they, the new residential owners, are responsible for the up keep. Steve thought that five to seven acres be enough for the gasoline and food area. Think out laud "we don't want to run competitive business in the nearby towns. These private homes will generate business for restaurant and marina too" was my plan.

I have been doing some research on this development activity to insure success. We have gas for heating and electric. We can do more solar work to cut electric demands. We were able to pay for having water piped to us from St. Helens, where we all pay surcharge until the water company recovers the cost. We have large sewage unit that can take care of us which is connected to the city sewage system too. We need to address if expansion would be necessary for the development across the road from us or should we connect everything directly to city sewage.

I have my usual check off sheet of possible costs. You never think about so many little things. We have great county agencies that help us from falling into any minefields of problems. Ron has been great building this support system. It has not been one way help because Ron has helped the city get grants passed through for the much needed improvements i.e. roads and general up grade services.

As I look up, there goes a grain ship, fully loaded riding low with all her lights on, going on her journey. It seems funny; we always refer to ships as her. I wonder why. It has been said because "she holds the men and her precious cargo like a mother holds her unborn child in her belly.

I better pack all this stuff up and turn in; I think Barbara said it was set for 10 a.m. I can be up and ready to feed my hungry wife before she goes to sleep and I go to work.

I had expected the night sleep would speed by so I could see my loving wife again. Instead, the night moved on slow pace as my mind integrates these new concepts and readjust perceptions that were based on old dysfunctional experiences and events. Mornings when I finally wake up, it seems I have been working as hard as I am in the daytime, I am exhausted.

Jenny came in later than normal this morning, saying they had to have reports and emergency had taken place. She did not want to talk about it. She only wanted some yogurt and sleep. She apologized for being out of it, gave me quit hug, kiss, and evaporated into our bedroom. I clean up the kitchen and then I went up to my office with my briefcase in hand.

Judy and Francis were there with some sketches to be considered. Steve and Ron came in a few minutes after me. Barbara had coffee ready and sweet rolls to keep the meeting very informal. Russell to my surprise was there before 9:30.

"Since it appears that all the principal parties are present, we open with the agenda for this meeting. I have Judy and Francis first, Steve, my boss and open to general information. But before we get started, I want to introduce Russell to each one of you and he is here as possible candidate to operate or lease the businesses." Barbara stated. Barbara always opens all the meetings, which get us off on good foot. She also keeps us tracking until we are done, then if we want to socialize, that is fine.

Judy had put up two designs, one that complements our project and another that was more 'eye catching' to attract travelers. She did a great job presenting up and down side of each. Open for suggestions for further options, especially if going to be leased property. Francis was great with her design activity. Judy always gets the assignment of presentation of their work.

Steve gave general ideas as to the lay out and options on needs that would make the project possible. Most of his questions that need to be answered were my concerns too.

From that point on, Barbara made sure everyone had an opportunity to express their ideas and thoughts and concerns. It was amazing as to Russell's ideas as to the layout of the store and gas station functional business fit into our vision. Ron was considering the permits necessary for this venture. When noon was upon us, we had run out information and were ready to quit. We scheduled another meeting in two weeks. Barbara will have a summary of the meeting in everyone's hands within a week to help with deeper exploration of the project. Without question, it will be a very viable piece of the whole operation. Regardless how the economy goes, we have enough fail safe systems to keep it solvent.

I invited everyone to lunch on the premises at Johnny's Restaurant so we could be acquainted with Russell and build relationship by using each person's strengths. The lunchtime kept building upon the meeting we just left and it turns out to be very productive. We have growing with Russell's involved. Every minute it seems like he adds more balance to this new venture. It is surprising, as how this new project was really coming together. When you are on, you are on and the whole world seems to flock to you to add to the success. After a couple hours, everyone was ready to quit for the day and get about his or her duties.

The afternoon for me was getting all the paper work moving with the construction of the new condos. Steve portable office shack was within 20 feet of our office, so we could keep up with the needs that affected us. We had great suppliers, because they knew we paid on time and there was lot of business coming their way. They must screen for defective material because, we always seem to get the quality and quantity we ordered.

The rest of the week was just usual work day. We sold two more of the new condos that were now under construction and they were busy customizing the interior they wanted in their new home. The back row has the living quarter on the top floor with 'almost floor to ceiling windows' facing the river. Great view and sleeping quarters were on the second floor. The first floor was the garage in front and Pullman kitchen with half bath on backside of the first floor to support sitting room and patio with small back yard.

Thursday night, out of boredom, I decided to go to bed early. I listen to my tape every night before I go to bed, at least part of it. I will also make sure I listen to it completely at least twice before the next session. I take notes of things that I need to pay attention to, to bring about positive changes in my behavior and make these adjustments become an active part of my life. I just shut off the tape and decided to get in bed. The front door bell rang. It was almost midnight.

There is Johnny at the door asking if he could use the guest room for the night. His lame excuse was that he had to be at work early for supplies that were coming in around four. It is such a waste of time to drive home, in a couple hours turn around, and drive back. He figured he would only have a couple of hour's sleep, which is not enough for a Friday. I would never refuse him anything. He had done this drill before, so I had nothing to do but go to bed. Before darkness totally invaded me to take to the land of sleep, the thought wandered across my mind, Johnny is here by truly why. Before the answer was disclosed, I was gone.

Chapter 25

As the darkness of sleep crept in, my dream emerged by starting out in beautiful setting however it flowed quickly to that strange space where I start to feel uncomfortable. Unknown fear slides in like the fingers of fog. Every fiber of my body feels like it is on alert, but what is it? The fog of time evaporates very slowly and I am witnessing a lad appearing to be in state of great turmoil. Damn, it is I, on that god-forsaken island back in the 2nd Century B.C. I was already wailing out cries from deep in my soul. My panic was on the loose, I felt like I was ready to explode. Then I felt this warm hand touching mine. My God! I am not alone. I turned to see Kevin sitting very close to me.

Kevin gently spoken to me "Alex, you are down loading from your soul all the pain you buried there from this experience. You are not Altair any more, that was just an experience you had on earth in that time and with that name. I want you to continue to hold my hand as we journey to understand what really happen then. This will help you to release that pain so you will be able to deal with later lifetimes related experiences. Are you ready to journey with me?"

I made a very feeble reply, "Yes" and I held his hand tighter. I kept telling myself I would need to trust my spiritual advisor for he is my healer. The panic raging in my physical being started to subside until it was manageable. I was aware I was still shaking; still it was not out of control. "I am ready. So what is this that we are going to do? I was informed that I would witness the hell of abandonment, the lost love of my family and get to know the captain that I had uncontrollable feelings for. ""Please don't make me relive it again? Right now I am in really very anxious." I pleaded with Kevin.

"Here is where trust comes in. You have said you trust me. What is there to be afraid of; I am here with you on this journey. So hold my hand and I am going to show you some scenes of understanding so you can know the "why" of your pain. Here we go and I want you to listen and the only interruption that will be tolerated is if you don't understand. You have to hold in check your physical emotions until, to experience, by seeing the whole event in your present physical understanding. You have seen these scenes hundreds of time when you were in spirit, between lives, without physical body's emotional reactions whereby you can intellectualize the experience but you are missing the emotional aspects of the experience of understanding. Remember, we talked about this many, many times to building your knowledge to finally understanding this course of action. How best to resolve these past lives experiences that, damage your soul, your psychic, and release of this into your physical body in this lifetime. Your present body has to be somewhat related to the physical form that existed during that past life experience. Yet, no match is perfect and this activity still causes some unknown side reactions we have no way of knowing could exist. You know about DNA. You have an understanding how you can trace ancestors' way back in time. The plan is to have the DNA as close a match as possible to help the soul to heal these past life events by releasing those traumas into this new physical body and then release it from the present physical body to be finally free from it. The best laid plans most of the time don't work out as planned, but we keep working on perfecting the process.

Before we get lost with details of how it works, let's try to unravel the experiences. Remember we are just going to witness the events, don't get physical involved if that is possible. We see you are on Ethan's ship and listen to the crew members. They are out of control because they are very superstitious. They witness red clouds in the morning, birds flying to the land and the wind filled their sails when they found you. These are signs of bad omens for sailors they are very destructive. Maybe these are truly warnings from the Gods of impending disasters that are going to befall them. They, the crew, went into the 'survival mode' and had irrational justifications to solve their perceived problems. They wanted to throw you over board immediately.

Ethan, the captain, who cared about you in many conflicting ways tried to save you. He suggested to appease the Gods was to put Altair on the island. He rationalized the Gods must have planned this because he and the sailors found this island when they were blown off course coming to Athens. Ethan was trying to reason this tragedy out. They could not take you back because of winds and tides. They could not get you back to port before everyone there would have lost their reasoning power. History had demonstrated what happens to kidnapers. There is the problem of mob mentality, the madness that exists in these kinds of events. Altair's father had power and the people of city would avenge his anguish on Ethan and his crew. Altair's parents already knew Ethan was not coming back for a year. You had demonstrated a very unnatural attachment to this captain that even was an additional concern of your father. You put them, the whole crew, in very precarious situation. You also had received warning not to do this, but you did not heed these warnings. So here we are, caught up in almost unsolvable dilemma.

The island would be the best solution, with the possibility that someone else could save you. Now that places the burden on you. What did you do? You went in a state of uncontrolled emotional behavior. You were unable to utilize the supplies they left for you to survive with until spirit helpers could attract someone to rescue you. Your own pity party blinded you. The goats even tried to make friends with you; you would not have any of it. There was enough food on the island to survive for over a month. They left you all the tools to fish, an activity you always day dreamed about wanting to do on your ridge overlooking the harbor. Yet! What did you do? You starved yourself to death; by refusing, eat or drink what was available to you.

Only if you would have tried to see this an experience, as an adventure, that you used to dream about before going to sleep at night. You, the mighty lone survivor, of all ship wrecks you conjure up in your fantasies. We, spirit helpers, were projecting every survival idea to you. We were trying to build in fail safe system encase something like this might happen. It truly happened. You were stubborn, bull headed, rejecting any help as usual, and a historical attitude, which resulted in your death. By historical attitude we mean in previous lives you exhibited the same behavior in similar situations.

Within a month, you would have been rescued by other vessel. We had begun the inspiring ship's captain to sail in your area.

We, spirit helpers, were building guilt level in Ethan to find a way to get back and take you off the island. That one would not be the best arrangement because of his crew. You would have been sold off when they got to Sicily, because the Gods wanted you to live, that would have justified that action. What a mess and it all could have been avoided if Ethan had not come to Greece, but he did. You could have heeded our warnings, but you didn't. Out of the mess, there could have been a lot of learning. However, we are now trying to make sense of all of it and to facilitate healing to move on. So it has taken 2200 years, it was not all wasted because for other learning lessons were accomplished during that time. Yet! We are now in your evolution of development where these "omens" [nervous laughter] need to be healed, corrected and integrated into your soul's journey to get evolving again. Before you reply to all of this, I want to thank you for not interrupting and justifying your past behavior." Kevin stated as matter of fact, without any emotions.

I now had a chance to say something, "I have to tell you honestly, every time I wanted to butt in, your hand just squeezed mine so hard, I knew better not to interrupt. What you have told me, just again sets my head spinning. Here I am again blaming everyone out there for my disastrous life. I guess my character flaw have at times got in the way of resolving problems that could have been solved by me. Then I carry the karmic pain from lifetime to lifetime limiting my participation and growth.

These kinds of events have always colored my world, to leave me less than satisfied. Then every lifetime coming back to spirit upon my earth death to you, and blaming you for what happen to me. "It was always your fault that our plans were not complete as laid out. As I also remember, I would never admit that I could have been to blame. These dysfunctional events had very significantly shattered and crippled the foundations of my being.

If, now, my earthly love for Jenny right now is limited unless I do heal and correct all of these human frailties. Not to mention, Johnny, whom I realize is Ethan in that lifetime; he is still standing by me with so much love.

Am I entitled? So much is offered, so little involvement from me. Why you haven't given up on me, is truly beyond me?"

"I am not going to go there," replied Kevin. "I will continue to enter thoughts into your dreams and stay the rest of the night. You need to process all of this without guilt because all of life's experiences are experiences. You need these experiences for growth. Without them, your soul has many experiences but no knowledge of understanding or wisdom. Wisdom only comes in the physical application of knowledge and then truly you own it. Adrian, I hope you understand what I just said to you. For those statements are true basis for the spirit journey in physical body and the process of evolution. However, for now, you need to shut down your conscious mind and get rest. I will be talking with you today at Roger's session and maybe if you integrate this, in second thought, I may have Roger postpone your meeting until next week." Kevin gentle ended the session.

I woke up with a start because Kevin had indicated he had left, but how is it I am still holding his hand? I looked down and it was a hand, a real live hand. It was connected to a body that was fast asleep on Jenny's side of the bed. He was still sleeping. I should have known that Kevin put Johnny up to being here tonight. I just closed my eyes and lost in darkness of a much earned healing sleep.

When I awaken by my alarm clock, I look to see that I was truly sleeping alone. I got out of bed and went into the spare bedroom and there was no Johnny. I am confused. Did he stay last night? Was he in my bed? I am not sure what is what now. Oh! Damn I forgot he had stated he needed to be up early to receive supplies. I went to my bedroom window, there was the truck, and it was being unloaded. I keep forgetting that these condos are so sound proofed you don't hear trucks, cars and most ships. Occasionally, a ship will lay on the horn for some reason and you can hear it, but still it sounds far away.

They were just finishing unloading; I am not sure if it was by chance or what, but Johnny looked up and saw me standing in the window and waves. Then he turned to continue the work that was needed. I really don't know how I would make it through all of my past life healings events without him and so many others. I am so bless and grateful yet I can't find the words to express those feelings.

I should get clean up and dressed, because my wife will be home soon, I need to be looking sharp. She is most always cheerful in the morning; I hope that one trait that will rub off on me.

The phone rang and I answered it, there was Roger's voice stating, "I am unable to meet with me today because of emergency and other commitments. You are rescheduled for next week at the same time. I am sorry I can't talk, I am driving right now and I don't like using the cell phone, even though it's not in my hand. Right now my attention needs to be on the road and in the present, so see you next Friday."

Jenny came in just in time to see her breakfast consisting of eggs and glass of juice on the table. Enough to keep any of her hunger pains from existing but not too heavy to prevent sleep. "You are a love; you have fixed something different every morning, which I am grateful for, thank you. You must be tuning in on me psychically, for that is all I could think about wanting for breakfast."

"It just another way I can say I love you. You look like it was another heavy night. I looked at the calendar and we had a full moon last night. She was a beautiful full moon and I bet you had your hands full." was my reply

"The 'establishment' keeps saying there is no connection between 'full moon' and people needing service. I would like them to come and work with us a week before a full moon and see how as days come closer to full moon, so does the needs. However, that will never happen. [Ha] Life just keeps going on and I am thankful for that. Would you draw me hot bath? I need to soak; I am not sure what part of me hurts the most. We have had busy times, but last night had to be the worse. Maybe it is stimulated by the coming of holiday season also, whatever! You have a very tired wife and I probably won't see you until tomorrow morning. Thank you, I'm going to eat your prepared meal, get soaking, and sleep" the exhausted words dropped from her lips.

I have never seen her looking so exhausted. I ran up stairs, filled the tub, put in some water softener that smelled very relaxing and laid out everything she would need. As I turned, she was standing there in bathrobe. I gave her a quick kiss and was on my way. I understand her need for this lone time and she deserves it.

As usual I had the breakfast at the restaurant, special is always great, and Johnny joined me with a cup of coffee. "You were at the house last night, weren't you?" I asked.

"You must be getting old and forgetful! Sure I was there so I could be here bright and early, have you forgotten already." He replied.

"I have to ask and I all ready know the answer, but I am going to ask it any way. Did you sleep in my bed and hold my hand last night? Because I remember waking up thinking Kevin was still holding my hand and it was you." I stated with a sense of knowing.

Johnny did his usual semi-denial but with his big grin, "I had a hunch you were in for an evening and I thought I better be there just in case. I have to tell you, you are handling these experiences with less rebellious struggling, more humility, or something like that. I could hear you talking but lot softer and smoother. Your body was not skirmishing with whatever going on, and you aren't doing those awful sweats. Holding your hand was pleasant experience, and I could get some sleep too."

"What I am learning from my past lives, I was not always there for you or I caused you lots and lots of grief. The place we are in now, whatever it took to get us here, I am thankful and grateful. All I can say, you are always there for me. In this lifetime, you and your sister are the best thing that has ever happen to me. Before I get mushy, I want to just say thank you." I concluded.

I went on to say, "So here I am spending my time and day just sitting here lamenting over what happen already this day. I am glad that I got the call from Roger; I will have a week pardon. I will now get a different take on my tape of last week as the result of the nightmare of last night. There has to be lot of processing. All my soul's experiences that were colored by the 5th and 2nd century are going to be reshaped in this life. Someday, I will have to ask Kevin why it is you, Johnny, that seems to have your act together sooner than I did. Look what you have been able to do for me in all of this. I haven't bailed you out of anything I know of this life time."

Johnny replies, "The only thing that comes to my thoughts was that other lifetimes you helped me to work mine out. That is why I can help you now. Of course, your goals were always requiring a head strong person to make them happen. You have always have been a shaker and a mover, an out-front kind of man. While you were doing your thing, I took on lesser goal and roles. We both will get to the same place. You wanted more depth of experiences and understanding, so that's the price you have to pay. When it all pencils out, your goals for your soul's journeys were different then mine but we will finally get to the same place when it is all said and done. Listen to me talk!"

"This getting in more than I can handle right now, let's move on to something else. We will take this up when I am finished with Roger. I expect it will be soon, yet I feel a storm is brewing that has to do with Spain. You know, Jenny had some weird experiences when we were there too. She was more than happy to get the hell out of there. She told me after we were back. She had thought it had to do with my illness, but it was something different. Her comment was like her 'world vanished without warning'. She did not know what that meant, but she felt lost."

"I pushed to get on some other topics. Is there anything I can help you around here? I had blocked out this morning and was available to work since meeting with was cancelled. Oh! By the way, we had a meeting with the gang and Russell. I expect you already know all about it. Am I right?" I inquired.

"Now to be honest with you, Judy, who you know I sleep with, talks in her sleep sometimes therefore I do know that happen. However, honestly, I like both proposals and I think this will serve this project was well as the area and travelers. I would never have guessed that Russell would have so much to offer as to how it should look, what is needed. Judy said he has been planning to do something like this for a year, but like most of us, finances sometimes get in the way." Johnny explained himself.

Johnny went on to say, "I am glad that this is moving, I suspect that development will really be needed when we have this place full up, plus the motel, which will have small functioning kitchens in them. I can't believe my dream of owning this restaurant would end up being part of our own town. I should say community."

"In addition, it still surprises me with the cash flow out of this business. I am starting to get bookings for wedding receptions and parties, which I had not expected. Judy has been a great help in helping create all of this. You know I have to thank your ex-wife for hiring those ladies of the evening.

Especially, since we were their first customers. Who would have known, we were led to their business that helped design and made it happen for us. I would never have Judy in my life. She is more than a treasure. If you hadn't had me to share that evening as your guest when you ex-wife hired those ladies to entertain you, I would never met her. That was special gift from you. In fact, my time with Judy that evening was how I found out about their real business. Again, they would not be working with us to make all this happen. Being with you, you attract the greatest things, I will never let you out of my sight. Every day is adventure of some kind." Johnny replied

"Before I forget, Judy and I are going to buy one of new back row condos that are being constructed. She loved that full wall of windows looking out to the river. We will not have to have drapes. The master bedroom windows have some view too. Most of all, she has wanted to decorate her own home. We like most the same things. We are taking the end one on West side that is next to wet lands. We also get a larger patio. I will not have to drive to work and her office is still the same distant. I want you to know we are not moving here to keep eye on you or Jenny." the words flowed with the love of true friendship from Johnny.

"There is another one! I didn't know you put a bid on a condo." Was my surprised remark "I am glad to have you in the neighborhood. I truly believe this will be a great community. We have new support system already in place should the need arises.

"I had thought of a community building for functions of condo association but the groups don't seem to want that. They are still working their way around the idea of community support system like an extended family but not developing groupies or clicks. Barbara is still working on her degree and she has been bringing in speakers on different subjects of interest to our community to assist in this experiment. Time will tell. I still believe if develop very functioning and supporting home environment, person can be all they really want to be" I stated

The waitress came over to inform Johnny that there was a customer who wanted more information on the availability of the space for a party. He excused himself to tend to business. It gave me a chance to leave and go to the office to finish any paper work that still hanging. I wave to him as I left.

Whole afternoon was busy talking to couple of interested condo buyers. I walked them through the guidelines of living here. We will not sell them a place unless they can afford it. They can design the interior within limits. Should they decide to move, we would buy it back at a fair market price. There is no sub-leasing or renting of any units. When the decision is made to go ahead with the purchase, we do all the final checking on background, ability to afford the unit, and related material. We will not be a Big Daddy in this operation with condo owners. We are just giving them tools to complete or heal their innate unknown needs. A support system; not a disabling co-dependent system, but build a system for co-creative to maximize whatever they want to do with their lives. You know co-creative is helping a person find their life's tool or talent, assist in empower their talents and positive support of their creativity. Help them find their passion so they can really enjoy life.

I had all my work done and with a clean desk, I left before the staff. So far, I have nothing on my scheduled for next week. Next week isn't here yet, there are always surprises. That is what I like about this project. I also had a few investors from the Washington side to look my operation over and they are considering doing something similar. They wanted to hire me to put it together for them on a contract. That would not be a bad deal, since it's on the other side of the river. I could hire most of my gang to make it work. Barbara could take over the daily operations of this place to give me the freedom to do this.

As I left the office, my dear wife waved at me as she drove past for work. I need to get home, something to eat, take a sea salt bath, and do some homework on me.

CHAPTER 26

Saturday morning was upon me and I received a call from Ol' Johnson, who asked me to go fishing today. My wife was fast asleep when I went back to check on her before we left. Therefore, we started out right after breakfast. The day was cloudy, with a hint of winter coming our way and breeze was little on the cool side. We motored down by the old Trojan Atomic Power plant to try our luck there. After throwing out anchor on the Oregon side of the river, we settled back to see what our luck would be. Johnny told us that the chef would cook whatever we caught for lunch when we got back. I am not sure that was good offer or not. It will really depend if we catch some fish, if we don't, there can be lot of joking about our failure.

Ol' Johnson started to ask me "Everything is moving along smoothly, a lot better than I expected. Would you be satisfied living a life that was not as challenging?"

My reply was "I am not sure. I am still working on stress factors that I inherited from my past lives. It appears that I have one large thunder storm ahead of me yet. With a clean slate, what it would be like? These past life stressors are keep me hopping. With them out of the way, I am not sure what I will be like. I know I believe I would be in love with my wife more than I am right now. Still, I wish I knew what life would be really like. And yet, I can park all of this activity to give full attention to developing projects. I have an investment group that wants me to look at and possibly consider being the general contractor/manager of proposed development on the other side of the river. They are not sure whether to have it closer to

185

Longview or Vancouver. We are only in the talking stages. You know how it was when we started this project."

"Boy! Do I ever. I want to tell you that I am glad I did not get out like Fred. Running the marina, and having a first class houseboat, this is what makes me happy, content and at home with myself. The more simple things of life just keep me ticking along. All the work you conduct makes my head swim. Still you make it look so easy, like there nothing to it. I am sure glad I am part of all of this. That is another reason for you come fishing with me. Everything is settling down, so I can get to know you better. I must admit, the hell you have gone through with that wife of yours, oh, I mean your ex-wife, what is her name?" asked Ol' Johnson.

"I try to erase her name out of my mind. It was Marian. We were a pair and what kept us together should have never happen to anyone. The price of my freedom was cheap at any price. I have not heard or want to hear anything from her ever. Not that I hate her, for I found my peace and I mentally thanked her for the growth I gain out of that relationship. Without being married, and finding a method to break the commitment I made to her over 4500 years ago in another lifetime, I am not sure how many centuries would have passed before I could finally be free. If you don't mind lets drop this subject" I half way pleaded.

"I didn't mean to pry, but you seem so back to earth up to and including being married to that sweet Jenny. I wish I were 40 years younger. I was handsome man; I would have given you a run for your money with Jenny. Now you are back at being somewhat different again. Is there anything I can do to help you? You both make a great pair, but something is a foot" looking right me.

I might as well spit it out "I have been having night mares again, but this time they are different. It is more about healing me. It appears that many of my lives were more destructive to me than I expected. You know I believe in past lives. It seems that I was good warrior for protecting people, but with the affairs of the heart, I did miserably. I not only broke my heart but others. I am trying to heal those broken heart, with my friend Roger. In some ways, Jenny is connected or because of past broken heart with a wife or woman, there is something blocking me now so I can be free to love her unconditionally. I have to tell you, as I am telling you this, now it doesn't make total sense to me yet. However, I am really working on this mess and I am yo-yoing again. Lucky for me, Jenny has been working nights, doing her internship and day sleeping, so I don't have to keep up great front for her while this is going on. Frankly, I thought I was pulling it off so no one could notice it."

"You have been really up and going all the time. Nevertheless, I have seen you a couple of times sitting by yourself in the corner of the restaurant and you seemed to be wiped out. Still, when someone came near you, you flash back to that regular guy we all know and love. Johnny told me not to worry but I want you to know if there is anything else beside my boat, I want to help you" in friendly and very fatherly voice, Ol' Johnson just sat there looking with concern at me.

"Right now, I am doing fine. Using your boat has made my trips up to see Roger easier and everyone who may have noticed something, has not said anything, which is great too. I have always related to our crew on this project as part of my family. So your concerns are really respected. Damn, there goes your bobber under water; I think you have something on the line. You better pay attention if we want to have lunch," I yelled with joyful song in my voice.

For the next few minutes, the battle was on with man against fish, and it appeared that Ol' Johnson was winning. I was busy getting the net ready and to pull our lunch on board. The pole was bending almost in two as he reeled it to the boat. It was a fascinating tug-a-war and I was sure Ol' Johnson was going to win. I had the net in the water just a foot or so where it would come out of the water. The fish made the last desperate effort by going under the boat and it worked. He or fish broke free. Leaving two astonished men in the boat who can't believe what just took place. We began talking away at what had just happened. We finally settled down, baiting our hooks, tossing it in and hoping for lunch.

The next couple of hours were spent just being in each other's company. Men as well as women need this kind of bonding time. It seems to fill some void spot in our heart. That was the only strike we had. Finally, it was after 12; we pulled the anchor and headed home. In addition, wouldn't you know that smart ass Johnny was standing on the dock to see what we had to cook for our lunch? Secretly, I think he knew we were empty handed, and wanted to do some gloating. After we secured the boat to the dock, and we were standing on the dock. Here it comes.

"How successful were our mighty fishermen? I don't see any fish. Does this mean we will hear tall tales about how they all got away? In addition, the mighty battle that was fought but this giant of a fish or fishes got away by some strange stroke of luck. I will not spoil your stories, I will listen with an open mind of compassion" laughing to point where he could hardly contain himself.

I dropped my gear and started to lung at him in jest, but he must have expected my move, turned quickly, and started out on a dead run laughing so hard and loud you could hear him everywhere. I went charging after him, not knowing what I would do if I caught him. Fortunately, for me, he got through the kitchen door and shut it before I got there. He kept looking at me through the glass laughing his heart out. The only thing I could do now was go back, get my gear, and prepare to have lunch with my fishing buddy who will of course share whatever deluge we will get from anyone who wants to join in this kind of horseplay. We stored our gear in the Marina's locker and journeyed into to face the music. It wasn't too bad. It only took an hour for everyone finally let it be. That kind of good clean fun is another way to bond, isn't?

When I arrived home, there was another note from Jenny. She was going to be done early, because she wanted to be home by eight. She wanted to go dancing with her man tonight. Johnny has a great romantic group coming tonight and I am in the mood.

I felt like a school boy going out on date. I was all cleaned, dressed up, and full of expectations for our 'date' tonight. Jenny was home by eight and retreated to the upstairs to get ready. I stayed down stairs to keep out of the way. I could hear the commotion going on while she was getting ready, sometimes it was burst of giggles and laugher and then times of frustrations. I have to say I glad I was out of the way. She arrived at the foot of the stairs, looking like a walking dream and bubbling with life. She gave me a quick kiss and stated, "we better get over there, because there are no reservations and I want a good table near the dance floor so we can get with it".

We charged out the door, holding hands. We seemed to float over to the restaurant and up the stairs to dance hall. The place was already filling up. We were able to get second table in off to the side that gave a great view of band area and the floor. The clock struck nine and the music melted the evening. It was like a lovers' night, slow, cuddling, and enjoying the one, you hold feeling the music that carried that closeness throughout your total being. The evening evaporated all too quickly. The evening was like when you share great intimacy after lovemaking, that glow that keeps glowing that you don't want to end.

We also talked with many of our neighbors and friends, but interesting no one asked us to dance with them. I guess they knew by our dancing that it was our night to be together. They also knew that Jenny has been working many hours for her job and was finishing her degree. In caring community, they make a conscious effort work to support each other. The activity tonight was to allow us to grow in our relationship.

It was almost two when we finally got clean up and in to bed. Without saying a word, it was time for sleep and being close to each other. The night was somewhat restless for both of us for some reason.

She was up first and prepared breakfast, and called to have me join her. She thought I was still sleeping, but I was up and quiet like a mouse. I was down stairs and standing in the hallway. When she walked to foot of the stairs to call me, I quickly grabbed her and after she relaxed from being startled, she granted me a kiss. We spent most of the time at breakfast just exchanging what had been happening in each other's world. She served Champaign with the breakfast that is a mood setter.

After putting everything away, being a beautiful day, we agree that a slow walk around the place and maybe look at our new acreage across the street was in order too. The new condo activity was moving right along. The weather was holding which made building possible. We crossed the road and walked around in our weed-filled land, thinking about how it would look when it is all put together. The priority will be the grocery and gas station first because they will be required to assist in the cash flow. We have required permits in the works now. I don't envision any problems because the people of the area expressed great approval because it is a necessary for them as well.

We were still in the middle of the area when I witness a car drive off the road and down the make shift dirt road toward us. The guy got out and walked over to us, and introduced himself as Robert P. Stuart. He thought he recognized me and I would be Alex that bought the acreage and wanted to talk with me. I acknowledge I was the co-owner representing our company.

Robert spoke rapidly and started out with "I am not a condo man but I like what is going on here. I have used your marina and restaurant most of last summer. You probably don't remember me with all the people coming and going. To the point, I was wondering what you were going to do with this land. I had heard that maybe a store and or gas station. You know how words spreads when you want to know what is going on. I am interested in having a home in this area. Is this area being urbanized into homes with yards? I hope you are not considering trailer park. I want home around here and if that is your plan. Here is my card; I want to be notified as soon as designs are available so I can make my bid for a place. If you have it in the moderate range, they will go fast. With the new schools and other activities in the area, they should sell out fast. Will you do that for me?"

"First I want to introduce, my wife Jenny, [gave them time to acknowledge each other] and yes, we considering homes for sale on the rest of the property. We are not planning on trailer park, but modest homes that people who live here can afford them. We really don't have much on the drawing boards yet but have a go on a possible design to present to investors. I will take your card and put it with this project and we will notify you of our progress. It may not be until May or June before homes will begin to be ready. Will that fit into your time frame?" I questioned.

Robert stood there thinking for minute of two about what I said, finally he broke the silence "that will work fine with me. I have been living in a large apartment complex closer to Portland and I have had about enough of apartment living. My job is secure and living here will save me time when I come up here to use this area. I know my family is ready to move and the new school should be great for them. I really want in on this, so I will check in with you from time to time about the progress. You can see by my statement, I expect it will be ago. We, accountants, are rather definite in our approach to life. I will contact you later for I have a few more errands to run for the wife and get home to take the family out. I will be talking with you soon" as he walked back to his car and waved goodbye.

We watched him turn around in the weeded field and head back on his journey. Jenny looked at me saying, "It appears that I have married a very successful lucky guy. Here we are just looking over what is been bought and we have someone wanting to buy what we have not yet designed let alone built. I knew a good catch when I see one!" With those words, she broke away from me and began running down the dirt road to the highway. Giggling, laughing, and taunting me to catch her if I can.

She had a good lead on me when I finally came around to what was happening. I wouldn't predict it. I start out running full out but traffic was with her and she was across the road before I got there. I was detained with traffic going both ways and she was taunting me from the other side. When she saw there would be a break in the traffic, she ran off towards the marina's office. She was inside before I was 30 feet from the place. When I got to the door, I was totally out of breath. Open the door and there Jenny laughing with the employee about our game. I just stood there looking at her, trying to defend myself "I want you to know Sue, that she had a head start, I got hung up by the traffic. So it is not my fault she beat me here. [Acting in the mood, I stuck out my tongue], so there. That made them laughs even more. A man just can't win."

"By the way, why are we here?" I asked.

"If you were truly were a romantic which you tried to demonstrate on the dance floor last night, you take me for a ride on the river while it still nice day. You can do that can't you? You want to impress your loving, caring wife, don't you?" purred out the words from Jenny which created more laugher and entrapment.

"It appears now this request was done with an audience; therefore, I will have to succumb to your request." I was trying to playing along with the mood.

Sue had the keys ready for me and the cushions very quickly, giggling all the time. "Now you will have pay for any time over an hour at the hourly rate, we do not allow special treatment to anyone. Everyone is treated the same. Do you understand that?" Her voice was wedged between laughter and giggling, which was delightful.

"I know the drill, thank you very much, 'come along girl', and your man is taking you for a ride." I could hardly contain myself.

We got in our rental and we quickly motoring out on the river, when Jenny asked if we could drift for a while. I saw no problem with that because there was no traffic on the river.

Jenny had something that was bothering her and wanted to get it out and over if possible. "I am not sure if it was because we have not been sleeping together, or what is or was going on. We had such a great evening, I always dreamed about when I was single. Then it seemed to trigger something or maybe not, I am not sure. I keep having a half way dream of being lost and I cannot find you. It seemed to go on and off all night long. If you ask me to explain it, I cannot. I don't understand it. It is beyond me, so I ask you do you have any insight to it? It is very out of the ordinary and puzzling for me. Oh! I remember it was something like I was experiencing in Spain. Since you are the one who getting help from Roger, maybe he can shed light on this subject? It only seems to happen when we are very close and loving, and sometimes even awake I have this creepy feeling I can't find you or I am losing you. I do not like it, so I am looking for answers. For me, I want you around me until I leave this planet. I love you so much and want to be with you. For some reason you fill my heart."

"I am lost for words; I have to tell you that I have asked Roger about this subject a couple of times. I have not told her about my spirit teacher, Kevin. I don't think I have what the answer. His play on this is that, we both shared an event and it needs to be revealed and resolved. It is about something that happened to us, not between us. He would not say. I too had a restless night, with about the same dream I could not find you. I am pushing Roger to find the underlying cause of it too. I love you more than life I really don't what to say only that within a month I should know some kind of answer. Can you hang tough until then?" I inquired.

"As long as you are working on it, I am fine. It's more than a little unsettling but I am not going anywhere and you had better not even consider leaving. I had the judge tie the knot to last this lifetime, and I know he will be my "champion" should I need one. I just wanted to know the unknown thing that keeps popping up when we are lovingly close. I will never let that dream drive me anywhere, because leaving you is not a part of my life. Still, I would appreciate it if there is an answer. I would truly like to know" was Jenny's way of making her point.

Having said what she wanted to say, letting me know where she stood with it; that was the end of the conversation about it. She spent the rest of our time on the river expressing her appreciation of what was around us and what a great place this is. Just then, a hawk flew over looking for a meal had added to the activity of the moment. To see the old abandoned power plant was so sad, but as with all things, when they are no longer useful, it is time to quit.

We finally fired up the engine and cruised back slowly to drink in all the beauty around us. We docked and locked the boat up and headed back to the office. Sue saw us coming and had my bill waiting for me. To our surprise, we were gone over 2 hours, which meant I paid for three. I handed her my credit card and she gave me the receipt to sign. I think she was bracing herself against any verbiage I may hand out because we were over 2 hours. I mean really over. I kept her in suspense and finally broke the silence with "Have a great day, and thank you." as we walked out.

We went home, spent time making and eating a light lunch, and the mood was recaptured from last night. We retired to a shower and same time that melted the afternoon away.

That evening they went over to restaurant to visit with her brother and friends who are living here. The place was quiet because it was really after the dinner hour when they arrived. Their usual spot was vacant, so they made their way to the table and waited for the waitress.

Helen was working tonight, "do you want menus, or do you know what you want?"

"The special on the board sounds great to us, and we would like wine with the meal, we will leave that up to the cook what would complement his creation" I replied in very soft mood. The glow of the day was still with us.

Helen left without saying another word. I guess she could see we were acting like love bugs. Jenny broke the mood with "I have a very honest question to ask you. It really concerns both of us. I have been asked by the school, could I on completion of internship hours required, continue same number of hours because the hospital are running short staff. This short staff problem seems likely it will not be solved for couple more weeks or so. When I have my required hours in, they will start paying me for any hours over the requirements. This looks like I will be doing anywhere from three to five days like those that I have been doing in the past two weeks. I would like you to think it over before you reply. I, for myself, would like to have it all over with before the holidays sets in. We don't need the extra money but I would like the experiences plus I will want to spend more time with you over the holidays. Just think about it.

My mind was racing in all directions. I have freedom while I am dealing with the issues that developed in the sessions with Roger. I would also find myself alone more for a while, I'd miss her, but she has a life too. We have seemed to be able to take care of our needs over these past weeks. I think I always go for completion to have the rewards at the end. "Jenny, I have been working on my answer while you were presenting your case. To be honest, I miss not having you around more. The realistic part of me says are you able to physically and mentally to handle the extra work. I do not want a wreck of wife for possible more time together over the holidays. I love you more than I love enough to say, it is your world and I will support whatever you can handle. It appears only temporary, and you have been working and going to school for such a long time, part time, I understand closure. Therefore, you decide and that decision will be the best for both of us."

Jenny just looked at me for a while. I didn't know if she believed me or wondered what was going on. Finally, she slowly said, "I want to get this over, for one. I really want to expand my experiences to be ready for the duties of the degree. It is a push, I agree, but for this limited time, I believe I can do it. I will be honest enough, if it begins to be beyond my abilities to function effectively, I will back down. These two weeks have been within my limits, although some days were little much, it appears I can do it. I know with your demonstrated support as you have done in the past two weeks, it will be a no brainer. I am going for it."

I took her hand and looked her in the eye, "I love you for you. This is part of you; therefore, I will support your decision as you have supported me up to this point in our lives. What's not to trust? This is part of a co-creative marriage."

We sat there "mooning" at each other when the mood was broken with Helen words "All right you two, the honeymoon is over. This behavior just makes the rest of us jealous. So break it up. Here is your salad, and the rest of the meal will be with you in about 20 minutes. This soft red wine recommended with the meal. I opened the bottle at the bar, I hope it meets with your approval" as she pour some in our glasses.

Jenny tasted it first and it was all right by her. Helen didn't wait for me to taste it before she left. I looked a Jenny, "It appears she does not care if I like it or not." All Jenny did was giggle, the evening melted away with meal, a small amount of social interaction with other customers, and finally Johnny spent about half an hour with us before we left. We walked home, finished some household tasks, and then off to bed, another great day ended.

CHAPTER 27

The week began like last week. That is the way of life. I spent time at the office while Jenny was about her work and sleep. We had late lunches together whenever it was possible. I received a call about meeting with the investor that will be postponed until next Tuesday. They asked for permission to have it here at my office. The motive was to keep a low profile on this project until it is a go. I agreed to host the meeting and the time will be determine later in the week.

Roger called on Wednesday to get us back on schedule. I will be seeing him Friday morning this week. Next week it will have to be in the afternoon, there would be more discussion about this Friday.

Friday finally rolled around, as usual, I had to get on my way to see Roger, but it started to do a little misting. Had breakfast in the restaurant, and I witnessed outside the mist was becoming more of light rain. As I was leaving to go home to get my rain gear, Johnny handed me his slicker and hat as I walked pass telling me I will need it. Since we are the same size, why not accept his offer. I'd get wet going home to get my own gear. I put them on and went out on the dock to use my friend's boat as I have been doing on Fridays. I only uncovered just enough to get in and sit down. I was going to use the cover to help keep me dry and it work okay.

The journey up to Rogers was little on the rough side because the wind had started to pick up. I did not dally tying up the boat and pulling over the cover because the light rain was now turning into real rain. I hasten up the path and on to the porch. I placed the slicker and hat on the top of the rocking chair, my shoes on the porch. Roger was waiting inside with his cup of tea for me. We did our greetings I started out "For some dumb reason, I have begun to understand my complicity in the final outcome of my life in the 2nd century B.C."

"From a year ago and now activity, it is crash, crash, crash, until the reality is revealed. I really have to tell you, being human, trapped in the emotional aspects of living life, we are in a bind. We don't see the forest for the trees. We have so damn many warnings to prevent the grief we are walking into and don't distinguish them. I should say we, when I really mean me. How in God's name could I have been so dumb acting when I had so many people trying to help me prevent tragedies that affect my present life? Let's get to work, before I get sappy," I sadly state.

We began our normal routine, through the house, down the hall and into our special room. The chair was waiting for me as I slipped into it. I took long drink of tea and sat back forcing myself to relax. Roger began using his very smoothing, gentle, guiding tones with every word, which leads me down an imaginary hall to the gateway to my past.

There was Kevin, as always, waiting for me, ready to take me on the next journey. Only God knows where that will be. I had lot of mind adjustment since the last visit with him. I suspect he also has been helping me rearrange my perceptions of past events.

"Well! Kevin it has been a continual adjustment at night during the past two weeks I am starting to feel some feeling the freedom. I suspect you were busy helping with my homework. Last week, Thursday was the hardest, I know you must have had something to do with Johnny being there." was my statement.

Kevin just looked at me then said, "You have been more receptive to working ideas and thoughts. It has been easier in some respects because we made it through that night with a lot less drama. You might have made it through the night without losing it, but Johnny's hand appears to help you stay ground and centered through it all. Sometimes you surprise me by comprehending what is going on and then sometimes you don't. I think we need time to resolve your unreasonableness, inflexibility, and at times, downright bull headedness because they have held up your own growth. If you correct your behavior, you will bring it back into your world of growth.

If I force you to accept corrections, we know the answer to that one. You don't. This free will entitlement sometimes gets in the way of person's progress. I know it is the only way to evolve, but with you, there is no short cut. That is water over the dam, as to speak, let us get on with our work. I should say your healing and freedom. Before you ask, we will get to those feelings of confusion with Jenny but everything is connected. So we will work our way there."

Kevin continued, "I have done some major research on the creation of your soul and it purpose. Evolution just fine-tunes it for your purpose. For instance, you are unable to sort through the clutter of what is going on and to find the best solutions. It is not a skill that can be taught it has to be experienced. It is a distinct way of thinking and a special perspective on the world around you. These past activities brought out the achiever skills your soul also has. You start out every day at zero. By the end of the day, you must achieve something tangible in order to feel good about yourself. The further driven with that events or things happen for a reason and the quest to find the cause to understand the reason.

In the time of the Pharaoh & "The Keeper" in Egypt, 4500 years ago more or less, the Pharaoh realized your strength as he watched you demonstrate your natural innate talents. You moved quickly up through the ranks to where you were captain of your own unit. When Pharaoh wanted to reward the Priest, the Priest knew your strengths were part of your soul and he knew you would fit into his plans. He accepted you. He established great rewards of items of value. Besides, he offered all the physical pleasure possible because you were not born to the privilege class. What he gave you was beyond any imaginations you had ever imagined. He had over shadowed your goals and had your head swimming all the times with pleasures of the flesh. The Priest justified the experiences you had as empowering your driven strengths. You focused on striving to maximize your talents in the Pharaoh's army; you never gave yourself permission to sample physical life. Here it was being offered without limits and you got drunk of pleasures of the flesh."

"In every lifetime, these would be your basic tools for dealing with the world around you, no matter what you are doing. You were a great candidate to be a protector for him every time he wanted to come to earth for his experiences. That is why he gave you all those earthly pleasures of the flesh to hook you. Again, you had never experience them before and they filled the place of lust in your physical form. It would have been a hard gift to refuse when you thought it would never end. It would not cost you one coin, so when he offered you an eternity with all those goodies, it was hard for you not to accept.

Nevertheless, because of your original soul created goal by your creator, you knew some level in your soul's goal that this may not be what you would always want in the future. Because your own soul evolution drive and the thought you may not want to be tied to this person forever regardless of gifts. That is why the "three yeses" you needed to extract from the Priest to be released if you ever get tired being his lackey. To finally break that obligation, it took until this lifetime and Marian [the Priest in woman's body] to break that forever commitment. It was good thing that the Priest did not want to re-incardinate as often as you were. That way you were able to enhance your natural abilities and talents. That also caused you extra frustrations on how to break that bond to be free. For every time you came back with him, you were his 'lackey'. . . there to protect and do his bidding. Of course, he did furnish lots of earthly pleasure for you as payment. Even those gifts became distasteful over time because those types of activities were activities without feelings or love besides they did not feed your natural quest for your soul evolution.

When you came back on your own each lifetime, you really pushed your normal skills: such as an achiever, connectedness, and a conductor of complex situations, strategic applications of your skills and of course learner. You had not time to develop political compromise skills, which would have enhanced your natural abilities. That compromise energy was consumed in your quest to find the solution for your freedom from the Priest. That mission presented you some great learning lessons along with some very painful experiences. It has not been until the last 700 or 800 years have you finally understand the application of political compromise where it necessary to keep moving forward. The political compromise is really about people skills. In addition to resolve issues where there can be a win-win situation for all involved. By not applying those skills, before that time, it prevented the further expansion of your normal innate skills.

The Priest was aware of your increased drive and performance when you were on your own. From time to time, he would maneuver you into situations that caused you great pain or painful deaths as punishments. If you stayed close to him, those events would not happen. This has to have been the sickest part of this relationship.

I must admit that I did not see all of this before, partly because you always attacking me out of your frustrations when came back to spirit. I even partition the committee to be removed as your advisor because I could not seem to effectively communicate with your. They would not release me. In my own frustration, I did not explore your basic core causes. You are not the only client I have. I am not using these as excuses. This has been a mess for so long, I just wanted out and that was not possible for me either. Yet! What can I say; sorry doesn't seem to fit a justification for my not coming to your aid sooner. For now, I am working full out with you to resolve it all because you are finally committed without any reservations. Also I want to thank you for not interrupting me while I talked all this information with you."

Adrian [Alex] quiet replied, "We have to be in the now, I really can't go back and relive all of it nor fixing the blame doesn't resolve anything. With the chain broken with the Priest, my mind has been energetic seeking answers to my greater questions. I have always worked on the premise that we are all connected on earth and have tried to empower people to break traditional, cultural limitations, but when any one in authority caught on to what I was doing, they would box me in, and that forced me to rebel. That did cost me unnecessary pain as I begin to understand now; still those were great learning lessons. No experience is lost in the accumulation of knowledge and experiences. However whenever I hear the words, "connected to anyone forever" sends chills up my spine."

"This is something I don't do often with you, but realizations that I have these innate drives are really normal for me. That is a great mental relief. I know it in spirit but by the time I am adult in the physical world, I forget these drives are normal for me. Most of the people I am around don't understand what comes natural to me or it is natural, since they either don't have those gifts or can't understand them. I try to offer them more but I often find myself at odds with people."

"So most of the time, I go it alone. It is hard to find people who trust me to understand I know what I am doing. They could complement my goals and could understand the process within their abilities, or could benefit by being part of the action but they don't. I guess my abilities shows because that is why I am very successful in this life and can be on my own without Marian's [Priest] help. Remember with your help, we arranged with a group of people, who were with me in spirit, knows who I am, and were willing to take the ride with me. A ride where everyone benefits because they are free to add their strengths to my journey, therefore, it becomes our resolution. Their efforts widen the scope of experiences of the applications of my innate talents. It becomes a win for everyone, and I really enjoy that."

"Before you get lost in this information, which now seems to flood in my mind and body, since I given permission for it to happen, we need to do some reviewing to get to Jenny and me. Jenny has asked me to tell you that she sometimes has strange feelings around me. They started for her when we were in Spain. I told her I would ask, knowing that you will decide when that would happen. Am I right?" was my statement.

Kevin took a long look at me and slowly stated, "We will get to it in time. It will be a while yet, for we have some ground to cover freeing different lives that will lead us to the solution. I expect that we will have it done by your Christmas as a present to both of you. The major goal now is to resolve as much as stressful experience energies as possible. Then when we tackle the time in Spain, it will make it feasible to enable you to observer what happened, the why and to answer questions that you have asked us since that experience. That experience was so injurious to you, because this is the third time on earth to heal that damage to allow you to go on. I have to admit again, you have called upon every ounce of your inner strength to tackle all you have done so far. Your commitment has forced us to give you all the support possible to complete what would be considered two life times activity in one."

"Now let's begin resolving some basic problems and strengthen your resolve. We begin with the experience you relived in Rome this year, where you charged in to face the fear of taking a shower in the morning. You know the one where there was blood everywhere and the sword was sticking out of the front of your body. We gave you the rest of the story, the killer was terminated too. To continue the process of changing the perception you have of that event, we will begin there."

"The two aspects of that learning experiences were you could have use some political compromise with the politician and slowly checked mated him where he would have lost his power over the people. Being an over achiever along with your other talents getting the job done, you are not wanting to learn a slow evolving game of diplomacy. We tried to show you that your death could have been avoided if you use your cunning skills, which would have taken maybe 4 or 5 months to complete your goal successfully. You died and the people got nothing because your need to do it your way. That was loss number one, which was major."

"The second cause for this crisis was when we tried every way that was possible to show you that the officer that killed you was not to be trusted. However, he used his subservient friendship to feed into your innate drives and your ego. With all the negative evidence presented from your fellow officers and us, you went ahead and promoted your own executor. Do you remember all the road blocks that were sent to you about him? That was major because you were just trying to learn about compromise and maneuvering political officials. That lesson was 'killed'."

"As you were talking, I could see it in my mind's eye, you were right. I was stubborn because friendships were important to me. I spent too much time on betrayal of the experience instead of what or who made it happen. Plus I was really mad at myself for failing again the lessons in compromise. This has to be my weakest skills" I replied.

"Then there was that building project in Rome that you headed up for the Emperor. You again thought you were invincible which resulted in you falling off the scaffold, which resulted in you being crippled, and that reduced you to a beggar's life. You always looked at the degrading life as beggar was somehow inflicted on you; nevertheless, you caused it by not being in the moment and being safe. We have spent time on this before but you would only half way admitted it was your fault. Still there was lot of learning lessons on humanity gained from that experience once you got past being the victim."

"I think I will take on one more events, because I want you to really integrate the information learned today in physical system of your present life. We are in that non-feeling world. Because you are not, you need to properly integrate those physical experience of knowing with your soul, so you can release the misconceptions that exist there. In simple terms, replace incorrect information with true valid information about those events while in a physical emotional body. That is how the releasing of past events. We will keep giving you insights when you get stuck in the process when you are not in these sessions."

"Now, I would like to take you to the time you were the Abbott of a monastery which was about 100 km north east of Rome. It was in the 6th Century A.D., remember, don't you? I will just go on. You were running *your* monastery away from the present doctrine of the Holy Mother Church. You were doing demonstrations of healing, teaching the people they can pray directly to God, along with quite a few other violations. You were summoned to Rome, to talk with the Pope about mending your ways and being good leader for the Church. They kept you there for almost a week, brainwashing you into submission. Out of desperation, you would submit and signed the papers to that fact. That was an early lesson in understanding the art of political compromise. You were thinking of how to appease them, find ways to keep your own faith and to get the hell out of there. They would not let you go until you would submit in writing."

"Back at the monastery, you followed the letter of submission for a year. The brothers kept putting pressure on you to go back to spiritual ways again. You tried to convince them they could do it among themselves but not to violate the rules with the public. They did it anyway and the message got back to Rome. The Pope sent an emissary and his assistant to remind you of your letter of submission. You tried to explain, it was the brothers that were violating the rules, and you were trying to bring them back in line with the teaching of the Church. Offers were made for the immediate dismissal of the violators in the emissary presence, and then post the letter of submission on monastery door."

"*You* could not let your old supporters go in such disgraceful manner. You counter offer was that you would go about removing them over time but you would post the letter of submission on the door now. The emissary told you that was not acceptable offer. You refused to comply with their request of discharging those violators immediately. The emissary announced that he was leaving the next morning for Rome with your counter offer. You did not know he was under strong directive, submit totally or your death. He was given an order if you did not comply, he was to terminate you, and his faithful assistant would now be the Abbott.

The next morning, the emissary asked for a blessing for him and his assistant for safe journey back to Rome. The travel during that time was not always safe even with his armed escort and the emblem of the Church. They knelt before you; you placed your hands on his head, and you were praying for a safe journey. Mean while he quietly pulled out a knife as ordered, stabbed you in the stomach and you were dead. A brother saw what happen. They loaded your body into their carriage. The emissary called all the brothers together, and informed them you were journeying back to Rome with him at the pope's request. They were also informed that emissary traveling companion, with the blessing of the pope, would be in charge until your return.

Afterwards the brother quickly reported what he witness to the rest of them. Some of the violators fled for their lives except those few who would submit to save themselves. Those who stayed to insure their employment would of course report the violators the new Abbott. The violators that stayed and recanted eventually murdered in their sleep. There are those drones, which can live under any conditions; it did not matter to them who was the Abbott. As you know your body was dumped in the ditch and covered half way back to Rome."

Kevin continues, "I have to admit, it was lot of submission, but trying to save those brothers who did not care what happened. That was too costly, especially as you know some of them still stayed under the new rule did not last. All you could have gained was lost trying to protect the violators. The violators either did not, or would not support the larger picture that you were attempting. It was really about them instead of your goals. Your monastery would have been the keeper of the wisdom and a haven for the seekers until it was safe to share with the rest of the world."

"Still, you had begun the development of the art of compromise to make possible what you considered the greatest good for the greatest all. There are people worth saving you have to choose from the soul and heart, not from your ears and head. You needed to learn the motives of your followers.

Who will stand tough and who will turn and run in a minute. There was knowledge and wisdom lost because you could not see your own greater picture. However, most of all, the wisdom of understanding the role of steward protecting the gifts of your Abbey for the future of humankind, was major. We can't show what would have happened if you really did the right thing, because it never happen. It would be only speculation that is not a goal. The events and knowledge's speaks for its self.

I will continue to help you work all this information through your thought or dream system in the coming week. I believe we have covered a lot of ground today. In fact, we have covered more material than I had planned. You again need to relate your abilities to these events. How you could have completed them effectively. How to view the results differently are to be learning lessons as well as not getting lost in a victim status or punishment. The only true punishment were the lessons for your evolution that did not happen, so you have to keep trying different methods in different life times until you do. Remember there was lot of learning going on regardless of the outcome of the events should you understand both sides of the activity and come to positive co-creative resolve. By getting the new resolves organized and down loading then into the soul level to replace the restrictive miss-information with corrective balance information of those events, your freedom, and your healing of yesterday continues to grow" were Kevin's final words

I was back and aware that Roger again was handing me the tape of this session. "When I signed on to this activity with you, I never realized that these sessions would help me solve questions that I have been trying to get straight in my head also. I am glad we are working together and I will see you next week," Roger stated as he started out the room and through the house. I looked at the clock. I realize we went over and he must be late for another appointment.

At the door, we embraced and I walked away without saying a word after I put on my rain gear and shoes. The path was getting slippery; I was not doing well walking because my mind was racing with what I have heard. The day stayed the same as I came here; raining was still coming down in buckets with increase wind to assist in splashing it around. The river water was very choppy even thought there were no other crafts on the river. I wish this boat had a windshield to keep the rain from blowing in my face. It was great sight to see the dock and Johnny, in rain gear, was there to help tie up the boat and cover it. We ran laughing back into his work place. I was in great need of coffee to warm up and thankful he was there to help me. I forgot gloves and my hands were cold from the rain, and they hurt as I placed them around the cup to warm up. Johnny knew where I was and he did not ask any questions. Still he could sense that there were slow but permanent changes in me, because I demonstrated a greater command with what I was saying. There have been examples of some compromises in the development of this project. My goals at first were for all of us to be involved but I only let them get involved within their abilities, with room to expand their skills as they could do so.

As we were sitting at table over-looking the river trying to warm up from the damp chill, I asked, "Johnny, your face is way off in space."

Johnny looked back at me as if he was waking up, "No! I keep kicking or pinching myself to see if I am awake. The whole world of mine is far greater than I could ever imagine. My life is just one continual surprise I am never bored. Out of all of this, we are able to live with a mixture of people successfully. I first thought this project might be an impossible dream, but with all our impute it is real. I love the support system we are developing with each other. If you create an environment that is supportive, those who can resonate with it will come. My mind keeps wandering all over the place; I just want you to know you are the best thing that has happen to all of us." He finishes gratefully.

"How do I answer that? I guess only a thank you." I replied. "I better get home to see what your sister, my wife, has planned for us. I will see you later. Maybe for dinner, for I think she is trying to get all intern time possible so we will be free for Christmas. By the way, we need to get everyone living here and the business owners to decide do we want to decorate for the holidays to complement or just do free style for Christmas Season. It is only short time away. I will have Barbara send out flyer for the meeting and see what happens. This is not getting me out the door. See you later." As I got up, put on Johnny's rain gear again, made a beeline to the front door to splash and dash home.

Jenny was in the kitchen preparing supper and was surprise to see her husband home so early. "I have called the school and they informed me I can keep the same schedule for a couple more weeks. However, today I have to go in early, to be there by four. We just got off the phone. So if you don't mind, I going to refrigerate what I have made so far and have it tomorrow for late a lunch with you." She came around the cooking island and we did my enjoyable past time of little necking and hugging. As she pulled away, "it will be 6 to 11 and my normal shift from 11 to 7. I am sure I can do this because you don't make me feel guilt if I don't spend time with you. I'm glad I married not only a very understanding husband, but one who is great lover and allows me to make time for him whenever possible." With those words, she took off and that was a cue that this is one of those times.

At 4 p.m., I put on rain gear and went up to the office to check on what work that was waiting for me. I informed Barbara about sending a flyer to everyone on the project about Holiday Season lighting. She told me one of the office staff was already working on the design. It will be completed and sent out to everyone on Monday. Don't look shocked by her reply stated Barbara. Johnny had already called to inform me what you were considering. He is just being helpful.

By five, everyone was packed up and gone. I stayed around for another hour since I did not want to go home yet. I devoted time looking at the future diagrams in the conference room of what is done and what is being done. I heard a rapping on the door and I went to see who it was. There stood Steve and he motioned he wanted to talk with me about few things, if I had time.

I opened the door and said, "Welcome! What can I do or help you with?"

"I saw there were lights in the office and I suspected it was you. As you can see we were rained out today, and the weather report is cloudy for Saturday and Sunday. The subcontractors wanted to know if they could work over the weekend to keep this project moving. They are working on bid bases, so the hourly rate does not apply on weekends. They want to put up some of the framing because the footers are cured. We tested them to be sure and they passed the test. They also want to be able to get the plywood siding on along with the roof and shingled. We need to dry the interior out before we finish the rest of the interior framing. This action will allow us to keep moving between these rainy down days. We really have a great group of supportive subs. In addition, they want to bid on building those building across the road. There are no secrets around here." Steve was all business with me when it is business.

"I have not a problem because they have commercial contractor's licenses. That project will not start until most of the condos and motel are completed. This 2nd phases condo operation, they are working on now, does not interfere with the 1ˢᵗ phases residence. As far as activity at Marina, it is almost to a slow halt. I expect there will be deliveries and whatever. I am so glad you are running this part of the operation so these are not my problems to solve."

"By the way, this coming week, I am going to have a meeting with some investors from Washington State, across the river. I would like you to sit in with me. It appears they want to do something similar to what we are doing here. They want to know if I would consider overseeing its development. I was think maybe we could form a company with everyone to do this kind of development work. It is something for you to consider. Even if you see something wrong with their offer, we could think about developing a company where we could get our subs involved too." I was kind of thinking out loud.

Steve stated, "I will notify the subs to come in tomorrow and Sunday. If the ground isn't too wet on Sunday, we can do some earth work for the next units to be built. The long-range weather is we will have spotty rain for the next month. If that true, we can get a lot of work done before Christmas. About the meeting, I would love to sit in; just let me know, but I have to get because my wife will be holding dinner for me. Thanks again for your offer. Talk with you on Monday." Steve opened the door and was on his way.

Well! I think I need to get some things working in my life to satisfying the drives that keep me on the edge. I can goof off for short time, but the internal part of me keeps screaming, "Feed me, feed me". There is no rest until I am in that creative mode. I need to check to see if everything is secure and I think I'll wonder down to Johnny's for dinner. I should go home to pick up his rain gear he lent me first. Have dinner then and go home early. I need to listen to the tapes again and begin doing more of my emotional and mental work completed. I have a dead line ahead of me and I need that stimulation to keep going regardless of how I feel. There are no excuses not to face the music!

After a quick dinner, I went home, after a shower, I retreated to my third floor office. I relaxed out in my favorite chair to listen to this week's tape. I keep taking notes on what course of action I need to focus on most of all. This way I can give myself permission to be free of guilt, pain, and stupidity of my past lives' events. Those negative activities keep restricting my growth and causes stagnation in my present life, which is worse.

Jenny arrives home. Her first thought was she would find her husband out of bed. The house was quiet as tomb. She thought,' "maybe he is gone". She journeyed through the home and entering his study to find her man fast asleep still in the chair. She went over and gave him her usual soft kiss but this time his eyes did not open. She just stood there looking at him. She had the sudden thought just leave him alone for now. She needed to get something to eat and ready for bed. She decided to do another 5 to 12 tonight to shrink away those hours.

Upon her entering our bed room she found that he had gotten up and was dressed for the day.

I asked, "You are home already?" as I looked at the clock. "Boy! I must have been dead. I found myself in the chair where I sat down about 9 last night and here it is nine, that 12 hours sleep and I did not get up once. I am a little stiff sleeping in this lounge chair, but I will survive. Well! How was your day, should say night?"

"Believe it or not, it was quiet. Even the time I spent doing PA duty, it was slow. I guess it is slow cycle. My crystal ball will not give me any hints about what to expect, but now I need to get to bed and sleep. I still have a 5 to 11 tonight. I want to have dinner with you before I go to work. Therefore, I am off to dream world and I hope you have pleasant day, but be home by three so we can have dinner or lunch together. The main part is together." Her voice drifted off as she went into the bathroom and she started the shower running.

I grabbed something for quick breakfast and up to new construction site to see what is happening. The morning was taken up with a couple of people looking at our condo operation. We still had a model to show them the possibilities; we give them a packet about whom we are, and what we are trying to develop here. If they are still interested, they need to bring in their financial information to insure they are able to afford living here. We keep stressing we are selling a life style, not just a condos.

At 3 o'clock I beeline it home so we can spend an hour or so together which seems to be the ritual now and will continue for a while. This activity seems to make our relationship stronger. When I did not have the answer to her question about what is going on with her that started in Spain, she accepted my reply that the answer was forth coming.

Sunday came and went with a blur.

CHAPTER 28

The investor from Washington called Monday morning early to inform me they decided that they would meet with me on Wednesday afternoon. They would be here for lunch and then we could do a small tour of the place and finish up with a meeting in my conference room. I had informed them that my project builder would be sitting in on the conversation to assist us with ideas as to its feasibility.

We have golf carts. We use to chauffer people around in who are looking over our Condos or are interested in buying. On Wednesday, when the gentlemen showed up, we had the carts ready to go. Wednesday came on so fast. They were here at 10:30 a.m. Sidney Olsen was first to introduce himself, then he extended the introduction to Daniel Shinn and Alan Lind. I, then, introduce Steve Holland, my contractor, which resulted with handshakes all around and me. I pointed to the golf carts to begin to show them around our facility. Steve and I did the driving; we went to the model first to show what we were selling in the condo business. After that tour, we drove around the streets explaining about the lay out and through the park area to show our retaining wall to prevent erosion. We were at the restaurant just the before noon hour. We took them first around the deck that circled the restaurant and then entered to be seated in my usual corner to have the best view of the river activity. Sometimes I find these meals "getting to know each other" a little boring because I want to get to the point of why we are meeting. I usually have meal afterwards, but this time it did not work as possibility. We killed about an hour and we went over to my office and conference room. Barbara had it all set up with refreshments. After everyone was settled in, I began the meeting with a few questions to assist in getting to the point of this exploratory meeting.

"Is what you are proposing is strictly for making a profit? Is it a development where you sell out enough to get your money back? Are you to lease the business to keep getting a return on your investment? Is it to be a cash flow as we have here? Or is it a combination of all of the above?" I laid out my beginning questions; exploring their intentions.

Sidney rolled out plans for two locations and placed them on our cork board for everyone to view. "The one near Longview, we were considering apartment, housing mixtures with harbor/marina, restaurant, and possible boat repair. We would only be operating the apartments and leasing the restaurant and the marina. The one nearer to Vancouver, we were considering, apartments, condos, and restaurant. The problem with Vancouver; we don't have an enough area between the channel and the land to consider a marina. We have a mixture of investors; some want their money back with profit as soon as possible, some a little of both and those who want a steady income from their investment. We have sufficient funds for one, not both. We need someone outside of us to look at this and give us some guidance and a possibility of being the general contractor for the project we decide to go for now. We have options on both sites. We could build one and then the other. We are at a point that is confusing and frustrating because everyone will not come to an acceptable decision among the investors."

Steve got up and took a closer look at both projects. I looked puzzled for moment, and then I said, "I take it this is your baby. Which one of them do you want to do and why? You need to exclude the investors' interest at this point. We can always get investors when we finally come up with plan that works for the project; that is no problem."

Alan injected the basic problem, "we have these friends that are would be investors and want to be part of our dream. They are a mixture from each of us. They keep adding confusion and throwing their weight around at every meeting. I keep telling Sidney we need help, before this whole program goes down the tube."

"First I will tell you, having friends as investors are worst business arrangement. In most cases, it doesn't work unless you really know them and this is "fun money" they are lending to you. If they lose it, it is no big deal and they want nothing to do with the operation of the project. They would be strictly hands off investors who want to help you develop your dream.

Second, if this is a well-conceived project, we can get investors. You need the support of the government agencies so they won't prevent it. A project manager to keep the goal moving is major. What does the project looking like with that just the three of you and your combined dream? Maybe I should have started with that last statement as a number one goal." I stated in an almost demanding tone, to cut through the dream, confusion, not being grounded, and whatever else that destroy this project. Their visual design for the land has great potential. This whole area on the river has great potential. It has be developed right to make it a livable program.

Steve turned to look at the group as I finished my statement and he stated, "I like both designs. I need to know a couple pieces of information. The Longview Project, could the area support something like this? There might need to be considering some different mixes to make it work. The Vancouver project, is little off the main drag and without a marina, it might not work. There is main highway nearby for people who want to live by the water and work in the city. I think to make it happen; we should give it more exploration with some of the guidelines you used, Alex. One more thing, I know this part of the river. Would you have any chance to obtain the land west of your propose project? There may be just enough water space for a marina."

Sidney looked at both of us and replied "I been so frustrated with this and I'm glad I came to talk with you. I thought I had all my ducks in a row, but now it seems like I don't. We need to go back to our basic plan design. We need to remove all the suggestions or restrictions from our friends. Then to complete the fact-finding we would need to consider if what we want to do is possible. Would you consider meeting with us again soon? I know of your reputations in the financial world. I know you are not active in at the present time, and what you have done here with funds you have. I want to hire you as consultant. What do you say?"

"I would like to see what you come up with at the next meeting. I also need to develop more activity to keep life interesting for me. I will have my office manager give you material you need to research before the next meeting. She would also start you on retainer fee because of your offer. This activity is purely business. When you keep it business, success usually follows. Are we done at this point? We need to keep in touch to keep this moving to either build or leave. [Our guest nodded their head in affirmative] I will take you to meet Barbara and she will set up the next meeting for you. I know this can work if we clear the deck for action and follow the course as close as possible."

We again began the hand shaking around and I showed them to Barbara to complete our verbal commitment.

Steve stayed there, so it gave me reason to go back to conference room to see what was on his mind. He was still standing looking at their project maps they left for us to keep looking over. "Well! Steve, what do you think?"

"If they do a few corrections on the Longview project, I believe they will have a successful operation. It appears their friends wanted them to build the place for their benefit, even if they failed, their friends would have their ideal place to live. I know a few of the people over there and the area is ready for development like this. The people driving always to the coast or trying to find something on the river for personal retreat is a hardship. Keeping the price right, this could sell out fast because there is really no competition on that side yet." Steve's words just flowed as thinking as to what are up and down side to this.

"I believe we will see them again. Business is business when it comes to a large project like this. I hope they can straighten out their act. We also can have something more creative to do" were my closing words.

With that statement, Steve opened the door and stated he would talk with me later. He had to see how the boys were doing today to keep us on schedule. This left me with my mind confused since I now have something cooking on the back burner to keep me busy in the future. I looked out the window as my wife honked her horn and drove out to her internship and work for the day. Another day to find something for me to do by myself, but it is not forever.

The evening finds me at home, early soaking in sea salt while listening to the tapes of past session. I keep a voice tape machine available when I am bathing to record my thoughts to speed up healing process I am working on. There always seems to be lot more on the tapes than I remembered during the sessions. Was my mind to busy processing, that I missed some of this? Who knows? I don't how Roger is able some times to record Kevin's conversation with me on the tapes from time to time, but sure helps me. After an hour, I would get out, dry off, and dress in a bathrobe and retreat to my office. I found myself re-listening to my thoughts I glean from the taped sessions. With the sea salt helping to drain off the negative energy that existed during those activities, there are less emotional stress. This activity allows you to visualize the action that would be like watching a movie of those events without the emotions. I can now deal with the event without all the painful emotions that distorts what is happening. I am able to see the causes, effects, and sometimes the reasons but best of all resolve them which sets me free from those nightmares. I am getting so relaxed; I had better head for bed so Jenny will not find me again a sleep in this chair when she comes home.

The rest of the week was dry enough for Steve to move ahead with the construction work. The office work and thinking about the ups and downs of the Longview project played in my head when I had nothing else to occupy my time. I don't have appointment with Roger, some ways it is a blessing to take a rest from it. Still parts of me want to keep charging forward with it to get my freedom.

Saturday morning after Jenny got off work, we had breakfast at the restaurant. We needed make plans for the weekend. We have time to discuss how our relationship generally. She informed me that she was taking Saturday night off, so I had better find something great courting activity. She also covered that she was going to work on Sunday from 4 p.m. to 10 p.m. putting in her intern hours. That way she can sleep in if her loving husband should keep her out after midnight tonight. Before I could get into answering or suggesting options, we started to be inundated with friends joining us at our table. I should have known better to bring her here; I will not make that mistake next weekend.

Jenny went home to sleep. I stayed to continue the conversations with those who had joined us. By lunchtime, the crowd continued to shift from breakfast to lunch. I told them I have to beg off for I needed to get reservations for this evening. My wife and I are going courting. After a few phone calls, the evening was set in motion.

I told Jenny to dress casual and we were off for an evening of surprises. I would not give a hint as to what we were going to do but got her attention as we traveled Route 30, then 84 and on to 205 going south. She kept asking questions, but I would not give up the secret. I got off at Clackamas Town Center and pulled into the plaza's parking lot. She started to give me that look and I put my fingers to my lips to be quiet. We walked into the Center. She just kept looking at me from time to time until I got us to the ice skating rink. Her eyes lit up, "You mean you are taking me ice skating? I have not done that in years. It was one of my most favorite sports, but how did you know?"

"As if you did not know that your brother can not keep a secret. That is why you are dress casual and I thought you might enjoy a couple hours before we go on to the next activity" was my self-confident statement.

Jenny couldn't get her rented skates on fast enough and she was out on the ice. You would have never known it has been about 5 year ago was her last time on ice. I took my time getting on my skates because truly, I am an amateur. I never had the strong ankles to do this sport. The stalling lasted about an hour and then the truth was known. Jenny couldn't stop laughing at how I was making it look like a very hard task. After half an hour, she took mercy on me, sent me to the benches, and enjoyed the remaining time being free. Time was up, she came charging in and being out of breath, "you are so special! What an enjoyable time. Thank you; of course, the night is not over. What next?"

I had to hurry her along because the next place we had reservations at nine. We flew up 205, off on Marine Drive and as we pass the airport. I pulled off, saying we have 2 hours to watch the planes land and take off. She gave me that look again, that this will not fly. I could hardly hold back the laughter as I pulled back on the Drive. Down road a short distance, we entered Salty's on the Columbia River parking lot, I parked the car, got out, open her door, and ushered her into the restaurant. We were greeted as we entered the restaurant. The headwaiter showed us to our table where we had a great view of the river and the bandstand. As we past the marquee Jenny saw they had blue grass music tonight, she had a collection of CDs with this kind of music, and she squeezed my hand with great delight. Their seafood meals are the best in town. We had their lobster thermador for a main course that is all I remember out of the delicious full 5-course meal that lasted while we were there. We were just bubbling away at each other through the entire meal. Then the band came on, Jenny would only let me talk during intermission. We did some dancing to the music but mainly she just enjoyed listening and watching them perform. At 1 a.m., we retired to our car, Jenny's head was on my shoulder as much as the restraining strap would allow. We were completely quiet all the way home and as I pulled in the garage, she came alive "your Cinderella is totally wiped out. Sorry about that, going to leave you wanting at the door." As she got out of the car, running into the house, closing the door, laughing all the way as I was trying to catch her. We did have some playful time together before the lights went out and a peaceful sleep drowned us.

The next morning, the smell of a fully cooked breakfast filled the whole house and it jerked me awake. My wife was nowhere in sight. The mystery is solved. I went to get up and there was my wife coming out of the bathroom dressed for the day. "Well! It smells like you were busy while I was bathing and getting ready for the day".

I looked at her with surprised look "It was not me. I thought you were doing the cooking as surprise for me, since I am such a caring husband."

Jenny threw her hairbrush at me, missing me by a mile and charged down stairs laughing. If she did not do the cooking, I had better not charge down stairs in my buff. Who knows who is down there?

I quickly cleaned up. I dressed in casual clothes like Jenny, and went on adventure. Who to see whom or what caused the mystery of the smell of breakfast. Coming down stairs, I can hear voices in the dining room and lots of laugher. The sparkly sounds of laugher masked the voices so I was not sure who was there. As I entered the dining room, there was Johnny and Judy hooting up with laughter to my surprise. "Well! What is this?" I asked.

"Judy and I decided that since your wife wanted a courting night out, that maybe you needed some help with making breakfast. You are not as young as you used to be" laughter filled the air, which was infectious.

"Speak for yourself, my young friend, I was up for the task dealt to me last night and ready for any adventure today. That is, after I enjoy your feast." I tried to be as light with my words as possible.

"Action speaks louder than words. Who was first down stairs to investigate who was cooking the meal, I ask you. The answer was my sister. Who finally found themselves coming down a lot later to part take of the meal? The answer was you. I am not saying anything, again I rest my case" were smart remarks of Johnny's which brought out another round of laughter.

The horse play on words finally stopped and we all enjoyed the full breakfast, cleaned up the table, and were informed by Johnny that we were going with them for the day. The weather was great over at the coast and little beach walking and shopping at Cannon Beach would be great, with dinner in Astoria before coming home. It would be a day for the in-laws to strengthen our relationship and a change of pace which is good for everyone. We all piled into Johnny's SUV and we were off.

The day just sparkled with the pure pleasure of each other's company. The ocean was soft and gentle. The sea gulls were screaming at something, but who knows. They are always begging for food. If we had a crust of bread, we would attract an army of them. The gentle warm breeze danced across the sand making new designs on the beach. For a Sunday, there weren't many people out walking or shopping. We found more art items to fill our home. Johnny found a few metal art pieces that he wanted for his business decorations. I thought we would never run out of conversation as we shifted pairs all day long. I don't know why the beach sea air makes you feel little sticky but refreshed at the same time. The drive up to Astoria was pleasant when you can drive slow enough to enjoy the scenery. The bay restaurant many vacant tables so we had a window table. We are able to see where the ocean and the Columbia River meet. I never get tired of looking at the river, its traffic, birds; the list is endless. We could also see the bridge over the Columbia River from our table, which presented deeper depth to the view. Our meal was very pleasant with each ordering something different in seafood and sharing the taste with each other. The final leg of the drive home, Jenny and I finally have to share the back seat to do some cuddling. I am glad Jenny likes to cuddle, because I never had the pleasure as much as

I have had with her. I never understood the unspoken pleasure that comes from such activity. I sure do now. The pleasant soft CD romantic music filling the air added to the special family journey. Upon arriving home it was getting late, so with quick hugs and they were gone leaving us standing at our gate at the back door. I guess this is what it feels like; where love lives. We retired to bed. Little was said but much was experienced. Another day spent building bridges between us and our hearts were fed.

I left Jenny to sleep in because we were back to the schedule of working to get everything completed before the Christmas Season. Sunday was the time for me to catch up on loose ends that were on my 'to do list' for the week.

Monday I start the routine all over again by reporting to work at 8:30 and Barbara had coffee and rolls available for the staff and customers. After a long drink of her coffee, I was totally awake and ready for action. Steve started the day by asking if it was okay to start building down to the river. He was checking to determine how the sales were going to meet the needs of the demand. The back row of condos that they were working on are hot sales items now. The family section was beginning to make more demands, so I guess we need to work on that next. Should the weather hold for building, we might have most of the units covered to have work for the crews on the inside? We do the basics on interior and we wait to see what the home buyer would want to customize the rest of the interior to their taste. It is surprising when you see the unified appearance on the outside but once you enter the door, I don't believe there is one of those condos that look alike. The baring walls are the same, but other ones are different. This system seems to make everyone one happy to appear the same on the outside but inside we are different.

Our motel will or should be ready by May 1ˢᵗ. That will be on scheduled for the tourist season. The property across the road, we still have some meeting to determine the appearance of the outside of the station and grocery buildings. We are moving along with very little problems because all the subs are working together, cutting waste, and completion time.

Barbara put a note on my desk; it appears the complex has voted totally on complement decorations for the holidays with red and silver dominate colors. That will give us a lovely feeling of connection. I will have "the staff" give us a couple designs for to carry out our theme. We will need to develop a scrapbook for each year.

The phone rang and it was Jenny, who was requesting my presence. She was at the restaurant for late lunch because she did not feel like cooking today. That was great as far as I am concerned. I hustled on down and joined her at our usual table by the window and for some strange reason no one joined us today. We had a couple of hours just planning the week, which really boiled down to the same thing that happened last week and the week before, and the week before that. Still, it will be over soon. I can feel Jenny itching to have a clinic in this project or across the street to serve the people of this area. I think Steve has it designed to be across the road to best serve the community and I don't blame her for wanting her dream.

CHAPTER 29

The week was just a blur doing the usual busy work and preparing to work on whatever projects I can get going. Oh! There was a break in the week, the Ra, my ex-wife's yacht, anchored off the restaurant. She and her partner came ashore to look over our place. They stopped to lunch at the restaurant knowing that would flush me out from wherever I was to come and see what she wanted. Johnny called me at my office, to inform me who was here if I did not already know. I went immediately down to the restaurant to test my strengths and check if I had any weakness that I needed to repair. We spent a pleasant hour, even though she worked all her usual zingers at me. Lizzie, her partner, got a kick out of seeing that Marian couldn't get rise out of me regardless how she played her words. I kept feeling nothing in her words that affected me. Again that felt strange when I realized I had acquest to her demands for over 4,000 years.

She is now just another stranger passing through my life. It must have been very disappointing for her to realize the tie was truly broken and her power over me was gone forever. She told me that she had been checking into my financial needs for this project and knew I was in great shape. She had nothing to get her hooks into. She began gloating about all her successes and growth and what I was missing. To think you could be playing with many millions and having the luxury life of creating more than what you have now, "but you chose not wisely". Try as she might, all her efforts were impotent. Finally, she realizing this adventure was frustrating her beyond words. As always, she quickly dismissed further conversation and was on her way with her lackey in tow.

Johnny and Ol' Johnson came to my table to join me. We all were watching her motor out, climb aboard and sail away with her back to us as her last gesture of rejection. The only thought I had was I hope she pays the staff well because they earn it with her.

"Well! How does it feel to know you are the winner for sure?" Johnny finally blurted out to break the silence.

I looked at both of them for few minutes and said, "That was the greatest holiday gift I could have ever had. I feel nothing for her but lots of pity and yet I am not sure I have that for her now. How ridiculous she was in her controlling behavior. I am so glad that nightmare is over forever. In addition, I have to say, you all helped make it happen. So let's celebrate and have the waitress bring another round of coffee" as I broke out in an almost uncontrollable laughter of relief. They just sat there laughing along with me. I looked up and there was Jenny walking through the place.

As she reached the table, she asked "what was all that about. I looked out when I got up and there was the "Ra" parked out there on river. I know she must have come to visit and was holding court in here."

"You got that right, she was trying to hold court, and even her court jester could not be more amused by her failure to dominate or control anything" was my quick reply.

Johnny and Ol' Johnson both chimed in with, "you missed a great performance". Johnny continued with "a "has been" trying to make a grand old last-ditch effort to control. It was better than any soap opera and it appears that will be last of that old girl." Then they broke out laughing.

We spent over an hour just hooting and laughing over her performance and the pleasure of knowing I am free. By Jenny's expression, she knew her husband was truly free from her and past experiences that ripped up his physical body. That made my day for me. It wasn't long until everyone who had experience with Marian and her relationship with me was informed of what happen.

Nights, I would listen to the tapes either soaking or sitting in my chair readjusting my perceptions of the events, which released my stress and energy of the events from my soul and uncolored the events in this lifetime. There are no words in my present vocabulary to express the release and freedom that results from resolving the past negative karmic events, not to mention the reality of daily living. It takes on a positive creative nature, which makes my life more enjoyable, for truly I am now living in the present. Most of all, I have the entitlement that I thought I could never have, which allows me to be a co-creator with my own life plan and my required evolution.

There was the usual Thursday night conscious and subconscious mental house cleaning, which sometimes raised havoc with my physical body. That is the price of undoing the self-destructive activity of past lives. I could say of my past errors, they were all accidents; however taking ownership of them makes it easier to clean them out. I can't be thankful enough for all help Roger has made possible for me to obtain my freedom. I have to do the corrections myself. He just helped me go there to make it possible.

There are times now, when I meet people; their behavior informs me that I am witnessing something from their past, and sometimes it's a very distant past. Again, I must remember I am a witness and not get involved. It is not my job to do anything unless my teacher informs me that I need to interact. My involvement, always under my spirit teacher's directions, is to insure a healthy outcome. As we walk it through the activity, I am able to make all the corrections in the process. The main point is that they, spirit teacher, do it under a very low, low profile approach. The person still has a choice to do something about it or not.

Here it is Friday morning, after another troubled night sleeping, but I am up and out of the house as usual. I had breakfast with Johnny to prepare for my boat trip up to Roger's house on the river. The boat ride was influenced by clouds with a cool wind, or I should say cold breeze coming off the high country, blowing it way down the Columbia River gorge, and out to the sea. I am dressed for it except for my face, which is rosy red from cold breeze beating on it. The faster I drove the boat; it just seemed to be much colder. Happy was I to see Roger's dock and on the porch he was with that hot cup of tea. I did not waste time tying up the boat and running up the path to get some warmth. Roger could see that I needed what he had in his hand, and he quickly passed it to me. I could not get the tea in my mouth fast enough. I even rubbed the cup against my cold cheeks to help reduce the sting from the cold. After few seconds, Roger opens the door,

I removed my winter gear, shoes and we did our usual parade to his office. He gave me a few minutes to get my composure and to settle down. "Roger, I think winter is coming on quickly, if today is measuring stick. Next week, I think I will wear ski mask to protect the face. I know I can take the long way by driving, but I still love the water and the river regardless. Soon, within a month, they will start having the boats decorated with lights for the holiday seasons cruising around Portland. They are one of my favorite holiday season enjoyments. I try to see them at least twice during the season. I think I have chattered enough and I am ready for work," I stated as I sat in my chair to begin. Roger just started his mesmerizing count down and I was gone.

Kevin was waiting for me as usual. Kevin stated we were going to do some spot reference of different lives to allow me to explore them further during this week when you were meditate with the tape of this session. We are just going to observe different lives, what happened or talk about the events; they are not major but they all are necessary in the healing of your heart. Your basic need to accept love, demonstrate it, and the development of unconditional love, which is a major part of living on this planet. Love feelings have been the hardest one for you. You have spent 2,000 years on this journey, trying to get to the feeling, knowing, and evolving concept of love. It is very important to understand that the formula of life is knowledge plus life experiences equal wisdom. With wisdom, you can control your evolution.

Let's begin, after being Abbott, you had enough being a monk. You lived in Bologna, Italy born to a wealthy family. Life was good until you were 17 when your parents forced you into loveless marriage for political reasons. You did sire two children, which you built your life around. After your parents died, and major part of their estate went to your older brother, and your wife grew tired of you. She had her lover, which you did not know, who helps to get rid of you and your children. You saw the children's throat cut before they purge out your eyes, so that was the last thing you saw. You were held in make shift prison for almost a year before your death. Your then ex-wife wanted you to suffer as you caused her to suffer in this seemingly long endless, loveless marriage. It was reported that you vanished and was declared dead. Short time after her lover married her, he found out how she could kill any love expression. He spent the rest of his life in a very controlling, vacant marriage. Nothing could ever pleased that woman and he found that out. The two of them were at war with each other for almost 20 years.

It was a horrible thing to do, kill your children and blind you. That crime payment is still being worked out even now. Therefore, you see what goes around comes around. You could never punish them more than what they did to themselves. Your children forgave them long ago. You can too.

The lessons could have been learned, such as how to deal with this marriage more effectively on creative, positive side where it could result in a positive solution or dissolution. We have checked into some of the events that went wrong in the marriage. Because it was prearranged, and in your defiance, you never realized that others were victims. Your behavior, which was supported by the culture of the time, justified your indifference and sometimes your malice drove her into rebelliousness for her own survival. You know the rest of the story.

However, if you had applied more diplomacy and consideration, who knows what the outcome would have been. Sometimes that indifference and malice came out from your soul when you interacted with your ex-wife, Marian. She did not know what caused it, so she dug in deeper to control you. Maybe that was a good thing, since it heated up all the issues to assist you in bring about the quest that obtain your freedom from her forever. I wonder could there been less destructive way to resolve that quest of freedom from her? We can review it more objectively, if this burden has been removed and you are free to see events as events, not colored by history of limitations.

Next, live time, you are in Venice and again living a very successful business life. You are able to apply your own natural talents as an achiever, arranger, and strategic themes to embellish your life without the aid of the "keeper". In fact, the reason you don't want to ever visit Venice because you were found floating in the canal with knife in your back from unknown assailant. As hard as you have tried, you could not find the answer to what caused that death. We had hard time to because the "keeper" was able to make it almost invisible. With you breaking the tie with him [your x-wife, Marian], we were able to discover what happen. You were successful in everything you were doing. The "keeper" was also alive during that time and his star was rising as fast as yours was in that community. He wanted you to back down and support him. You challenged him. He could not let that happen, you need to learn your place. Therefore, you were dead again for not supporting him. You have always thought it was maybe someone in the family, but it wasn't. You are here on earth, when he is here, you are to cater to him and his needs. Nothing can come ahead of his needs regardless of cost. He also realized you were getting stronger; he needed to break your will to keep you in your submissive role to him. I think now we can all let go of this mystery. In addition, you don't need him to be successful, you proved that, and you had whatever you want out of life in that lifetime. You can achieve it on your own. Here again, if you listened to us, used diplomacy, and what difference does it make in your life if he was number one. I ask you, was the loss of it all for to be top dog, worth it? You had more you could have learned, developed greater connection in your family, and the list goes on and on. Free choice, you did what you wanted and you will show him at all cost. In addition, you did, you were dead again. You decide now what you lost.

We went through all the stuff relating to your family, which came out of 1046. Of course, he again was there with you at that time as advisor. He was getting wealthy and had influences so you were no threat to him. You allowed him to live in your duchy where he was protected and he could do as he pleases. The only problem we found was he was one that really broke the love bond between you and your wife at that time. That true love is why you could help her heal her damage soul in this lifetime. During that lifetime, he again filled up your life with others, as many as you wanted. You indulge because your personal love life was destroyed. He had the vision he was in control and he was. You have resolved most of the karma in this one, still there are fallouts that are continually adjusting in your new marriage.

1210 or there about, you again married, authority, power, all the experiences to strengthen your innate talents. Then your children got greedy, they wanted to rule, and you were not about to allow that to happen because they were to self serving. They tried "bush whack" twice when you were traveling between estates. Their plan failed when you escaped. Try as they might to get rid of you or force you to let them rule some areas you controlled. You loved them still in spite of themselves. You died a natural death. They didn't rule long because of their own character fault. You truly did come into your own that lifetime. Now you are truly ready to find a way to break that "forever bond" with the "keeper". Also got a better grip on this love item, marriage and family relationships, which was good start in the right direction.

We are about ready to explore what happen in Spain that has you and your wife on edge. You more than her, because what happen to you then. I really want you to prepare for this. To prepare, I want you to listen to the tapes of this time as often as you can, because we will be injecting more information to you with each event to deepen your understanding and strengthen your options. Sea salt baths are necessary. I am also requesting that you have someone do "Rolfing" on you. That is very deep body massage to help you release any memories that are buried in the cells of your body. Sometimes, every part of your mental knowledge understands the process of releasing. Still the physical cells where the emotional activity is buried, they have to release the stress and energy connected with mental turmoil. Sometimes, the new body cells are reproduction of what was buried there; therefore, this Rolfing including aromatherapy should help break and give you the release you need. I have to tell you, this therapy will make you aware of every muscle in your body. I know the first session you will not feel any changes, but you will come alive. Finally, we may have to skip next week; there is a project that still up in the air. We will try to work around it. We love you and keep doing what you are doing it is working for you.

Roger was surprised that I came out of that session in such a short time. He reaches around for the tape for me while he looked at me. "I know the next deep issue will be last that we will have to do. I suspect it will take two or more sessions. I will have to call you later in next week to see what is going on with me if I am free for next Friday. Because when we get this rolling, we need to see it to the end. Therefore, my friend, it soon will be over. By the way, I have had Rolfing done to me; it may hurt when they are doing it, but man what great flexibility afterward. Deep muscle massage is good, but what you have and I had, you need the full deal. I will walk you to your boat; I need to stretch my legs a little. "

We journey through the house; he grabbed his foul weather gear, shoes and was putting it on while I was doing the same thing. The wind was picking up, but it will be at my back this time. Roger helped me untie my boat and shoved me off. The motor fired up on the first try and I was off. The wind seemed to be pushing me as faster than the motor was driving me over the water. I looked over my shoulder to wave goodbye but he was already on his way back to the house. It seemed like I just got in the boat and I was at our dock tying up. At the dock, I was busy putting on the cover and locking her down. When that was done, I ran into the restaurant to get out of the bitter cold wind and maybe hot lunch to heat up my bone.

I don't know where all these people come from, but Johnny's restaurant always seems to have almost a full house. I was invited to join a few of my neighbors at their table. As I walked over, I wondering what is this all about.

Dennis who lives over back of me was first to greet me as I sat down. Randy greeted me along with Jerry and Jeffery. I asked, "Is this a holiday or what? This is Friday is it not? You all have the day off?"

Randy spoke first "we had scheduled to have golf day. You can see how the weather turned cruel since 9 a.m. The weatherman reported that it could be cloudy but usual fall day. I swear, with all the equipment they have to determine what is going to happen, they miss it more than they hit it. Oh! Yes I have to agree when we have those continual sunny days during July, August, and September, they can call them."

Dennis buts in "this was going to be our last game for the season and a chance for me to win back a little of my financial losses in this past season. That is not going to happen today."

Jeffery jumped in "Dennis was the biggest loser, all of $5.50 for the season. Like that is going to break his bank."

They broke out with roaring laughter. I caught myself laughing with them. Just then, Jeff, the waiter, came over to take their order and to inquire if I needed a menu. I looked at the special, fish and chips. I ordered that with onion rings instead of chips and a light ale for me. As the rest of them formed a choir, sang out the same order. That caused another round of hooting and laughter. We spent the time just enjoying each other's company.

Finally, Jeffery after finishing his meal looked at me and said, "I hear you bought the land across the road. Is the rumor true? In addition, it's stated that a grocery and gas station was in the making. Furthermore, as long as I have your attention, there was a rumor that there could be clinic there also run by your wife. You now have the floor as to speak and we are all ears to your reply. By the way, that was the topic of conversation when you came in and was one of the reasons for inviting you to join us. So my friend, you can see we had agenda."

"First, you heard it right; we have bought the land across the road. As it looks now, we will have a gas station and grocery store plus a clinic. My wife will be finishing her PA degree in January. She has been putting many hours in to complete her internship before Christmas. After graduation, she will be working as a PA for the hospital until we get the clinic building built. There is nothing like that around here. This project will be nice fix with all we have going on around here. The rest of the land will be sold as homes and lots, and we will have about four or five different home designs for people to choose from. We are still not sure whether to do the designing or let the people who buy the lots decide the design. I am not sure, and the more I look at it, the more I would like to see some relationship to this project. We are really building a community. I think we have someone who is going to lease the grocery store he has lots of experience. All of this activity is going to be a good fit. I think we could have space over there to park vehicles that have their trailer attached. There is lot of fun things happening around here, is all I can say at this time."

Jerry spoke up "when I came here to see what this was all about, it seem like a dream. I read your objective for the place and it sound like something I wrote, a community I wanted. Since we have been here, it is all of that and more. I truly think the more. Although we are all different in many respects, we have found a place to blend successfully. There are rough edges from time to time, as there is in marriages." That brought out laugher from everyone. "I have to say, with everyone input from time to time has broaden every one approach to life. Even my work relationships have been more successful. I have place to practice because we have diversity at work but I had no idea of their cultural background or the standards they were raised by. I am using some of the technique I am learning here from our meetings. I haven't said it before, but I am saying it now, thank you for what we are enjoying so far."

"I have to say, we all around here feel the same way. If you want your privacy, that no big deal; if you want help, it is there. Barbara is a real gem the way she handle everything. The kids are enjoying it too because we are being real role model for them. I can't wait until the other part of this project is complete to see how all of this works out" replied Jeffery.

There was that all demonstrated silent approval of what has been said. There really wasn't nothing more to add at this time. The next hour just disappeared quickly. We all realization we need to get home before the wives will be wondering what happen to us. It is great to just walk home in minutes. As we parted from the group, we shouted out our final goodbyes.

As I walked through the door, Jenny met me at the foot of the stairs. "I saw you coming across the parking lot with the other neighbors. I wanted to welcome you home."

I put my arms around her, brought her up tight and was about to give her a lovers very warm passion kiss. Jenny bent her head back saying, "no you don't, I can feel where this could go, and I don't have time for playing around now. Besides, you shouldn't eat so many onion rings. First hand, they are great, second hand, well that is another story." I loosen my hold while she was talking. That was just enough she bolted away, laughing.

"Just get back here, woman, I am the man of the house and when you married me, there was that line that states you agreed to obey me" I said it in my cocky all together self.

From the kitchen rang out "don't you remember I had that deleted from my vows. Besides that onion breath is enough to turn off any flame of love, passion etc. etc."

I swaggered into the kitchen and these gentle words fell from my lips "there has never been a lover like me and women always swoon in my presence. So be careful, my love, some needy woman will carry me off and you will be truly sorry. Whether I have onions breathe or not, I am in great demand."

"You keep this up, I will open the door and invite them in" Jenny playing into his game.

Now where do I go for here, she called my bluff. "I will go up stairs brush my teeth and gargle so you will have fresh breath lover."

"Never mind, we have just run out of the little time I have left before I go to work. So my onion breathe lad, this all will have to wait until another time and another day, so there" Jenny stuck out her tongue as she walked out the door.

"Hey! Wait just a minute, it is only three. You have another hour before you need to go to work," I pleaded.

"Sorry, I must have forgotten, I need to be in early today because the hospital school is putting on an hour special training for us. Isn't that a great gift from them to do this for us? I am now blowing you a kiss from afar so until tomorrow, sweet dreams my love. I love you" flowed out of her lips as she duck to get into the car. In addition, in minutes, I watch taillights disappearing and I was alone again.

I love that woman more than life itself it seems. I pray what I will learn, in the next couple of weeks, gives me the freedom to love her without any reservations. I think I might as well retreat to my office upstairs since Barbara has not paged me. Before I do that, I need to call Barbara and have her find someone in Portland who can do Rolfing and aromatherapy on me next week. She has my schedule, so she can schedule a session for me. Now it is time for me to do more work on myself.

As I entered my third floor office, I put on my soft music CD, plugged in the tape, stretched on my couch this time and drift off to my healing space to continue my healing for freedom. As hours slip by again, I relived those times we talked about on the tape and found them less painful. I could feel the stress of those events losing their grip on me. However, somewhere in all of this, the lights went out and I was in deep dark hole. It is not a hole but a cave, no it is a room that is developing as the light began flooding every part of the space. There was my contract bride of Italy who we talked about this day, sitting at a table. She was asking me to join her. I walked over and sat down. She looked like she had not slept in weeks.

She began by telling me her story that she was miserable before I met her. For some reason she thought I could solve her problems of loneliness. She had envisions that she could be happy like I was when she first met me. However, a last, that turns out to be just a fantasy. Maybe there wasn't enough love you could have give or shared with me to vanquish my loneliness. My lover and finally a husband couldn't save me either. What a mess I created with you, our children for what? When they have shown me where everything went sour for me, it was truly my own fault too. You know I am still stuck trying to work myself out of this messy for the past 1200 years. The children forgave me quickly, damn if I know why. I now face you, who I had blinded, because you did not or would not help me. I kept you alive so you could feel the endless pain that I felt then. It was empty, hollow, and ever endless pain. You are the last person connected to this mess for me to deal with. Hell, I cannot really imagine you would ever forgive me. I have seen and experienced some what of the emotions you lived with those months with only the picture of your children's throat being cut before you were blinded. You had showered love on our children, I wanted you feel that shattering feeling of love loss the rest of your life, which was not that long. I truly don't deserve your forgiveness, but I am still asking if it is possible. I really need your help can you help me.

I could feel the acid taste in my mouth. My emotions were jumping all over inside me. I wanted to scream, yell, and maybe punch her out. Then as fast as it began, there was connectedness that was stronger than penned up "_____" which is beyond words I can express right now. Was the pity in her face? Was it, it doesn't matter anymore? I seem to lack the gentle words to express how I felt right now. I realized I too was very furious being sold to this woman for political reasons. How could my parents do such a thing? They must not have loved me because looked what they did.

[A life scene was interjected to me; I was observing my parents were in meeting with her parents. My parents were in a position that they had no other choice but accept my arranged marriage. They needed to protect "the family". Marriage would insure the protection they seek since they were unable to do so themselves. My family and their house, which means the family, were safe. In fact, that political alliance, keep my family out of harm's way as long as it existed.]

Then I was aware I was back in the room, facing this woman, who was for better word, appears bewildered. I have reached into my heart, remember what I have destroyed in my own life's journey, I said the following from the bottom of my soul. I not only forgive you, but in some ways, I thank you for

I am great person as result of this experience with you. Don't ask me how I know but I feel something that I never felt before in a space that was once a void within my heart. A void that just radiant the pain of nothingness that is beyond description of words. Now my heart has a gentle warm feelings of compassion and tolerance growing there.

As she looked at me, she now appears young like the first time I saw her. She was attractive and pleasant to the eye. My vision, when we were married, I never saw her like this because I was clouded with resentment of being sold off. Could I have helped her find her way back or rid herself of such antagonism? I will never know and I really don't want to know because it could not change what happen. We, she and I, can only now change how we view or feel about those experiences and what we can salvage out of it, to build better tomorrow. This has to be answer for me, for guilt of what was, would only destroy me in spinning wheel effect where there are no exits.

I reached across the table, took her hands in mine, and said something I never in all my life ever thought I would say. That is, "I am sorry I wasn't there for you. There is nothing I can do to change what has happen, but I love you now for making the effort and journey to be here with me. You have given me a freedom I am honestly been seeking and now I am giving you my unconditional love in the anticipation you can receive your liberation."

Now, her hands felt warm and very soft. Her face continual to looked like the girl at age when we were forced to this loveless marriage. Most of all, there was a glow, no, a warmth, no, a sense that all was right with our world right here, right now. The room began to glow with a mixture of rays of light that was dominated with a very light blue and loving pink I have never known before. The room faded away from me as I floated back to that dark hole which did not seem to change. My eyelids slowly fluttered open. The night had now graced the room and I was back. I laid there wanting not to shatter or disturb the mood that now embraced me. That emotional burden I carried all these years has evaporated and my heart is feeling the bliss I have never known. My eyelids felled together and sleep swept over me.

Some hours later, nature call brought me out of that most restful place I have never been before. I hurried to take care of business. On the journey, I witness the clock that told me that it was already after midnight. Well! I am up; I might as well shower and get to bed because tomorrow or I should say, today. I am not sure whether I am to pick to courting activity or is it Jenny's turn. I am not thinking straight, I just need to be to be about my showering, slipping into bed in my usual way and sleep. After I closed, my eyes and my last thoughts were "We shall look forward to un-encumbered love".

I woke up early and left the house so when Jenny comes home, she will get to sleep to be rested so we can have evening out of courting. As usual, the restaurant for breakfast was my first act of business. After killing an hour or two, I walked up to the office to see if there is anything there for me to do. I got there just when we had two separate families who wanted tour and some special time for a one on one conversation to address their questions and concerns. Patty, the clerk, took the older family and I was left with family that had two very busy young sons.

Samuel introduced his wife, Sara and their two sons Ralph and Herman, whose ages were 13 and 14 and I did the same. I loaded them into the golf cart and took them over to the model condo. After touring both floors with explanations that they had choices of designs and some differences in lay out. With the two boys, there would be choice of their joint bathroom. I got a buzz from Patty that she was ready to show her group the model condo. I round up my family and offer general tour of the place to vacate the model. It was a modest day, typical November day in Oregon. As we past the restaurant, their sons cried they were starving and needed food. The parents yield to their request and I left them there and would be back in 45 minutes to finish the tour and return to office to answer any of their questions.

I did not join them because sometimes they expect you will pick up the food tab, and I was not going to do that. I had a hunch they were just shopping around and killing time. I went back when Johnny called to say they were ready. I picked them up and we went back to the office. In the conference room, I addressed their questions and concerns. Just on cue, the wife looked at her watch, reminded her husband of their appointment and they would take our information with them. Samuel got up, shook my hand, and said he would get back with me later in the week. They were on their way. [As I expected, they never contacted or came back my hunch was right on]

Patty was luckier than I was she made a sale. She had started the paper work to close the deal. It appears that they had stopped by before because they had all their necessary paper work to qualify for purchasing a unit. Their only child was going off to college next fall and they were in the process of downsizing their lives. What we had to offer in living space, they knew it would fit into their future life style. Patty had invited me in to meet them and answer any other questions they may have had. I looked at Louis closer and I remember meeting him at one of parties held at Johnny's place. Sure enough, it was and he introduced his wife Margaret. We discussed the life style we were designing here. Another feature they wanted in their new life was to be a part of that kind of community. When I covered all the information they needed, I excused myself for my stomach was making noises that it needed to be fed.

I walked down to the restaurant to have lunch because I did not want to wake up Jenny. After a couple hours of eating and socializing, I decided I better head for home in hopes that Jenny was up and we could plan the evening. She was sitting at the kitchen table when I entered by the back door. Her first words were "well have you been into those onion rings?"

"No" was my reply. "I have learned my lesson, if I want to be an x-lover with you; onions are a way to shut that door." I began to laugh because her face was beginning to have that affectionate smile.

"I was thinking, you were down to Johnny's and I might have to have a raw onion sandwich for breakfast for self defense" she could hardly get the words out with the giggling going on in her voice. "Then again, I am not sure you are really worth a raw onion sandwich for breakfast. It is a little tough even for me. So I am glad that you are not forcing me to such extremes to be able to kiss or love you back." At that point, we both enjoyed a good laugh.

Jenny had already written a note, which was on the table for me. It said, as I read it, that she had made all the arrangement for us that evening. That I had to be ready by five, dinner was at six. Dress was casual and I really needed to be hungry.

I looked up after reading the note, "I can comply with all your wishes or command as it maybe. For I am your slave for the evening, your very action or words I will give you my full cooperation. I see the clock is striking four, I think I was rush upstairs and get ready and be waiting at the door to escort you out for the evening." I was half way through the house when I yelled out the last sentence.

No one joined me in the shower nor was in the room when I was done. I dressed and took my time returning to the kitchen since I still had fifteen minutes. There she sat on chair she pulled over from the table, "I am not sure what a girl has to do to have her date, or escort arrive a little early to ensure that I am available or even waiting. Therefore, I have been sitting here for over 15 minutes so very lonely, I could cry. I guess the gusto has finally disappeared out of our courting. I am not sure what is in store for me over time. Maybe, there won't even be a breeze let alone being warm." With those words, she had planned to use the chair to block his way, as she open the door and was out by the driver door waiting for me to open it for her. She was laughing and giggling all the way.

I found that chair was barrier that I had not planned on. I got it out of the way and locked the door as I was leaving. I rushed over to the car door, with great showmanship, open the door, and gestured her to enter which she did with lot of fan fair. I could hardly contain myself through this lighthearted courting game. I went around to my side and she had reach over and unlatched the door. When I got in, she rewarded me with a light kiss and we were off to the city by her command.

She had made reservations at Greek Restaurant that was decked out as we were in Greece. The food was as we were there. They had violins playing and when we finished our desert, they brought out Greek dancers. The evening was magical. There was so much fun and activity; it was truly like being back in Greece with our newfound family. One of the male dancers came to our table, took my wife hand and she became part of dancing group. That must have been planned or he knew she knew all the dances they were doing. They were short one woman and she filled the bill. Her eyes danced and sparked every time she looked at me. What have I done to deserve this kept playing in my mind and heart?

When that performance was over, the male dancer introduce himself to me and how pleased he was that Jenny was here tonight. She had taken dancing classes from him about year or so ago and she has not lost her talent. He thanked me for allowing him to have a dancing partner and her again and was gone.

"That was fun. I did not know they were short a girl, lucky for me. I miss that dancing some times. I am pleased that you are not the jealous or possessive kind" as her words whispered from her lips as she lean over and kiss me gently.

"You do make me feel proud to see you enjoy that gives you pleasure. You brought back some haunting enjoyment when we were with our newfound family. I think if I live to be hundred, I know I will never be quick and light on my feet to do those dancing. So, my love, I enjoy watching you enjoy what you are finding pleasure in doing" as I held her hand and looking dreamy eyed at her.

"Now, now, no mushy stuff in public, we need to leave that to our private time. So behave yourself in public, people will think I am common." With those words, she could hardly contain herself.

The evening ended too soon as it always does when we are together. When we left it must been almost midnight and we had very quiet drive home. When we got into the house, I put my arms around her and pulled in close, gave her a gentle kiss. She pulled back slowly, looked me with her head cocked to the side. "If I remember your words you gave yourself to me as slave for the evening, my word was law and you would give me your full cooperation. Those words maybe not exact but close enough, don't you agree?"

"Yes [with hungry heart and body] of course that was about what you said. I expected you to quest after me with passion, ol' great lover of mine" slipped out of my mouth on breath of passion and desire.

"Your love boat would very much like to shower and have a pleasant night sleep before she would succumb to your and my lust. Will you grant such pleasure to your master, dear slave?" Jenny was pulling these words off very seductively.

"You should not have stimulated your slave by saying to hold all demonstrations in public to our private time. Now you have a slave in very wanting aching passionate mood." I couldn't hold it in I just started to laugh. "In all honesty, on the way home, I was dreaming about those lost times we enjoy in the morning. That loving would be the gentle dessert that romances the heart. So should you be serious, I will with great expectations for the future, I grant your request for a delay."

There were no more words said as we retired to our bedroom. Took separate shower and enjoyed sharing a bed in slumber land. The morning broke with music of love.

CHAPTER 30

It was Sunday already, while Jenny was getting ready for the day. I made breakfast and it was waiting for her when she entered the room. We were still in that rapture mode. After we feed our starving bodies, clean up after the meal, I suggested that we go for ride. I had destination in mind. As for the excuse for where we were going, I have a potential buyer for one of our condos I had to drop off some more paper work. After that delivery, we were free to go anywhere we wanted.

I requested that she would drive her car, I felt lazy. She gave me that look, something is up, but she did not say anything. I just would not acknowledge "that look" and I gave her directions towards town. As we got closer to our destination, I informed her that I had made the meeting with a salesman at his car dealership where he worked. As part of my surprise, I had a specific car and color picked out to be in full view when we got there. As I directed Jenny to pull into the dealership lot, and again informed her this is where the salesman worked who was considering buying a condo. In addition, I would like you to meet him for he could be our neighbor. Jenny got out of the car and joined me as I walked up to the salesman, who was leaning against a light blue Ford Fusion hybrid with very light tan leather interior.

"Hi George, how are things going for you today? I also handed him an envelope, stating it has all the information he requested," I stated.

His reply, "he appreciates my time, and for stopping by so we can talk. By the way, what do you think of this Fusion Hybrid? Isn't she a beauty? She has everything a person would want on a car, she if fully equipped." He opened the driver door to my wife who was already lost in looking at her dream car. She thought I had not seen her picture of her dream car in her car glove compartment.

The offer was there, so Jenny sat in it and just was busy looking around the inside and all the gadgets. "Would you like to take her for ride? I can't take my break for another half an hour to talk with you about my interest. The boss would be happy having me showing off our cars." Stated George in the usual salesman jargon

I jumped in back "why don't you try it out Jenny, we have time to kill and who knows?" I left that sentence just dangling there to set the stage to get her to accept the gift. We had figured out the trade, paper work was completed, all we had to do was sign the papers, and we would be on our way.

George got the dealer tags. I sat in the back so George could sit in front to assist him in his sale pitch and we were on our way. He had Jenny get on expressway, and some of the usual back streets. All the time explaining all the features to her and we parked on Airport Way for few minutes to enjoy the scenery and the pleasantness of new car. Jenny was like a little kid with a new toy. Her old beater was getting nervous but she wanted to wait until she was finished with school before she would ever consider a different car. She always talked about another second hand car, when the subject was injected in our conversations.

I finally leaned forward with my head on back of her seat, "Isn't she a beauty? It has everything. You can talk to your cell phone with both hands on the wheel. It is nice once in a while it is nice to try out a dream car to see if it truly the dream car for you?" I sat back and let the words tease her for a while.

Jenny started out again and we made our way back to the dealer. She drove to where we had gotten in and parked it. She just sat there while George and I got out and we knew she was weakling. Jenny finally got out and just looked at me. "You are a truly a very cruel man. You know I will have a hell of a time driving that beater of mine after this. You have a way of breaking a girl's heart. So we better go in so you two can have your discussion that brought us here today."

George said, "Yes, why don't you come into my office so we can have some privacy. I don't want the other employees know I thinking about buying a condo."

We followed him in and I watch Jenny keep looking over her shoulder at the car. Then her heart seemed to fall when she saw another salesman put a bright red sold tag on the windshield. When we sat down, I think she was pouting. I could not hold it any more, I asked George to slide over the paper work. When he did, Jenny saw it was registration for the blue car. She looked at me with questionable expression, blurted out "you mean that car is mine?"

"It is your Christmas and graduation present, so it is little early. All you have to do is sign the registration form and it is yours to keep." I replied.

Without a second thought, she signed the paper and threw her arms around my neck and gave me a kiss right there in public. I said "shocking to kiss your slave in public after what you told him last night". I just bubbled with joy.

They had the temporary tags already on it, all items from her old car in the trunk of her new car and we were on our way with full tank of gas. We took a ride up to Hood River on Route 84 for a late lunch. Jenny wanted to enjoy her new toy, and suggested we cross the river, travel back on Washington side on Route 14 because hills and there are different driving demands. Then we were on Route 205 north, then 5 and cut over to Longview on Route 432, then 433, cross the river and on Route 30 south and then back home. She had to drive up front of the restaurant to have her brother come out to look over her new car even if it was getting dark. I had called him ahead of time, to insure that he was there. We, men, know how to gush over a new car. I told her I wanted to talk to Johnny for a minute and I would walk home. She drove it home very slowly.

"Johnny, the more I love your sister, this pain in my heart keeps growing. I know Roger said it would take two or more sessions to find the underlying cause of last crisis of my past lives. It is scaring hell out of me. I know I can do it, but I am still scared." I stated with fear in my voice.

Johnny looked at me for minute, then "you know if you get in trouble, they will send for me and I will be there. It really can't be that bad, you lived through your family's trouble basket and all the hell getting free from

Marian ["the Keeper"]. If you were not concern, I would be, so my friend, we can do this without skipping a beat. Think of all the loving you will be living in when it is over. I, also, have to tell you, sis, has similar but different fear. The more you to become one in acceptance, the more she feels lost. So whatever is buried in the event in Spain, must affect you both in perhaps different ways but still needs to be resolve for both of you to have your freedom from it. The more I think about it, the thoughts that keep wandering around in my head, this resolve will only strength your marriage. Maybe, you two could think about making me an uncle, maybe a god father, or something" as he broke out laughing at the whole idea.

"If that happens, 'the something' could be a baby sitter, and how do you like those apples" was my rhetorical statement. "I better get home or my wife will think I abandon her or worse yet. I may find her bundle up in her new car. I never witness a woman being so over whelmed about a car."

Johnny was raising his voice as I was walking away "that is sis first new car. She has always owned a beater. I could be just excited as sis if you bought me a new car, but make mine green." At that point, I looked over my shoulder yelled back, "that will be the day" in laughter.

When I entered the front door, there wasn't a sound in the house, nor were there any lights on. I wonder did Jenny take her new car out for another ride. Maybe she is out there in it. I went to the door to garage and looked in. Her new car was there, but she wasn't in it. I went through the house and upstairs, and into our bedroom to witness my princess fast asleep. I guess I stayed away to long. When I went into bathroom to get ready for bed, there was her note: "you will get yours in the morning." That was open-ended invitation meaning what, I hope on the up side. Took a long hot shower, dried off, put on some of her favorite men's cologne on me and slide into bed very quietly.

Out of the darkness I was attacked, love enveloped us, we were lost in a world where oneness lives, and all is well with the world. I kept those ugly unknown thoughts that haunt me from time to time at bay because nothing was going to ruin our magic. The magic melted into deep restful sleep until the alarm shattered the silence that brought us back to real world and another new day.

The morning was announced with the ringing of the phone, it was Barbara and she wanted to know if I would be in this morning. Steve wanted to have some time with you along with Judy and Francis. It appears, Ron has gotten things off the ground with the county, and we could start on the project across the road by the first of the year, weather permitting. So my dear boss, can you make it by 10:30? By the way, I have a Tuesday 10 A.M. appointment for you at the Wellness Center for Rolfing and maybe aromatherapy.

My reply was I would be there. I looked at the clock it was nine all ready. I hung up the phone before she could answer because nature call could no longer wait. Quick shower, dress and as I walked through the bedroom, Jenny was still sleeping and I left quietly.

Quick breakfast of coffee and toast, I washed down some vitamins and I was out the door on my way to work. As I came through the door, Barbara was carrying in coffee rolls and coffee for the meeting. I looked at her and said, "I forgot you are so prepared, I could have skipped my burnt toast for breakfast. Did you get a hold of Ron; is he going to be here too?"

"It appears everyone was on alert, Russell will be here too. I had Johnny send up the sweet rolls and made reservations for lunch for everyone around 12:30. I hear some voices in the office; it appears they are here already. I will usher them in and have a great meeting" were her words as she rushed to meet the guest and direct them into the conference room.

It was like old home week, with all the chattering and general greeting of each other as they came in and took their seats around the conference table. Barbara was busy hanging up new drawing of what the new project could look like if it was agreeable.

I looked at Ron, which was the signal to begin the meeting. Ron gave a progress report with an update where we were with the county and state with signal light on the state highway. All the permits were signed and it was up to us when we want to begin the work. That presentation received a hardy voice of approval and appreciation from the rest of the gang.

Judy started next with the two designs for the two businesses. The drawing also displayed the clinic attached to the grocery. She spent time explaining the designs where to complement this project and maximized traffic flow to and from this project. The designs also presented high visibility to attract business. The arrangement of the gas station with fast food and beverages was on one side of the entrance and grocery complex would be on the other side to prevent miss use of space. The traffic would flow would be controlled by the traffic light This arrangement would also allow traffic from the sub division housing to use the traffic light because entrance and exit would be in the middle of it all. The drawings were very detail and made sense to assist in traffic flow patterns. As questions came up, Judy was able to give detail answers to them to everyone satisfaction. The only differences between the two drawings were the exterior of the building. One would complement the river front project and the other would have its own identity. There was round of acceptance of that presentation when she was finished.

I took the floor next with my questions. "The question I ask of you, do we want to complement this project or let it have its own design? If we go for complement, do we present buyers of the lots five or six designs what will be only acceptable being built on this land? If we go for its own identity, do we have designs that will complement it or they can put up any design as long as meets the sq. ft. requirements?

Russell was first to speak up, "I still would vote for the complement design because it would strengthen the community attitude and identity. It fits well with the landscape of the area also. That was his vote."

Steve was next to support the complement design because it works. The people of the area are already identifying this place by the design. Ask anyone in the area; it is about the design, not by its name. We also have our suppliers set up for general exterior material for all the building, therefore, we get it at a better price rate and besides it cuts down on waste.

"Well! I guess it appears we can take it to our investors to get their support. Ron, do you think we need to go to any government agency for anything that is not cover with the permits?" I inquired.

"As far as everyone one concern, we have the green light to begin whenever we want to but it has to be within 6 months. That means that we have to start before May getting this off the ground. They know we are going to building the businesses first and the housing project as needed. It is expected that the streets, water, gas, electric, and sewers will be put in the same time as the business to integrate the whole system. So the game is with you, Alex and Steve" was Ron's closing words.

Steve looked at me "I would like to be able to break ground by the 1st of the year. The land soil has very good drainage, so the prep and foundations work will not be delayed by any rain. The streets and all the lines will be done at the same time. I have looked into a system of building covers where we can work under it even if we have rain. Of course, as soon as we get the roofs on and sealed, the walls can be prefabed, and then the inside work can move ahead very quickly. Russell and Judy will have to agree upon the inside by the time the roofs are completed. I will have interior subs busy to meet our completion date. As soon as plans for interior are completed, I would like copies for the subs so they can prepare their bids and insure we have all the equipment on time too. I would like to have the business operational by sometime in March. I, already, have had a couple of gasoline companies sales reps contact me to find out who do they need to contact to make their pitch. It seems like even the chain grocery stores are sending out feelers. Who do we refer them to?"

I looked at Russell "since you want to run the grocery store, do you want to be connected to a chain? In addition, do you also want to be connected to the gas station operation? Alternatively, do we lease out the gasoline business? Will you have hand with the fast food section? We haven't covered this in depth yet, so I would like you to research these questions to determine how much of this operation you do want to manage. You can manage it all or parts, it is up to you. I want to give you a three-week dead line on your decision and your proposed lay out for interiors of the businesses you want to control. We will meet in three weeks here with everyone, so we are all on the same page. You all know how to get a hold of each other, there will be no excuses for delays. If you need help, I am here along with Barbara. If you do not have the answers, we will get answers as soon as possible for you. What I have said, it is clear to everyone." [There was verbal agreement of present] "We need to run a tight ship on this one to insure we can support everyone goals and objectives. We have been a team, and we are going to keep up that goal on this new project too."

Russell looked relieved that he was not required to give answers right then "I have been thinking that maybe I can manage the full operations if I can get the gas station manager I have in mind to commit to that assignment. March would be great to begin. I have explored being part of chain group and I have not made up my mind, should have answer by the next meeting. If I go with manager of the station, I will have him here also. So you will have my answers to both questions then."

I asked, "Is there anymore questions or information necessary before I close this meeting. We are having lunch at 12:30. As my guest I hope you can stay. Are you hungry?" Hearing no further questions, I am adjuring the meeting and lets us journey down to the restaurant where Johnny will have everything waiting for us.

Everyone was still busy talking and walking toward our lunch. As I passed Barbara, I asked her if she would have a summary of the meeting and have it available for everyone by the end of the week. I noticed that she had the meeting recorded for everyone benefit. As always, she replies no problem, probably have it by Wednesday. She keeps a progressive file on this project with all necessary information for our future information. She has cover sheet in front to refer to what meeting covered what material. I am glad I have her on my team. She also gave me a reminder written notice that I was to be into Wellness Center in Portland tomorrow at 10 and it included the address and directions.

I looked up just then to see that the gang was almost at the restaurant and I had to run to catch up. The luncheon went well. The meal together seems to build the bridges to help develop a full team. We seem to recognize each other's strengths. There is a knowing of how to blend the talents.

After lunch, Steve asked if he could use our conference room tomorrow to have a meeting with all the subs bosses and suppliers to keep them abreast what we are doing and schedules for the future. In addition, he would arrange with Johnny to feed them all.

I could speak for myself, I had no problem with your request. You have to do check the date with Barbara, and if it opens then it is a done deal. As for Johnny, you will have to speak for himself. We both laugh when I said that.

Everyone left; I was standing in the drive way of the marina and wondering what to do next when I saw Jenny at our front door, motioning me to come on over. I ran to her beckoning and when I got within voice sound, she asked if I wanted to go shopping with her in her new car. Any excuse to spend time with her is all right with me, especially since Barbara said I did not have any work assign to me for the rest of the day. If there were any problems, I was available on my cell phone.

There is nothing better than the smell of new car and spending a social time with one's wife. I must have done something right to have her in my life. I often think of what did I "pay forward" to earn the right to have her. I guess I will never know. However, for now, enjoy the time before she disappears going to work. This time helps endure the time away from her.

Tuesday arrived as a normal day; I realized I have to give myself a little over an hour to get to the Center if I wanted to be on time. The drive in to Portland and locating the Center was uneventful. Receptionist greeted me as I came through the door. She had some paper work for me to fill out before I could see the Rolfer. She also gave me information on Rolfing. I read most of the information before giving back the paper work. David, who was my Rolfer, was standing there to greet me and introduce himself to me. He showed me to his room with a massage table was waiting for me. David again explained this was very deep body massage and it can be painful at times.

I replied, "I am accustomed to pain, but I will tell you if it gets beyond my ability to with stand it. I signed up for series of 10 of them, once a week and it appears we will be seeing each other for that length of time. Per my office manager, you come well recommend, that is why I am here."

"I appreciate recognition of my talent, thank you. To begin, if you don't mind, I would like you to disrobe down to your shorts and socks. Then I will like to have you stand on that spot on floor so I can view your physical form to determine where I will begin. The first session I will try to take it easy on you." was his gentle manner.

After I disrobed, I piled my cloths on the chair, and then I stood on the spot as directed and I stood normally for me. David stood back, looked at me, and then had me turn slowly around. He remarked that I seemed to be somewhat out of alignment. He asked me to lie on the table face down and he would begin. He was explaining what he was doing as he worked on my back and down my right arm and back of my right leg. He asked me if I was into sports because my muscles were locked up. I explain that was not the case with me, just lots of stress from work and very bad divorce. I did not want to go into too much of the details. He spent the hour working my muscles with his fist, hands and elbow to get them to be flexible. He told me he was surprised that I did not cry out once from the pain. I didn't because I didn't feel any real pain. We didn't do much talking doing the session because he seemed to be busy. When he was through, he excused himself because he had another client waiting and he looked forward to see me next week.

I was also told to lie there because the next person will do the aromatherapy and Swedish massage to support the work that was done on me. Sam came in to perform the next phase of work. He asked me to remove my shorts and socks and handed me a sheet to place over me when I was done. While I was doing that, Sam left the room and returned in few minutes with essence oils plus massage oils to begin his work on me. I have to say that was most pleasant experiences especially the aroma from the oils. I could not believe another hour was over. I must admit, Sam could not have said 20 words during the session. My first Swedish massage and it was very pleasant to me. Sam excused himself to let me get dressed. I got dressed and as I went past the receptionist, she gave me my next appointment card and I signed charge slip for today's treatment. While driving home, I am glad that I was having that work done because I was beginning to feel physically great.

The week faded away with the usual busy work of the business. That Rolfing with Swedish massage was not so bad at all. I didn't have any sore muscles and still I seemed to move easier. I was witnessing Jenny coming and going, reminding myself, that this is not forever. My evening were spent listening to the different tapes, sometimes taking notes, and other times mentally playing along with them. There was a very subtle change going on inside me, that it is very hard to define. Sometimes it is perplexing because at times thoughts or understanding floats in space not connected to anything and the allusive feeling can be so discerning. Oh well! I just have to let it float until it connects with something. The Friday appoints is coming up and Roger called and said the deck was clear for the next two weeks for us to continue at the same time.

The Thursday night sleep went too smoothly which is frightening since that was a first time that happen since we started these sessions. I was still getting out of the house before Jenny gets home which was my usual ritual.

I never know whether I would be, I am edgy or out of sorts, so I don't want to unload something on her that I had no answer for as to why. She agreed that times after full night, she is in a space that is not comfortable to be in therefore I did not need to be subjected to it either. She also knows if she in good space, she can always joins me for breakfast at the restaurant.

I always seem to have someone joining me for breakfast any way. When the time comes, I excuse myself by putting on my outerwear as it relates to the weather and I am on my way. Today, it just cloudy and it was an uneventful journey up the river in the boat. It always seems odd to me, I am going south while going up the river. I think the Columbia is perhaps the only river that flows north to the ocean in the U.S. At this moment, it is not important as my mind chatters away until I get to Roger. I left it free flow to keep my mind off the next event I need to face, witness, heal and let go. The dock is always a pleasant sight along with Roger on the porch waiting as always with that hot cup of tea.

After tying up the boat, and as I was walking I was slip sliding away up the mud path. I arrived at the porch with big grin on my face. "Roger you are always a life saver with the hot tea. It seems to put everything into some safe place for me. Besides, it is great tea."

He handed the cup to me and opened the door where I took off my muddy shoes and weather clothing. We then began our usual ritual of journey through the house to our room. Today, he had my chair facing away from the light of the windows. I looked at him and was about to say something, but he jumped the gun with, he was trying something different today. It seems I am conditioned that I am gone before he gets started. He wanted to know if fast induction was cause by the environment or I. I sat down, took my usual sip of tea, and then sat back rinsing the tea around in my mouth before I swallow it. When he said the first word, I was gone. I guess he still doesn't realize that I want to get there as quickly as possible to be done with all of this. The lights went swiftly out and I found myself journeying down my usual hall to meet Kevin who is always waiting for me.

Welcome, as always were his beginning words. Remember, we are only going to observe the events. Therefore, you should be less physically emotionally involved in the action as we open the doorway to Spain. Before

I forget, how did you like the Rolfing? Your spirit team reported it was not painful for you.

I reported "it wasn't this time; I think the Swedish massage smoothen out the muscles prevented much of the pain, we will know more as the treatments continue."

Kevin began again with; let us begin with the pleasant time with you and your family in your villa outside of Madrid. You are going to observe your soul activity in the physical body of a Spanish male. You were not any man, but a relative to the Spanish ruler. How you are related is not important but what happens within that life's last days are. The events and their damage is why we are here, you will always have to keep that in mind. This will not be as difficult as you might think because you have prepared yourself with all the work you have done in the past four evenings.

We first see this very large spread with very large rambling hacienda home, a small apartment area short distance from the home for the workers of the land and home lived. It was very prosperous operation with about thousand acres of good farmland. Your name was Jimena and wife as Jazmyn, mother, Annabelle, children: Phelipe, oldest boy, Isabella, girl, and Vivana youngest boy. It will be interesting to how Jazmyn plays into your present life. Her name means Jasmine.

You were given an opportunity to be host to visiting representative from the Pope, Roxxo, and your own monsignor Antonio. You laid out the red carpet as to speak. They arrived in mid morning to spend day or two at your hacienda. You had a chance in the late morning to give Roxxo and Antonio a walking tour of your hacienda. When you dine for lunch, you had lunch with all the workers on your estate so they would have the benefit of meeting a representative from the Pope. The family was excluded at this time so this would be very special treat for our workers. Roxxo was very official but gracious with your employees. The afternoon was spent riding horseback through the rest of the estate at the request of Roxxo to see what a very productive estate it was. They arrived back late in the afternoon to allow the guest to rest and prepare for the evening meal.

At the evening meal was out on the enclosed courtyard, Jimena introduced his wife, Jazmyn, his mother, Annabelle, and his wonderful children, Phelipe, Isabella, and Viviana to his honored guest. Roxxo presented a gift, as was the custom to the wife for providing food and shelter. There was music and dancing for our guest entertainment. In all appearance, the evening went very well. The guest retired for the evening. At the present time all seemed very well at the estate.

The next morning, after breakfast, the guests made their regrets they could not stay longer but there was need for them to be back in Madrid that afternoon. You as well as your family were very surprised as this turn of events. They had spoke last night they would leave the day after. This was their choice, so there was nothing but accept their decision. The family and employee waved them off as they rode in their carriage out of the main courtyard at front door.

On the way back to Madrid, Roxxo was asking many questions about their host. Why they had crosses but no crucifixes anywhere? Antonio defended his host because they believe Christ has risen; therefore, no longer need to have him hanging on the cross. The more Antonio defended Jimena, the more visible upset his guest became. When they arrived back at the church, Roxxo quickly retired to his suite and called for his secretary. He didn't leave his suite for two days. Then finally, he summons Antonio to inform him that he was convening a trial for heresy. That he has the power and blessing of the Pope to do that wherever he found acts of heresy.

"Who do you suspect of heresy?" questioned Antonio.

"Your friend Jimena, I have researched and have built a case to try him. No crucifixes, well, he will be wearing the cross then" was Roxxo angry reply.

"You can't be serious. He is also a relative of the King. We will have to inform the King of the proceedings. You can't do this," replied Antonio who was totally upset by Roxxo actions.

Disregarding the pleading of Antonio, Roxxo began his orders with "I need one of your massagers that is not known to Jimena to deliver a message for me to get him here for his trial. Should you in any way block or interfere with my work, you will receive the same punishment or perhaps even more. You will plead, no you will beg for death and I will find great pleasure purifying your soul with more execrating pain before death finally loses your eyes. Do you understand me?" By this time, Roxxo was shaking in rage.

Antonio was white as sheet because he has had some firsthand experiences witnessing what happens to heretics. He had never bloodied his hand or never wanted anything to do with this kind of justice; still the fear of it could happen to him paralyzed him as he stumbled with his words "yes, I understand and I will have one of my new massager report to you as soon as I find him. Is there no pleading for my friend could or would change your mind?"

"Get the hell out of here, you wimp. If you are not careful, I will have the Pope remove you from your post and assign you to some hellhole Parrish or maybe a member of the maintenance crew for St. Peter's Basilica for penance. Get out of my sight before I put you on the rack too for practice before I work your dear friend over. He will beg and pledge for mercy. He will sell his family to the burning stake for quick death. Get before I." the words still in his mouth when Antonio ran out in desperate fear. Roxxo smiled to himself, what a little fear does to these weak creatures.

I, Roxxo [the Egyptian Keeper] know this Jimena. He has the effrontery to be born on earth when I am here and not be my servant. He has wander off the path of obedience before, but this time I will teach him a lesson he will never forget who his master is. Before this life, I have given him a quick death for his disobedience, but this time he has gone too far. His present successful life and that family wrapped around his loving heart, and he thinks he can have it all without me. He will now learn that life style will never be for him ever again, without my permission.

Roxxo sat down and with his best penmanship wrote a note requesting Jimena presence at King's Office of Justice as soon as possible. His king's official has great need of his service. Then it signed it so no one could read the signature. He also sealed the letter with wax that justice department uses because he had visited their office and witness their procedure. The imprint on the wax was smudged. I will have it delivered after dark. I will have the massager wait for him to insure he will ride back with him. We will bush whack him on the road, so no one will know where he is. I will put fear of death of my helpers so it will never be known what happen to him. What a great plan I have set in motion, what pleasure it will be for me. I am the master over Jimena regardless what name he has in this lifetime.

Just then, the massager knocked on the door to his suite and Roxxo's secretary let him in. Roxxo handed the message to the massager with these instructions "this message is to be taken to Jimena's hacienda estate with all haste. You will wait for Jimena to ride back to the city with you. You are to lead him down the street that passes the backside of the church hall. This is where he will be captured alive and brought to me. Is that understood? Failure to deliver him to me, you will be suffer the fate of being a heretic and you know that is a very painful death. God has entrusted you with this sacred mission and I again remind you a very slow death be your fate if you fail or ever tell anyone. Do you understand your orders?"

The massager was very young and heard of this man's powers. Also heard rumors of what happen if you fail. His words came forth with the tone of fear "I will do as I am ordered. I will bring him to you this very night without fail." He took the letter, placed it in a leather pouch, and left as quickly as he could.

He rode as fast as his horse would carry him. He was praying all the way to Jimena estate to complete this task successfully for this was a sacred mission and he did not want to die. The servant at the gate challenged him but when he realized that, it was message from the King's Justice Court he let him in. The massager rode fast from the gate to the house. Where again the front door guards again challenged him. They accepted his explanation of this presence and the need to see the master of the house. They had him to dismount and open the door for him to wait in the main hall.

As he entered the house, the head house man question the meaning of his intrusion. He was presented the letter. After viewing the dispatch, he told the massager to waiting. The letter carried to Jimena who had already retired with his wife to their sitting room. After Jimena read the letter, "I am needed in the city tonight, there is nothing in the letter as to why, but it must be important because it came sealed. However, why me? I have nothing to do with that part of the government."

His wife agreed with him, "Wait until morning, and then go to find out what this is all about. As you just said, you have not been connected with this section of the government".

"I think I need to go down and talk with the massager, maybe he can shed some light to the urgency to all of this" was Jimena reply.

At that point, he hurried out of the room, down the stairs and met with the rider. The rider, whelmed with excitement, explained that it was major for him to be there tonight. "My orders were I could not come back without you, it was that important."

"Are you sure", was Jimena inquiry. "Did the minister give you the letter himself?"

"No, it was his secretary that gave me the letter and instructions. I did not see the minister myself. Please come quickly, it very important you get there tonight" were the desperate pleading of massager.

Now we see you return to your sitting room, inform your wife that you had to go. You dressed for the night air and hurried down to join the massager on journey back to the city. The head houseman had sent word to the stables to have the master's horse ready and have it brought to front door as soon as possible. When your horse arrived, you both galloped off into the night.

As you entered the city, the massager led the way so you would pass the back of the church hall. You both were greeted with a huge blanket dropping on you both. This action knocked both of you off your mounts and brought to the ground into the hands of the rouges before you knew what was happening. The massager was killed as ordered but you were only ruffled up somewhat and bound. The four rouges opened the door to the hall and they vanished into the building dragging you. They took you to designated room in the basement, which was like a jail cell. There were no windows, the floor had straw on it, chair table and cot. They threw you on the cot, untied you, and left locking the door behind them without a word to why this was happening. The only light in the room came through the bar opening in the door.

We are witnessing you lying there stunned. Your head was spinning for answers besides hurting from the blows you suffered in bringing you into submission. Darkness finally flooded over you in sleep. Out of the darkness, you feel hands pulling you to your feet; they dragged you along not allowing you to try to walk. You then ended up in room that had a table, three chairs behind it. Very bright light of day sprayed the space where vacant chair waits. This made it very difficult to see anything from the chair they threw you into it. The two guards stood on each side of you until the three men came in dressed in dark robes and sat down. There was also a four persons, who was a scribe. The leader started reading the charges against you, which if proven to be true, you would be declared heretic. That death was punishable by different means depending on severity of the crime.

You asked for water because you could hardly speak because your mouth was so dry that prevented you to reply to their charges. After you drank the cup of water, you tried as you could to deny all the charges with explanations. The leading judge dismissed you answers and instructed the guards to return you to our cell so you could reconsider your answers when they convene the next day. The guards again dragged you out of the room, back to your cell where crust of bread and cup of water waited to be your meal for that day. We can see you spent most of your time rapped in your cloths because of damp air and pain of your injuries.

[Kevin asked Adrian [Alex] what you think of what you have witness so far. You can see it is not Antonio causing all your pain because we can see the total picture. Because of all hidden players and events during this trauma, resulted in scaring you to such a point, that resulted in you being afraid to become or fall in love ever again. We will walk through this one day at a time. I think we will witness one or two more days, which are about the same intensity. So let us view the second day of your trial.]

The guards came into your cell, picked you up by both arms and were about to drag you out, and you puts all your strength together throws them off. Free, you rush for the door, but one guard was able to recover enough to block your way. There was some scuffling, but in the end, you lose. One of them gave you a fist blow to your head where bruise was already showing deep purple. That caused you to almost black out. They again dragged you to the room where the four representatives of the church inquisitions were waiting this time. The guards dropped you in the bright sun lit chair where again you are blinded by the incoming light.

The leader again asked if the charges were true. Of course, you shouted out as laud as your horse voice would carry, "no. I want to see Antonio, he know that these charges are false. He knows I am a true Christian. Where is he?" You were making a pitch to find support for your cause.

The replied almost echoed in the room, "Monsignor Antonio is not here. He is on his way to Seville on important church matters. He isn't aware you are here anyway. So again, do you confess to the crimes against Holy Mother Church and the doctrine of the Church?"

Again, you answered, "No, these are all lies and if Antonio was here, he would support my true support of being a true man of the faith." At that point, guard hit you again on the bruise, and this time you were rendered unconscious. The leader of the tribunal realizes what has happen, calls halt to the proceedings until tomorrow. Telling guards to take you away and bring you back tomorrow.

The guards lifted you under your arms and dragged you out of the room and back to your cell, where they threw you down on your cot. They were chucking to themselves "that you will be burning soon". As they looked back at you, they yell out at you. "You wealthy dog will get what you deserve because you are wealthy; you think you can get away with anything. I hope you get the rack soon, you will beg like dog yelping, they all do." Then they both laugh.

Again, we are witnessing what happened the next day. You were just able to stand up. Water and one crust of bread is not enough food. The bruise was throbbing with every beat of your heart. You tore the sleeve from your shirt and wrap around your head trying to stop the throbbing. It did very little to relieve the pain.

For the last two day, you have been silently prayer that God will send someone to save you, to protect your loving family. It was no longer a prayer, more like begging for help. Yet! Nothing was different. You felt absolutely lost since you were raised in world of love and pleasures that come from true love. The ordeal that is happening doesn't make sense to you. You had heard about these heresy trials, only in passing. Now you are in the middle of it all and it is like a nightmare, you are now praying to wake up. This activity has never been even close to your world; it was for criminals of the city, not us nobles of the country. If the king knew you were here, you know he would come and rescue you. Your fears were that no one knows you are here. What did you ever do to have this curse dropped on you? Who, who would do this to you?

The door again opens, your two guards walk in and grab you by your arm and back to the room again. We can see you were very exhausted by the time they got you to where the chair uses to be. However, today, there is no chair. You were forced to stand without the aid of his guards. The leader of the tribunal stood up from his seat and yelling, "Will you now confess your crimes, and throw yourself on the mercy of this court?" while shaking his fist at you.

We hear your voice was just audible, "no, I am not guilty of these crimes you claim I committed. I am very devoted Christian and my God know I am innocent. I demand that I face my accuser, whoever he is, for he would be unable to speak his lies to me."

The court leader screamed out "You have no rights here. You can't demand anything, because you are heretic, even with your own wretched defense, you been unable to prove your truth. I believe you need the taste of the whip to remind you that we have the truth of your transgressions. So guards take him away, but before he is taken to his cell, he needs about twenty bits from the whip to awaken his tongue to the truth of these charges. He will beg for mercy before it is too late. Without mercy, you will live in damnation for eternity for your crimes. Take him away before I make it thirty bits, such a miserable creature you are."

The guards take you back to the area of your cell, remove your coat, shirt, tied your hands to ring that causes you to stand on your toes, and then the fun begins. The guards took turns laying the whip across your back bringing forth ribbons of red strips as the flesh separates caused by rough rawhide. As we witness you, lost consciousness before the deed was done. They threw cold water on your back, then take you down and then dragged this lifeless body into your cell. They threw your coat and shirt down on the cot before your wet, blood soaked body was dropped on top of them. The guards were laughing as they walked out because of the pleasures they were able to enjoy at your expense.

The next day, you were unable to do anything but to lay there. There was cup of water, but no bread today. Your back was throbbing to point it was totally out of control. Your mind couldn't process it any more. The guards came into the cell, stood you up, draping your coat on your shoulder, and dragged you back to the room. The chairperson again demand that admit to your crimes, and throw yourself on mercy of the court.

As we witness, today, there were no words leaving your mouth. The chair was there to hold your physical frame, but no response. The chairperson told the guard to give you a cup of water to loosen your tongue and it was done. Most of the water poured down the front of you. It did give some sense of presence, but word was still "no".

The chairman said he would consult with his two colleagues as to the verdict. With a few whispers and nodding of heads, the court "announced that they found you guilty as charged. Since you had not begged for mercy of the court, they were force to render the maximum punishment. The punishment is the rack to help purify your soul. Should you then confess your crimes a quick death would the result. If you still fail to confess, you be condemned to damnation for eternity because you will not receive the last rights from the church. Also your physical body will be submitted to the stake of fire." The guards were ordered take this miserable creature away, and submit him to the rack to loosen his tongue to bring about your confession. At that point, the three-man tribunal places a black cloth over their heads, got up and walked out. The scribed recorded the proceeds left at that time. You were taken to the room where humans beg for ------.

Kevin said to Adrian [Alex] we need to leave this now. You have seen enough and it is hoped that we will not have to witness much of what happen the these last days you had on earth as Jimena. You have to really police yourself that you don't take yourself to the pain of this event or get involved in it. You are to witness so you can resolve the trauma connected to this event. Your demonstration of your illness when you were in Madrid, Spain, was your body beginning the purging of the pain that you endured during and resulting in your death. We will work with you to help you understand what is about to happen. The torture was not the real damage to your soul; this event was to do with, abandonment of family, guilt, and betrayal. Everything seemed to begin to fade away and I was back in the room with Roger.

I slowly open my eyes to come out of this adventure. I was not sure what to expect from what happen. I remember seeing movies during this period of history and I was always shocked and disturbed by man inhumanity to man. The men, that did the dirty work, always portrayed as mindless. They were operating on almost animal level of being. Then there was the "mad men" who provoked and ordered the punishment. I used to be fascinated with the interplay of these scenes in the movies, yet they always troubled my being in an indescribable troubling way.

Suddenly I am aware of someone touching me, my head turned towards the direction of the touching and my eyes flashed open to see what is happening. There was Roger very gently touching my arm to help me to come back. I thought I was back but apparently, I wasn't.

"Are you alright? You seemed to slip into different space and I was not sure what was going on. That is why I touched you to see if you needed to be grounded." Roger was explaining his action in a very quiet voice.

"My mind took me to movies that I witness the macabre behavior of the middle and dark ages when inquisitions were control activity of the Roman Catholic Church. It went on from 1227 until it was abolished in 1800s. From time to time, I would read about it but if it were extremely graphic, I had to skip that part. The same in the movies, I found myself looking at the floor until that part of the movie was over. I seemed to be searching for answers to that kind of behavior and how could a church that reveres this champion of human's rights, Jesus, the Christ, perform such acts in his name. I finally came to the conclusion that it was the people who wore the robes that were the culprits not the philosophy. I guess I could walk around talking about man's inhumanity to man. It happened I can't change that. Roger, I guess I need to get going, my head is racing, and I need to find something else to occupy my thought patterns." I was closing down my thoughts and getting up to leave.

We retreated as usual to the front door without saying a word. I put on my outer clothing and shoes for the trip back home. For some strange reason, Roger put his arm across my shoulder, and gave a half hearted hug as he pulled me against his chest. We made a figure of a "T" standing that way. I felt great comfort and kind of lost at the same time.

"This will work out fine. We will have to skip next Friday because it is after Thanksgiving Day and I will be away with my family. I want you to busy your mind with getting everything ready for the holidays. Take a rest from this work we are doing, to give you the much-needed balance to finish that last part. Oh! by the way, I got a slinger from Johnny announcing his restaurant will be closed for Thanksgiving. I guess everyone who gets the slinger is invited. It's going to be a pot luck dinner at 2p.m. that day. Will you tell him my regrets that I will not be able to make it this year? Now get on down that path and start celebrating your coming up freedom from your past. I know we will only have to do this one more time and you will be able to unravel the traumas of the past. You will have the strength and tools to do it successfully. Besides I am always up the river from you in case you get lost." Roger started to laugh after the last statement.

I put my hand on his shoulder and thank him for his endless support through all this crap. I turned and hurried down the path, untied the boat, she fired up on first attempt as always and I was on my way. Maybe there truly is only one more of these trips. What a Christmas presents that would be for me, my freedom is the present. The sun was trying to break through the clouds to bring some cheer to other wise a drab day. I pulled close to the shoreline because a car cargo ship was heading up the river to deliver all those new cars for Christmas presents. I am always amazed as to their size. Load how low they are in the water on the way up to Portland and empty, how high they ride coming back. I never did the math, but there lot of weight resulting from all the cars in those ships' hold. A couple of the crew looking over the side, wave to me and as a normal reaction, I waved back. It seems such a simple jester, yet I am glad they acknowledge me and I them.

The ship slipped by so quietly and I gave my little boat full speed ahead to get back to our dock and greet what the day will bring. Ol' Johnson was on the dock waiting and helped me secure the boat and put on its cover.

"I never marvel at those huge ships sailing by and how they help us to be connected with people we never ever see. I also heard your engine coming on full so I knew you would be here soon. I wanted to talk with you about an idea I have to solve some of the parking problems, vehicles and their trailers, after they launched their boats. Why don't we have a sandwich and coffee at my place and I will lay my ideas on you. That is if you don't have any pressing business at hand." As he motioned me to follow him to his houseboat, he guessed I didn't have any pressing business.

His houseboat secured to last dock, out on the far end so he has clear view of the river and it was out of the way. He is the only one that has a houseboat as per our contract with him. It is always a pleasant walk out to his place. At this time of the year there aren't any boats tied up in the slips.

We went in and he must have expected I would be here because the table was set, sandwiches on the plate and coffee brewing.

Ol' Johnson pointed to a chair "have a seat, I will pour our coffee. I hope you like ham and cheese sandwiches with horseradish on them. The horseradish is to help clear your sinuses as I have been told. Get comfortable because I want to lay out my idea before you give me any feedback while I am presenting. You guys are always four or five steps ahead of me all the time. So I have you to myself, I want to take this slow and easy." He was chuckling to himself. "You have talked about having the vehicles and trailer travel across the road to park. I was thinking, since we are making a road to our motel; why not use the land between the road and the break wall for parking instead of a park. We can still have a walkway with benches for people who want to sit and watch. The motel will have grass area in front of it with benches. We could get 12 to 14 units parking right there. I kept track last year to see how many units were involved every day parking. The number average about eight but the most we ever had here was 13 at one time. Most of them rent slips for their boats that use the marina, so we have only cars or trucks to deal with. I just don't like the idea that we have people cross the road even if we have a light. You know those fools will probably run the light anyway. I can give you my daily tally and it runs from May to September. I would really want you to thinks about my plan. I am not jamming down your throat, but think about it."

I had finished my sandwich while he was talking and I almost finished my cup of coffee when he finally did stop talking. I kept eating so I wouldn't interrupt him. He is right, I am always thinking 4 to 5 steps a head most of the time. "I have to tell you, I am glad that you kept a record of the traffic. I figured we had to do one of two activity, the one you have suggested, which I have to tell you that it has been wondering around in my head when I working on this problem. There was been a strip of land offered to me, the price has been reasonable, which butts up against our property on the north, I could build a bridge across that little creek, gully and there is about 8 acres were we could park vehicles with or without trailers. This land is locked in so it has no access to the main road. For access the owner would have to get some kind of right away from us or person who owns the land between his and the road. The main road is really up steep hill and to connect to it would be a very steep incline from his property. Anyway, I found out that a road down to his property has been denied by the county because the access is on blind spot on the main road. When they widen the road, he sold the county the right away land at good price. He sold so much, that there was no flat land to make good access road to the rest of his property. In fact, he made more off it than it cost him for all his acreages. He must not have been thinking, because he didn't have access road included to his property included in the sale to the county. Bad for him, but maybe it will be good for us."

"Damn, I always wondered why that damn fool sold that strip to the county. He could have forced them to move the road over enough to get out, but as you say, he was counting his profits. I would vote for buying it because it could give us more parking, but also we could make a ramp there also for launching their boats. That would free up some of the traffic on our present launch site. We could also build some more slips and docks to expand our business. I can keep an eye on that area also. Give me something to do at nights when I can't sleep. This place is greater than I ever expected it to be. That Johnny keeps people coming back with his good food, entertainment and because of him. He is one hell of host. Therefore, I said all I have to say. I know we are going to be having a meeting of interested parties. I sometimes get confused, we have interested parties, and we have just investors and then us. I glad you have a handle on all of this." Ol' Johnson ended his pitch for his parking solution.

"I guess we have our operations broken up in three or four areas because we need people to help us hold the vision or purpose as we developed this project. We need money, but these investor are interest only return similar to CDs because of their wealth. Then there are steward groups, which are old money people. They like to support something that improves quality of life too. Then as you say, there are us. We are doing it for a living plus it just fun to be involved in something that pays dividends that enhances a quality of life. Look at all the friends and acquaintances we have made over this past year. Life has been good to all of us. One action that we have done that I enjoy being a part of and that is deferred payment or reduced mortgages of national guards that have been called up. Barbara has really developed supportive day care for children of parents that are working. I better get off my soapbox and hike up to see if Barbara has found any work for me to do. However, I will get with our team of designing the use of this extra land, and it should pencil out to be a good investments.

In addition, I cannot believe it, but if all inquiries materialize in sales, we will have most of the lots sold across the road for income. We have half of the new construction condos spoken for with down payments. We are really sitting pretty at the present time. We are not hundred percent slow down proof, but almost most. We are in the position to own everything without depending on banks and loans to stay afloat. I must get going, and thanks again for the food and ideas. I will talk with you soon as I can see any results. Thank you, my dear friend." As I got up leave, the last sentence just floated out with true friendship love that I am learning to express to people who are true friends to me.

CHAPTER 31

It was nice short walk to the office. The sun was now out full after having melted the clouds away. We have one of those super fall days when everything seems right with the world. Barbara greeted me as I entered the office. "You have someone who just dropped in to see you just a couple of minutes ago. I put him in your office. I was about to ring you and here you are."

I went directly into my office and to my surprise was the person I was talking about with Ol' Johnson. "Stanley, this is a pleasant surprise! What can I do for you on such a great day?"

"I know I just talked with you the other day about my land that is next to yours. I was in the neighborhood so I decided to stop in and ask if you were considering or had made a decision" Stanley inquiry.

"To tell you the truth, I had not spoken to anyone except Ol' Johnson about your property. I have given it a lot of thought and after talking with Ol' Johnson, I would like to buy your land. We are having a problem of what to do with vehicles and their trailers after they launch their boat. This could be a very good solution and your price that you offered is reasonable. Therefore, I guess we have a deal. What I find good for us, there is no other way out of that property but through ours." I said with conviction.

Stanley took a minute and said, "Do you suppose that I could pick up the money by Monday or Tuesday. I decided to buy a RV that is the end of the year model and at a great price, but it is about the full price of the land I am selling you. It has everything, and the dealer said they would hold it until first part of next week for me, to give me time to raise the money or sign a loan. I put down $5,000 to hold it. I have been looking and shopping around and this has all the bells and whistles I have always wanted. I am also taking the following week off to take my wife down to Medford to visit her family. It would be great to arrive in grand style. By the way do you think it is possible?"

While he was talking, I had buzzed Barbara and she was just entering the room when Stanley finished asking his question. "Barbara could you get a hold of Ron and see if he is available this afternoon to come on up here, I need his services." Barbara left immediately and was back in a few minutes with a positive answer to his request.

"Ron was on his way down here anyway this afternoon. I caught him on his cell phone. He should be here within a half hour" was her report.

"That is great. Stanley, can you stick around and when Ron gets here, we can draw of the bill of sale and I think we will still have time to record it today. Should we be unable to record it today, Monday at the latest. Do you have a clear title to the land?" was my concern.

"You must think me brazing, but I brought my deed with me just in case. You can call your title company while we are waiting to have them check, but I do have a clear title. I really want that RV and we have to keep this rolling. Would you mind calling the dealer to tell them I will have the money soon?" Stanley asked in a rather pleading voice.

I took the time out to do that, that action pleased everyone who is involved.

All Stanley's action was like a young kid about to have a new toy. I suggested that we take a walk down to Johnny's for lunch while we are waiting. Ron will come down there as soon as he gets here. We went outside, took our golf cart, and motored down for lunch. I was still full from Ol' Johnson lunch so I just ordered homemade fresh apple pie and coffee. Stanley did the same because he was too excited to eat much more. We had just received our order when Ron came walking in. I had ordered the special lunch for him. As he walked up to the table, I stood to introduce Stanley and he is the reason I needed to see you. Stanley has the 8 acres of land north of us and he offered it to us a very reasonable price. I am having the title company do the search while we speak. He has his deed to the land with him. I need you to do the paper work and maybe we could record the deed even today. If not, Monday, will be fine. Stanley bought himself a full-equipped RV with the money and he is very anxious to get his hands of it for trip with his wife.

Ron sat down after shaking Stanley's hand and we discussed the property and its use for us while we were eating. As soon as we finished, I paid the tab and we loaded up in the golf cart and headed back to the office. Barbara had all the paper work laid out on the conference table. The Title Company called and reported the land was clear. I then left Ron and Stanley continued their work of the bill of sale etc. Barbara was notary so we had one of office workers witness the signing of the needed documents. While they were busy doing their job, I also had Barbara cut a check for Stanley for full price we agreed on and had signed it to give to him when all the paper work was done. One of the office workers lived near the courthouse, so she ran the documents down to be recorded on her way home. We also called ahead the recording office to tell them we were coming in. That was the fastest land transaction I think I have been a party too were my thoughts.

After we gave Stanley his check and he was out the door heading to the dealer. I again called the dealer to report that we bought his property, so he will be in very soon to purchase the RV. I looked at Ron, "by the way, why were you coming down to see me anyway. It worked out good for us, but now it is your turn to talk about what is up?"

"I just needed to get away from the office this afternoon. It is such a great day and we will not have many more of these. I also got the invitation from Johnny for Thanksgiving. Is this offer open to everyone or to residents or what? I have my folks over that weekend and I would like them to come to the dinner too, if that is possible?" Ron inquired.

"We can walk back down and see if he is in now. As far as I understand, the invitations are his doing. I know he offered to furnish the turkey, dressing, coffee, and tea. The attendees have to bring their favorite dish to share. I believe some of his friends are planning to play some music for us for entertainment. It should be a great time. So let's go and see him" was my reply to his question.

We walked down and Johnny had just driven up at the same time. When Johnny was asked about the dinner, his reply was it was open to everyone who got the invitation and their guest. As you remembered, there was RSVP on the bottom that needed a reply by Tuesday so he would have enough birds to feed everyone. So far, there have been almost 50 commitments. It should be a great get together. We went inside and we sat at my usual table at the far end by the windows, drinking coffee and spending the rest of the afternoon catching up on everything that has been going on in our lives. Barbara called me on my cell, everything was recorded, and the land is ours. Just them Ol' Johnson came in and joined us. I broke the news; we now own the land that once was Stanley.

"I thought you told me just couple hours ago, you needed to walk it by some of the others and now, you tell me you bought it. That is fast" was Ol' Johnson reply because he still cannot get over how quick we move and how things get down on the fast track.

We all broke out laughing because the way he said it while shaking his head in disbelief. We settled back into round robin conversation until it was time for Ron to get on home and Johnny needed to prepare for the evening trade. I decided to go home and spend some time with my tape. I need to get clear with myself and prepare for maybe the last session. Some of the old timers joined ol' Johnson as we left, so he wasn't left alone.

I was walking very slowly toward the house, trying to plan how I will work with my tape tonight. Jenny has already gone to work. Upon entering the house, on the railing of the stairway, Jenny posted her note stating, "I was to plan our courting date for tomorrow night. Of course, it will include dinner and dancing, not that I am telling you what you should plan." It has one of this faces drawn on the paper with big smile, a few ha, ha, with Xs and Os. Man! I love that woman more every day. As I marched up stairs, I decided I would listen to the tapes first and then soaking. I got in my overstuff chair in my office on the 3rd floor, turned on the tape and it was 2 a.m. when I woke up. I can't remember if I listen to the tape or what. A fast shower and bed time, for I need to be in tiptop condition for my courting.

I forgot to set the alarm and I was still fast asleep when a very warm body slides into bed from her night shift. It only took a few seconds for her to get me from fast asleep to a loving Romeo. What a pleasant way to start my day and her regenerating sleep to be ready for tonight.

I went up to the office, to check on anything that I can do even on a Saturday. I also called the Atwater's Restaurant and Bar, which was one of my favorite places that is located on 30th floor of US Building in Portland. One of the major reasons for going to this place is to see if I enjoy it without any past history experiences with Marian clouding the evening. The food and dancing was good then, sure hope it is the same or better now. When the maitre d' answered the phone for my reservation, they had table at the window as I had before; the he even remembers my name after all this time, we got book in for seven. I guess good tipping pays off even after all this time.

A few people stopped by to look at our condos and I worked with the office workers showing them around and answering their questions. It turned out to be productive day because we received a deposit for two units and we set up appointment with Judy for interior design with them. We had two others that were still on the fence whether to have condo or wait and buy into stick house in our development across the road that will be developing after March. In many ways, having this development across the street is answer to prayer. Not everyone wants to live in condos, but I for one don't understand their desire to keep up all that landscaping activity.

I went home at five to get ready for our evening. Jenny had just gotten up and was soaking when I found her. She sent me on my way because she wanted her privacy and wanted no distractions for she wanted to be on top of her game for our date that evening. We were both ready by six and I made it a mystery date but when we pulled into the underground parking, the jig was up. She knew where we were going. The ride up the elevator was very pleasant since we had it to ourselves for some strange reason. The maitre d' greeted me as we walked in by my first name and showed us to our table. Jenny gave me that look "did the maitre d' really know you or was that to impress me."

I confessed that I used to come here quite often for business and pleasure and that is why he knew me. That is in addition why we have this great view of the city and river. I hope you don't mind was my reply to that usual look she gave me from time to time.

"I bet you also brought your wife here too" Jenny was quick to reply to my general conversation.

I looked at her with confused look "I really don't know how to address your question. Yes, I brought Marian here for business reasons and courting activity. I wanted to know if I could spend time here without any ghost of yesterday clouding the evening with you."

Jenny was not going to let me off the hook easy when she came back "Well! When were you going to tell me that I am not your first nighters date with this place? Was I going to be measuring against your history with this place? Can I fit in your social world is the question? What is it you?" At that point, she broke out laughing. When she finally got control of herself, "the look on your face when I fired those questions at you was priceless. I glad you can't guess when I am pulling your leg or being serious. That action keeps us alive."

"Ha, ha, you caught me cold. You saw through me. What can I say?" I was trying to play along with the game. "But really, this is a great place, with great dance music plus I wanted to know if there are any ghost of my past haunting this place for me." I replied.

"The view is great and I am glad you got us this table." Jenny wanted to shift the tone of the evening back to courting. Just then, the waiter brought over menus for us and told us the specials of the evening. From that point on, the evening just romanced away. The food was great but I don't remember what we ordered. The music was for courting, but for the life of me, I don't remember the name of the band or any of the dance songs they played. I have never been so lost in the love courting game before in my life. There was ghost in my past relationship showed up from time to time, but I kicked them back into the closet. A few friends and clients remembered and greeted me. I had an opportunity of introducing them to my new wife. All in all the evening was great, the added bonus was the how well my friends and clients accepted Jenny.

The drive home was part of the rapture of the evening. From the time we drove into the garage and until we were cuddled in bed, I have not a clue of how or what happen. The soft smooth ecstasy of just being us is what happened. Sleep and dreams embraced us throughout the night. The spelled was finally broken with phone ringing at nine a.m.

The phone rang and when I answered. Wouldn't you know it was Johnny and Judy at our front door, wanting to come in? I made a gasping sound aloud; "we got company", as I hung up the phone. I grabbed my robe, and out of the corner of my eye, I say Jenny dashing for the bathroom.

As I open the door, of course, they had their comments about newlyweds and Sunday morning. I asked them to come in, make yourself comfortable and keep your remarks to yourselves; we will be right with you.

I could hardly believe it; Jenny passed me on the stairs dressed in jeans and a sweatshirt. I told her I would be right down. While I was getting ready, all I could hear was howling sounds of laughter from down below. When I finally arrived, they all looked at me with the look, "what took you so long?"

Before I could say anything in my defense, Jenny told me she forgot to tell me that we were going out to brunch with them today at this time. Her excuse was there goes our perfect score for communication. That caused us all to laugh. We are still building family history. Within minutes, we were out the front door and into their car for ride to Astoria for brunch. The whole day was pleasant to be with people you are building bonds, bridges and family history to support you in the future when or should you be in "an hour of need". After brunch, we took the long way home stopping from time to time to view the scenery. By late afternoon, we said our goodbyes and thank you for a day well spent. They were gone and the rest of the time before bed was getting everything ready for the next week.

Monday morning at eight a.m., Barbara calls me to ask if I would be up to having a meeting with Sidney, Alan, and Daniel who had stopped in before and discussing the Longview Project and Vancouver Development. I looked at your calendar, which is clear. They really wanted to talk with you this morning. I told them that 11 a.m. would be available. "Are you up to it?" She asked me.

"You better get a hold of Ron; I think we need him here also. If he is not available, I will still meet with them" was my reply.

I slipped out of bed and prepared for the day. Jenny didn't hear the phone ring, so I tried to be as quiet as possible. I grabbed a cup of coffee before heading up to the office. As usual, coffee and the bakery goodies were available, whenever we have a meeting. Barbara told me that Ron would be here because he met with them last week and found some big problems. I guess they want to discuss it with you because of it.

Sidney was first in with Daniel and Alan tagging behind. We all went to the conference room, grabbing coffee and sweet pastry on the way. Just as we were sitting down, Ron came rushing in. After all the greetings and comfortable conversation to get things started. Sidney began "Ron came up to see us last week at our request. He found glitz in our contract with our investors. We talked with them about changing the clauses that were on the last pages of our agreement where they determine the time line development of these two projects. They told us verbally that we were in control of both programs that was in there to insure we would be timely with completion of the different phases. They would not modify or change any of the words. I adjourned the meeting and we would meet next week again concerning these projects. The major investor was very explicit that there would be no changing of our agreement. We have to take the blame for these problems. We were busy making changes in the contract every time anyone felt uncomfortable with things. Instead of realizing how these changes affected such a large project. Since they want to hold fast to our present written contract, there wasn't a need to press our concerns then, and that is why we wanted to meet with you today."

Ron stepped in immediately, "Alex, I went over their contract with their investors. Those hidden clauses means they direct what will be build, when and all the responsibilities of any failure would be on these guys. I even talked it over with a couple of my colleagues and they agree that the clauses could be and is a killer."

"I am confused, what can I help with this?" Replied Alex.

Alan stepped in "well! We really don't have the experiences with this kind of thing. I guess we don't know should we trust our investors and go with the project or what? Those clauses 'could be a killer' are they really?"

I replied, "I had a friend investigate these investors because their names sound familiar to me. He dug deep, low and behold; these guys have taken other developer down this same road. They were the only ones that benefited. The other developers were truly lucky they broke even. If Ron tells me they have that clauses in there and the clauses bothers him, I guess I have to ask Ron can you get out of the contract."

"I have copy of the contract they gave me. They can get out of it, but there is a termination clause. That clause states they cannot build anything similar within 40 miles of either or both sites for 10 years. These foxes have you up short. There really is no way around those clauses. I was going to talk with you this week Alex about this but I glad we have this meeting now" stated Ron.

I got up and paced back and forth, then excused myself to get something from my office and I would be back.

While Alex was gone, Ron looked as deflated as the contractors did. When I walked back in, I stated, "I called my source and their recommendation was cut your losses and run. I had found out that they have friends in county that would keep them informed if you tried to slide by them if you didn't build for them or tried develop it elsewhere. I have trust Ron and my source on this. Can you get out of the contract and what is your cost?"

Sidney looking stunned "Ron and my lawyer tell me, it would cost us about $50,000. Which we have to cover emergency and I guess one would call this an emergency."

"I looked over both projects and I really like the one in Longview. Liking or owning a project that could kill you, is not worth taking the risk. I support Ron that this is almost no win for you. If you break even, you would have to be truly lucky. I know it is hard to see your dream go up in smoke. I have found two alternatives for you guys. There is a site closer to the ocean and one up the river towards Hood River, which is outside of their restrictive boundaries. These are options. I believe we could get the support you need if you take the one up the river toward Hood River. You would have both major cities to draw from and the area is depressed, which could really be to your advantage. There could be so very viable concessions if you build there. It is something to think about, but first you have to decided, do you want move ahead with the contract, or not. What Ron has said, I will be honest, I don't believe, Sidney, you will want to take the chance. If I were in your shoes, I have to follow Ron's lead on this for myself. The ball is now in your court."

Alan shook his head and said "we had a feeling we were doomed with these two projects. We have been so wiped out about this since we found that we could be had, that we can't think straight. We have enough work to keep our business alive that is not a problem. We don't have anything on the drawing board to replace this. We were in state confusion, a place where we have never been before. This was to be our chance to be in the big time."

Sidney jumped in with "still you have given us idea where we could pull this off. It is small hardship, but still we are still mobile enough to do it in different place. That is another of the reason we wanted to meet with you again. You are up straight with us. We need your help, because we are in that place where it could make or break us. I know we need to trashcan the two projects still it is better than we be trash can. Maybe some of the designed we could maybe use on the site toward Hood River."

"Should you explore this alterative and want to bring it into reality; I will work with any lawyer you have to insure you do not get boxed in by any one especially your investors. I know Alex will assist you as much as he can because he likes what you are proposing. So as you can see not all is lost, just that your dream lives at a different place on the river" was Ron closing remarks?

The next hour, we began working as team with options and possibilities for moving forward for them. The contract was dead deal as agreed by the company's representatives. When we got to a place where everyone was comfortable, like all meeting, we adjourned for lunch. We would meet again in the future after they were free of these current construction contracts and ready to do all the groundwork on a new site.

Tuesday and Wednesday was very busy time for everyone who was involved with the Thanksgiving Pot Luck at Johnny's restaurant. We designed programs for after dinner for those who want to participate. We had people volunteering to keep the children occupied after dinner. Decoration group were out scrounging whatever they could get free. The big day came and went with the grace of a swan gliding across the water of a smooth pond. It was like a family gathering that you dream about and this one came true. The only expense was for those who wanted beverages from the bar. Even the clean up was done with everyone pitch in. It was rather warm day; some of the people took time out to fish off the deck. There was lot of hooting going on when someone caught anything. Everyone enjoyed the music, with everyone in the family taking part in the different dances. We even did the chicken dance along with some square dancing. Great day had by all.

Jenny was called into work because the hospital found itself short staffs do to the demands of the public. Life seems to go on even on holidays and sometimes the holidays cause health issues that we call accidents. At least she did not miss much because she left just after six. I stayed around helping putting Johnny's place back in order. We still had food left over after to feed everyone who stayed around for late supper. I finally rolled in to bed by eleven exhausted.

This night, sleep did not come easy. I am not sure, if it was from all the food I consumed, the freedom of interacting with people who care or because it is Thursday night, the usual night before seeing Roger, whatever. The nightmares troubled my sleep all night long, one after another.

One of them I remembered took me back to Spain. I was in kaleidoscope of events. I was squirming all over the bed. The scenes were racing into each other. Words didn't hang together to make a sentence. Parts of people interacted with me but before I could respond, everything changed again. Colors, sounds, flashes of people, events, began to spin out of control. The continual struggling caused my body and bed to be soaking in my sweat. I finally screamed out in pain and terror, which brought me back to my bedroom. I was sitting up in bed, just soaked and shaking, and so grateful these condos are sound proof.

I sat there for a while trying to make sense of what happened in my nightmare, but I couldn't. I felt a chill race over me that brought me back to survival mode. I need to get into shower to get control of my body. As I was busy washing off the damp dank sweat and I was running my tub at the same time. When the tub was filled, I went in with sea salt and spent the next hour just spaced out. I didn't let my mind travel anywhere, kept focus on letting go of all the craziness that I was dealing with from my horrendous, tortuous sleep.

When my world seamed sane again, I got out of the tub and put on bathrobe to prepare to change the bed. Even the mattress cover was soaked and it needed to be changed. I put on some soothing music to calm the room down. I remade the bed, took all the bedding to the laundry room, and started the washer. I retreated to the kitchen for something; I ended up having a small glass of red wine and played a couple games of solitaire. When the washing machine completed its function, I transferred everything into the dryer. When back to my bedroom, slipped in to dry bed and my eyes closed on the clock reporting it was only three a.m.

Jenny got home at four because everything was under control at the hospital. She smelt the warm fragrant air as she passed the laundry room. When she opened the door, she was aware that Alex must have done the laundry. When she took the bedding out of the dryer, which was still warm, she knew he must have had one of those nights from hell. He always does the laundry when that happens. Even the mattress cover was here, that is not a good sign. She finished folding the bedding and carried it up stairs. As she looked into their bedroom, Alex was fast asleep in a fetal position. I have seen this before, she talked to herself, and I know he needs his space so I guess I will retire to the guest room tonight. I never know how he will react after one of his nightmares. Jenny was using the guest bathroom to reduce any disturbing sounds and she gave herself the feeling of being a guest as she rolled into bed under the covers and the sandman rolled her into a deep relaxing sleep.

When I got up it was almost ten, I must have forgotten to set the alarm. Jenny must not be home yet, because her side of bed is undisturbed. I went about getting ready for the day. Maybe she decided to sleep at the hospital; she does that if she too tired to drive. I went about my day, making brunch and decided to go for a walk since it was nice day. I could stop by to see if Johnny needed any help to kill time since the office is close today. I realize I needed some alone time, I walked out on the deck and found a vacant comfortable bench facing out over the river. The weather was clear and gently warm enough to spend time being lost in the daydreams. Suddenly I felt a hand on my shoulder; I came out of my daydream state of being to see who is disturbing me. My out of focus eyes slowly came into focus, and there stood that lovely woman who shares my life.

"Jenny, how did you find me? I thought you must have slept at the hospital since you were not in bed this morning. You can see I have been just wasting the day, doing nothing, just waiting for you to come home. Oh dear, I forgot to write you a note to tell you where I was. I guess I am guilt of my first omission to our marriage." I was trying to be amusing but by the look on her face, it was not flying.

"My dear man, you can try to fool this old girl as much as you might, but she knows your tricks. Best you give it up, and come clean, about what you have been up to when your wife has been slaving away at work. You better chose your words carefully, mister, because I have hired detectives to watching you daily to protect my investment." With those words, Jenny laughed aloud, bent down, and kissed him. She slid in beside him on the bench and they sat there quietly side by side.

"Well! My dear lady, how did it go yesterday? Did you earn your money or was it a false alarm?" again I was trying to keep conversation light while I was trying to clear the cobwebs of last night's terror out of my head.

"Wouldn't you know, people just like to put on their acts of craziness and we had a full night? The emergency trucks were out collecting customers for us to insure we would be busy. Overall, I think it was worse than Labor Day Weekend. All the beds are full. We had a break, lull, and plenty of staff so they let me off early so I came home at four. You were in such a sound sleep and I was bushed, I decided to sleep in the guest room. You know that maybe a great place to retreat to when we have our off days." Jenny was trying to be informative and loose at the same time. She was getting to read her husband better to know when he still coming out of these shattering nightmares. "I have to say dear husband of mine, if you want to keep me in good spirits, you better buy me lunch or brunch because your working slave is hungry. I thought with all the food I ate yesterday, I would not need to eat for a week, and that is not true."

"Let it not be said that the master of the house starves his slave," as I grabbed her hand, jumped up while pulling her to her feet and pulled her close for a kiss.

"No! You don't; none of that until your slave is fed. You are not going to take advantage of your slave in such a weakening condition as I am in now. You will be rewarded with a kiss when you earn it with food." Jenny broke out of my grip and starting running down the deck laughing that laugh of catch me if you can.

I half-heartedly ran after her. She made it through the door, closed it quickly to slow me down even more. She was sitting in our favorite table by the time I finally came through the door. I began arguing with myself, 'I can't understand why I can't snap out of these funky moods when I have someone I love so much'. Still! There is that fear 'am I deserving or entitled or - - so many mixed emotions'. The closer I get to be free of my karmic past, the greater the ugly monster grabs me. The monster of 'what if' is dominating my every thought. 'What if it can't be corrected? What if it will be worse that it is now. What if I lose her in all of this? What if, what if, what if, goes on and on causing my eyes to dance in ocean of water. My body shaking like earthquake. I slow down to walk, in fact, dragging my feet. Suddenly a hand pushes against my back with a jolt; I looked over my shoulder into the face of my grinning brother in law.

"Come along little doggie, you are keeping my favorite sister waiting. I can be a mean dog if you don't keep her happy" with his chucking voice. Johnny could read his old boss, and he was in one of those far out spaces. He is aware that Alex is cooking again, something is about to erupt. All the signs were there, so I had better be on guard again to help him. "By the look on her face, you have been starving her, and that is unacceptable to me, especially when I run a restaurant. I have the menus in my hand, so let's move a little faster." Laughter still masked his true concern.

"Just three months of marriage, dear brother, he is starting to neglect me. Just taking me for granted. What do you suggest I do about it, oh wise brother of mine?" Jenny playful matter was to keep the kidding going.

Johnny was quick on the gun "sister, you give me the word, and I will deck him for you. That should teach him to honor you in the correct way and in keeping with his marriage vows to you. I was a witness, so he can't crawl out from his obligation."

"Enough you two, I surrender, so feed the fair maiden before she evaporates away. My dear brother in law, you can put it on my tab, excluding any consideration of a tip because of the way you treat your most valuable brother in law." I replied to this badgering.

The spell was broken, from that point on it was just friendly jibbing and trying to make the mood lighter. Johnny and Jenny are very aware that I am going into one of those devastating emotional house-cleaning activities. Johnny ordered our food and when came back and spent the mealtime with us. He also took the time to plug his Jake's Country Western Band that will be here on Saturday and twisted our arm to attend. We finally agreed to show up. Having made his victory, he excused himself to get back to work.

Jenny and I sat there for another hour just watching the activity on the river and having a quiet time together. The rest of day just marched by until she needed to go to work. Jenny also informed me as of 1 December, she would have completed all her requirement for graduation. The best part of it; she will be assigned to the day shift for the coming month, the first Monday of December. We will have more time together.

However, before she went off to work, she dragged me out to do some Christmas shopping because of the after Thanksgiving sales. This is our first year for decorating for holidays; we went to the craft store Michaels to get everything we need. With the coupons and sale items, we almost save as much as we spent. What a deal. We got home just in time to give her kiss goodbye and I am left alone again.

I took a walk around the construction site to witness that the back row of condos had their roofs on, some siding, and windows. That will mean that with a little luck in the weather, we could have at least one row completed before Christmas. We have a buyer who would like to be here for the holidays. We may not have any of the landscaping done, but they don't care. That is good for us.

I toured the new acquisition beyond our motel area to see how that will serve us. When you hold the vision, sometimes, supplementary things happen in the best of ways for you. We have most of July and August reserved at the motel and we have not begun to build it. I am so glad that I can separate my own personal problems from the business. I know that by giving the positive same attention to my own stuff, I will be free of the past very soon.

I look out on the river where the motel will be and what a view. A car cargo ship was quietly slipping down the river, riding high to tell the world its delivery has been made. The evening is settling gently on the river, and the man made lightening lamps are coming alive. The waves from the ship and the lights sliding across the river, gives your imagination time to wander to wherever gives you pleasure. I am slowly making my way back home and I hear my name echo over the water.

Ol' Johnson was calling out to me a greeting and at the same time he was motioning me to come on over to his houseboat. I thought, now, I have nothing else to do now. I walked out on his pier and joined him in his floating home. He saw me wondering around and wanted some company for little while. He offered coffee. We took our mugs into the living room where we could look out over the river and sat in overstuffed rockers. We just talked for a while about everything and sometimes nothing. When the clock rang out nine, I decided to head for home, so I excuse myself and was on my way.

Arriving home, I remembered I did not bring all the decorating stuff in from the garage that we bought today. That was another hour that was washed away. Jenny wanted to get started on this project this weekend so as December comes crashing in on us we are ready.

I finally went upstairs and let the bed consume my body as I was awash in night of darkness. When the alarm went off, I felt like I just lying down. I think I will get up and have breakfast ready for my wife since she made a big deal about starving her yesterday to her brother.

CHAPTER 32

I had farmer's breakfast plate ready as she came through the door. For some strange reason she called as she left work, it usually takes her 30 minutes on good day and that is how long it takes to put this creation together. I made toast, coffee, juice and had peanut butter nuggets for something sweet to end the breakfast. She made a stab at all the food I prepared, but I could see I made enough for four instead of two. I love being married with these special moments we share. I could see the candle of light going out in her eyes, time to let the sand man in if we are going dancing to night. I didn't have to convince her it was time for bed. She was gone in staggering flash. I cleaned up my cooking mess and spent most of the day in my office study on third floor. I was working on the layout of the parking area of the land we just bought and determining if a boat-launching ramp would not be bad idea from that space. It would reduce traffic and would be convenient for everyone. There are always small projects, with low priority that you leave until you have nothing else commotion, and then is when busy work completed.

I just finish cleaning up and dressed for the evening and I heard Jenny was about. I found her in the kitchen, warming up some of the left over breakfast because she was hungry. We greeted each other, I informed her I was going over to help Johnny get things ready for tonight, and I would be back later. I got back in time to escort my date to a late dinner at the restaurant and enjoy an evening of dancing and plain old fun.

Sunday was consumed with opening all the boxes of holiday stuff we bought on Friday. We had to rearrange the furniture a couple of times to get the right presentation. The artificial twelve-foot tree and all the decorations took up most of the afternoon. A glass or two of wine made the day pass easy. By nine o'clock, the whole downstairs glowed with decorations, but when she went up to my study, she decided that it would require decorations and maybe a tree for the middle window. I wanted to say no to her suggestions. When she gives me that look, what is a man to do? That will have to wait until tomorrow morning so we will have it all done before she goes to work. That night was as nice as honeymoon as you can have.

When morning arrived, Jenny had breakfast on the table, quick meal and out the door. The store was opening early and she wanted to be sure we could get the decorations to match that what we had. I was blessed with 7 1/2ft narrow tree with all the trimmings. Most the afternoon I was doing the work myself because Jenny needed to sleep before she head off to work. Few more days of the PA training and then she will be back on day shift, I thought it would never happen.

The whole week seemed to be kept busy doing many miscellaneous items. The end of the month reports that eats up most of the time. When Barbara balanced out the books, we were in great shape with the business. Every night was some dark journey for me but nothing that caused the sweats. The whole condo project had finished with its outside decoration for the holidays. They were all on timers, when it comes on at dark until twelve midnight we are all lit up. All of our streets were alive with color along with the yards that were decorated complementing each other. Our decoration came on from five to midnight every day now. The holiday spirit was gaining momentum and it showed on everyone.

The Thursday night before I was scheduled to see Roger, I had another one of those all nighters. I changed the bed twice. I never understand where all that sweat comes from. I got out of the house before Jenny got home because I did not look great. I even stole a little of her make up to put a little color in my face. It is dam hard to do this when you have not done it before and make it look natural. My face was remade about five times before it looked okay to me. When I arrived at the restaurant, the waitress gave me that look but did not say anything. Then Johnny came over and had to say it, "the blush does make you look better, but must say, maybe you should have a professional help you" as he was trying to stuff his laughter.

I quick took my cloth napkin and tried to wipe off what little I had on, and I guess it just made it worse. I excused myself and in the men's room, I finished removing it. Back at the table, my food was waiting and so was Johnny.

"I am not sure if you look better or worse with or without. I guess I have to vote for the "with". You must have had one of those nights again. They will soon be over because I keep getting that feeling, maybe this will be last day with Roger, and you can have a normal life. Then again, with you, what is normal?" Johnny was trying to be supportive knowing his friend and what he is about to face this day.

"You are hell of lot of help, with this with or without. At least I was able to make it through last night without any help from anyone. That was a good sign for me. Of course, I had to change the bed twice. I really thought those nights were over when I got rid of the ex-wife Marian. This Spanish era distress has me running on the edge. Kevin keeps telling me, that we are not going to deal with the destructive activity of my physical body then but the real cause that the players did to me, my soul. I have no idea what is going to happen, but with Roger and Kevin, I have nothing to be concerned." The soft words flowed out of my mouth almost to a whisper of disbelief.

"You better eat something, it is almost time for you to take your boat ride, and I need to get back to work. This job takes more time, than I thought it would, when I made the move to have this business. I found the recipe on how to make "Texas Hot" as they do back in the northeast. I am going to make them available for lunches for now on. That sauce was the hardest to master, but I got it now. It will be great to have served in the summer time when you charcoal broil the hot dogs. Here I am running off at the mouth, you better get a move on because your time is about up" were Johnny closing words as he walks away to insure that I get going.

I put on my winter outfit even though the day seems mild. The run up the river was uneventful. Made the dock, tied up, hasten up the path to Roger who waiting with my tea and took off my weather gear, and shoes. I began maybe my last journey into the past. I will also know why I have this feeling of loosing Jenny too. A few words pass between us, as we were to make maybe our last journey to "the room" and the chair that holds me while I face my yesterdays. I took long drink as I sat down and settled back to begin. Roger reminded me, to take my time and to know he is here if I need him. He just started his words and I was gone.

Kevin was waiting for me. We mixed a few words because I was beginning to feel up tight and afraid. Again, he assured me that the worse was over because they were working with me during those sweats to remove what was necessary. He went on to say we are going to be observers of the event, so if I can keep my emotions in check, we can get through this final phase. I have reviewed your records; this is the last activity to set you free. It is nothing you have done, really; again, it important to remember it was a crime against you. You just put too much faith in people and when they don't live up to their pledge to you, you take it a personal injury.

Lets look at Antonio, the priest, who professes to be your most dear and trusted friend. A man of virtue, a man of the cloth as to speak but has never been tested to see if his words and his actions match. We are going to witness, Roxxo challenge him and his own fears eat up all his wonderful words, for self-survival is major to him. He ran away so he was not present at your death. Look at him, he's just human, and nothing more or less. His professed belief in his God and Jesus could not sustain him at this time. You were expendable. However, let us go fast forward to after your death.

He travels to your home and prays for your safe return with your family, knowing that would never happen. His fear that someone will find out he did nothing to save you haunts him night and day. Then one of Roxxo's hired men to capture you, sold out to a government agent who was tracking down the crime. The letter summons you, that you left in your haste, was given to the government agent turn out to be fraud. You don't kill a relative of the king and get away with it. Roxxo realized that he may be in danger, had notified Antonio that he was being called back to Rome. He skipped town to save his own skin. It was less than 2 months; an arrest warrant was out for the hired captures. Antonio thought he could hide behind the church, but some very interesting poison found its way into his communion wine that cause a very slow painful death.

Therefore, you see, being betrayed by a man of the cloth, as in the 91st Psalm, "vengeance is mine saith the lord", what goes around comes around.

He received his just rewards. He had violated many moral and spiritual laws before you were involved. For which he will have his karmic payment or atonement to live within a life upon this earth should he ever want to heal his soul. There is no free ride when you violate the rules our souls are govern by.

Now let us look at the last moments before your death. You stayed your course that you were never a heretic to save your family. We placed your soul in a comma like state for almost 100 earth years to deal with the event that was not to happen to you. This truly was a wild card as we call it. We knew the "the Keeper" was born and lived in Italy and his name was Roxxo. We never conceived in our wildest dreams he would ever come to Spain, let alone meet you. Just before you died, you finally understood who Roxxo [The Egyptian Keeper] was and your anger went off the scale. This is where everything deteriorated.

You cried out from your soul the following: Where you never ever going to be free from that bond? The bastard has caused my death in other times because I was not serving him. Is there no method, system, or God that can free me from this unholy curse that I entered into because of my lust and greed for a good life? I have grown, I found my spiritual path of evolution, but still I am tortured by that damn pledge. Your inability to deal with the violence of your death as a result of your commitment, the loss of your wife and children that had finally open your soul to the spirituality you always wanted and seeking in physical form, and you went into deep dark hole of depression we could not reach you. The only healing we could do is put you in a comma and to send your soul healing energy to bring you back.

This lifetime, you did find always to finally break that commitment to "The Keeper". The anger of your death in Spain gave you the strength to push for final dissolution of the agreement and your freedom. The Keeper's revenge was really his undoing, for which we are all thankful. The loss of the family was also part of the push to make it so."

"Kevin did I ever find my wife or children after I got out of the coma? Did I try to find them? What happen to them? I abandon them, myself, what have I done?" My voice was slipping way, darkness was flooding over me, and I am lost.

"Adrian [Alex] listens to me. Not all is lost. Adrian come back" my God I am losing him.

Kevin now is pleading with "Roger, I am in trouble. Alex is slipping away from me. You need to get Johnny and Jenny here as quickly as possible. I don't know what to do exactly. We have a team working on this now. We had considered he might fall into that black hole again since he was there before. We thought we had all the bases covered, but I am afraid not."

Roger was on the phone to Johnny who was informed what had happen and that Kevin needs him and his sister as soon as possible. We are in trouble with Alex. Please hurry, Kevin is trying to hold him from falling in to a deep coma he was in before as much as he can but he needs help.

Johnny hung up the phone, raced over to Jenny's condo and with his key, he let himself in. Knowing Jenny is probably sleeping, he ran up stairs and into their bedroom. She was out cold in sleep. "Jenny, Jenny wake up, wake up, we need your help" was his crying words.

Jenny sat up quickly, caught between sleep, awake, and emergency. "Where am I? Johnny what are you doing in the hospital? No, where am I? What is happening?" utterly lost.

"Jenny, Alex is with Roger and something went wrong and they are having a hard time bring him out of hypnosis. They need us there as soon as possible. I am not sure what we can do, but we have to do something. I'll go down stairs and make some coffee while you get dressed and come down." Johnny rushed out of the room before Jenny could say anything and heading for the kitchen. He had to keep busy so his mind would not get lost in "what if".

Jenny stumbled out of bed, still in daze, trying to put on her slacks and sweater, which seem like forever activity, and grabbed her shoes while heading down stairs. Upon entering the kitchen, Johnny was pouring her coffee, that microwave stuff. "Jenny, I don't know anything about what has happen, so please don't ask questions, I can't answer. We can take my boat, thank God; I did not put it way last weekend. [Jenny was busy drinking down this awful tasting coffee and finished dressing] Are you ready?" Jenny replied "yes".

They ran from her condo, to the dock, into Johnny's boat, cast off, fired up the engine and they were off. It seemed forever to get to Roger's dock.

They could see the boat Alex was using tied up there. As soon as Johnny's boat touched the dock, Jenny jumped out and ran up the patch to Roger who was waiting. Johnny quickly tied up the boat and followed as quickly as he could. On the porch, Roger greeted them and showed them the way to the room where Alex was sitting in the chair.

"Johnny," the voice coming from Alex's mouth was that of Kevin "Alex is slipping into a "black hole of comma" that was used when he lived in Spain and had that devastating experience. We can't seem to bring him out of it. The only solution we can come up with is Jenny needs to let Roger hypnosis her to bring her to me. We will have to work from here. Of course, Jenny needs to want to do this. She will really have to trust us. One because she has never really experience hypnosis and this period of history, Spain, and all has been problems for her too. Therefore, I need to address you, Jenny. Will you help us?"

"Of course, I will, just tell me what I must do" was almost her panic response.

"Jenny come sit here in this seat, I will walk you through the process, and you just have to let yourself go. The more you are relaxed, the faster this will happen. So take a few deep breaths. Slow in and out, in and out. Try to relax, you know the drill, you do it a lot where you work. Get centered, block out everything, and listen to my words. When you are under, your soul will meet Kevin, who is Alex's guardian and he will be directing what you can do to help" with his most assuring words, Roger could muster.

"I will be ready in a minute. Let me get focus, centered and ready." There was this long pause and finally she said she was ready.

Roger started the process of slowing talking her into the space where she can step out of the body and she was there looking at Kevin.

"Welcome Jenny, what we have to do first, your name while with me is Jazmyn. That was your name when you were in Spain. Alex knew you by that name because you might as well just jump in with both feet. You were his loving wife. His name is Jimena. You think your life now is good, it was ten times better then. Alex so overcome with grief etc. that he again is slipping into that black hole of a comma where he was before to keep from being destroyed. It is a place where healing can take place. You need to call him by his name Jimena with as much love as you can. We believe that you can bring him back or talk him out of the comma. The last time, it was 100 years. We don't have that time now. I am not going there with any explanation. Just start calling out his name. Roger has you sitting next to Alex, I want you to take your physical hand and lay it on top of Alex's hand. Now begin calling his name slowly and lovely as possible. Kevin now tells Johnny, you take a hold of his physical hand on the other side away from Jenny to act as ground and be there for whatever we will need to bring him back. If we don't get him back, his earth body may die or go into a coma too. I am here to tell you that will not happen on my watch. I have the best spirit doctors here monitoring to reduce any unexpected risk. We did not plan or suspect this would happen, so we need to be on our toes on this" were Kevin's instructions.

Jenny began by squeezing her hand on his as she could see this man lay before her. He did not look like Alex but she felt she had to do this. After saying his name a number of time and with as much feeling as she could for this stranger, all of a sudden, she knew him. She was Jazmyn and her long lost love was there before her eyes. Such passion and love flooded over and through her that almost cause her to swoon. She had marvelously found him. After all this time, how her heart still ach for him. No one could ever fill that void since then except for this man called Alex, which caused more questions than answers right now. She became to stroke his arm and finally in this dream state, she ran her hand over his head.

He appeared to her as he was laying on a gurney. She felt like she in the hospital and we were in emergency room. She took her time walking around the gurney while talking to him. He did not respond to any touch. He was not cold to the touch. What must I do to help wake him up, no pull him back, damn if I know what. She remembered she would blow her breath on his face when he was sleeping. It would not take long for him to awaken with a passion for her. She kept saying his name as she blew her breath on his face. She bent over closer to his face. Continually breathing and blowing on him, saying his name in a rhythm as she always said it. She took her finger and slowly moved it down beside his nose and gentle back and forth across his lips. Still no response, but the skin was feeling warmer to the touch. She bent down and gave him a very gentle kiss as she used to. They used to tease each other that it was bunny fur kiss. It always raised the passion between them. His body seemed less lifeless as she pulled away. She found herself getting up on the gurney and laying beside him. The gurney seemed to expand to make that possible. She kept breathing on his face and calling his name. Then she remembers she would run her finger down his chest and find his belly button and push some pressure on it. That used to arouse him also. She kept blowing on his face while saying his name repeatedly. Now she slides her finger from his lips down his chin, throat, and down the front of his chest. The finger finally found that very touchy spot of his, his belly button. She gently massages it as she used to while pressing her body tighter against him. His body seemed to begin to respond to what she was doing. His lips parted and that was her clue before to give his bunny fur kiss while gently blowing her breathe into his mouth. She was slowly oh so slowly lost in their old lovemaking. Jazmyn [Jenny] found she was being caught up in the process and this action caused her to hunger for him more. These past hundreds of years have left me wanting the man she loved with every cell in her body.

Kevin kept watching what has happening. The other spiritual doctors were monitoring him too. It appears that he is fighting his way back out of the black dark hole of nothingness.

Jazmyn slide over on top of him. Keep breathing on him, chanting his name with all the love she could give. His body began to respond as men do. She knew she had found her husband again. His breath began to pick up speed in the rhythm of hers. He began to feel alive. He open is eyes.

"Jazmyn where have you been? I have been looking all over for you. I should have listen to you and waited until morning, but I didn't. No." he screams out as he held her tight "they killed you too. Oh! I am so sorry" he began to cry.

Kevin realizes he slipping, comes to them, "Jazmyn tell him you are not dead. He is not dead. You are at home. He had a very bad dream."

Jazmyn [Jenny] realizing when patient is going sour; you need to get some action going here. "Jimena, my darling, I am just wakening you from a very bad dream. You are not dead nor am I dead. The children and your mother are waiting for us to take a buggy ride to town. Remember you promised you would take them to the fair that is in town. On the other hand, would you rather make love to me? However, I have to tell you that

I would want you to take us all to town. Now let's get up and not let them wait any longer for us. Come my darling, we need to go."

Jimena open is eyes again, "you mean we are not dead. That was such a real dream; I thought I lost you forever. Well! Let us not keep the family waiting. Take my hand and let's see what the fair has for us today."

I open my eyes and I was back. Jenny found herself back at the same time. I started to cry and was shaking uncontrollable. Jenny just put her arms around me and kept repeatedly whisper to me, the nightmare is over. I have found you. You have found me. That is all that matters. That horror able nightmare is really over. Because you finally understood why it happen, you can let it go. That history is finally over and we can live again.

I began to settle down and was just lost in nothing for few minutes. Roger had gotten some fresh tea to help settle me down. I realize Johnny was there holding my hand also. We all sat there in disbelief and belief of what had happen. If everyone had not done his or her part, who knows what would have happen. We don't want to go there.

"Alex, now I know why I had that lost feeling when we were in Madrid and sometimes when I go away, I was not sure you would be home when I got there." Jenny explained.

"I miss you too to point it sometimes uncomfortable, not knowing why. Still I was haunted by unknown fear that could not be explained." I replied.

Roger knowing that there were loose ends that needed to be addressed. Addressing the group, "we don't explore this event without Kevin's help. I want both of you back here next week together this time. We need to finish up and there are many loose ends. You both may get clues during the week. I would like you to journal them down, talk them out and bring them with you next week. I am so thankful that Johnny and you, Jenny, were available today. I am thankful nothing destructive took place. This is why we try going at a safe pace and with as much support as possible. We really don't know what totally happen in the past, and what you came here to heal. Saying that, we really have no idea how this physical form is going to react to all that happen back then. The healing sometimes is painful too. With love and support, we can always be winner. Therefore, you guys, I will see you next week. I will be here if you need me. Johnny, you better come along also, I want to make sure we have all the bases covered this time."

We all just filed out of the room, at the porch Jenny and I gave Roger a hug and slowly walked back to the boats, without saying a word. It was like being in shock or how do you organize it to make sense of it all. We tied my boat to Johnny's and headed for home all of us in Johnny's boat. It was very quick trip. Johnny offered dinner, but we passed this time and went home. It seems strange but without saying anything, we went in, got undress and went to bed. Jenny set the alarm to get up for her last night shift for while. We just hugged each other and quickly lost in sleep. The alarm when off and Jenny left and I didn't hear either one. I was so exhausted from that experience which I still don't want to process it yet.

At nine a.m. I felt a cold hand on my shoulder and I came charging out of nothingness back to reality. My eyes flew open, there staring at me was good old Johnny.

He looked at me for a minute or two, then piped out "you bum; you can't lie in bed all day doing nothing. I have some errands in the city and you can come along to keep me company. I will not listen to any lame excuse of why you can't. So get the hell out of bed, shower, and let's get going. I will at least make you a cup of real coffee to assist your day." He turned and walked away to the door, where he stood to make sure I got out of bed and was heading to the bathroom.

The shower felt good and in some manner, I got dressed and went down stairs following the aroma of fresh brew coffee. It was poured and Johnny made himself at home, eating my last sticky bun. You get to know someone, and by his or her looks, you can tell what they are thinking. His thought was, your poor unlucky not to be up or you would have this hot sticky bun for your breakfast.

"I knew yesterday was a rough day for you, so let us keep busy doing busy work and enjoying the day. I know you should prevent your mind to travel or try to make sense of yesterday. Your present mind needs a rest from it all. Therefore, my dear brother in law, I going to keep you busy all day long, until Jenny get home. Then it is her job. Kevin told me that he really would like you both not to discuss yesterday until maybe Tuesday night. Your spirit team and Jenny's spirit team are working on away to reduce the complexity of it all. You have tried two life times before to deal with the events of Spain with no success. The "Keeper" was born last lifetime without you, and ended up captured as young Greek man and sold into slavery for his full life. That was his punishment along with a few other zingers. That is why everyone was working on breaking that bond to him this lifetime. Therefore, you severed that bond forever. You did a splendid job.

Now you have been working on the healing of your personal love lost these past months. That has been a heavy too. I have found my peace between us and know the pure friendship love we had 2500 years ago. I am glad our personal relationship is back in balance. Everything I am doing lately flows that loving energy around and through it, makes my life's journey more of a fun game. So before the day gets away from us. Finish your coffee and let's be on the road" was Johnny demanding voice as he headed out the door expecting me to follow post haste.

We got in his waiting truck and headed for wholesalers in Portland for some items he forgot to order on his last shipment. We talked about everything but most of it was about how I worked through the struggle of breaking away from my ex-wife. He had a spirit team working with him then as now. Therefore, the review was to remember the strength that exist and I can do this. [We did not discuss the black hole coma that was strictly off the table for now].

We stopped at wholesalers, pick up the supplies, and we were on our way back within a half an hour. The conversation seemed to die for most of the trip back home. He even kept me busy unloading and storing the goods. Then busy work around the restaurant to keep me occupied. I knew it was for my own good, so I made a game out of it and kept telling myself no job was beneath my dignity. Cleaning rest rooms, a downgraded work far from my life aboard the yacht "Ra" where I didn't nothing. Everything was performed for me. Still I wouldn't go back to that shell of life for anything. What I have now, a life that gives me pride in myself. The rewards are the real people that live in my life to add meaning and purpose to their life as well as mine. I was busy in the last rest room upstairs when Jenny poked her head in demanding to use the facility since it was for women only. We both got a laugh out of that and I was especially glad to see her.

"Your brother kidnapped me and has me doing the worse job in the world. I am glad the maiden has come to rescue me. Thank you, thank you." With all the pledging voice, I could muster.

Jenny laughed back "not on your life, you have earned the right of having this job and I will not take your prize away from you. So I will see you down stairs when you finish not only cleaning but remember to sanitizing too."

Jenny was gone before I could reply. I quickly completed the task and put all the supplies away. I cleaned up and joined her at our favorite table looking out on the river. She had a craft of wine waiting for me on the table and appetizers as reward for completing my assignment. During this time, it transferred into quiet time after she told me about her day. We both wanted not to talk about yesterday either. The place was filling up and we had some friends of the project join us at our table to keep the conversation light and easy. Johnny had music right on schedule, which gave us excuse to get up and dance. I never understand why people wait until the first couple to break the ice, before they will come out on the floor. Fast and slow, western and jazz, there was action for everyone. By eleven, we bid everyone around us good night and we escaped to our home. The timers had all the Christmas lights on and the house, which is our home, welcomed us with blazing love. We retired quickly and that day was done.

CHAPTER 33

Sunday morning crept in, I found myself feeling like a little cuddling, and whatever time, but I found the other side of the bed cold and vacant. I got up and dressed. Made my travels to the kitchen to find breakfast was about to be served. So much food, I protest that if I eat it all, I will weight a ton. Jenny laugh saying that we were going walking for next couple hours with some of the friends we spent time with last night. You must remember you were the one that suggested that we hike the old road to town and back for something to do. I expect you will have a crowd about 10 plus people at our door in about 20 minutes. So eat what you can, we need to be ready. The weather was just warm enough to make the walk pleasant along with some sunshine.

They were all on time, and I glad I stuffed myself. Two hours later, we were back and I still felt full. The day was just great with full sun, little breeze and the trees naked of their leaves gives completely new view of the countryside. In Oregon, we also have the landscape filled with dotted areas of green from our wonderful pine trees

Jim invited for last ride on his 27 footer on the river at one because he was hauling her in for the winter and get her ready for next spring. We cruised the river nice, slow, and easy. Coffee was served because drinking and boating does not mix with our crowd. By four, we were done with riding around and I helped Jim get her on its trailer. That is always a couple of workers' activity. Jim towed it to repair yard and storage. Jenny and I walked over to new land I bought and wondered if we had enough space to build boat storage area for the people living here. We did lot of discussing on how it might work, but I think we decided that Francis and Judy would have to tell us if it would work.

We finally went home and made a small light supper. After supper, we did the most comfortable activity I have ever done before. We put on some real nice soft love music. We turn off the lights and bath in the holiday lights from the decorations and the tree. It seemed like we just settled into the mood when we hear the clock strike eleven. It is time for bed. Jenny needs to be into work by seven. I sent her on ahead, and I finished putting things way and then I headed for bed. Jenny was fast asleep. For some strange reason, I went up to my office, I thought I would sit in my easy chair for little while before I turn in. My lights went out and when the morning sun flooded my eyes, I was back. On my blanket was love note from Jenny who will see me late this afternoon.

All week long seemed to be a blur of continual activity of some sorts because it seems busy but nothing stands out as important. Except that Roger called to tell me that, he had to hold off our meeting on Friday to Saturday afternoon at two. I told him that okay with us, because we would have had to make special arrangement for Jenny to get the time off on Friday. If the weather permitting, we will motor up the river to be, there on time for maybe the last river trip.

I truly do not understand what happen last week session because we did not discuss the experience. I have had some real strange dreams where I am falling in and out of black hole. Some I am screaming and some things where beyond description with no sweats. I found myself sleeping in the chair in my office upstairs, but Jenny did not seem to mind. We would take some side remarks about how strange our night sleep has been this week. Yet! The remarks were more in passing, rather than point of exploring what they mean. Johnny did his check in on me most the weekdays along with Barbara. You would think I was going to do something crazy. I do not have that madness I experienced trying to break away from my x-wife. Still it was more heartrending where I could cry without any apparent justification. My mood swings were all over the place when I am alone, still it is strange when Jenny is around, none of that happens. I was not conscious of what was causing it I just let it happen. We both kept a journal as requested by Roger.

The Friday night, I went up to my office to look over some blue prints that Francis sent over to me about boat sheds and how much space they would use. I started to look at them, and began to cry my eyes out. The water was leaking everywhere. I wasn't making any noise, which was so strange; it came and went with waves. I finally got up, dropped into my easy chair, and pulled the blanket over me. I was lost some place in time but I don't remember where. Jenny shook me to wake me up because it was time to go to bed. For some reason she was not going to let me get lost tonight in my chair. I followed her down stairs to our bedroom. We both got ready for bed and as we hugged, the world slipped away from us both.

The light and very strange feelings crept over me. I could feel the passion moving over me in waves. I was struggling to bring myself out of my sleep and for some reason I was having trouble break through. There was this pungent fruity gently air drifting across my face. I wanted to break through to awaken to what is happening and still there was the sweet pleasure that held me fast. A soft finger slide across my brow and down the side of my nose, finally it was resting on my lips. It gently moved back and forth as if it was sending signals to different areas of my body. Those areas were becoming aroused. Then that soft finger slide down my chin and neck on to my chest. It ventured over to my nipple on one side and then gently on the other side. Finally, it continued it journey to my belly button where it kept delicately sympathetically sensitively circling that area. My body began to race with hormones, heat, and pounding blood. I kept fighting to awaken still it eluded me. Then it stopped, I felt some motion, as if someone was hovering over me and slowly allowing our fleshes quietly touch. I was aroused I was awake. My eyes wide open, looking into Jenny loving caring face and we were.

Saturday was here; we finally dressed for the day, and had brunch over at Johnny's restaurant as usual. He joined us for a short while and we talked about going to see Roger. He decided he did not need to hitch a ride with us. I kept getting the thought everything will be o.k.

It was almost one, so we got on our winter coats, and hat for fast ride up to see Roger with expectation that this will be our last journey for healing the past karmic trauma. The river was like glass because there were no boats were out nor was there any wind. We were experiencing a one of our normal gray winter days, enjoyable, with the sun trying to burn its way through the overcast.

At the dock, the usual drill, tie up the boat and hike up to Roger who was now holding three cups of tea. After removing our winter coats and shoes at the door, we went through our normal greeting but I could tell he wanted to get this project on the road. Roger handed us out tea and ushered us through the house and down the hall to our room. It was set up with two recliners besides each other with coffee table between and he sat opposite us. We gave him our journals that we were to write our thoughts during the week for him to read.

"This should not be very dramatic; most of it will be in the hands of Kevin. I will take you both in at the same time. Just follow along with me you will be there quickly. Have a great trip and let's get all the housekeeping done this time" as Roger words began to fade for me, Jenny had to be walk on in. While you are gone, I will take the time to read your journaling.

Kevin was there waiting. It just took a few minutes and Jenny was with us. Kevin formally introduced himself this time, when she came last time; he was too busy trying to hold the space to prevent any additional problems. Jenny acknowledged him.

"The reason for this meeting is to clear up a lot of pain. First, Jazmyn [Jenny] you spent the rest of your life in grieving over disappearance and the loss of your husband. You knew some how he was dead, that he had not abandoned you and the children. You also placed so much blame on yourself; you should have prevented him leaving. Your prayers were unending about forgiveness for failure to do what you should have done. This guilt has prevented you from having a healthy, loving relationship with a man ever since then. You have spent the last two life times being an unmarried woman. You have this cloud of fear with this marriage.

This past week, your spirit team has released layers of energy and guilt off your soul because you allowed them to do so. We are again going to show you what happen that night he left. See it for real and we will be prepared to help you deal with your emotions of that time. [There was viewing of the kidnap, trial, very little of torture scenes for Jimena and Jazmyn for observing what happen only stopping to ask pointed questions.] When it was completed, Jazmyn realized there was nothing she could have done different. There was no blame or guilt attach to this event for her.

The same was for Jimena; he could not have done any different because of the man he was. Jimena was having the hardest time with this because of the guilt that drove him into the black hole comma. We, spirit teachers, spent time going repeatedly with Jazmyn while he was in spirit helping him understand this could not play out any different. The good that came out of this was Jazmyn was able to run the estate successful while raising the children. The spiritual, moral goals you both set for the family and for those who work for the estate did prove to be enlightening and empowering for everyone. The strength to forge forward with such a great loss to you really proved your strength and commitment. Therefore, you both have looked at loss, but proof of your commitment and strength was tested tremendously. This was what we call a wide card, both were not prepared for this experience, but you both proved your core strength. You, Jimena, when they were destroying your body to force you to declare yourself heretic, you refused. Your love of your family was greater than your life. It has been an emotional disaster, we have to agree, and the experience developed some positive soul growth.

When you plan your life on the earth, you come equip to deal with all the events that you design for your soul growth and development. We can never cover all the things at would or could happen. We call this event a wild card because no one could predict it would or could happen. However, it did. Again, I have to emphasize it also gave you, Jimena, the hidden strength to finally shatter that bond with "the keeper". There was such uncontrollable hatred that came out of you toward this person, you could finally harness that power to give you the strength to master the challenge thereby have a real loving life you have dreamed about between lives.

We have always been mindful of the black hole coma that you had experienced. We now know that you are strong enough never to fall into that space again. From this experience, you both developed your personal strength to survive. You both know how to use mental, physical, and spiritual energy in positive direction to create an environment where a wild card cannot enter. Should one appear, you have the ability to push it away or master it as it happens. Your evolution has taken you both to that place of command.

Therefore, my dear friends, you both have this lifetime to continue the love life that was cut short before. Your life together will only strengthen and embellish your core strengths and development. You have each other to work on your empowering of self and others. You have a life-style and business to practice your talents to greater depth.

Now, are there any questions, your teachers, or I can help you resolve? The next hour, we explored our unresolved concerns by going with, through, past misconceptions and old history that would stand in the pathway of your committed goals. We both now understand how we have listened to our spirit teachers before without realizing it but at times did not act on their advice for our protection. Now we truly have to take more pro-active use of their support and our commitment for creativity. We will have a live what we create and continually evolve with for our highest and greatest good. Our co-creation bond is strengthen where it will be win, win, for everyone we are involved besides ourselves.

Suddenly, we were back, with Roger handing me a tape of what happen should we need reminding we are the winners. Jenny hugs and kisses Roger on his cheek to thank him for getting her husband back. I just hug him. He reminds me that if I have any problems in future, he was here, but he knows he has lost a good customer. He gave back our journals with comments for us to work with later. We paraded through the house as usual, and for the last time, maybe. We put on our weather gear and shoes, walked silently out and on our way. How do you say goodbye to friend that brought you back from your living hell to life of co-creation and love. Jenny and I just walk so quietly down to the dock, entered into our boat, and cast off. We looked back but Roger was gone from sight. The boat drifted for a while, we were not in a hurry.

Darkness was now creeping behind us because the light source in front was fading fast. We just kept drifting, lost in our thoughts of what had happen. If I had listened to my wife in Spain, I would not lost my family, I would not have suffered such damaging death, and all those years lost in trying to heal the damage. What a price.

I was breaking out of my thoughts when I became aware that darkness was creeping in with its blanket. The man made light sources were coming alive to flood their designated area. We floated around the bend just in time to see our project come alive in holiday lights. What a welcome sight to come home to. We could see our own home flooded with its bright color lights, what an additional welcome sight.

Jenny turns her face towards me, while very quietly whispered, "You are going to be a father. I found out Friday for sure. I love you." Now all is right with the world. The prayer that floated through my thoughts, will this begin where we left off in that other life?